So very nice to meet you, Mr. Yeats . . .

The fourth Yeats sibling turns from closing the parlor door and touches his ear as though my voice had been deafening. Taller than his father and more slender, with dangerous eyes behind delicate glasses, he smiles at me. A twisting desire ignites behind my sternum. It beams down the backs of my knees, and they puddle. It flies out of my eyes into his.

"Call me Will, please." His eyes touch my brow and chin, and slide over my cheeks and jaw with the greedy reverence of a priest's lips on a bishop's ring. It makes me want a mirror. "Are you ill, Miss Gonne?"

"Not at all," I say. "Just a little faint."

He takes my elbow, and my body—this statuesque frame of heavy full breasts and robed thighs—is at once wholly mine, strange and unfamiliar though it is.

Will steers me from the window to the sofa. His touch radiates from my arm into my ribs and belly. He sits beside me, and I have to remind myself I'm dreaming.

"Miss Gonne mentioned she admires your 'Isle of Statues,'" the older Yeats says, and I'm so grateful. I can't remember anything Maud has said.

A shy smile touches the young poet's lips. The vacant space arcs between our bodies . . .

Berkley titles by Skyler White

AND FALLING, FLY

IN DREAMS BEGIN

In Dreams Begin

SKYLER WHITE

BERKLEY BOOKS, NEW YORK

A BERKLEY BOOK
Published by the Penguin Group
Penguin Group (USA) Inc.
375 Hudson Street, New York, New York 10014, USA
Penguin Group (Canada), 90 Eglinton Avenue East, Suite 700, Toronto, Ontario M4P 2Y3, Canada
(a division of Pearson Penguin Canada Inc.)
Penguin Books Ltd., 80 Strand, London WC2R 0RL, England
Penguin Group Ireland, 25 St. Stephen's Green, Dublin 2, Ireland (a division of Penguin Books Ltd.)
Penguin Group (Australia), 250 Camberwell Road, Camberwell, Victoria 3124, Australia (a division of
Pearson Australia Group Pty. Ltd.)
Penguin Books India Pvt. Ltd., 11 Community Centre, Panchsheel Park, New Delhi—110 017, India
Penguin Group (NZ), 67 Apollo Drive, Rosedale, North Shore 0632, New Zealand
(a division of Pearson New Zealand Ltd.)
Penguin Books (South Africa) (Pty.) Ltd., 24 Sturdee Avenue, Rosebank, Johannesburg 2196,
South Africa

Penguin Books Ltd., Registered Offices: 80 Strand, London WC2R 0RL, England

This is a work of fiction. Names, characters, places, and incidents either are the product of the author's imagination or are used fictitiously, and any resemblance to actual persons, living or dead, businesses, companies, events, or locales is entirely coincidental.

First edition: November 2010

Library of Congress Cataloging-in-Publication Data

White, Skyler.
In dreams begin / Skyler White—1st ed.
p. cm.
ISBN 978-0-425-23695-6 (trade pbk.)
1. Occultists—Fiction.   2. Yeats, W. B. (William Butler), 1865–1939—Fiction.   3. Gonne, Maud,
1866–1953—Fiction.   4. Ireland—Fiction.   I. Title.
PS3623.H5788816   2010
813'.6—dc22   2010027419

PRINTED IN THE UNITED STATES OF AMERICA

10 9 8 7 6 5 4 3 2 1

To my tall, redheaded daughter, Kaki—
an old Irish nickname for Katharine (and Kathleen)—
for whose dreams I learned responsibility, and
whose soul for love and imagination has ransomed mine.
And to Scott, my hero.

In wise love each divines the high secret self of the other and, refusing to believe in the mere daily self, creates a mirror where the lover or the beloved sees an image to copy in daily life.

—W. B. Yeats

In this world, time is like a flow of water, occasionally displaced by bits of debris, a passing breeze. Now and then, some cosmic disturbance will cause a rivulet of time to turn away from the mainstream, to make connection backstream. When this happens, birds, soil, people caught in the branching tributary find themselves suddenly carried to the past.

—from *Einstein's Dreams* by Alan Lightman

1

LOVE IS BUT A SKEIN UNWOUND BETWEEN THE DARK AND DAWN

When you are old and gray and full of sleep,
And nodding by the fire, take down this book,
And slowly read, and dream of the soft look
Your eyes had once, and of their shadows deep;

How many loved your moments of glad grace,
And loved your beauty with love false or true,
But one man loved the pilgrim soul in you,
And loved the sorrows of your changing face;

And bending down beside the glowing bars,
Murmur, a little sadly, how Love fled
And paced upon the mountains overhead
And hid his face amid a crowd of stars.

—"When You Are Old" by W. B. Yeats

When I'm old, I'll say I married in black today because I put cute ahead of lucky. I'm a modern girl, not superstitious, and I look my best in clean, black lines.

At the wedding, I blamed it on the awards dinner I have next month. If you're going to buy one expensive dress and wear it twice, black's the reasonable choice, right?

But now, already almost dream-soft and full of sleep, I'll tell the real and secret story: In a depressingly not-atypical moment of wandering attention, I left my white, purpose-made, gorgeous, bias-cut, silk dream dress on the MAX line coming home from the seamstress shop after work last week. This pisses me off because I had planned to go barefoot, and had to wear heels. Because Amit and I looked like badly matched storm clouds—me in black, him in gray. And because I still have no idea where my real dress ran away to. Nobody turned it in. I can almost feel it out there, living its own life. And my ridiculous imagination is worried it's having more fun. Dreaming freer dreams.

Amit says we must have ransomed it for the weekend's unreasonably brilliant weather. Having paid such a high price, we made full use of the shockingly clear, high blue sky and the first smells of dirt and roses in Portland's long, wet, and usually cloud-filled spring. We didn't even set up the tent we had rented. Our friends poured out into the sunshine and the grass of the Japanese Gardens with their cake plates and little "Laura and Amit" bubble-wand bottles, and I wound up shoes-in-hand, dancing with my new husband in the koi pond. It was exactly what we wanted for our wedding—an old-fashioned free-for-all with friends and family who won't ever be all together in the same place again unless one of us dies young.

I hope our honeymoon can be the same—exactly what we want, even if not how we planned it. We had planned to be somewhere over the Atlantic right now, but young graphic artists like me don't get many chances to pitch huge ad campaigns for banks, so when my boss asked if we'd push the honeymoon back two weeks, Amit and I decided it was a reasonable sacrifice to make for such an opportunity. Now, beside me in our expensive wedding-gift-to-each-other Danish bed, he is already lost to dreams. I'm waiting for sleep to claim me, too, and overthinking it, my crazy imagination pondering what pieces of a person can wander like attention on a train, or drift off like awareness into sleep.

The wicked, peat-smoke whisper catches me just as I'm falling asleep. "Maud?"

I don't really fall asleep. I only float up into it. I try to be graceful so my body won't feel it's dropping behind and jerk me awake. But how can I be falling or floating if I'm right here in my bed? And how can I be so clumsy about it, when my athlete's body can do pretty much anything easily but dance?

"Maud?"

In the coming wild two weeks, I will come to listen hungrily for this husky lilting whisper—and it will learn to call me by my name—but it's my wedding night. I wanted to sleep through it.

"Are you truly mesmerized then, Maud?" The inviting Irish whisper keeps finding me—it sounds like from an ocean and a hundred years away—just as I start to lose consciousness.

No, you don't lose consciousness when you sleep—that would be irresponsible—but I feel like I could lose mine permanently tonight, and my mind.

No, I will completely lose my heart. I'm going to look like shit at work tomorrow.

"Maud, you are entranced." Her whisper has grown a new spine of bright, almost erotic excitement. "Submit your will to mine!"

I crave sleep the way a locked-up junkie wants a hit, but I've never actually heard voices before. So maybe I'm not asleep. Maybe I'm falling apart. There's been enough stress with the NorPac pitch materializing just two weeks ago, and a wedding to plan, and putting the honeymoon on hold. I crack a lid to check for crazy.

What I see spectacularly fails to reassure me. Hellfire-blue eyes probe mine from a ghost-white face. Gaudy, bright brass posts wreathed in cloth have sprouted from the foot of our slim platform bed. Nightmares on my wedding night. Fucking figures.

But at least I must be sleeping. And the bed I'm dreaming is better than mine. It smells more of smoke than fabric softener, and I *am* tired. Tired enough to dream about sleeping, anyway. I nuzzle into my dream bed's warm, intimate softness, wishing I'd imagined myself under the covers. It's chilly. But I'm sinking into the crisp outdoor smell of woodsmoke, and the warm, interior scent of someone else's body. Not Amit's, which should trouble me. But I'm coming un-moored—mind from worry, muscle from memory. I'm floating up. Adrift.

And overthinking it still.

Dammit. I have got to get out of my head.

But if my carefully compartmentalized, pinned-together, modern self really falls apart, where will the pieces land? They'll wander off, I guess. Not sluts or renegades, just pilgrims, hunting their truth, or god, or you.

"Only keep your eyes closed, Maud," the Irish voice whispers. The mattress bends to buoy her weight perched on the edge, and infant-soft fingers fan my cheek. They spin into my hair, running through it, teasing out long strands with a hungry tenderness.

I wear my hair short, and it's way too curly to finger-comb with-out swearing.

"Maud, you are mesmerized," she whispers, her breath quick and trembling. She turns her ear to my mouth, and I struggle to keep the slow and steady breath of sleep. Her lips blaze my cheekbone to my lips, and open, whispering, "You will not remember this."

She kisses my mouth once in a slow luxury of stolen sensuality, and a delicious pull blooms between my legs. Hell no, I'm not forget-ting this. This dream shows more imagination than I knew I had.

"When you wake up, you will remember only what you have seen with your soul's eyes," she whispers. Her voice strokes my lips. I want to kiss her back, but she clearly wants me asleep. So I peek instead, just enough to see the BBC miniseries loops and coils she's worked her hair into.

Okay, she's right about the closed eyes.

My slammed shut eyelids and her old-fashioned clothes create a silent movie flash of jumping, jerky movement. All I need now is organ music and a man weeping in the dark theater. But it's only her voice again. "When you wake, Maud, you will have no bodily mem-ory at all. Although you may realize you love me more than you knew before."

Her lips grow less tentative, the tip of her tongue reaching. My fingers and belly, my breath and mouth are too awake to fake it anymore. Maybe I'm dreaming this creepy Victorian bedroom, complete with oversexed ghost, out of guilt for postponing my honeymoon, but it's only going to help me make it up to Amit in the morning.

I cave open under her kisses, into the entwining sheets and luscious smells. I kiss her.

The sound she makes is something between a gasp and a moan, and for a moment she does not move. I reach my mouth for more, and she kisses me again, with a new decadence on her lips. Despite some desultory dabbling in college, I've never had such a powerful effect on a woman—on anyone, really. I'm impressing myself.

"I had not thought your physical body could respond to touch, your astral body having left it," she says.

I have no idea what this means, and I don't care, riding the deep erotic current rising in my belly. Float me back to the liquid blossom kisses.

"And it has left, has it not, Maud?"

"Stop calling me Maud," I whisper. Such a ridiculous, old-fashioned name.

"Maud's spirit left." She's clambering off the bed. "But some other voice speaks through her."

I curl into the comfort, away from the crazy. I want more kissing, but I'll settle for the drift back into drowsy unerotic. Anything but waking up to stare, sleepless, at the cold Portland skyline out our massive, modern window.

"It must be the ghost of Maud's dead father," she mutters. "How peculiar. I only made a show of conjuring him, but here he is all the same, devil damn it!"

This is why I prefer not dreaming. Dreams' dark and restless whispers carry you away into deep and deeper water. Can't I ever just stay shallow and sexy?

She clears her throat with a fussy cough. "Captain Gonne, I regret to inform you, you are dead."

Talk about peculiar.

"Sir, you died two years and two months ago this day."

Through my heavy lids, her delicate face hovers, fringed with smoky wisps of hair the same indeterminate auburn ash mine would be if I didn't dye it darker, to a deep, sleek black.

"I believe you knew my father, sir. John Jameson, the whiskey distiller? Do you have a message for your daughter, Captain Gonne?"

Well shit, it's a guilt dream. Whiskey and daughters. I've been clear with Amit: I'm not sure I want kids.

"I don't have a daughter." I can hear the irritation in my voice, feel it prickling me awake.

One night, when I couldn't sleep, Amit told me about an old literature prof of his who said dreams were where we explore our fascination with what's difficult. Or maybe it was books. Either way, we meet our demons in some imaginary place, whichever it was, so they won't destroy our real lives. It makes sense, I guess, to dream adultery on my wedding night.

"Not Maud. Not Maud's father?" Her voice sounds like an empty aerosol can.

I open bleary eyes, and struggle through the heavy, twisting bedding to push myself into the sinking pillows piled behind me. I'm waking up, but the dream is not receding.

"What the fuck?" I mutter.

She stares at me with flaming eyes. I have no idea what she sees, but my own gaze is whipping from the convoluted vase of peacock feathers behind her, to the fireplace, to the God-help-us-it-really-is wallpaper where my plate-glassed city view should be.

My fear is mirrored in my nightmare's face. "Those aren't Maud's eyes!" she whispers sharply, backing away. "Some evil spirit has possessed you!"

I am waking up in a different body, in a very strange place, but my breasts, swollen, full and unfamiliar, weigh pleasantly on the sluggish body that does not want to sit up. The massive, bright bed is piled with blankets and canopied with webs of lace and ruffled flounces.

"We were playing at séance. I untethered Maud's spirit. But I didn't summon anything! You—You shouldn't be here!"

I thoroughly agree.

"I'm not," I say. "I'm at home. Asleep. In Portland."

"Portland Gaol?" The trembling Victorian nightmare gapes at me. Now this is just ridiculous.

I push at the twisting sheets winding like water plants around my hips and legs, and lug my unresponsive body upward. I stumble to my feet, but I'm too tall, and everything is wrong. Auburn pours down my back and over my mounded breasts. I'm wearing a corset. I can't breathe. My mouth makes a noise like tearing metal. My loft is gone, my husband is gone, and my too-awake dream rises in solid potted plants on every side of me. Green, aggressive stalks reach for wallpapered walls, which vanish upward into shadows or soot stains.

There are never ceilings in dreams.

I can't remember my husband's name.

But I've known this strange woman since childhood. I know her mother's and her brothers' names.

"You can only be a lost soul or a devil," she whispers. "Nothing else floats free."

I stumble in my unfamiliar body and crash into a parrot cage. The birds shriek, and my hair—no, not my hair—falls into my eyes. Panic claws along my arms. I tear at the lace buttoning my throat, as the third woman I've ever kissed edges farther away, backing herself toward the fireplace. She looks so close to coming completely unhinged that it forces a kind of calm on me.

"Okay," I say in the slow, controlled voice we save for cornered cats and other people's children. "Let's be reasonable. I'm not Maud, right? We both know that."

She takes another, imperceptible step back, but her lower lip slips from the fierce grip of her baby-small teeth. "Anyone looking at you would swear otherwise," she whispers.

It's cold out of bed. I'm not fully dressed and trailing tangled blankets and complicated layers of underclothes. But rather than tear the bunching fabric from my too-large, too-soft body, I stand the parrot cage upright again, and look around the cluttered room. Everything is layered. The windows are robed in velvet over linen over lace. Every flat surface is draped with tiers of cloth and crammed with lamps or flowers, tiny portraits in ornate silver frames or fragile porcelain figurines of peasants.

Shivering in the chill out-of-bed air, I run my hands over an equally upholstered body that is equally alien, although I feel my touch across its exposed skin acutely.

"I'm in another body," I whisper. "This one isn't mine."

"No." I barely catch the whispered answer from where she's backed herself against the velvet-draped mantel. Her hungry eyes trail my hands. "Maud would never touch hers so."

"What's your name?" I ask, but insanely, I know the answer. Her name is Ida Jameson. I remember climbing deep under the rhododendron of Dublin Castle with her when we were girls. We dreamed up mansions and husbands for ourselves in the leaf-roofed hollows between the huge old trunks and bottom branches.

But my dearest childhood friend shakes her still baby-soft curls at me. "I must not tell you! We have kissed. If you had my name as well, it would be enough for power over me."

"That's cool," I say, striving for a calm, grown-up voice. "Let's start over, okay? I know we can figure this out. What did you say about a séance?"

Her mouth trembles. She's pressed against the fireplace, and I worry about how close she's coming to the grate of burning coals with the elaborate fabric bundle perched on her ass.

"Did you hypnotize Maud so you could kiss her?" I suggest.

Ida's sharp little teeth catch her lower lip again, but the pretty lilting whisper doesn't waver. "Maud's beauty—your beauty—is the kind born only once a generation."

She's not much younger than I am, but innocent tears gather beneath her tender black lashes and tug me toward her. Maybe I really won't remember this. Maybe I'm always such a sensualist in my sleep.

Ida's burning blue eyes, so bright they're almost white, meet mine recklessly. "No woman—here in London or back in Ireland—none of the European beauties compare to you." The tip of her tongue pokes through her trembling lips, vaguely snakelike. Somehow threatening.

"Beside you," she whispers, "any woman is in shadow. And every man aflame."

I want to take the hands of this timid, lustful side of myself and hold them, but she's twisting them behind her, so I just step a bit closer. Her eyes dart from my face to the fire behind her like a wasp between flowers. "We can think this through together," I promise, but I've already figured it out.

It's guilt. For not taking my honeymoon right after the wedding (but the bank pitch will be huge for my whole tiny agency if we land it). And for marrying a man I'm not ass-over-elbow crazy in love with (but crazy in love is still crazy, and I'm never doing that again). Still, it looks like I'm conflicted enough to dream myself into this made-for-fucking body trying to calm a paler, frightened, too-thin version of myself. Apparently some body image bullshit, too. Fuck.

"Start at the beginning," I suggest.

Ida nods her delicate, wary head, but doesn't say anything. Does some part of me really feel this backed into a corner? So I ask her, "Ida, are you in love with Maud?"

Her face washes ice white. Her eyes never drop mine, but they fill to overflowing. She nods.

"I don't think she knows." It's my clumsy attempt to comfort her, but saying it, I'm certain it's true. "No, she doesn't know. She loves you, of course, but she's in love with someone else—a man."

A tear shatters down Ida's dimpled cheek. "Who?"

"A Frenchman," I tell her.

His name is Lucien, but I find I don't want Ida to know this. I feel Maud's rain-soaked arm beneath his scalding mouth.

"Are you going to kiss me again?" she asks, misreading my shiver. Her eyes dance wide and restless again.

In the moment before it happens, I know I'm not this crazy, and I turn away from her whispering, inviting lips. I am stumbling back as she whips the little silver-handled fireplace broom from behind her back. She brings it arcing, with all her slender strength, directly at my head. I step back. My foot catches in the tangle of bedclothes and long skirt.

I'm falling. And if it didn't all ignite in exploding roses of pain, I would be laughing. I've just literally been hit over the head by a dream.

Fair enough, Ida-my-Id. I get it.

I stagger into a little wooden writing desk which showers paper on the re-up-ended parrots.

"Return to Hell, devil!" Ida shrieks.

The bird screams offer the same suggestion.

I will wake up beside my new husband, and chalk up my headache to hours of dancing on nothing but champagne and frosting.

I hit the florid carpet with my face and knees.

I'm not the sort to fall apart. I'm the girl who didn't try suicide once in four years of art school. I never get carried away. But okay, maybe I have some things to work out. My arms splay and my thighs fall open on the blackening rug.

I have fallen. Asleep.

The rising dark hides the carpet's color. The parrot voices grow further and further away, screaming with their green wings that it's crazy to reason with your dreams. And I drift into a blackness spotted only by a swimming, dreaming crowd of stars.

"Maud?"

Crouched over the beautiful, inert body of her friend, Ida Jameson swallowed hard against the creeping, twisting chortle threatening to burst from her pursed lips. Outside the closed bedroom door, Maud's dog began to howl.

"Hush, Dagda!" she called to it. Could Maud go nowhere without a menagerie? Stopping in London for only one week, she shared her rooms at the Grosvenor Hotel with that howling Great Dane, three rabbits, five budgies, a falcon, and a squirrel.

Maud moaned, but did not move. Ida chewed her lip. No matter what powers a soul or a spirit may have, it depends upon the body to contain it. Break the pipe, and the flute cannot play. And although Maud was not her body any more than Ida's little silver flute had been music, still, when her father, whiskey-sick one morning, had thrown the slender silver pipe into the fire to twist and close, Ida had been then—and since—without music.

Ida replaced the pretty little broom in its holder beside the poker and tongs. It had been one of those she'd hoped to brandish against whatever was possessing Maud. Drawing blood could break a spell. That she had seized the soft, blunt broom instead was Ida's typical misfortune. That Maud—Dublin's famous beauty—now lay sprawled at her feet, was an equally symbolic, but atypically delightful surprise. Ida licked blood from her lip. She had suggested mesmerism only for a moment's pleasure kissing her beautiful, wild friend's senseless body. Now a devil possessed it.

Such things always happened to Ida.

But Ida had a knack for grubbing through the ashes of her own disasters. Even ugly lumps of melted silver fetch a price. And secret cash is secret power for a fluteless girl.

A deferential rap at the door made Ida stamp her foot in pique, missing Maud's furled palm by the width of a pinky. "Miss Ida?"

"We're fine, Emily, thank you," Ida called to her parlormaid, forcing the smile into her voice. "Miss Gonne and I are learning a new dance. Take Dagda downstairs. I can't carry a tune over her singing."

Ida returned her gaze to her fallen friend. What fun it was, looking down upon a celebrated beauty! Maud towered over every woman and most men. Yet, inexplicably, her height only added to her allure. Even in the awkward posture she had adopted insensate, with both knees bent and an arm thrown over her face, Maud still possessed the unearthly beauty of an Irish fairy or Greek muse.

Ida twisted the gold band on her left hand, a twin to the one she'd given Maud as a token of their friendship, and tried again to calm her mind. She had studied the occult for months now with no sign of a magical gift, yet Maud, easily mesmerized, had channeled at once a fully formed and speaking demon. And Maud was completely untrained—uninterested in training. Another thing Maud did not value and Ida craved, freely given to Maud and denied to Ida, despite grueling effort and humble request. The friendship ring came off in Ida's twisting fingers and she nibbled it absently. If she had Maud's

beauty and good luck, she would enroll herself in Madame Blavatsky's Theosophical Society. The small-minded, old Russian woman
would not deny Maud as she had Ida.

Ida almost swallowed her ring as the thought struck her. If Maud
had added words to her copy of the golden band, it might explain
the day's unsummoned visitor. Slipping to her knees in the puddle
of red hair, she separated Maud's limp fingers, and grasped the ring
encircling the slender thumb. Ida yanked. Maud moaned again.

"Devil damn!" Ida grunted. She knew too well how pain linked
body and soul, and she needed Maud's faint to hold. Neither the
woman who belonged to the fallen body, nor the devil whose appearance might presage Ida's first occult gift, was welcome back into it
just yet. Ida worked Maud's ring in a careful spiral up, and holding
the limp hand, remembered her brother's bleeding ones.

Quarantined at home, Jamie had dropped school pages like breadcrumbs onto the green spring grass at Airfield to lure Ida with Latin
into his forbidden sickroom. There, he had taught her the origin
language of her daily words, the occult and secret heritage of sounds
beneath the English and the French she knew. Jamie had trained her
to prick his fingers with sharp pins to keep him conscious when the
fevers came.

One fine morning, sitting on his bed, hatpin ready, but unneeded,
Jamie's warm laugh and affectionate patience with her childish lisp
collided with the stories they shared of their secret lessons and their
private knowledge of their modern words' hereditary stains. It all
combined to carry Ida's small nine-year-old frame away with joy. Its
freedom and power spread strong boughs of love to wind around
their sprawling house and ever-expanding family, and dove below to
root in the subterranean warmth of history, origin, and mystery. It
pinned the moment, with its taste of occult knowledge and whiff of
freedom to her forever. But Jamie had died, and their mother had
stopped getting dressed in the morning.

Maud opened her eyes. "Ida?"

Ida dropped the squeezed-blue finger and cloaked her disappointment with a mask of worry. "Do you know your name," she whispered.

"Edith Maud Gonne," Maud muttered. "Ida, where am I?"

"You're with me, darling. You fainted." Ida studied the luminous, brown eyes. The strange gold light in them was gone. Ida forced tears into her voice. "My father died."

"Back in Dublin, yes." Maud nodded.

"And you came to see me . . ."

"To say how sorry I am. Ida, my own father . . . Oh God!" Maud jerked as if to leap free of her body. "Oh God," she said again, going pale and falling back into Ida's encircling arms.

"Your father died when you were nineteen," Ida prompted. "We were having a séance with my new mesmerism. I said I'd try to contact him."

But Maud was crying, the soft white chemise slipping from her shoulder, and love—or the heady mix of envy and admiration that passed for it—moistened Ida's lips again. She coaxed the exposing lace away, and congratulated herself on having suggested Maud remove her belted suit and under-bodice before they began their mesmerism. Maud was always in a passion—mostly of righteous political rage since she had returned from France—but this frenzy was something different. Ida smoothed Maud's tumbled hair, revealing whiter skin. If Ida had Maud's beauty, she swore she would be happy. Beauty was its own power, and she would not seek for more elsewhere, nor mar her looks with anger and scowls, politics and the supernatural.

"I never told you," Maud's voice came low and muffled against Ida's still-buttoned waistcoat. "I never told anyone."

An unnamed man in France, and now a new confession? If Ida weren't being eaten with curiosity, she would be hurt by how much Maud had kept hidden. "Tell me all," she murmured.

"I killed him," Maud swallowed a sob. "I killed Tommy. It's my fault my father died!"

"No, darling," Ida soothed. "Captain Gonne died of lung hemorrhage."

Maud shook her head, her cheek rubbing.

"The night he fell ill, I prayed," Maud whispered, tear-choked. "I prayed not to God, but to the Devil . . ."

"What devil. Any devil?"

Maud lifted her mottled, tear-splotched, and radiant face to stare at Ida in confusion.

"No, nothing dear," Ida held out her arms again. "I didn't mean to frighten you. Come back." But Maud shook her head and propped herself against the wall, drilling her fingers on the leg of the little writing desk.

"I should confess this, Ida. Maybe you can help me. I know you've been studying these things." Maud wiped the tumbling hair from her face with white, impatient fingers. "I prayed to the Devil for my freedom, to be able to direct my own life, and in exchange"—Maud gulped, and dropped her eyes from Ida's searching gaze—"in exchange, I offered my soul." Maud's strong fingers clutched Ida's hand for courage. "Ida, tonight, I think, the Devil came to claim his prize."

Ida willed her hand not to tremble as she stroked the delicate wrist. She had never noticed before how much too small Maud's hands were for her large frame. "Just because he came for it, doesn't mean you must cede it to him," she whispered.

On the other hand, if Maud had truly sold her soul to a devil, Ida might borrow his power while avoiding his price herself. Patiently, she waited until she could bend the eagerness in her voice to comfort. "Maud, could you see this devil while you were entranced?"

"No, but I felt it possess me. It slipped like warmth into my body." Maud's strong fingers gripped Ida's arms, shook her until their eyes met. Ida held them, gazing into the fathomless depths. Maud's beauty, Maud's drowning, fascinating, enslaving beauty could almost negate what hung in the balance. It held an almost equal power. "Ida," she gulped, "I can still feel it near us."

The squeal rose in Ida like a belch, and she bit her lip savagely to contain it. Her body lurched forward, rigid with the impulse to throw her arms around Maud and laugh, to clutch her melting flesh and taste her lips again, but harder and completely.

"Close your eyes," she whispered.

"No!"

"Maud, I will channel your devil into you again. I'll . . ." Ida groped wildly for the right incentive. "Oh, Maud, I can see him leaning over you! Quickly. Close your eyes and keep them closed. I'll offer him my soul as well for more time before he comes to claim you."

Maud took the gift of Ida's soul without hesitation. She closed her eyes.

With more care than she had employed the first time, Ida positioned her blunt fingers in the famous auburn hair, planting her squat thumb at the center of Maud's high, white forehead. If Ida could learn the devil's name—she already had its kiss—she would have power over it! She repeated the slow, smooth downward stroke she had seen Miss Hunt perform in her public demonstrations, and recited the words exactly as they were put down in her *Private Instructions in the Science and Art of Organic Mesmerism*: "Close your eyes tightly—tightly—and keep them closed."

She repeated the thumb's sliding stroke again, and then again, watching hungrily as Maud's proud body lost its vitality, gave itself into its own weight, and melted down the wall.

Ida touched the rosy, parted lips. They did not move. Her fingers slipped over Maud's hard chin and down the swan's throat. Maud gave no response. Ida skimmed the smooth flesh stretched over the deep bones, and hesitated.

"Maud?" she whispered.

She gathered both hands around the generous swell of Maud's breasts, and pressed their swollen weight for one shuddering breath, eyes held to the perfect and impassive face. Ida could free that sensuous flesh, and taste it now. She could call Maud back into her body with its pleasure, and blame it all on a seducing devil. She could say Maud, the devil in her, had driven Ida to this, and had stolen her own innocence. Ida sighed. She had stroked many tender breasts, raised dun and coral nipples, scarlet and damask ones to hungry peaks, but Maud was a virgin yet. And Ida had a devil waiting.

"Devil, can you hear me?" she whispered.

Maud's eyelids pulsed.

"Devil, I conjure thee into the body of Edith Maud Gonne!"

Maud's perfect, inviting lips parted. Ida stopped her breath, wishing madly for time to consult her library. She knew so little about possession. Who could have guessed her occult talent would lie in channeling devils through her childhood friend and adult obsession? Mayhap she should have.

"Tell me your name!" Ida worked to make her voice commanding.

Maud's eyes opened and were not Maud's eyes. "Laura," she whispered.

Devil damn.

Ida shook her head. Surely only a very minor, weak, and unimpressive demon would have such a stupid name.

Ida tried again. "Demon, reveal your true name!"

"My married name you mean? It's brand-new. Tonight's my wedding night."

Ida could not summon demons after all.

The eyes that were not Maud's eyes drifted closed. Ida bit her lip. Still, she had summoned *something*, channeled a ghost mayhap. Or a pilgrim soul.

"When were you born, spirit?" she whispered. A birth date would mean a human soul, and the ability to work an horary and natal chart.

"The winter solstice."

Minions of torment take Maud's damnable pride over that vagary of birth! It was an auspicious day, yes, the only day of the old Celtic tree calendar without a name, but it was Maud's birthday, part of how she played at being part fairy, and not what Ida needed. It also signaled the possession was somehow not complete. Maud and the spirit were intermingled in her.

That, at least, Ida might remedy. She could deepen Maud's trance enough to discover the nature of the spirit she had channeled, and whether it had any power Ida could use.

Never taking her eyes from Maud's beautiful face, Ida unlocked the drawer of her little writing desk, and groped until her fingers found the yellow paper box of Egyptian cigarettes secreted at the back. They had been a gift of sorts, from a young architect who had shared one with Ida, hoping to seduce her with the fashionable decorations and artifacts of his Oriental smoking parlor.

Careful not to inhale any of the somnolent sweet, gray-green smoke herself this time, Ida propped a lit cigarette in a bud vase between Maud's parted lips and elegant nostrils. The fragrant coils of smoke shuddered, responsive to Maud's faint breath, but flowed readily in on her next inhalation.

Whilst Ida waited for the smoke to set Maud's spirit farther adrift and draw the possessing spirit nearer in, she explored Maud's handbag for clues about the unwelcome Frenchman. She found an embossed red leather diary and flipped backwards through the gilt-edged pages. She saw next week Maud would leave London for France again. It had made no sense to Ida before—that Maud would fight for peasant Ireland from stylish Paris—but now she understood what drew her closest friend away. Devil damn the seducing French lout, and may he rot in his wretched city of magic and cruelty.

Maud had not thought to notate her call on a bereaved childhood friend today. There was just one entry for the thirtieth of January, 1889: "3 Blenheim Road, Bedford Park. 5 o'clock." But the name beside it sent a frisson of icy comprehension spilling over Ida more stimulating than if she had found her own name in the luncheon timeslot wreathed in tiny hearts. She stood motionless while an intricate fabric wove itself from what had been, moments ago, only solitary and unrelated threads. Maud's teatime appointment explained all.

Ida replaced the book with trembling hands. She had heard the rumors, of course, of sex magic practiced in the Hermetic and Masonic societies, and here, on the very day Maud was to meet with one of Madame Blavatsky's theosophists, Ida had conjured a bride! A spirit on her wedding night! Ida poked a rosy thumb between her lips and chewed it. Surely Madame Blavatsky had sent this spirit as a summons. Or a test. Ida's mind whirled, eyes wandering Maud's beautiful, slack face, crowned now in heavy coils of sweet smoke.

Ida cursed and leapt to Maud's side to stub out the stupefying cigarette. Why must her remedies always turn to poison in her mouth? She fanned the air with frantic, flapping hands. The single inhalation she had taken with the architect had painted her lids in lead and dimmed her wits—perfect for the long interview she'd planned with Maud's body-squatting spirit, but now, disaster! Even the architect, despite Ida's practiced fingers working down his fly, had fallen asleep with his cock in her hand. She had taken the whole packet of cigarettes in recompense.

"Laura!" she hissed, flailing the limp body against the wall. "Laura, I conjure thee! Return to the body of Maud Gonne!"

Ida barely dared hope her luck had turned at last, that Madame Blavatsky and her fabled Theosophical Society might accept her as a student after all! But how could they not if she delivered the equally famous Maud Gonne to them possessed by a spirit Ida had channeled! She sprang back to standing, and shouted for Emily.

"Laura, I conjure thee by name!" she whispered. "You must wake up! It is vital that you meet Mr. Yeats tonight!"

Ida's sweet-smoke whisper finds me again, through the white peppering pain of chair-bruised ribs.

"Laura?"

My epiphany is gone, and Ida's sharp chin tilts with pride when she sees me in Maud's eyes. "I know who you are, Spirit," she announces. "And I know why you have come. You are my annunciation. I am ready to answer my summons." She kneels beside me in a gust of accordioning silk. "I only wish to serve."

I have no idea what she's talking about, but I like her better incoherent and over-awed than incoherent and violent, so I give a solemn nod. I should make up something impressive.

"You called this your wedding night, Spirit. Am I to give myself to you?" Her fingers hesitate on the buttons at her throat.

I think that's a fine plan, but my eyelids keep sliding down, curtaining the charming image. I haven't felt like this since the art school days. In a minute I'll remember what it means . . .

"Maud? Maud!" I hear Ida pop back up to standing. "Devil damn! We'll just have to get you to Mr. Yeats. Can you stand?"

"Yes," I hear myself say. "Where's Dagda? I still have my slippers on." But it isn't my voice.

In the cab's closed darkness Ida starts her whispering again. "Spirit, I applied to the Theosophical Society two months ago, but Madame Blavatsky would not meet me. It's because she likes to send spirit summons, isn't it? As a test. Will she be at Mr. Yeats's house today? Do the Theosophists hold their meetings there?"

In the rattling dark, her urgent lips mutter too fierce to kiss, and I catch a glimpse of menace under the distortion of my dream. I am being dragged by a dark horse through Victorian streets toward nightmare. I press myself farther into the hard green of the hansom's interior, but Ida's soft body only leans closer. "I will pass any test you set me," she promises. "I want to be initiated."

Yes, I know marriage is an initiation. But Ida's body and my corset, the bone-jarring streets and industrial darkness crowd too close for me to think it through. I will pass any test my dreams set me. I just want to wake up in my rational, twenty-first-century life.

But the cab rattles to a standstill and then I'm standing—not only asleep, but stoned—on the cold, hundred-year-old London doorstep of a man I've never met in what, apparently, is my personal, twisted version of the forgotten-pants dreams of schoolchildren. You'd think I would have had enough of humiliation yesterday, dancing barefoot in a fishpond.

I can't remember why I danced.

The nineteenth-century London door before me opens, and my modern real life is not standing there behind it. An elegant, tall man, stern black tie knotted tightly at his throat, holds the door open by its center-placed knob.

"So very nice to meet you, Mr. Yeats," I say, hoping that's right. God, do Victorian ladies shake men's hands?

"The honor is mine, Miss Gonne." But he takes my elbow to usher me over the threshold and I don't have to figure it out further. I can pull this off if all the men are so confident in their control. "Mr. O'Leary speaks highly of you," he says, "and I remember your letter in the *Times* on the topic of a certain song quite clearly." He chuckles indulgently.

The heavy fabric of my dress rests against my thighs, and hefts weirdly about my legs but he leads me down a dark, firelit hall with ease. I would have tripped over all the layers on the front steps if my hands hadn't lifted my dress like they were accustomed to having to carry my clothing ahead of me. It's only the things I pay attention to that trip me up here.

"Yes, I've always rather hoped God *won't* save the queen," I answer him.

And wish I hadn't. Shit, this is London of the perpetually bereaved Victoria. What am I thinking? The faces of the two women arrayed to greet me before a genteelly threadbare settee turn pink and then pale. But their imposing father ushers me into his front room parlor with a flourish, and shakes his head at them.

"I had heard you were opinionated, Miss Gonne," he says cordially. "Allow me to introduce my daughters, Elizabeth and Lily, and my son Jack. My wife, I'm sorry to say, is ill and won't be joining us."

Elizabeth executes a practiced laugh. "We Yeatses are actually in possession of that old literary trope—a madwoman in the attic," she says. "Call me Lolly." She's prettier than her sister, but her hair sweeps back from her face in strange, uneven little ridges and depressions, like a badly made bed. I know, without knowing how, that both women's clothes are rather plain and more than just a little out of date.

"Susan had a stroke some years ago." The old man's voice carries a threat of something I can't quite peg. Lily's protruding lower lip trembles.

"My mother passed away when I was very young," I say, standing stiff and anxious by the big bay window because I don't know who sits down first. "I'm sure you're grateful to be able to care for yours."

I guess because I'm dreaming, the less I think about what I say, the more easily I talk to the tall, attractive man I somehow know Maud needs to impress. I find I like earning his slow smile, and let the unfiltered fiery words of nationalist politics and even revolution spill between us. I breathe the subtle white petal smell of the almond blossoms on the window ledge, and Mr. Yeats inclines his gray beard toward me. His eyes register my height, my borrowed beauty, in blunt, warm appraisal.

My attention wanders back to Ida, waiting across the treelined street in the cold London January for something. A sign or an invitation. I swear I'm colder indoors than I was in the cab. It's terrifying not to know the rules of the time and place. I feel awkward and ridiculous, and my gloved fingertips are numb with nerves, but I'm doing well enough with Yeats and his son, as long as I stay on automatic pilot.

The hollow concussion of some furniture-heavy thing crashing to the floor overhead startles me and I'm suddenly fully back in the strange present. My past. Jack has started to his feet, but Mr. Yeats only shrugs.

With an imperceptible shake of her head Lily stops her brother. "He won't need you."

Jack's pained smile apologizes to me. "Only my brother can manage Mother when she's feeling poorly." He reseats himself. "I don't know what magic he works."

"It has nothing to do with magic," Lily snaps.

"I think he just listens to her," Lolly says.

"God knows we all do that, Lolly," Old Mr. Yeats grumbles.

"He listens with love," she says.

A descending clatter on the stairs ends with the arrival of the missing Yeats.

"So very nice to meet you, Mr. Yeats," I say again, figuring it did okay the first time. He turns from closing the parlor door and touches his ear as though my voice has been deafening. Taller than his father and more slender, with dangerous eyes behind delicate glasses, he smiles at me. It's a warm, but perfunctory smile that turns quizzical, slows, and deepens mysteriously. He has seen something in me. A twisting desire ignites behind my sternum. It beams down the backs of my knees, and they puddle. It flies out of my eyes into his. I seem made of raw emotion in my dreams.

"Call me Will, please." His eyes touch my brow and chin, and slide over my cheeks and jaw with the greedy reverence of a priest's lips on a bishop's ring. It makes me want a mirror. "Are you ill, Miss Gonne?"

"Not at all," I say. "Just a little faint."

He takes my elbow, and my body—this statuesque frame of heavy full breasts and robed thighs—is at once wholly mine, strange and unfamiliar though it is.

Will steers me from the window to the sofa his sisters have been guarding. His touch radiates from my arm into my bruised ribs and belly. He sits beside me, and I have to remind myself I'm dreaming. I am more aware of my body's boundaries than when I am awake.

"Miss Gonne mentioned she admires your 'Isle of Statues,'" the older Yeats says, and I'm so grateful. I can't remember anything Maud has said.

A shy smile touches the young poet's lips. "My ideas of poetry have changed a bit since I penned that," he says. "I was overly concerned with form in 'Statues' I now believe. It was altogether too cautious."

"Leave it to Will to wish he'd been more reckless." His father laughs.

"Not less careful, but more concerned with the power and responsibilities of poetry than with its structure. I'm more interested in what poetry should be."

"And that is?" I ask. It's crazy to hear someone talk so unselfconsciously about art.

"A poem should be a thing that, when you are alone, makes you less lonely, but no less peaceful."

The vacant space arcs between our bodies. I will never be peaceful again.

"Not that you'll be an argument for peace yourself, Miss Gonne," Will's father teases me. "I'm not quite sure Young Will would have agreed with your refusal to have the national anthem sung at your recital." The elder Yeats chuckles in that indulgent way some parents have of fondly suggesting their child is a very special breed of idiot.

"If there's a worse poem in the English language than 'God Save the Queen,' I have never heard it," Will replies calmly, pushing a chestnut lock of hair back from his forehead with paint-stained fingers.

"My son puts the beauty of a song over its politics."

Will studies his hands in his lap, passion flaring in his cheeks. I know he's angry with his father, and my temper cracks in sympathy.

"Well," I say, "you can't hum dogma."

Yeats Sr. laughs and nods. "It's true. But Will's ambitions extend beyond simple songs to sing. He wants an Irish poetry fashioned from our land's ancient stories and wild imagination."

I will not join in his winking invitation to ridicule Will's dreams. Mine are crazier.

"I want our people to be proud of their artists, not just because what they create is Irish"—Will's eyes hold mine with a bold defiance—"but because it is Irish *and* it is beautiful."

I cannot open my ribs against my corset. I want to be Irish and beautiful. God, I haven't talked capital *A* art since college. This should be embarrassing me, not turning me on.

"Irish artists may repudiate the form and style of our English occupiers," he continues, "but what do we have to offer in replacement? Things we know to be crude and poorly made? Things only Patriotism, through its deliberate blind eyes, can see as beautiful?"

I don't know the rules. Should I answer him? I only know what is fundamental to me belongs here with him. All other kinds of belonging—to an era, to a body—are simply possessions. My job, my city, they're things I own, not things I belong to. And I don't know where I belong, except with him. I believe, and for once without my constant modern doubt, every word we're saying. Our words are more true than anything the real me has said in a long time.

"I'm so pleased to find you a kindred spirit, Miss Gonne." His voice crackles with a powerful, controlled intensity. It reaches all the interior space of a body I can't quite inhabit, and draws me to the surface. It touches me beneath Maud's flesh. It gets under the padding of his sisters' polite formalities.

"You want Art to offer a vision of what could be, or of what once was," I say. "You demand Art advocate for a new way of being, not just oppose the present way, otherwise . . ." There is nothing to protect me. I've lost Maud's confident voice, and the close, smoky air catches in my throat. "Otherwise, we only play the defiant child, whose self is simply the inverse image of his parents."

The subtle glances and quick eyebrows of his father and sisters speak from a subtle codex I can't interpret. It's terrifying. I don't belong here. But Will's eyes hold mine, and I don't want to leave.

"Precisely so," he says. "With the Irish imagination colonized, how can we even dream ourselves free?" He turns his body to me, almost reaches for my hand, but stops. I am dreaming.

"We must imagine our own images." His tender, resonant voice claims something in me that was never awake before.

I nod, mute.

"What have you been doing since your performance with Miss Jameson, Miss Gonne?" Lily asks.

"I've been in France," I answer, remembering the man, the kiss, and the rain again, but as my attention wanders, Maud's voice grows clearer. "I adore Paris, but I want to find somewhere in Dublin as well. I'll never own a house in London."

"It is a hateful place," Will says, passion heavy in his Irish voice. "You can't go five paces without seeing some wretched thing broken by poverty or wealth. I long for Sligo and Dublin. For Ireland."

"You long for an Ireland of bards and fairy tales," his father mocks him. "For the *daoine sidhe* and the *Tír na nÓg*—the Host of the Air and the Country of the Young! Miss Gonne, surely you would wish Ireland's artists to be more practical."

I touch Maud's fingers to the still-sore places on my cheek. "I think I understand how one might have nostalgia for another time," I say. "Even for one that must be imaginary."

I am no longer alone in my unbelonging. It makes me smile, and Will catches and returns it. Like me, he belongs nowhere, in a country and time that don't exist.

"Have you seen much of the West Country, Miss Gonne?" his

father asks, and I let Maud answer him, allowing my mind to wander, trying to remember why I feel more displaced in time and country than I could ever explain, even to Will.

"Will has been chasing ghosts and fairies since his teenage years, Miss Gonne," Will's father complains congenially. "But you may be interested in his latest fascination. He's been working with the old Kathleen Ní Houlihan story, trying to show some native Nationalism in all the mindless tales of newborn babes and new-wed brides carried away by the *sidhe*."

He's laughing, but his words terrify me. Is that what's happened to me? "I'm sorry?" is all I can muster.

The old man's accent broadens with his laugh. "Ach, Miss Gonne! If you had spent your childhood roaming the wilds of Ireland as young Willie here has done, you'd know the country people will never praise an infant's disposition or a bride's beauty without adding a 'God bless her!' for protection."

"From what?" I whisper.

He laughs outright at this, a loud rumble that echoed from the mantel to the windowpanes. "From the *sidhe* that might come and steal her away of course!"

"What do fairies want with brides and babies?" I ask.

He leans across the worn rug with a conspiratorial wink as though imparting some dark secret only to me. "Sure, the old folk say it's because the *sidhe* cannot dream. They have no imagination of their own, so they carry away the living who have the most dreams wound round them."

"The Kathleen story is actually a variation on the stolen bride motif," Will says softly. "It bears a resemblance to the German myth of Faust as well, for Kathleen ransoms her soul to feed the hungry of Ireland."

"It's a childish act, to sell one's soul," I hear Maud say. "It isn't really yours to sell." But her voice shakes in my throat.

"It's an ancient story"—the gentle Irish of Will's voice has my full attention again—"but I felt drawn to it, as most of our mythic heroes are fighting men. She is more beautiful and brave to me because her battle is with herself. Hers is a more tragic, and more Irish heroism." Will is talking only and directly to me. "Kathleen is not *sidhe*, but shares with the fairies a wild restlessness. Her pilgrim soul wanders Ireland searching for our nation's high, mythic self. I want our poetry to create the Irish soul she sought. If I can reimagine Irish freedom, not as simple violent rebellion, but as its own wild and creative dream, it would be worthy of her ransom, and her heroism."

I want to be wild and creative for him. But I don't believe in heroes.

"Enough of politics now, Will." This is one of Lily's coded communiqués. "I believe Miss Gonne has been struck quite speechless."

"Not at all," I say. "I'm a deep believer in the power of words to inspire men to action." Advertisers bank on it, after all.

But Will blushes and stands. The sisters rise at once, levitated by their brother's agitation. "We'll go in to tea, shall we?" He holds out a slender, artist's hand to me, and I put Maud's beautiful small fingers into it. Understanding leaps between our flesh, and almost jars me awake. I stagger in the unfamiliar bone and clothing.

I am waking up.

His sharp inhalation drives a torrent of heat across me. I will refuse to blink.

"Laura?" A voice they don't hear, sleep-muffled and distant, pulls me further from the troubled, polite glances. Tears sting my held-open eyes. I squeeze them closed. I don't want to leave this stuffy room of uncomfortable women and formal furniture.

"We must go to war," Maud says—it is not what I mean, although I would fight to stay with him—"with words and weapons. There is no price too high for freedom."

Over his shoulder, the scowling father says, "Had you ever seen war, Miss Gonne, you might have less enthusiasm."

No. I opposed the war. I had a bumper sticker . . .

Will's hand steers me away from the sofa and the window. Away from Ida, angry and waiting outside in the horse-drawn cab. Away from the mother secreted away in the room above. And toward . . . I don't remember what.

Was it toward anything? Toward reality? No. Only this man is real.

"Will . . ." But he can't hear me.

"Go back to sleep."

Only his eyes can hold me here, but the power of what I feel when I look into them wakes me.

"Miss Gonne?"

"Laura?"

Help. Oh God, help me.

Mr. Yeats did not come down.

Although millions of middle-class and high-class ladies now thought of themselves as spiritualists even more than Christians, although even Mr. Conan Doyle could write magazine articles about the séances he attended, still Ida had been unable to gain access to the occult knowledge she knew underpinned it all. She did not want to be another one of the thousands who packed the public lecture halls, she wanted to be the mesmerist they came to see. Or the medium invited to give séances for the royalty and aristocracy of Europe and Russia. Only not so public or so visible. It wasn't the fame or the income she needed, or even the access to the palace or the White House, it was the knowledge itself, and the belonging to an inner circle of initiates and members. Belonging to the spiritualists or the spirits, it didn't matter. She only wanted to be chosen. Not left forgotten again. Not abandoned in the barren London suburb of Bedford Park with its no-longer fashionable Aesthetic Movement houses and winter-starved gardens.

But Mr. Yeats did not come down, and by the time Maud emerged, the sun had set, and Ida was seething in disappointed rage and the wicked, creeping suspicion she had been mistaken.

"Home!" Maud's careless alto called to the cabman, but she added the cheery clarification, "The Grosvenor," before climbing into Ida's hansom cab. Maud reclined against the seaweed-green velvet. "Ida! Whatever are you doing way out here?" She graced Ida with a surprised but perfect smile.

A hard fist of fury twisted Ida's empty stomach. "Do you not remember, Maud?"

She had waited alone, while Maud shone, wanted and beautiful, in the Yeatses' golden window of firelight and tea. Without her, Maud would have slept straight through the appointment. "Do you not remember our drive here?"

Maud cocked her proud, round chin. "No," she said, without even the humility to be surprised. Every turn of her head showed her to advantage. All the small nervousness of the afternoon was gone from her proud frame, like the gold from her eyes.

"Close your eyes, Maud."

"No, I think not." Maud pressed her spine to the seat back, rattling too quickly away from Bedford Park's red brick and white wood facades, and Ida's stranded fantasies of an awed Will Yeats rapping on the cab window, and inviting her inside. "Welcome to the Theosophical Society, Miss Jameson," he would say, and they would speak of Maud as a mere conduit, a beautiful vessel. He would sit between his two guests in his father's gaslit drawing room, and turn his eyes to Ida.

"No, I will not close my eyes." Maud's honey voice was hard. "I don't believe I like your new mesmerism. I felt even less myself after the second time. I was scarcely able to pursue my goals this evening. But I think I made a good impression all the same. Certainly the young men liked me well enough."

Ida chewed her quavering lip. She could not lose both Madame Blavatsky and the spirit she had channeled. It would be too much disappointment, even for one deeply familiar with its sticky knives.

Maud lit an impatient cigarette. "I don't know what O'Leary sees in Yeats, with his English paintings on the wall, and his sons in English art schools. It was only my courage in calling for battle that stirred his Irish spirit at all. He's full, domesticated Englishman."

After hours waiting in the London January dark, Ida's fingertips were bitter, even through her gloves. "You work with such dedication for the cause," she soothed, despite the bile bleaching her smile. She knew Maud loved everyone, including her, only to the degree they hated England. If Ida stopped working for Ireland, she would lose her beautiful childhood friend at once. And she would be alone.

"I could not rouse them tonight!" Maud exclaimed, grinding her cigarette into the floor of the hansom and turning her face to the blind, black window. "I was but half alive, listening to my voice from a distance, and not caring so very much what it said. I felt . . ."

Ida's pit of anger, nested in her lap, coiled tighter. "You felt what?" she spat.

"I felt . . . removed. And the oddest thing is, the farther away I felt, the more keen the one son became."

"Will Yeats?"

Maud nodded, and Ida had to bite the fleshy inside of her cheek to keep from smiling. So Will had met the conjured spirit? Mayhap it had been a Blavatsky test after all, but they did not want Maud to know? It had not been Ida, but Maud who had been found wanting!

"No, I shan't play at séances ever again," Maud said, and Ida almost struck her for a second time that day. Even sitting on the offending hand, she feared her own anger. How dare Maud so coolly dismiss all Ida's new power? "It is because you are afraid," she whispered.

"I am not afraid!" Maud rounded on her, straight and dignified. But the carriage rattled across the pocked streets, jiggling all the flesh and hair of her. Not so elegant now, Lady Aspic. "You know I am afraid of nothing," Maud snapped.

"Oh yes. I know," Ida mocked. "'Not of anything, not even of death.' Your father's last commandment."

"I am not afraid. If you knew the things I have done!"

Ida snorted. "Fear is the only reason to refuse a message from the Beyond."

"You have no understanding of what I experience while that devil or ghost—that soul—inhabits me. I've stolen into Russia with secret documents sewn into the hems of my dress and been in less danger. It's unnatural."

"Because you are afraid."

"Ida, my soul, my awareness, goes to someplace else. Someplace better. It—I—like being removed from my senses. It makes everything seem too easy, like falling into the most gorgeous, restful sleep. I don't want to awaken to what's here . . ." Maud's defiance puddled away.

"Your soul traveled somewhere else?" Ida could not keep the awe-tinged envy from her voice. "And you remember?"

Ida would give three front teeth to be able to accomplish what Maud complained of, but she had no skill at astral projection. The British Museum's one book on the topic made it sound like a rare and wondrous power. "Poor thing." Ida held her voice to just above silence. "You're so very tired."

Maud's heavy head bobbed. "Yes."

"You can rest." Ida whispered. "You needn't carry the weight of Irish freedom alone. You can be free a little. Close your eyes." She forced her voice to pull hypnotically on her words again. "Tightly—tightly—and keep them closed." The cab rattled, and Maud shook her head. Ida wordlessly cursed the cabby to seven years of testicle-eating ants for his jostling haste, and waited.

Did her commands still hold some power over Maud? Ida extended a cautious hand and stroked her stumpy, gold-ringed thumb down Maud's high, porcelain brow. "You are entranced," she whispered. "Submit your will to mine."

The heavy rich teal of Maud's bodice lifted and fell. Ida had done the buttons up herself that afternoon, and her fingers twitched remembering the lush ribbed fabric.

"Maud, tell me where you are."

"I am in Hell."

Ida grinned into the darkness. Maud had always had visions, but this was a new thing altogether, and very exciting. "What do you see?" she whispered.

"It's dark, and peaceful. It makes me feel at home." Maud said. "It's a waiting room, but lovely. I know my body sits there in a cab beside you, but I find I don't care. I'll just slip in a bit deeper here. And rest. It is so peaceful here. And numb."

Was it possible Ida had been where Maud now was? Ida smelled sour smoke and whiskey. She remembered the cruel top button of her uncle's fly had ground against her hip, and a fiercer truncheon battered where no hard bone could save her. On that night, ten years ago, Ida had sent some part of herself to such distant calm and waited out her uncle's midnight visit. A waiting room, yes.

Hell's waiting room.

She clawed hard into memory for some prompt to offer Maud. "You can still feel," she recalled, "but wrapped in cotton wool, or quilt batting."

Small tufts of the white stuff had peeked out at each needle puncture in the quilt thrown over her face. And she had wondered, as Uncle sawed at her, if she would also always be likewise leaky.

Maud's deep nod bowed her heavy head, chin dipping. "I slip into it," she whispered, "like water." Her famous profile tipped across the velvet to rest against the cab wall.

"You are back there now, in the warm, safe dark," Ida intoned, but she picked up Maud's limp hand and held it against the cold and violent loneliness that had seeped into the rattling cab. "Tell me all you know."

"Tonight, it was as though I was bathing there, floating in the quiet distance, and while I could see myself with Mr. Yeats, I didn't mind what happened. It was all happening to someone else. Nothing he said could reach me. I tried to argue, but I was so very far away. Too far to be convincing. And too at peace."

The cab jolted, tossing the drowsy copper head, but Ida caught Maud's face between her hands and steadied it. If she could hold Maud here, keep her drifting, she might still call the wandering spirit, summoned by accident that afternoon, and learn what its nature was. Ida held the drooping face in her blunt and bitten fingers, and squinted into the shadows. What were the first words of conjuring?

"You are entranced," Ida muttered. "Submit your will to mine." She broke off scowling. It was all she could remember, having read the damnable book only once through.

"Maud, can you sense the spirit you channeled today? Is she with you still?"

Maud nodded.

"I must speak to her, darling. I need to know if she is human."

"She is one of the *sidhe*," Maud whispered. "My dark fairy."

"The Gray Lady you've seen since you were a child?"

Maud nodded, and Ida longed to shake the head she steadied, to rattle the fanatic mind in its heavy skull, but she stayed motionless, and made her voice sweet. "Maud, only let your spirit wander a little farther from your body, so I may speak to her again." Why had Ida not thought Laura might be one of the Host of the Air? She had wasted time sipping from a puddle when a fresh fountain flowed nearby. "Maud, the spirit came to us for love. If we refuse her, she must serve us!"

"No," Maud shook her head, and her hair, drifting from its tethering pins, crawled over Ida's wrist and wisped against her face like spiders. "I never want her near me again."

"If you bring her back, I will banish her. Spirits must be dismissed or they will linger."

It wasn't quite a lie. Ida didn't know a thing about banishing, but she knew Maud had been haunted since childhood by the image of a watchful veiled woman. Ida was certain Laura, the spirit she had seen take possession of Maud today, was something new. And much more powerful. Ida would have promised to exorcize Queen Vickie from Balmoral to usher Laura back. It was to Ida, and not Maud, after all, that the spirit had made love.

"Laura?" she whispered.

Maud shook her head. "No, but something with *L*s, both his daughters, Lily and something else, but not Laura. And Jack, and . . . another son." Maud's eyelids sagged. If her countless admirers saw her thus, head lolling, eyes adrift, she would not be so proud.

"And his other son was . . ." Ida prompted.

Maud's insectial hairs swarmed Ida's cheek as she leaned closer. Rigid with suppressed shudders, Ida waited, and hoped.

". . .Will!" The eyes sparked open gold. "Will?"

"Laura?" Ida put her lips to Maud's. Let the crawling hairs keep crawling until they crawled away, and not bite inside her eyes and nostrils.

"Where's Will?" Laura demanded. The cab reeled into the smoother streets of Belgravia. A mixed curse. Here, it rattled less, but it did not slow, and the fairy no longer wanted Ida's kiss. Devil damn!

"I've never met anyone like him, Ida!" the not-Maud, but not-very-fairy-sounding voice exclaimed. "He has this ferocious, heroic imagination. He thinks poetry can do ridiculous things! Nobody believes art has that kind of power." Laura laughed with a freedom Ida had never heard in a woman's voice.

"You believe it," she said.

"No. Not really. It's just a stupid dream."

They were getting dangerously close to Victoria Station with its lights and crowds.

"But I want to dream it again." A romantic, wistful softness crept over Maud's face, and a slow, deep, very human, erotic flush. "We felt powerful. Like we could create something real out of our wild imaginations. Which is ridiculous, I know. But it's sure a nice dream."

The cab rattled to a stop with a final shudder of reins and a thwarted whinny from a horse who'd rather run than stand in the cold. Ida understood the protest in the warm stench of fresh horse shit.

"It wasn't a dream," Ida muttered. Who would have such dreams?

"Home, madam!" barked the driver from above.

Eyes that weren't Maud's searched Ida's. "I don't want to be home yet," she pleaded.

"Tell me your birth date," Ida whispered into the face she held.

"December twenty-second." The voice was a scraped whisper.

"Damn you to Hell with a month of solstice birthdays!" Ida spat. Rage, desperation, and the scuttling insect-hairs overwhelmed Ida, and she dropped Maud's head in disgust.

Maud gave a gloved hand to the cursed cabman and unfolded her long arms and legs like a spider from the coach's black interior. Maud came smiling back from Hell where Ida had brought away only memory, her uncle's shame, and a murderous hatred for the once-favorite doll she had ruined with the blood he left behind.

"I invited Mr. Yeats round to dine tomorrow night. Do join us, Ida dear." Maud smiled into the blackness at Ida. "Didn't you have something metaphysical you wanted to ask him?"

Something golden wavered in Maud's dark eyes.

"Tell me your entire name and the year of your birth," Ida commanded.

Maud laughed, but Laura answered.

Ida swore the whole way home.

from *A Servant of the Queen: Reminiscences*
by Maud Gonne MacBride

1938

Ida's family were large Whiskey Distillers and her Dad had loved the golden fluid of his famous vats so well that, though he lived on, he had ceased to count among the living and was only occasionally visible on the grounds of Airfield in his wheeled chair, attended by a valet nurse. Ida was the youngest of a large family, all of whom had married, a strange girl, with a lovely voice and curious psychic faculties . . . She could see things invisible to others, and I had a little of this same gift; it was the basis of our childhood friendship, for she knew I was not making it up when I spoke of the dark woman with the sad eyes, who stood by my bed, and I knew she really had seen the big black dog, with eyes of fire, said to haunt the Donnybrook Road, and of which the servants were very afraid . . . Of the dark woman, so strangely associated with my life, I shall write later; there came a time when I had to banish her because our wills clashed and after I joined the Catholic Church I realized that unless one is very holy, the tearing of the veil which separates those in flesh from the inhabitants of the borderland, may let loose forces dangerous, if uncontrolled, for those we love.

In the rose garden of Airfield, I told Ida I had come back to work for Ireland's freedom, and about my disappointing interview with Michael Davitt. Ida was eager to help; her family were Unionists. That afternoon, Ida went into town and ordered two gold rings with Eire engraved on them, which she said we must both always wear; she also said she had arranged for us to go to tea next day with a student of Trinity College, Charles Stuart Oldham who was a Protestant Home-Ruler, and she thought engaged on important work for Ireland. Her mother must not know about it. Ida loved to dramatize life, even more than I did.

2

A MAGIC THAT CAN CALL A DEMON UP, UNTIL MY BODY GIVE YOU KISS FOR KISS

If you will give me all your mind awhile—
All, all, the very bottom of the bowl—
I'll show you that I am made differently

. . .

We have fallen in the dreams the Ever-living
Breathe on the burnished mirror of the world.

. . .

All would be well
Could we but give us wholly to the dreams,
And get into their world that to the sense
Is shadow, and not linger wretchedly
Among substantial things, for it is dreams
That lift us to the flowing, changing world
That the heart longs for. What is love itself,
Even though it be the lightest of light love,
But dreams that hurry from beyond the world
To make low laughter more than meat and drink,
Though it but set us sighing? Fellow-wanderer,

Could we but mix ourselves into a dream,
Not in its image on the mirror!

—from "The Shadowy Water" by W. B. Yeats

On the first drowsy morning of married life, my body wakes up ruthlessly alert and covetous in the indeterminate light of not-quite dawn. I'm itchy the way you'd be when your favorite boutique has a sale—half off everything—and you're peering in the window, drumming on the glass, wanting. I wind my body around Amit's sleeping bulk, and reach back across the terrain of our lovemaking past, rehearsing routes from sale rack to bin. Usually, I get up and shower, and come back to bed clean and damp, but I want him too much. I want him every way he's ever touched me—the way he first kissed me, courteous and restrained, and after our first big fight, furious with his fingers pinned to my hip bones in the basement bathroom of my parents' house. I run my hand across his cobbled chest and into the wooly dark. He groans and pushes his back against me. His cock yawns in my fingers

"Good morning, wife," he says, a smile in his sleep-heavy voice.

I grunt and dig my sharpening nipples into his back. I want him in a way I can't quite explain this morning, our first morning of husband-and-wife. I guess that's why. He rolls onto his back, arms over his head, mouth open. He stretches silently into fine tremors of flexion, then baskets his head in his woven fingers and grins at the ceiling. His thickening cock in my stroking fingers makes the highest point below his nose, its regal and ancient profile, dark against the pale morning. I re-twine my leg over his, my humid sex against his hard thigh.

Amit smells woody and warm and he's starting to match the tug of my hand with his hips. He flattens my hair, crunchy with the lacquer that slicked it into an elegant, adult updo for our wedding, away from his face, but it's just habit.

"Are you still going in to work today?"

I nod against his chest, but kiss it to make up for giving the wrong answer. My eyes close with the taste of salt flesh warmth. But when he slides a hand down my arm, another unfamiliar shiver slips after. Who at the wedding yesterday could have touched my elbow just there, to make this shiver bloom deeper and erotic? Or in my dreams?

I never remember my dreams.

Amit rolls on his side to face me and his heavy cock drops onto my belly.

Too much.

I twist up, straddle him, and push the open fork of my legs against the underside of his cock. His slow grin slides through the dawn gray between us and his eyelids, the color of rich, old woods, shield his shadow-black eyes, focused on the place where our sexes meet, slippery together. His large hand holds his cock upright, hard away from his belly. He's surprised, but pleased. I am desperate.

I grip his solid shoulders and raise my hips above him. He levers his cock farther back and slots into me. I ease my body down, seal my open legs to the tangled, rooting nest, and rock. My strangely small breasts miss some cushioning heft, but his fingers pluck them to aching, and I close my eyes to trace the blooming waves rolling between where his fingers and his cock touch me. I am drowning in feeling, and I am the feeling that drowns me, falling into myself, into tides of pleasure coursing from breast to belly and back. How can you smother in what you are?

Is this what it is to fall in love? My face feels congested with sex, and I don't want Amit to see me bloated with it. I press my electric breasts to his chest and sink my teeth into the secret soft of his neck. He swallows a growl and grinds his hands in the meat of my ass.

Did the wife in me wake up while I slept?

God, I do everything backwards. Fall crazy in love after I'm married.

But Amit, groaning now, stifled and urgent, bounces my pussy on his cock like a rubber ball tethered to a paddle by a bit of elastic string. I squeeze my eyes closed against another everyday-dawn, reaching for the lingering, whole dark of my wedding night. I know I have fallen in love.

We move faster, and the string cannot fully extend.

I wore a black dress, but it was still a wedding dress. We said our vows outside, but we still swore oaths. Victorian bridal customs we ignore and those we can't flutter against my skin like snowflakes or bird wings. The vows still say forever. Until death.

I plant my clit at the root of his cock, and grind against the bouncing. My flesh dissolves in the dissonant waves of his pound and my push.

But how can you promise anything forever? Hell, I don't have any idea where, much less who, I'll be in ten years. Till death do us part. Death—the end of the self.

The orgasm, just below the horizon, stains my thinking a swollen, brilliant pink. And I am falling. I don't believe I have a soul. I have a self—a construct made of many component parts, some of which change—like my body and my ideas about stuff—but some of which don't.

But what if the parts of me that change are the parts that he loves? Or if what I love in him changes? How do I know the parts I love in him won't change? Or wander off?

I am no longer swimming, I am being swum.

We wore our tattoos under silk. He had a tailcoat and his small hoop earrings and deep eyes to drown me, and I am falling more in love, into the center of the radiating pleasure, into blind desire, into something deeper than a simple wedding night. And ancient as darkness. But I am modern, and my modern distrust of my own thoughts and processes—my sense of myself as fragmented and malleable—is one of those unchanging parts of me. We are both still modern, even in the primordial dark of sex. And the orgasm breaks not like dawn, not in a progressive rise over the line, but in a theater blackout that leaves the vanished light burning on your retina.

My pussy contracts. I cannot hear the beats of my orgasm pulse—individual but outside time. I am deaf with desire for a man I don't know.

I've known Amit for years.

His shout, molar-ground into something animal, scares me when he comes. His hands claw my waist, pull me down over him to smother it. His fingers touch my elbow. I come. I come again. I've just met my deep, powerful love, just wakened to soul love, past time, past coming, my mind finally rattled into silence.

"Laura?"

His deep, resonant voice is playful and light, but I want the blanketing darkness.

"Laura, you didn't hear the alarm?"

Alarms mean danger. I open my eyes. A peacock-blue sky fills the bedroom's huge window, stretching over Portland's skyline. It all looks safe enough.

"I had a weird dream."

"You should do that more." He tweaks my sleepy nipple and grins. He likes me dreamy, but I know not to trust anything you can see with your eyes closed.

"No," I mumble, pulling the bedding over my head against his bad wish. "I think I drank too much."

On nights he didn't come home, Grandma used to say ol' devil drink had taken my grandpa. I imagined a jazz-age lady in red satin slinking her arm through his, twirling long beads on a skinny red finger. He would give her all his depression-rare dollars and in exchange, past that first delicious saunter down the lane, get not a moment of pleasure. But still he went, and for the first time in my life, I'm glad I'm adopted. Granddaddy's dangerous lady can't reach through my genes to crook her marriage-blasting finger back at me.

"It's bad," I mutter.

"I don't know." Amit wraps his body around my back like a human turtle shell. "I liked it. Besides, I'll bet it was less the champagne and more the lack of anything more substantive than wedding cake."

I groan into the pillow. I need to get up, shower, and go to work. Corporate identity pitches don't invent themselves, but I am desperate to fall back asleep. I can't remember why.

"I didn't sleep well," I mutter. I wonder if I'm getting sick, sleep pulls on me so hard.

"You slept lots, but you slept weird." His hand coils around my breast, swallowing the subtle flesh in his much larger hand.

"What do you mean 'weird'?"

"You talked in your sleep. I've never heard you do that before."

"What did I say?" I push myself up against the smooth Danish wood of our new headboard.

"Nothing I didn't already know."

I don't know why this soothes me.

"You mentioned you'd just gotten married. And you told me your birth date."

I shake my head.

"And then right before you woke up, you said your whole name."

An ice shatter of fear detonates behind his exploring hand.

"Just saying good-bye to my old self I guess." I toss off the summer-weight quilt and spring out of bed.

But I can't find my glasses.

"It wasn't your old name you said."

"Not Inky, you mean?" I grope the bookcase by our bed, my half of the pair of new Danish nightstands.

Amit laughs. "I haven't called you that for years. No, you said your married name." His eyes roam my body, leisurely and fond. "And just as a point of observation, I'd like to say that the new you looks every bit as good as the old you."

Kneeling to pat down the floor by the bed, I am ridiculous and exposed—alien—in a body more slender than thin, athletic, and modern. I never realized how much the soccer showed. He's holding my glasses by one stylish metal arm.

"Looks," I remark, "can be deceiving."

I catch myself washing my hands before I shower like I did back when all the drawing I did earned me the nickname "Inky" from some guy named Amit who sang in a band with my art school friend Otto. We knew each other a long time before we went out. I get in the shower and turn the water on full and whisper to myself, "No more drinking, no more dreams. No more drinking, no more dreams," until it sounds like cause and effect, instead of two separate promises.

Ida raised her eyes—it felt leagues and leagues above her—to the distant window where the massive ceiling came to a terrifying domed summit. The impossible space yawned vast and weighty despite holding only barren air and pregnant whispers. She shivered and dragged her eyes from the cavernous peak, down the roof's rounded, gleaming ribs, to the sightless gaping windows which ringed the vault's middle space and enclosed her within a circle of wild, open sky. Beneath the windows, soundless figures patrolled tiered balconies like shopgirls or prison guards.

Across the starburst of radiating desks, Will Yeats pushed through the great swing doors and stepped into the sacred circle of the British Museum's reading room. From her accustomed nook by the encyclopedias, Ida watched the poet's direct stride to the interior circle. Swathed in a billowing black Inverness cloak that swirled about him like a magician's cape, he already possessed much of the occult knowledge that drew Ida into dreary Bloomsbury. He took a seat, almost half the wheel of desks away, and occupied himself in unfolding the leather-covered shelf from the partition above his table.

Ida had seen him here before, the Bohemian set haunted the reading room like ghosts down Donnybrook Road, but as she watched the tall poet set out his tools like a priest—ink, steel pen, blotting pad, paperweight—and arrange them upon his humble altar, a queer shiver of new lust passed through her. She had seen him several times in the last months, engaged by choice as she was of necessity, in self-education. She knew he walked the long miles here from his father's house in Bedford Park—she suspected to save the tram fare—and she knew he made the pilgrimage, as she did from Belgravia, to read poetry and mysticism.

Ida's mind reached out toward the museum's secret shelves hidden beneath and all around her. They held even the *Kama Sutra* in translation, locked away. Forbidden to women, of course, its simple, mysterious proximity still contributed to the deep erotic song in the silent air. How much was likewise hidden here? Every forbidden secret, in its original Sanskrit or antique Latin, every true answer waited somewhere on the open shelves ringing her, or in the catacombs and archives underneath. Ida blinked against the jealous tears. He was in the Theosophical Society with Madame Blavatsky and all the London mystics. Maud was in France with her lover. Ida was without even the spirit she had channeled into Maud. Even having worked a complete natal chart and horary, she had been unable to summon the ghostly bride again, and despite her brave face and months of research, Ida had found no scorched and twisted good in the ashes of her disappointment.

A stray beam of raw spring sunlight pierced the distant clouds and shot through a high, arched window to anoint the handsome, bowed poet in a solitary streaming beam as if God himself reached forth to claim this man for His own. A fervent believer in signs, Ida closed her eyes. Swaying with the hum and whisper of all the world's knowledge—open and occult—dancing around her, Ida could not find a solitary voice. How do you pluck a single seed from a field of poppies, a solo voice from a chorus, a guiding star from a night sky?

Mr. Yeats glanced absently up, and he saw her.

Ah, mayhap that's how. Had she not read, just recently, in Mr. Wilde's new magazine, that domed spaces were extraordinarily conducive to telepathy? Ida smiled at the magus, and made a little wave.

The dome above her collected her power and magnified it. And with the knowledge of the ages surrounding him, with all that men have learned and understood and discovered ranked in stacks on every side, above and below him, here he came, walking past the bowed heads of scholars, past the superintendent on his high platform at the room's hub, out of the sun, drawn by the concentrated force of woman.

"Mr. Yeats!" Ida smiled into the deep, mysterious eyes of a true poet. His dark, mesmeric gaze held hers a moment, then scanned her face.

"Ah, hello! What a surprise to find you here. Have you accompanied Miss Gonne?"

"William Morris signed for my card," Ida snapped. "And Miss Gonne is in Paris." *Miss Gonne is in Paris, where she will doubtless consummate her smoldering affair with the very married Monsieur Millevoye, you stupid love-stricken cow,* she amended telepathically.

"Yes, that's what I had heard," he nodded, his extrasensory hearing apparently keener from afar. "But it was at her lodgings I made your acquaintance, of course." It was a question.

"Yes."

"We talked quite late into the night, and toasted cheese over the grate." He grinned widely. "We talked philosophy and Miss Gonne spoke passionately of Irish independence." He surveyed Ida's modest desk, the virgin sheaves of writing paper, the abandoned book ticket, even while his caressing voice enfolded Ida in the memory of another evening eclipsed by The Gonne. "And what brings you into the belly of the Imperial British beast?"

"Shakespeare," Ida lied with the confidence of old habit.

"You haven't finished filling out your ticket," he observed. His strong and graceful fingers twisted the telltale empty sheet to face him. "May I be of some assistance, Miss Jameson?" His intimate smile acknowledged both the theft of her name from the top portion of the slip, and the lie she had told him.

"It is more boneyard than belly, really," Ida muttered.

His laugh turned several gray and jowly heads their way, but Will Yeats folded his large frame with surprising grace into the seat beside her. "I think you're quite right," he whispered conspiratorially.

Ida flushed at the implication and the man's proximity. It was all very well for Maud and the Bohemian girls with their heavy workmen's boots and short skirts, to sit and talk with men so publicly, but Ida squirmed with the familiarity she craved. "I can't remember what I meant to write for," she confessed.

"Mmm." The poet smiled, stretching his feet to the heated footrest beneath her desk. "Memory is a ticklish proposition. Is it a present-life or a past-life memory which eludes you?"

Ida blushed a furious pink.

"Miss Gonne mentioned your interest in the occult the first night I met her at my father's house," he explained.

"Oh?" Ida folded and unfolded her guilty ticket. Maud professed no memory of that night. She did not remember meeting the poet or his family, and had seemed genuinely puzzled when Ida spoke of the spirit that had possessed her, or the time she had spent in Hell. "That is most unlike her."

"To speak of other women?" The poet's eyes sparkled with wit, but Ida swallowed humiliation. Was her envy of Maud so obvious?

"To speak of anything but Ireland," she replied.

The poet nodded curtly, and a shadow, distinct as the sunbeam had been, focused darkness over his strong face. "She was not so bloody-minded, the first night. That night I thought . . ." He stopped himself a moment, and directed a keen and searching glance at Ida before turning his eyes up toward the reading room's domed ceiling. "Mr. Wilde says the path to Truth is Beauty"—he winked with a forced charm—"but we poor men, dazzled by the pavement, risk mistaking the road for the destination."

"And do you believe Miss Gonne to be your road to Heaven, Mr. Yeats?" Ida asked.

The poet scrubbed at his face ruefully. "I think it much more likely she would lead me quite the opposite way."

Ida laughed. "And would you follow her, even so?"

"I believe I might. But I have always had a terrible sense of direction."

"So if we cannot trust Beauty to lead us, how shall a seeker find his way?" Ida asked, and caught her lips between her teeth with terror for having asked so boldly what she wanted most to know.

Mr. Yeats leaned into the mahogany-backed chair, the wood's deep brown a striking compliment to his Irish coloring, and stroked his red-brown beard. His eyes glittered. "Well, our friend Miss Gonne would say we can only find our way through politics and rebellion," he suggested.

"And yet she cannot vote."

He raised a wry brow. "Quite so."

"Nor can she study with the masters at Trinity or become a priest or a Freemason. Women are denied access to the structures of both formal and occult knowledge."

"And so?"

"And so we must get beneath the structures of formal power, to power itself."

"You are more like Miss Gonne than I had realized."

"I am nothing like her!"

"Perhaps you have heard of the Theosophical Society, which not only admits women but, in fact, is headed by a very powerful and charismatic one? I should be happy to introduce you, if you are interested."

"Madame Blavatsky may well head the society, but she is hardly welcoming to the weaker sex," Ida snapped.

Yeats chuckled. "I imagine that's so. Did you know she expelled two ladies last month? One for flirtation and the other for gossiping about it?"

"I had no idea," Ida whispered, struggling to master her voice lest it reveal how personal was her knowledge of Madame Blavatsky's imperious dismissals. Ida's cheeks still burned with rage and shame. She had been rebuffed by that grotesque, cigar-smoking Russian sorceress as surely as she had been turned away by the emaciated chaplain at her parents' church.

Ida's stinging color deepened remembering her ardent and consuming love for Christ. He had been her first love, and had promised her not even death, or life, or angels, or principalities, or powers, or things present, or things to come, or height, or depth, or any other creature, could separate her from His love. Since it had taken much less, when she was nine, to separate her from her mother's, she had hoarded her new love like the rare and precious life-sustaining possession it was. She wore her knees out with praying, groveling at the altar rail. Until she learned Christ was not monogamous. She could not have Him for herself alone. Even the skinny chaplain with the drippy nose was loved by Him, the harlot. Ida had challenged her rival, and lost.

It must never happen again.

"And are you here on Madame Blavatsky's behest today, Mr. Yeats? Or do you find time for personal researches, too?" she asked brightly.

Mr. Yeats cocked a quizzical brow. "Has someone instructed you to ask?"

"No." Ida flushed under the brilliant man's fierce scrutiny, something between curiosity and despair floundering in his deep eyes. "Why?"

"Did she say something to you?"

"Who?"

"Maud Gonne."

"About you?" Ida glimpsed hope, deep and stony, submerged below the dancing questions. "Did Maud say anything to me about your writing?"

"About *The Countess Kathleen*?"

"Whoever is that?"

His laugh cracked, Ida startled, and several heads snapped around to glare at the explosive poet. "She is a title," he said with another laugh, more sob than shotgun. "Miss Gonne mentioned an interest in amateur theatrics. She wanted something Irish she might act in Dublin."

"You're writing a play for Maud?" Ida's mind curdled. This man's "The Stolen Child" still wrung tears from her with every reading, and yet her haughty, thoughtless friend could order from his genius not just a poem, but an entire play—tailored to herself.

"I believe it will be my best, certainly my most Irish, work yet," he said, but Ida could only think: *Away with us he's going / The solemn-eyed . . .*

"How intriguing," she said. *He'll hear no more the lowing / Of the calves on the warm hillside.*

"I am hoping to capture," he whispered, all lightness stripped from his voice, "something I thought I saw in her the night we first met."

The rage ran out of Ida.

With a fairy hand and hand.

It left her hollow and white.

For the world's more full of weeping than you can understand.

"Miss Jameson?"

"What did you see in Maud?"

"Are you ill, my dear?" The poet leaned solicitously near. "You look as though you've seen a ghost."

Ida took a careful sip of air. "Or as though I know you have," she whispered.

The sadness cloaking the poet since Ida started watching him in the reading room four months ago slipped from his broad shoulders. They became taut with the gathered strength of a warrior's, and Ida was surprised, when he gripped her elbow, that he managed not to hurt her. "What do you know?" he demanded.

Ida's mind spun like a waltz. The poet, forward in his chair like a pointer who's found his downed bird, trembled with attention and leashed desire. The focus and the hunger in his eyes might not change their color the way Laura's spirit had altered Maud's but it was every bit as potent as a channeled devil. Against propriety, against her nature, Ida summoned Maud's easy way with men, the unchaperoned, impromptu dinners over the grate, the way she talked and laughed in the street so naturally.

"Shall we go someplace more private?" she said.

I take long strides on my walk to work, riding on legs that feel strong and free. The morning sun has split the cloud roof and the whole city is waking up squirmy in the sudden clarity and warmth. I should stay outside in this, with Amit on the day after our wedding, walking the Pearl, coveting through the shop glass, or wandering Mount Hood in the absurd, matching, high-performance hiking boots his parents gave us.

I stop into Prized Possession for a coffee, but it's just habit— I'm wide awake. The coffee shop's walls are plastered with pictures of people with their favorite object. I'm on the wall somewhere grinning with my first little golden pencil award, but Amit hasn't brought a photo in for his free coffee yet. I bet I could find one of him with his guitar from back in the days when he and his college buddies had a band. I should do that.

I catch myself bouncing up the stairs to the office before I reach the landing. There's no way to avoid being ribbed today, but I don't have to beg for it with every tired stereotype of newlywed glow.

Every one of the seventeen people employed by I+D was at my wedding last night, but only four of us are coming today. As artistic director, it's alright for Amy to have been the first on a Sunday morning, but I should have been second. Not last. I endure the trio's smattering of ironic applause, and hang my light jacket on the Eames coatrack at the top of the stairs.

"Gosh, I'm sorry, kids," I say with a stagey wink, "I must have overslept!"

They laugh and I'm off the hook. Amy and Ben turn back to their monitors.

"I'll be right over," Charlie calls from his.

I nod and unpack my laptop. I plug in and drag a chair over to my desk from the conference table in the center of the airy, open space. Charlie arrives with a notepad and a sardonic grin on his craggy, Irish face.

"Don't say it!" I caution as I roll away the physioball I usually sit on and plop into the chair. "I'm not sore, I just don't feel like having to balance myself this morning. What have you got?"

"Good morning yourself." He grins.

"I'm sorry," I say. "Good morning, Charlie. How was your weekend? No, wait—I know how your weekend was because I saw you both nights. You had a great time at a really cool rehearsal dinner Friday and danced the night away last night at the best wedding you've attended in years. You and Chris both had a touch too much to drink and took a cab home."

He laughed, a warm cracking sound. "It really was a great wedding, you know."

"Thanks."

"We were talking about it this morning." He lifts his ball cap and palms the top of his head in an unconscious gesture I assume is left over from when he had hair to stroke back into place, studying me with his miss-nothing eyes.

"I'm not in trouble with Chris for making you come in today?" I ask, unaccountably nervous.

"Hell, no. He just thinks you're crazy. Besides, it's not you making me come in. Amy said she would have assigned me to write this damn bank pitch no matter what. I am capable of working with other artists, you know."

"I know."

"I just don't win shiny gold pencils when I do."

"So it's not me, eh?" I tease him. "It's just the Clios?"

"You know you're the only woman for me."

"It's only because I can keep you on task. And I'm not even the only graphic artist for you, so don't give me that." I push my laptop back on my desk, grab a notebook, and give Charlie my complete attention. We've worked as a writer–artist team on maybe twenty campaigns, and a ton of pitches. But never one this big. "Okay," I say. "Talk bank identity to me. Amy wants two different angles and you were going to take first crack since I had some, er, personal things to take care of this weekend."

Charlie and I both like to work on paper in the early concept and design phase, so we could have done this anywhere; but corporate identity is hard, and our shared instinct brought us into the office where all our award-winners have been conceived.

"I started with position statements, but they all suck."

"Okay."

"I moved on to taglines. I've got two I like."

I close my eyes to listen.

"'Northwestern Pacific Mutual—Towering Standards, Fluid Innovation.' Cause, you know, they're right on the river."

"After everything that's happened in banking, don't you think 'innovation' sounds risky?"

"Yeah, I wondered about that, but we can't really say 'trying nothing new for over a hundred years,' either. They came to us because they want to update their image."

"We could say something about stability."

"A stable platform for change?"

"Can't say 'change' when we talk about money without suggesting coins, small change, small amounts of money. How about 'stable ground for growth'? We could do a visual with seeds underground. Maybe some play on 'not buried in the backyard,' or a protected environment, like a greenhouse . . . Or the Japanese Gardens."

Charlie stays quiet, thinking it over. "Banks have been saying 'grow your investments with us' for ages. It doesn't solve the innovation question."

"No, but it dodges it nicely. Everybody knows you have to choose between risky investments that might pay off big and lower risk, lower yield vehicles."

"You've been reading the material!" Charlie shakes his head, despairing of me altogether.

"Yeah, but it's no different than anything else, right? You gamble on your groundless, optimistic confidence. People play the stock market, or the lottery for that matter, because they think they're smarter than average. Or luckier. That they have some power to either control or predict the future. Which, of course they don't."

"Well, I always say, 'Why invest when you can spend!'"—Charlie lifts his coffee in a decadent salute—"but Chris tells me less now means more later. What do you do, darling? Keep all your earnings safe in Mason jars?"

I shrug. "No, I invest it, but I know *invest* is just advertising-speak for *gamble*. Look, if you can't predict or control the game, the best you can do is protect yourself—you don't invest everything in just one place, or count on just one thing for everything."

"Are we still talking about money?"

"Yes. No. I mean, money . . . time. You don't spend anything all in one place, eggs and baskets, right? You spread your investments out. Work time, play time, time with family, time with friends. You diversify. You can't expect one person to be all things to you, right? Or your job to mean everything? We all know about risk and benefit, but we're tempted by the goodies. Our own optimism and confidence make us take irrational risks. The guy who works eighty-hour weeks so he can cash out and retire at forty. The woman who puts every-thing into raising her kids, cause they are going to make her whole life worthwhile. There are a million ways people keep trying to find a surefire way to quick millions and lifelong happiness."

"NorPac Mutual: We'll make you a millionaire. Risk-free. Super-speedy. Guaranteed!"

"You should write jingles," I tease him.

"Yeah, damn those truth-in-advertising laws. It would never work anyway. The public's too cynical to believe promises like that any-more, even if we were allowed to make them."

"Tell that to the weight-loss industry."

"Okay, okay." Charlie closes his eyes and I look away from him, up into the cobwebby corner of the high wood-beamed ceiling. "Some Microsoft millionaire bought NorPac a couple of years ago, right?" Charlie never reads the research.

"Yeah," I say, "but he's gone now. The bank was founded back in the robber baron days. He bought it trying to make the Muhammad Yunus microcredit thing work in America after the bubble burst. It was supposed to be all ethics-based and green-friendly, but it made a ton of money and he left."

"Who runs its now?"

"I dunno, bankers?"

"Well, yeah, by definition . . ." Charlie snorts at his own joke and doodles. My eyes float back up to the spiders, spinning away.

Corporate identity is a mask for a faceless face. It helps people hand over their money to the idea of the market, or some other ab-stract concept, trusting it to take their time and energy and turn it into more than they could on their own. Because ideas are hard to relate to. An idea is ephemeral and people don't trust what they can't see, so we make the idea corporeal. We incorporate it, form a corporation—a corpus—a corpse for the idea. And we give this life-less thing—that has no conscience, no life span, no morality—legal status as a person, constitutional rights, free speech, due process. And we go to work inside it like maggots. And because that's gross we hire advertisers who ask themselves questions like "What color hair would NorPac have?"

I turn around for the cube of Pantone pens on my desk.

Not black . . . brown. All the stability and sobriety of black, but with warmth. I'm sketching hair, deep, deep brown with an even deeper red, rich and soft, falling over eyes behind glasses.

Corporations don't die, they outlive their founders and workers, and we adapt their names and logos to a human time frame: American Telephone & Telegraph, AT&T, ATT. They're immortal, like gods, like we promise love will be.

"Who's that?"

Charlie's head is twisted around to my notebook. I look at the face I don't remember drawing. It bears a mild resemblance to Charlie—goateed, beautiful, but twenty years younger, without Charlie's time-carved sharp angles.

"Edison?" I guess. "I was thinking about the 1800s."

"It's really good," he says.

And it is. I never thought of myself as having much talent at portraiture, but this man is compelling, deep eyes behind old-fashioned glasses, an almost grotesquely sensuous lower lip. Definitely not Charlie's mouth. More like Amit's. I retrace the soft line of it with a lighter pen, and envy the ink sliding its caress across the hungry paper.

I turn over the page and start doodling the NorPac logo, twisting it, embellishing, inverting. But every line turns erotic suddenly, and I turn over the page again, embarrassed I ever drew in front of people.

"We could do a series of spotlights on NorPac customers." Charlie picks up my notebook and flips back to the man's face. "A portrait of maybe six different real people, different demographics, and how the bank has helped them. We could pitch it as the bank that sees each customer as an individual and tailors its services to suit."

"Yeah, but it doesn't. They have three kinds of checking accounts and four savings." A ridiculous possessiveness in me hates Charlie holding that face.

"Okay, we could cut that bit out. Just the bank that sees each customer as an individual. 'NorPac, we see you.'"

"It's a little Big Brother."

"Crap. You're right." Charlie drops the sketch pad in frustration, and it skates across my desk.

We fall quiet again. I close my eyes, and the man I drew comes slowly into focus. He's sitting at a desk, but his face is turned to a smudgy window. He looks the way Charlie does when he's working on a headline, abstracted and distant, but keenly focused. I move a little closer to him. I want to see his face more clearly, check my work, but his head turns.

"Hello?" he says.

I've heard his voice before. I recognize its texture and weight, its gentle Irish inflection.

He looks right at me.

"Jesus Christ!" Charlie looks ready to punch me. We're motionless, both standing, his face painted in shock, then anger, then confusion. Then he grins. "Damn, Laura, what the hell got into you?"

The lid of my coffee exploded when it fell, and four stained pant legs accuse me of not having had a sip out of the full cup.

"I'm sorry," I say, numb, looking at the mess.

But Charlie's laughing now. Amy and Ben sit back down.

"It better be one hell of an idea," he mutters, following me to the kitchenette, all remnants of the dangerous man he once was erased from his face. "You've never jumped up screaming before."

"I didn't scream."

"You're right, it was more of a squeal."

"Nuh-uh."

"Whatever, but something made you leap to your feet. Dish, sister."

"I was just thinking, what if we could find a way of talking to the past? Maybe dig up the founding documents, touch back to the ideal the bank had when it started? To its founding spirit?"

"Okay . . ."

"Maybe old diary entries from people a hundred years ago . . ."

"The more things change, the more they stay the same?"

"Yeah, something like that." We blot our jeans on designer dish towels and wander, thinking, back to my desk. Charlie almost runs into the partition that shelters my workspace from the openness of the floor, making me think it was hangover more than discipline that kept the ex-boxer from decking me earlier. "We could do chunks from then and now on the same page. Show what's changed and what's the same, the particular versus the universal."

Charlie is nodding. I start sketching. "People use banks for pretty much the same reasons now as they did a hundred years ago, right? To keep their money safe. To save for the future."

"Borrow for their dreams . . ."

I turn my notebook back to face him.

I've drawn three raggedy rectangles. "Check it out," I say. "First we've got Mr. Sideburns." I rough in an old-timey face. "We put some quote about saving money and at the bottom, the date." I write "January 1889" under the man. "Then we do someone from today." I sketch a quick modern profile, wild curly hair. "We give her a quote and the date the spread runs. Then in the last pane, we put the Nor-Pac logo, or a photo of their big building downtown, and where the date goes we put 'constant' or 'consistent.'"

"I'm not sure either is the right word."

"Well, you're the writer, figure it out."

Charlie plops back into his chair. I mop up the spilled coffee on the floor and start Googling "turn of the century portraits" and then "Victorian portrait photography."

"Are you going to practice tonight?"

I look from the stiff and serious sepia faces to Charlie's grizzled grin. I have no idea what he means.

"Tell me you're not going to soccer tonight," he scolds.

"Oh. No, we're going to dinner with Amit's folks. They're staying in town a few extra days."

"Dinner with the in-laws on the first night of your honeymoon, wow!"

"And the second night. But this is not our honeymoon! We're still going to have one. We just postponed it till after the NorPac pitch."

"God, Laura. You're such a romantic!"

"Romance is for children."

"Oh, *now* you sound like a wife."

"Part of me is now. Not that kind of wife, but . . ." I sigh, feeling muddled. "His parents came from Canada for the wedding, and Amit has a really good, close relationship with them. We're having dinner tonight and tomorrow night. Then on Tuesday they go back to the Golden North where everything is Done Correctly, thank you, and we'll have the loft to ourselves again until the pitch is over and we're off to Italy. Besides, Amit understands how important this pitch is, and Amy paid the airline change fees, so we don't lose anything by delaying for a week or two."

"Not anything?"

"Not anything real. It's just timing." I turn back to the solemn eyes peering out from my screen. All these men are dead now. The dogs are dead. Even the little children.

"That's what I love about you, darling. You're so grounded."

I grin over my shoulder at him. "One of us has to be."

"I think you should buy me a coffee since you threw yours at me." Charlie stands up stretching. "Come on. We've had our Big Idea for the day. We'll come back and do the work." He holds out a hand to me, and I take it, and the compliment it stands for.

In the refreshment room of the British Museum, where Ida had never dared to take tea alone in her long months of study, she and Mr. Yeats sat down together across a small table to regard one another through the thin eyes of boxers. He ordered coffee and asked polite questions about her researches. But Ida's telepathic hearing worked perfectly well at close range. If Laura's ghost had proved a disappointing key to the Theosophical Society's front door, it might make a tolerable crowbar to its back window.

"Miss Jameson"—the poet's soft baritone whisper poorly masked his ardent interest—"what do you know about the night I met Miss Gonne?"

"Does your study of the occult extend beyond the Theosophists?" Ida quizzed him.

"It does. Next to my poetry, it is the most important pursuit of my life."

"And Madame Blavatsky?"

"I have quarreled with her some. I am more interested in the Hosts of the Air, ghosts and fairies, than she would like. And I have recently begun several experiments of my own to test what supernatural phenomena are real. But magic is at the center, Miss Jameson, of all I do and that I think and all that I write."

Ida smiled, and leaned across the small table. "Maud is a medium," she whispered. "The most beautiful woman you have ever seen is a channel for something else."

He sat rigid on the upholstered bench. "For what?" he whispered. Fear and desire warred too painfully in his face, and a terrible tenderness soaked through Ida.

"I don't know," she lied. How could she tell him a ghost had claimed his heart? "But at your first meeting, she was not herself."

"I knew I saw something extraordinary that night!" he said. "Can you tell me all you know about it? Start at the very beginning, if you please, Miss Jameson. What rituals had you performed?"

Ida allowed herself to bask for a moment at the center of the poet's impassioned curiosity. She would not confess her humiliations to this man. Let him think her a dilettante if he must, generally inhibited rather than expressly denied. "I have no formal occult training, Mr. Yeats. The day you met Miss Gonne, she and I had been experimenting, somewhat inexpertly, with possession."

"She was possessed!" The poet's face lost all its rich color.

"I tried to summon her father."

"It was not a man I met."

"No."

"Do you know the spirit's name?"

"Yes." Ida knew more than that, but she wasn't in the practice of surrendering information gratis.

"Miss Jameson?"

"Mr. Yeats, you are much more expert in these matters than am I."

"Miss Jameson! I beg you to tell me the name of the spirit I met that night."

"You are part of Madame Blavatsky's inner circle, a member of her Esoteric Section."

The poet's good manners conquered his exasperation. "I have tried to make a serious and thorough study of the mystical and occult," he said, earnest shoulders hunched under the weight of his knowledge and Ida's expectations. "I will offer you what I can."

"Must a disembodied soul be very powerful to possess the living?"

His polite nod did not conceal his impatience.

"I had guessed as much. And what are the most powerful spirits?"

"Gods," he replied swiftly.

"Or?" she asked.

He sat at the small table, a man rusted in place by the creeping corrosion of understanding. Ida waited for the truth to eat through him. "Or the inverse of gods," he whispered.

"If I told you the name of Maud's possessing devil"—Ida leaned closer to the handsome immobile poet whose unseeing eyes looked through her still—"it might gain some power over you as well. It is better that only my soul be forfeit."

"It was no devil I saw in Maud."

"I have seen one there."

His eyes locked with hers. "Whether I learn her name or not," he said, "I am already lost."

Ida saw it was true.

"Laura," she said.

"Laura." Will made the ghost's name an invocation, and Ida thought, if she had any soul within her breast at all, it would have stepped aside to admit his pilgrim's prayer and answer it.

"Laura," he said again, and the pity of his loving tugged at Ida with small mute fingers.

"Say her name a third time," she whispered.

"Laura."

But nothing happened.

"We must find a way to contact her again!" The force of the poet's passion caught Ida unaware. She let his heat soak into her. It touched her, sweet and private, but insistent. His eyes were fevered, and burned unfocused, a distant search beam alighting on Ida by erratic accident. "What I saw in Maud's eyes, what I felt . . . She might be a disembodied spirit, a ghost perhaps or errant astral traveler of our own age. Did you ask her origin?" he asked.

"No."

His disappointment struck Ida as a rebuke. "I asked her natal date," she blurted.

"Did she give it?"

Ida blushed. She should have stayed silent. "No," she confessed. "Maud answered."

"Are you certain?"

Ida deflated. "It was dark, and I would swear I saw her eyes change, that I glimpsed the other looking through Maud at me. But then she gave Maud's birthday."

"Perhaps they share a natal date. It would serve to link them, and explain much."

Ida hadn't thought of that. If Madame Blavatsky had not refused her, Ida would not be floundering after the pitiful breadcrumbs dropped by this man's better trained—but inferior—mind.

"She must have died young then," Ida snapped, glad for something intelligent to say. "At no older than fifteen. You cannot channel a living soul, and they rarely return immediately after death. It was just this Christmas that Maud turned twenty-two." Ida ground her molars against the Irish that bubbled up in her voice when she was agitated.

"They were both born on Christmas?"

How could she know infinitely much more than he, but only, at the moment he rehearsed her knowledge to her, understand its meaning for the first time? She could love him for that enlightening power. Or envy him.

"The winter solstice," she whispered.

"That date changes."

"Yes."

"Of what year?"

If he leaned any closer across the table, it would be near enough to kiss her, or bite off her nose. "Sixty-six."

"That is what she said?"

"Yes."

"Exactly what she said?"

Why? Ida shouted silently. Energy flew around the great man's head in mounting spirals, like a whirlpool. It radiated in and streamed out, and washed her in magic. And she did not understand.

"Yes!" Ida snapped.

William Butler Yeats, distinguished poet and artist, political writer and essayist, leapt to his feet with a strangled cry. "And that is all?"

Ida nodded. Again alone. Again uncomprehending.

"She could have come to me from anywhere in time! She might have been born in 1766, one hundred years to the day before our own Miss Gonne. Or even five hundred years before. She could be a spirit come from our nation's history." The poet stood among the boring startled faces of the refreshment room's few diners. "Or its mythic past." He sat. "She could be the Countess Kathleen herself!" he whispered, turning pale. He looked about the refreshment room as if Ireland's legendary, soul-selling heroine might walk in and have a bun. "I must learn more history!" he muttered.

I must learn more magic! Ida countered silently.

"If only we had her family name."

Ida saw the poet alone, carried away over horizonless sweep of history. *I have not only that, I have her kiss to bind her to me.* Ida's brazen declaration went unnoticed by the soul-deaf poet. "She mentioned a place name," she said.

Mr. Yeats refocused his distracted eyes. "Miss Jameson, you are full of surprises. Is there no sounding the depths of your knowledge?"

"The metaphysical is, by its nature, uncharted, Mr. Yeats. And I am untrained with either sextant or compass."

The poet laughed, a harsh, sad sound.

"Miss Jameson, I am at your mercy."

Ida pondered whether she quite liked sharing her exploits, and decided she did.

"She spoke of Portland Gaol," she said at last.

Surprise, fear, and then delight gusted across the subtle features of the poet's fine face. Finally a smile dawned slow, warm, and bright. "Miss Jameson, that is excellent news! Indeed, I have never been so pleased to hear of a lady's incarceration."

"Not all of Portland's prisoners are Irish rebels, Mr. Yeats."

"Quite right, Miss Jameson." His cordial smile betrayed no shadow of disappointment or doubt, despite the obvious implication his newly beloved had been previously hanged as a traitor. "English jails themselves have claimed as many lives as the hangmen they employ. And a hundred years ago, when the crown was less enlightened, women were hanged for debt as well as sedition. No, the English have hanged and starved the Irish in a multitude of jails for a fistful of crimes. But"—he grinned at Ida—"they have always kept meticulous records!"

He would go down to Portland and scour the Royal Prison Archive and find her—a "Laura"—worked to death or hanged, and learn her family name with the way she died, and Ida would no longer have anything to offer him in trade. "Have you seen the spirit since?"

Mr. Yeats took a guarded sip of his cold tea. "What makes you ask?"

"You were not surprised to learn the woman you entertained at your father's house was a body unmatched to its indwelling soul," Ida explained, "and you did not seek another, more scientific explanation."

"Miss Jameson . . ."

"If this spirit can inhabit Maud without my assistance, I would like to know."

He leaned forward and took her hand gently across the table. "Miss Jameson"—his voice rang husky with emotion—"my dear girl, I pride myself on my scientific disposition, on a dispassionate search for the truth. Every experiment has a control, and every phenomena, a cause. But your rebuke is not misplaced. I leapt to acceptance without proof, not because I had further corroborating evidence, but because the explanation pleased me."

It required a distinctly unladylike gulp to choke down the knot in Ida's throat. "Pleased you?"

"I had believed everything—everyone—I encountered that night was lost to me. It pleased me to think the woman I met that night was not, in fact, Miss Gonne."

"Why?"

"Because Miss Gonne does not love me."

"I don't understand," Ida said. How could any woman not love this man, this tall, proud, artistic man, whose soul wept into his eyes, whose pen could channel Truth as deftly as Maud Gonne channeled devils?

"I had feared the woman I met that night was lost to me."

"But she is more than lost to you!" Ida exclaimed. "Maud, at least, might come to see you for the man you are. She might learn to value your subtle gift for shaping minds over politics' crude work at changing laws. Law can only silence the voice out of tune with the song of the powerful, but Art welcomes it and creates harmonies. If Maud understood, she might yet yield to your suit. You are a man. Laura is a spirit without a body. How could you ever properly love her?"

"In a room of other people, when my father, my brother, and my sisters all met Maud Gonne, I alone saw the channeled spirit. Her divine, secret self was visible only to my soul. You ask how I could ever love her. I already do. I love her with a soul blind to reason, for which you so rightly chastised me." The intimacy of his confession took refuge only slightly in this gentle self-ridicule. "Such an overwhelming spiritual love is only explicable by something supernatural. Believe me, Miss Jameson, I have a scientific soul. Only magic can account for Miss Gonne's possession, my feelings, even your own experience, Miss Jameson. You, yourself are scientific proof of the power of the unseen!" His smile acknowledged his words' bravado, but his eyes behind his glasses shone shockingly uncertain and arrestingly open.

Ida smiled back with genuine courage. He wanted to do more than solve the mystery of what they had both seen.

"Mr. Yeats, there are some books I cannot write for, but with some additional study, I do believe I could contact her again."

"Miss Jameson"—his hand gripped hers—"would you?"

Ida took a moment to master her emotions.

"Yes."

He caught her hand to his lips, and although his mouth just grazed her ungloved hand and Maud's gold ring, Ida knew suddenly how like a bite a kiss was, how much a stylized assault, a kitten's nip of a wild cat's disemboweling maw.

"But I am clumsy and untrained and Maud does not like being separated from herself."

"Have you tried a more willing medium, or do you believe it must be Maud we use?"

Ida bit her lip. "I know it must," she said. "But leave Maud to me. I can bring her back from France."

He closed his eyes in gratitude. "And Laura?" he whispered, eyes still closed, beautiful, vulnerable in hope.

Ida was more so, but kept her eyes open and trained on her best chance to win by deceit what had been denied her by fate. "You must bring to me all the secret teachings of the Theosophists," she said. "But, Mr. Yeats, Madame Blavatsky cannot hear of our association."

He met her eyes and nodded. Ida could count on his gentleman's honor not to mention a lady's name. Let him think concern for her reputation prevented her, and not the blood-inked name of Blavatsky herself. Convict or queen, Laura would be brought back. With her newly acquired skill and the access Ida would soon possess to all the secrets of Theosophy. This poet might be Laura's love, but Ida would be more than that.

"Miss Jameson," he said, "my very soul is in your debt."

Silver or souls, there is no distinction between debt and power. On earth as it is in Heaven.

"It has been my pleasure, Mr. Yeats," Ida said, and stood. As before, so again. As above, below. The only question Ida couldn't answer was how far back and how far down.

from *Flowering Dusk*
by Ella Young

1945

[Maud Gonne] has a beauty that surprises one—like the sun when it leaps above the horizon. She is tall and like a queen out of a saga. Her hair is burnished gold and her eyes are gold, really gold . . . I see her standing with W. B. Yeats, the poet, in front of Whistler's Miss Alexander in the Dublin gallery where some pictures by Whistler are astonishing a select few. These two people delight the bystanders more than the pictures. Everyone stops looking at canvas and maneuvers himself or herself into a position to watch these two. They are almost of equal height. Yeats has a dark, romantic cloak about him. Maud Gonne has a dress that changes colour as she moves. They pay no attention to the stir they are creating; they stand there discussing the picture.

I catch sight of them again in the reading room of the National Library. They have a pile of books between them and are consulting the books and each other. No one else is consulting a book. Everyone is conscious of those two, as the denizens of a weedland lake might be conscious of a flamingo, or of a Japanese heron if it suddenly descended among them.

Later, in the narrow curve of Graton Street, I notice that people are stopping and turning their heads. It is Maud Gonne and the Poet. She has a radiance as of sunlight. Yeats, that leopard of the moon, holds back in a leash a huge lion-coloured Great Dane—Maud Gonne's dog, Dagda.

Destiny swept them closer to me. These two moved through my life for some years, with a background at times of Paris, at times of Irish play-houses, at times of Irish mountain and pine-wood, always with a sense of far-off splendid happenings, of queens of long ago, and of that prince who had the strangeness of hawk-feathers in his hair.

3

WHEN SLEEPER WAKE
AND YET STILL DREAM

My Soul. *I summon to the winding ancient stair;*
Set all your mind upon the steep ascent,
Upon the broken, crumbling battlement,
Upon the breathless starlit air,
Upon the star that marks the hidden pole;
Fix every wandering thought upon
That quarter where all thought is done:
Who can distinguish darkness from the soul?

—from "A Dialogue of Self and Soul" by W. B. Yeats

"It's too soon!" Maud wheeled to face Ida, her famous apple-blossom skin white as frost.

"You were late coming down to tea," Ida choked, standing uncertain in the doorway of her London town house's best guest room. Framed by the December sky, its milky light still warmer than her face, Maud lost even another shade. Her always-majestic body curled around her distended abdomen in a gathering wave of pain. It pushed a thin wail from her.

Afraid Maud might fall, Ida slipped into the room and locked the door. "Come away from the window, darling."

She unfurled Maud's ashen fingers from the clawed sill, but not until the pain passed would Maud allow Ida to steer her to a chair by the fire. Above the haughty, pregnant belly and rich, swollen breasts, Maud's white face was pinched as poverty's. She looked up at Ida from purple-bordered eyes. "The baby should not be born before the new year. Or the solstice at the very soonest."

Ida perched on the chair's arm. She would never have been indelicate enough to mention Maud's obvious condition, and had been obliged to eat her curiosity since she had met the Club Train from Paris at Charing Cross. Maud had said nothing in her letters, only that she would be crossing to London for her sister's wedding and would like to stay with Ida instead of in her usual rooms at the Grosvenor.

"You're over-tired, dearest. I'll ring for Emily to bring the tea things to us up here."

But Maud shook her head. "No. I can't eat. I've had no appetite since October. Dr. Pozzi says I must to keep up my strength, and at first I ate quite well, but now . . ." She stopped speaking and sat forward in the deep chair. From her proud, bowed head to her gripped knuckles, there was no movement in Maud's body. All her force and strength of thought were ground to stillness by the process her body must endure. When the pain passed again, Maud gasped and closed her eyes.

"Do you have a doctor in London, Ida?"

Ida shook her head. "Only in Dublin."

"And mine's in France." Maud's high brow was stained with cold droplets.

"Any physician can bring the chloroform and forceps."

But Maud shook her head. "The child must not be born in England!"

Ida considered the blight of an English-born infant to Maud's politics and image, and groaned with her friend. But her childhood habit of mining devastation for burned and twisted treasure raised a promise in its singed fingers.

"Maud," she whispered, "do you remember when you came to see me, after my father died?"

Maud scarcely nodded.

"We had a séance. I mesmerized you, and your body went to sleep, do you remember? All but your breathing stopped. You couldn't feel a thing."

Maud's eyes found Ida's.

"We might try again," Ida whispered.

Maud nodded.

Ida's guilt-hot fingers plucked the pins from Maud's upswept hair. Some gifts, like those blackmailed from overeager uncles, require you have no more scruples than they, and this would cost Maud nothing. Help her even, mayhap. And surely Maud's unlikely crisis was a sign that Ida was meant to pluck opportunity from its ashes.

Ida positioned her eager thumbs and watched the proud face soften and blur beneath them. The harsh pain-carved lines between the high brows dissolved, and the famous, full lips opened. A deep sigh of suffering came from them, and although Maud's face showed no sign of distress, her body, reclining in the chair, tightened yet again. Ida chewed her lower lip and saw how Maud's arching back raised her overfull breasts and engorged belly. She lapped the bitten spot with a thoughtful tongue, and waited.

The spasm eased at last, and in a strong, calm voice, Ida conjured the spirit that had possessed Maud almost a year ago using the spirit's name, as much of the birth date she knew, and finally, fearful lips pressed against the lax ones, a slightly blood-tinged kiss.

"Maud?" she whispered. "Laura?"

A slow, easy, safe, and satisfied smile filled Maud's perfect mouth. It was not Maud's smile.

The head lolled against the upholstery, and loose fingers climbed the huge globe of Maud's deformation.

"Laura, what year were you born?"

Still, Maud's blind hands explored the inert body.

"Oh, wow." Maud's eyes slid open and were not Maud's eyes. The lazy smile grew into grinning. "That's so intense."

"Is it another pain coming?"

"This is incredible." Laura rubbed the risen belly, looking down from Ida's inquiry to her stroking hands. "I'm dreaming about pregnancy. That's so cool."

"You are not dreaming."

It was a foolish smile, really. An imbecile's smile. Maybe in life, Laura had been feebleminded. It would explain quite a bit.

"No, it's good. I had an amazing day at work. Really cool stuff. And now I'm dreaming about creation and fertility." Laura undulated Maud's voluptuous body in the stiff chair, and closed her eyes again. "Much better than falling in love."

Ida sat down on the hassock, puzzled. What constitutes an "amazing day at work" for a prisoner of the crown?

"What is your profession?"

"I'm a graphic artist," the spirit replied without glancing up from the body she clearly reveled in inhabiting.

Ida shook her prim head. In the eight months since she had encountered Mr. Yeats in the Reading Room, Ida had carried constant worry that Laura might be an astral traveler, rather than a ghost or a devil. If Laura belonged to a body of a living woman, she might find her way to Yeats without Maud, or even Ida. But no lady could be an artist by profession, and no devil would want to be.

"I remember you." Laura's dim eyes reached Ida's face. Ida cursed her sex. If she had been permitted to study history at Trinity as her brothers had, she might know what culture and what time had employed women in art, and not merely diverted its prosperous ones with it. "You knocked me out."

"Yes," Ida agreed. "I mistook you for a devil."

Laura snorted and rubbed Maud's belly. "Then we went somewhere with horses and I met a man."

"You met Mr. Yeats."

A flood of warmth colored Maud's thin face. "I'd like to see him again."

"You're very bold. It's not for a lady to seek the attention of men."

"God, what bullshit. How would you stand up and give a pitch or ask for what you're worth when you take a new job if you believed that?"

"You do that?"

"Of course." A distant confusion clouded her face. "I think so. I can't remember exactly, but it seems right."

"And can you vote?"

"Sure. I don't always remember to."

Ida sat down carefully. Laura was no ghost, imprisoned and killed on her wedding night. This was a stranger soul than Ida had imagined. Nowhere on the earth could women vote. She was from some other realm.

"What is your profession?"

"I . . ." Laura's eyes searched Ida's face. "I don't know."

"What is a 'graphic artist'?"

"I don't know." Fear pinched the corners of Maud's mouth again, but there was no whisper of her left in her eyes. "I want to see Will Yeats again."

Ida took a dangerous risk. "He wants that, too."

Laura's smile was shockingly her own.

"But you cannot see him now," Ida cautioned.

"Why not?"

Ida reconsidered her imbecile theory.

"Because you are heavily pregnant with the child of another man."

"I'm married?" Pure terror washed Maud ice white.

"No," Ida said. "But the child's father is."

"I had sex with a married man?"

"Well, Maud did."

"Oh." The degree of Laura's relief was almost comic. What outlandish ideas this spirit held! What world could she inhabit that gave consent to women's suffrage, but could not comprehend the arrangements made by the unhappily married of both sexes? Certainly no human realm. Mayhap she was an angel of some advanced degree. Or an oversoul from some distant plane where men and women, equal and virtuous, married for love and remained faithful, not only in appearance, but in actual deed. A realm where the distinction Mr. Ruskin spoke of between the public and the private spheres had been erased, and morality was self-policing rather than obeyed for fear of social censure. It would be a very advanced and spiritual place indeed. But she had clearly said Portland.

The ideas of Mr. Ruskin and Mr. Darwin collided in Ida with such force she jumped from the footstool and stumbled into Maud's chair. Not "advanced," she corrected herself, "evolved!"

"Laura, if you want to ever see Mr. Yeats again," she whispered, steadying herself on the chair back and leaning close over Maud, "you must allow me to bring Maud back into her body a little ways. Only when hovering between your world and ours can you see into both. I must know the exact year of your birth, and you can't remember it now, can you?"

"No." It didn't seem to trouble her. "But what if Maud won't go away again?"

"You may be lost to this age forever."

"And Will Yeats?"

"He will be here."

Laura shook Maud's fierce head. "I won't go. I won't let Maud take her body back from me. This is fun."

"She was born to it, she can overpower you."

"She won't. She couldn't get out of here fast enough."

"She was in pain, but sadly, it won't always be that way. Laura, if I can learn your natal date, I can bring you back whenever I will. And I can channel you through Maud when Mr. Yeats will be nearby."

Laura stood up and staggered, awkward in the unfamiliar weight and height. Facing Ida across the chair back, she used Maud's height to intimidating effect, and Ida knew she was just as accustomed to getting her way, but with less artifice and subterfuge. Laura might ask, but Ida could wheedle. Laura was bold, but Ida was subtle. She must not let her excitement ruin her advantage. If only she was right in her new belief.

"Mr. Yeats is not here in London now," she lied, but Laura paced the room, her grace in Maud's body growing with every stride. She stopped before the window and gazed out at the tumbling snow.

Maud had been standing exactly thus when Ida's hesitant rapping inquired why she had not yet come down to tea. Maud, in profile, had been held absolute and certain by her proud spine, unyielding to the grim burden her belly carried. Laura rocked it now, her hands wrapped low, swaying its weight between her hips, back and forth from foot to foot and humming.

Ida crept up to her and touched her arm. "We must risk this. If you are to see him again."

Laura nodded. She shrugged off Ida's cold fingers and returned to the chair. She closed her eyes.

Ida started her whispered invocation and watched the perfect lips soften, admit a gentle pull of air, and release it, groaning.

"Maud?"

Maud's hands twitched, groping for her stomach.

"Laura?"

Maud's fingers found the waist of the long frock top tenting her distorted body, but she whispered, "I can hear you."

"Don't open your eyes."

"This thing hurts me." She yanked the rich fabric across herself, twisting.

"Tell me the year of your birth."

Laura grunted and groped beneath the heavy folds. "Nineteen sixty-six."

The snap Ida heard was miles away.

"Tell me the year of your birth," she said again, her voice stifled and rough.

"Nineteen sixty-six."

"Well, Devil damn us," Ida whispered. She had been right! Laura had been born not a hundred years before, or even five, not the shrouded past, but that undiscovered country of what was yet to come. Yeats would never think of that! Unheeding, she watched Maud's possessed fingers work beneath her dress, opening buckled straps and twisting. With the spirit's full name, birth date, and her kiss, Ida would not need Maud's cooperation now. She could almost summon Laura while Maud slept.

Ida considered what to say to Mr. Yeats. Since she had seen him last, Ida's occult education had encountered more obstacles. In Blavatsky's magazine, *Lucifer*, Ida had read an article by a Mr. Mathers. In a bookseller's barrow down Farringdon Road, Mathers reported, a mysterious, ciphered manuscript, lost for centuries, had revealed itself again through a miraculous intervention of fate (but really magic, Ida was certain). With its decoded rituals and curriculum of magic, Mathers had established a new society, the Hermetic Order of the Golden Dawn. Ida had been frantic to join. The order was powerful and growing quickly, open as Blavatsky's had been to men and women equally. But not, of course, to Ida.

Full of excitement and nerves, she had met the energetic Scot in a decrepit eighteenth-century terrace on Fitzroy Street, a studio shared by two artist-friends of Mathers, and appealed to him for admission to the Golden Dawn. Lean and handsome in his military jacket and crisp mustache, he had welcomed Ida and the family wealth she might contribute toward his planned conversion of the little studio into the order's first temple. They had laughed flirtatiously as he prepared to cast the ritual initiation horary. But even Ida, ignorant as she was, saw dark patterns of warning and disappointment in the cards upon the table. Mr. Mathers was sorry, deeply sorry, but the cards foretold the destruction of the entire order, should Ida ever be ordained.

But she was never one to despair! What she deserved, but was denied, she could steal, or borrow. Convincing Will to join the Golden Dawn would be easy. He was as interested in the occult as she. Ida's bitten lips split with her grinning. She could offer him Laura's full name in trade for what he learned once initiated. It mattered not that he would surely kiss the channeled spirit at his first chance. He would never guess the year of her birth, and her name would be enough to stop him searching prison records and turn his search to the occult, as he must do. And Ida would help him interpret what he learned. He would need to report everything he learned from Mathers to Ida, to further their shared aim!

When Ida thought to look for her again, Maud, her naked back turned, stood before the canted looking glass in the room's far corner.

The tailor-adjusted waist of her skirt had been pushed dangerously down beneath her obscene, exposed belly and breasts. The distended flesh stretched taut but luminous, cream soft, but peach firm. Ida stepped over the abandoned pregnancy corset and the discarded artfully concealing blouse.

She crept up behind Maud. "Tell me the year of your birth," she whispered.

"I already told you." Laura met Ida's eyes in the dark, mirrored glass, but the last taste of Maud had slipped away. "I remember saying it. It was . . ." For a moment the golden eyes were frightened, but Maud's hands, which had never ceased from stroking her swollen belly, captured her attention again. "I don't remember," she said, her reflection strangely shadowed as if even the mirror sought to mute the image thrust upon its surface of Laura, brazen in her undress, massaging her guilt without shame.

"Where do you live?" Ida asked.

"I don't remember." Her confident hands stroked the taut flesh. Ida watched their movement in the glass.

"Do you know who I am?"

Maud's small smile came quickly. "Of course, Ida darling. Haven't we known each other all our lives?" Ida saw Laura had gained access to Maud's details as she lost the facts and realities of her material self and time.

"Do you remember meeting Mr. Yeats?"

"How could I not? I've thought about him all day. Or not really thought about him, but I've felt him, felt something . . ." Ida watched the fluid movement of fingers over flesh. "I don't think I really remembered . . ." The famous translucence of Maud's complexion was stretched to near incandescence across the growing child she carried. Her thin, small-boned hands ran down the rounded dome to the obscured waist of her skirt. "Besides, it was just last night." The hypnotic stroking stopped. "But I wasn't pregnant then. Wow. Dreams are crazy."

"You are not dreaming."

"Yeah, you keep saying that." The hands moved upward once again. "But if this isn't a dream, what is it?"

"Astral travel," Ida said.

Maud's hands did not slide down again.

"You have come a hundred years back in time," Ida said.

The long, lithe fingers split and spread. They gathered and weighed.

"You are in London. It's 1889. Eleven months since you met Will Yeats."

The dough of breast pushed between her fingers like tongues through pursed lips, and beginning in her own breast, a twitching blush heated Ida's throat and cheeks. "Laura, you have not been born yet," she whispered. "You won't be born until after I've died."

The white of Maud's fingers pinched the pink of her breasts, and the swollen peak contracted. Ida's blush raced down her body to between her own soft legs. Maybe Maud reincarnates into this slattern. Ida took a careful step toward the gently swaying body, her curiosity at war with lust. In the glass, she saw Maud's eyes close, and gave her own a free and greedy rein. She longed to wrap her thin fingers over Maud's strong ones, to test and crush the tender flesh they held, to make them shudder with the same violence burning her. In the still-dark mirror, Ida saw Laura's eyes open.

"If this were just a dream," Laura invited, "we could fool around."

"It's not."

"But you want to. And I like sexy dreams."

Close enough to touch her, close enough to drink her smells, Ida stood behind Maud's overripened body and saw Laura wink at her in the smoky glass. Without dropping her eyes, she caught Ida's cold hand in her own.

"I woke up from last night's dream buzzing with Will Yeats, and it worked out very well for me," she said.

"How?" Ida asked, but the desire rising in her voice twisted the word.

Laura carried Ida's starving fingers to Maud's full flesh. "I didn't know there were Victorian lesbians," she mused.

"I'm Irish. I am not Victoria's!"

Laura shrugged Maud's sculpted shoulders. "I meant 'women from your time, from the sexually repressed, pre-feminist, old-fashioned times.'"

"Women from my time are better off than in my mother's," Ida retorted, but she placed her palm over the mushroom-navel. "We may have to go to rather extraordinary lengths to avoid scandal, but we never avoid romance! And the younger members of both sexes are quite adventurous. But we are not equal. Of course, as long as women must depend upon men for physical protection from other men, and for the financial support of our children, we can never be equal."

But Laura stepped back to put Maud's high rounded derrière against Ida's flat stomach. With a reluctant shiver, Ida closed her eyes and leaned into the bare white back. "I have channeled you into Maud twice now. I don't know if she'll let me do it again," she whispered. Her lips touched the cool, honey skin. "But Will Yeats is in love with you. He will want to help me now. Now he will join the Golden Dawn if I suggest, and bring MacGregor Mathers's secrets for me to comb for help in returning you."

Ida lifted her cheek from Maud's soft flesh. "I don't know why your spirit traveled here today, or even how I channeled it into Maud the first time, when she wanted to contact her father."

"I think I came for him."

"For Captain Gonne?"

"For Will. The way I feel about him, you can only dream that kind of love. I have a ridiculous imagination, believe me, Ida. Hell, aren't you living proof? You're crazy as a bogeyman."

Ida craned her neck to see Maud's smiling face in the glass. Eyes still closed, cheeks blooming pink, she smiled at Ida, teasing. Laura was in love with William Yeats. Ida began to work her fingers free. Why not with her? Why was it never her whom people loved? Even without Maud's beauty blinding her, Laura had chosen someone else. Maud's delicious breast mounded in Ida's hand like new snow over old. She had always been a pale ghost beside this tall tower. Ida's angry fingers slid open over the unprotected pink blossom of nipple. Laura, the only lover Ida could not lose to Maud, loved the poet Ida had insisted she meet. Ida's fingers began to bite.

The poet Ida had hoped would mark her occult initiation marked instead the only thing she could not compel. Her fingers clutched the too-tender flesh which slipped away from them. He would no longer need her. There was nothing to stop Yeats and Maud from channeling Laura without her. Ida twisted the dawn-pink flesh and looked for pain on the muted, reflected face, but Laura's full lips smiled beneath closed eyes. Ida watched her own stingy fingers gather more and more. She would twist and press the shy and hiding flesh, she would wring feeling from it, make it feel her, know her touch, submit to more than should be asked. Bring Maud into labor, bring Laura into passion. She would have affect. She would cause sensation. She would kill if she must; she was certain she could . . .

Ida stared. She dropped the darkened flesh she held and pushed the swaying body before her aside. Ida stepped closer to the mirror and took a deeper look into the thunderclouds gathering behind the glass. They had massed like smoke beneath the image of Maud, but this was something else beyond the woman and the room, the reflected lights and fireplace. These were other eyes. Behind Laura's rubbing fingers, behind Maud's distorted frame, yet one more figure. Another set of smoky pupils in an unknown face. He met Ida's puzzled gaze. And smiled.

All the heat went out of Ida. She closed her eyes and looked again. He was beautiful in a way no European man could be. Exotic. Unreal. Primal. And Ida knew at once that dark secrets were hidden in his inviting smile. He knew things she could not imagine or even dream, powerful, magical things, she was sure. Ida put her fingers to the glass.

"Who are you?" she whispered.

He answered with a slow and satiated sigh. A sigh from lips whispering behind her. Ida whipped around. Laura's eyes were opening. The glass-bound Maud was rising. Ida swore a long and violent oath and reached for Maud's discarded dressing gown.

The next sigh was fully Maud's, but still untouched by pain.

Ida helped the long, pliant arms into the wrap and lay Maud's unwieldy body on the bed.

"You will need to go un-corseted to your sister's wedding. The pains stopped when you took it off."

Maud struggled up from beneath her belly like a worm she had set a stone upon, to bestow a contented smile on Ida. "Don't be stupid, darling. Kathleen is my sister. It would take more than this to keep me from standing by her today. The infernal thing works well enough for English decency."

"You will have to register the child, if you birth it here."

"You don't have sisters, darling. You wouldn't understand. And I feel entirely well. Better than I have in days." Maud levered herself to standing, wrapping the heavy dressing gown around the magnificent tumults of flesh. "Besides, if the pains start again, you'll work your magic for me once more won't you?"

"Of course." Ida retrieved the tangle of buckles and whalebone from the ground.

"That's my dearest friend! You are so very good to me." Maud sat heavily before the vanity mirror and pushed pins into her tumbled hair.

Ida took the porcelain stopper from the speaking tube and told Cook to send up Maud's little French lady's maid. Then she collapsed into the fireplace chair. "I could come with you back to France," she said.

"No, I don't wear the blasted thing there." Maud caught Ida's eyes in the dressing table mirror. "Don't look so somber Iddie! I'll not have Marie tie me in so tightly."

Ida gave an absent nod, searching the reflection of Maud's perfect face for shadows, but the glass was clear and bright.

Maud laughed. "Ida, darling! You have grown too serious living in London. Honestly, I don't understand you! Your mother wrote you had an invitation from Madame Sarah Bernhardt herself, and did not go. She said you spend all your time in libraries!"

"I like my studies. I have no more interest than you do in the high and mighty." Ida pushed herself onto unsteady feet and stood behind Maud's straight back again. "Maud?"

Maud cocked a brow in the mirror.

"What do beautiful women see in a looking glass?"

Maud laughed outright. "The same things you do, I imagine. Let's have tea brought up here, I'm so hungry."

Ida rang for tea. Maud had never had much imagination.

✤

The knocking could be in Portland or Ireland.

After dinner with Amit's parents, I went to bed early, haunted by the sepia faces I'd been combing through for work. I wanted to dream about them, but it's different than the first two nights, first in love, and then pregnant. I'm insecurely situated in Maud, and Ida is no-where nearby.

I can't stand. Hidden under the white drifts of a summer dress, Maud's legs root me to a high-backed chair by an empty fireplace. Through the hotel's tall, open windows, a tentative summer breeze lifts occasional corners of paper or edges of fabric, and I feel equally carried. The fall into Maud's body still drops my stomach, but I fell asleep hoping for this, and it didn't frighten me this time.

The knocking is here.

For what feels like days, no one has been around—Maud has sent even Marie away—and she sits, in her gorgeous, white-and-blue-flecked dress, and doesn't move. I float in and out. Time moves much faster for Maud than me, and I don't know if it's her sense-muffling grief that lets me see through her eyes without Ida to summon me, or whether it's keeping me from feeling as alive in Maud's body as I did the two other times when Ida channeled me into it.

Maud's mind, farther from me than it has ever been, is only trying not to remember. I trace the outlines of her sorrow. I know what has happened. And just as certainly, but all at once, I know Will Yeats stands on the door's other side. My heart sticks in Maud's throat. The freezing fingers of old panic attacks slide down my motionless hands. I am feverishly in love with an absurdly romantic Irish poet from a hundred years ago. He's just outside the door from me. And I can't move.

Maud's heartbreak has crippled me. I can't stand up or open the door. Loving someone gives them power over parts of you. And they can use that power to banish those parts to places from which they sometimes never come back. Lucien's brutal betrayal of Maud will claim me, too, if Will leaves, because I can't speak.

"Will!" I hear Maud say.

And then he's here. He throws the door open and strides across the room. He kneels beside my chair. "I got your letter. Maud, I cannot say . . ."

His eyes run across my face, and he hesitates. Still kneeling, he takes Maud's hands in his. An exaggerated stab of concern shocks me at the blisters marking his slender, beautiful fingers. I want to ask what happened to his hands, but I don't know how to open her mouth or shape the sounds. I meet his eyes.

He shrugs. "I spent yesterday evening with an old school friend at his father's house in County Down." His grin is wicked. "We occupied ourselves by letting up fire balloons and hunting them across the country. We manufactured them from tissue paper, great globes of it, ignited them and chased after them. The better our skill in manufacture, the longer the hunt!"

The laugh comes without my calling it. It sounds unlike what I've heard of Maud's voice, and I know exactly why he's staring at me.

"Maud, your letter . . ." I hate hearing him call me by her name. I'm not Maud, not the proud, sad, beautiful woman he thinks I am. I can only try to memorize his face, the disobedient shock of hair tumbling in front of his glasses, the strength of his shaven jaw. I want to take the limp hands he's holding and touch the hard planes of his face, or tighten my fingers around his. I want all the obscure minutia of affection that I think are silly or cliché.

He's looking into my eyes like a fisherman into a river full of fallen trees.

"You wrote of a dream . . ." I cannot nod her head, but with my eyes I try to encourage him. I don't remember Maud's dream, or writing to him, but I've been drifting in and out of the hotel, her sadness, and his eyes. I never feel this way when I'm awake.

"You dreamed we had been together, a past life in Arabia together. We were sold as slaves, as sister and brother. You saw us traveling together across endless desolate landscapes all of sand. I have no memory of that life together, but the journey, the horrendous, fruitless march . . . I feel the same. And I'm certain our souls have met before."

What if it's never shared past lives we've had when our souls recognize another, but an as-yet uncreated one ahead of us? What if, for some people, the future resonates more than the past, these dreamers to whom possibility can whisper loud as memory? Why do our eyes automatically look back? The past is a landscape we love to retrace, but the future is vast as the sky, patternless, and as lonely. Still, we give preference to What Has Been when What Might Be has all the power. We retread the narrow, leafy, night-shadowed roads we know rather than look into the pathless, star-crowded sky of possibility, and we beg for promises as talismans against the hollow pain of doubt, when the only thing we know for certain is that we can poorly predict and are powerless to change what is coming.

Is that why I've gone back in time to dream of wild romance?

"Maud, I don't want to upset you. When we spoke last, you hinted at some unhappiness, some disillusionment, and maybe there is something from this vision you have had of our past lives that can build some peace for you. You have told me before now that you are not interested in the occult, but if you'll let me try my cards with you, we might learn something that would give you a measure of comfort."

He pulls a soft brown leather case from the inside pocket of his coat and removes a packet of handmade cards. He sits on the footstool and turns them over, one at a time, onto the low table where Maud has left her breakfast things untouched. He has the grace of a falcon or owl, some big hunting bird, even without the huge black cloak he's set aside. His arms unfold like wings, too large to be swift, but somehow lifting and airy all the same.

The vibrantly painted shapes on the uneven heavy cardstock look crudely cut out and pasted on. He turns over each symbol softly, pulling the cards off the pack the way you'd pull a brush through hair, strength and tenderness in the gesture. He loves these designs and patterns beyond their individual beauty and grace. They resonate for him. They pack years of meaning into such a small space, time into material, and whisper, as he turns them over, one by one in his beautiful hands, what would take even poetry hours of language to say. But the strength of his feeling for them goes even beyond what each pattern means.

"This is a card for power," he says. "It stands for the ability to access and maximize the self and its environment. It means freedom—the ability to use all one's resources as one deems best."

I can nod Maud's head. I've seen this somewhere.

My scream surprises me more than him. It's a strangled sound, from far away. From me alone, with nothing in it of Maud. And I realize in the same instant he's not only unsurprised, this is what he's been expecting. He turned up a card on the table. A symbol he knows, that stands for something. A symbol I doodled yesterday in a notebook, a hundred years from now, as I tweaked a corporate logo.

His keen eyes spot the trout beneath the mossy, submerged branches of my eyes. The tenderness and hunger of his gaze are almost enough to bring my voice through the strange, numb lips I'm trapped behind.

"This is another card for power," he says.

I can nod Maud's head. I've drawn this, too.

"It stands for the negative force of power—and the tendency of power to corrupt those in whom it is invested. It's exploitation, the 'power over' rather than 'power to.' Power over others, their lives and freedoms."

He's thinking about nations, Ireland and England, but I'm thinking corporations. And banks.

I nod Maud's head.

He takes the card and puts it in my hands. My fingers, Maud's fingers, move to hold it. I can feel my trembling breath. I can feel the grain and flesh of the card in my hands. He wraps his fingers over mine and they're warm and real. There is nothing now between our eyes.

He whispers to me. "Laura."

"Yes." My voice is my own, but nearly sobbing.

"You are the spirit I fell in love with the first night I met Maud. Laura, it was as though you had seen into my soul, and imagined there some sacred inverse of all the demons that had been plaguing my work."

I can only nod Maud's head. "I know," I say. "I thought I was falling apart, but you took the crazy wandering pieces and made a real and secret story. You saw a whole me."

"I saw poetry."

This is crazy.

I mean, beyond the obvious *a hundred years before I'm born in the body of another person* crazy. Who believes in love at first sight anymore, for one thing? It would be ridiculous to base a whole life on a snap decision made by some mysterious, subterranean part of the self. That's worse than crazy. That is irresponsible.

"Laura, I'm so sorry. I haven't known. I have been pursuing Maud, but she has never again been the person I thought I'd found."

"I've tried to reach you, too."

"And Maud has been in France."

"Ida channeled me another time, near Christmas."

"Laura, there have been three Christmases since we met."

"Ida . . ." I start to say *Ida lied*, but something in that knowledge frightens me too much to say it out loud. I'm remembering the baby's birth, Maud sobbing and the chloroform. Baby Georges, in Paris with his Irish nanny now. Reeling, I grope through the torrent of Maud's emotions, and memories I didn't have dreams for. The weight of lives, hers and mine, that don't make sense with anything I feel right now, my hands woven into Will's.

"Can I ask, do you feel . . ." He clamps his earnest lips too hard together. "Laura, I love you."

"Yes," I say.

"Marry me."

I will. I have. My soul has hunted for his forever.

"I can't," I say. "I have another . . . I have other . . ."

"Responsibilities," he whispers, and his eyes let go of mine.

I'm drowning.

"To who you are when you're not with me here," he says, "and to the life Maud has made that you inherit."

The gorgeous Irish of his warm voice slips over me. "I do want to," I say. "I want to be your wife."

"I know." His eyes hook mine again. "But how could you?"

"The part of me that's here with you now, this part of me will always love you. I swear it. And parts are all we ever get of anyone."

"No," he says. His fingers are so warm around mine. "I give you all of me."

His low voice is beautiful in its agonized restraint. "I give you my past. My memories. The man I have been, and the man I hope to be. All my nights' dreams. I spread them under your feet, and swear by the night and light and the half-light, that all I am and have been, all I will and can be, are yours."

"How can you say that?" I ask him. "You have no way of knowing the man you will become. How can you promise anything on his behalf?"

There is no doubt or fear or hesitation in his eyes, and this is his life. His whole, real life. Maud's hands are shaking with my fear. He raises them and kisses the knuckles one at a time, slowly, as if each kiss locks his promise to my skin.

"I only swear to the truth of what I say." He holds my hands in his against his chest. "I cannot control or predict the coming times, but not being able to see into them will not make me look away from what is at stake."

"Why would you take that kind of risk?"

"The eyes are ours for vision. The self is for experience. You would not blind yourself to avoid seeing. I gamble with my self because it is only a symbol, and what it stands for ends only at death. It only symbolizes what is integral, that which—in you—I love. And experience is its purpose."

"Not the experience of pain!" I pull my hands away and they fallen woodenly into Maud's lap.

"Not primarily, Laura." He tenderly reclaims my fallen hands.

"But not primarily the avoidance of pain either. The purpose I have chosen for my life is the creation of the Irish soul. How could I do less than give all myself to it, when its image appears before me in the face of a beautiful woman?"

But now it's Lucien's face I see. I see the memory Maud has been fleeing. It is because of the pain he's inflicted that I have been able to slip into Maud at all. I see Maud holding the child I felt twisting inside me before his birth. They named him Georges after the revolutionary general Lucien admires to the point of jealous love. This bastard child is not Lucien's first son. His wife has given him two others, and he's clarifying for Maud's dumbstruck understanding what he has just suggested. Maud's every thought is only not to cry, and so it's me listening to Lucien.

To Maud—who loves him completely and has never loved another—he suggests she place her greatest asset, her extraordinary beauty, in service to the cause of revolution. Many minor French officials would welcome her attentions. Their base desires, Lucien is telling her, are too powerful a weapon to flinch from using in the name of freedom. Years in advertising make me smile. Same thing still. Sex sells.

"Let's go out to Howth tomorrow," Will says. "I want to show you the places I explored when I was small. We'll watch the gulls, walk along the water."

"My old nurse has a cottage by the lighthouse there." It's Maud's voice, and Will sits back as if struck.

"Laura—" he whispers.

But Maud's thoughts cluster around my own. Sex sells. Lucien's suggestion that her favors might help their shared political cause meant only that. Only that he loved the cause. As she did. More than life, more than mercy. How could she be willing to spill men's blood and shrink from this?

"Laura? Can you still hear me? Stay a little longer! I shall write Miss Jameson from Howth, and tell her what we've done. She can help us channel you again, but more strongly as you were the first time, so that we may speak more together. Laura . . ."

Maud pulls her hands away from him.

"I know there is a part of you," his voice cracks.

"No. Will," I say.

"Laura, the next time will be stronger. But we must have a sign between us. One Miss Jameson does not know. I cannot trust her entirely."

We are all pieces of selves, and parts of our past live with us. Cruel bits and loving ones. Political parts with romantic ones. Secret pieces and wicked ones, and how can you know what of another person is real, or lasting, or integral, or imagined?

"I have a secret name," he whispers, "a magic one I chose when I was initiated into the Golden Dawn to which Miss Jameson will never be admitted. Laura, can you hear me?"

"Yes."

"I will tell it to you, and it will be a sign between us."

We have parts owned by other people. Lucien and Amit both own pieces of me. I hate this transitional time when I can remember them both, am half asleep in two times.

"Will you remember? Laura?" His voice is fading. *"Demon est Deus Inversus."*

from *Theosophical Manual* No. VII
Man and His Bodies
by Annie Besant

1909

When a person "goes to sleep" the Ego slips out of the physical body, and leaves it to slumber and so to recuperate itself for the next day's work. The dense body and its etheric double are thus left to their own devices, and to the play of the influences which they attract to themselves by their constitution and habits . . .

For the normal man it is only at death that this separation takes place, but some abnormal people of the type called mediumistic are subject to a partial division of the physical body during earth-life, a dangerous and fortunately a comparatively rare abnormality which gives rise to much nervous strain and disturbance . . .

If such a person has not yet learned to link together his astral and physical vehicles, if there be a break in consciousness when the astral body slips out as he falls asleep, then, while he himself will be wide awake and fully conscious on the astral plane, he will not be able to impression the physical brain on his return to his denser vehicle the knowledge of what he has been doing during his absence . . .

At other times when the astral body returns to the physical, the man succeeds in making a momentary impression on the etheric double and dense body, and when the latter awakes there is a vivid memory of an experience gained in the astral world; but the memory quickly vanishes and refuses to be recalled. Or yet again, the man may succeed in impressing new knowledge on the physical brain without being able to convey the memory of where or how that knowledge was gained.

4

I THOUGHT HER SUPERNATURAL, AS THOUGH A STERNER EYE LOOKED THROUGH HER EYE

Though I am old with wandering
Through hollow lands and hilly lands,
I will find out where she has gone,
And kiss her lips and take her hands;
And walk among long dappled grass,
And pluck till time and times are done
The silver apples of the moon,
The golden apples of the sun

—from "The Song of Wandering Aengus" by W. B. Yeats

Hidden in the Jameson family mausoleum, Ida found herself capable of something besides mute rage for the first time in the two months since she'd gotten Will's letter.

Railing against Laura and Maud, furious with each that either would allow Yeats to meddle in their magical triangle without her consent and participation, Ida had found in the larger world a mirror for her wrathful despair. Publically accused by Mr. O'Shea as his wife Kitty's lover, Ireland's best hope for freedom without bloodshed,

Charles Parnell, had, on the very day Yeats wrote to Ida, been felled by a heart attack.

Ida's blunt fingers stroked the cold October cemetery stone. All Maud's fabled nationalism aside, Ida knew it was not Parnell the famous beauty mourned, gone too thin and swathed in black, breakfasting with Mr. Yeats in the Nassau Hotel's dining room. No merely Irish tragedy would have brought Maud home from France. But leave it to the small minds of Dublin, on a day of national mourning, to find something to grouse about in a woman's dress. The biddies were whispering it was typical of Maud Gonne to dress like the widow herself, coming home to Dublin on the mail boat with the fallen hero's body.

But home Maud was, somewhere within the vast, umbrella-scaled beast grinding through Dublin, glistening with rain. Somewhere in the black streets or among the white graves, Maud Gonne walked with a hundred thousand others, alone in her secret mother-grief.

From her damp hiding place, Ida allowed herself a rusty smile at the elegant layers of cruelty. Parnell's heart had done him in, but the funeral wreaths said "killed by priests," as if the people knew any mouth that has the power to bless can curse just as well. But Ida knew neither his heart nor their priests, but Beauty alone killed Ireland's uncrowned king. And now his people came carrying his body toward her to Glasnevin Cemetery, *Glas Naíon*, "stream of the infants." And Maud, whose beauty had cursed her infant son just as surely, came with them. It was a dangerous power, a woman's beauty. Through Beauty a woman may hold sway over a man's wealth or political muscle, take his knowledge into her own hand. Beauty was a conduit. A medium. Like Maud was a medium.

Ida nearly knocked herself out leaping to her feet in the foreshortened second floor of the mausoleum. She had been a fool! She had spent her energy and rage in vindication of Yeats's blind betrayal. Yes, he had transgressed. He had written from the little beach town of Howth to say he had glimpsed Laura through Maud. Without Ida's help, without even consulting her, he had summoned the spirit Laura, albeit imperfectly. Yes, Maud had been under great emotional strain, but still, it had enraged Ida. Now the poet might believe he no longer stood to gain from helping Ida. He might cease to bring her the secrets of the Golden Dawn. But he would not think the same of Maud. And Maud, especially now, would be insecurely rooted to her vessel. Her child was dead. This was a much more potent grief than the previous loss of her faithful Frenchman.

Ida lowered herself through the hole in the floor onto the raw earth beneath. If she could pull a spirit into Maud, how much more easily might she slip into the vacated body herself? Ida would take Maud's beauty, would look into the world from behind those luminous eyes, and reach through that body to Yeats. He would deny her nothing then.

Careful not to soil her new funeral dress (so prudent to have ordered it two months ago), Ida pushed against the metal gate that opened from below the mausoleum into the moat around the O'Connell Tower. She climbed the stone stairs and joined the throngs crowding the old cholera mound where graves of hundreds of nameless poor would now carry only one man's name forever. Parnell. The man unkinged by a kitty.

Ida composed herself, grateful for the fine black mesh of her new bonnet. She veiled her smile and slid into the mourning masses, a light heart on a leaden ocean, a brilliant comet in black, thick night. She bobbed a demure nod to a tall, broad-shouldered man and felt herself protected by him and his Gaelic Athletic League mates. They carried their hurley sticks like mage's staves, wrapped in the black net of mourning. They have buried their chief, and would soon hoist another player into place, position a new man to lead them. But Ida already had more magic than mere men. They might find new players. She would change the game.

But Maud. Would Maud agree to one more séance? Ida marched with the crowd through the cold rot smell of grass and open graves, chewing on the question and a little corner of her veil. Yeats would be easy to persuade, but Maud might be afraid, and she would not agree just to please Ida. The new idea blazed like a falling star: What Maud would not risk for Ida or Yeats, or even for Ireland or Lucien, she would brave for the child whose death had served to summon her from Howth two months ago. Although she had spent little of his two years with him, content to leave him in France with his Irish nanny, now that her child was dead, Maud would do anything for Georges. A séance for the departed child would offer a welcome respite from her pain. Words lisped from beyond the grave might hint at future sessions. Smiling behind the trembling veil, Ida flowed with the stream through Glasnevin's gates, weaving graveyard ivy through their buttonholes and whispering about the night's sky's strange lights and Home Rule's fallen star.

Ida's terrible voice holds none of the gentle pull it did last night. And if she had sounded like this on my wedding night, I would have jerked awake instead of falling in love. But tonight, I'm sleep-addled and blind, stumbling back from the bathroom in the dark without my glasses. I tumble back into bed beside Amit. He grunts in his sleep and sandwiches my cold feet between his quilt-warm legs.

I close my eyes and reach back for Will on the cold rippled sand of Howth where a fierce wind blows in over shallow, submerged sandbanks, whipping the water up in sparkling sprays that look like waves driven shoreward by the speeding chariots of tiny, invading ocean gods. Ida shrieks, "Stay away!"

I cuddle into Amit and reach out eagerly for sleep. It welcomes me, warm and heavy as my great-grandmother's quilt over our shoulders. Amit curls his naked brown arm over my waist; Ida's slender white hand holds mine.

"Miss Gonne?"

My eyelids are leaden, but I'm already smiling.

"Whore!" Ida screams.

Her outrage sets my heart thundering, but I refuse to let it wake me, even when I realize the shriek came from my lips, in Ida's voice. A grassfire of whispers circles in a darkened room far away. I cannot see. I push my senses deeper. Maud's rich winter dress blankets my shoulders. Bone corsets my waist.

I am Maud Gonne.

I open my eyes.

The strong face of Will Yeats swims into focus through thin afternoon sun and candlelight. Chair pushed back, half standing, he reaches, torn between leaning across the table to me and coming around to be at my side.

"Spirit, can you speak to us?" asks a deep growl from my left. I turn my heavy head to track the voice, and choke on a fit of laughter. A man in a long blue nightgown, with a leopard skin draped on one skinny shoulder, sits on a raised platform several feet away from us. His oversized, little boy ears poke out white and wiggly against the Egyptian-style headdress tied to his forehead with a piece of string. He looks like a Sunday school pageant pharaoh. "Spirit, are you present?" he demands.

I nod, not trusting my voice to hide the giggles. Will's eyes snap to mine, probe them. I want to jump up and run to him, tell him I'm back, it's me, but something in his guarded gaze cautions against it.

"Have you a message from the Other Side?" intones a woman's voice beside me. I turn to see her, the weight of my piled hair rendering me vaguely fish-like with my eyes darting ahead of a slower-correcting body. She's much prettier than Ida, her shimmering hair loose beneath a crown of paper flowers. I take a cautious breath of dust and candle flame. Five of us sit at a large round table in the center of a long, musty room a little distance from the man seated on the raised dais. Only he and she are robed. The rest of us, Will and Ida, plus a man I recognize, but can't name, and me—Maud Gonne—are dressed warmly against the chill of a November London afternoon.

"Devil damn the Golden Dawn!" Ida screams from her seat.

"Miss Jameson!" The man on the platform shouts and all their heads whip her way.

Ida sags in her chair between Will and me, and although I try to catch his eye now, he's watching her intently as the rest. They're chastising and clucking, the two men, and the other woman, all talking at once. But Ida's eyes are closed, her body slumps in the shabby, high-backed chair.

"She's left her body," I explain.

"Who said that?"

"Another voice speaks through Miss Gonne!"

"Did Miss Jameson succeed in channeling a soul through Maud?"

"How do we know it is not evil?"

"I'm not a devil!" I say. What is it with these Victorians that they see Satan in any unfamiliar face? I should pull myself together before these people come after me with fireplace tools. Every face at the table shows an eager and innocent interest, except Will's. He's looking at me, but the shadow hasn't left.

"Demon Est Deus Inversus," I say.

"The Devil is the inverse of God," the bearded man translates. "And the inverse of a devil would be . . ."

"A god!" whispers the man on the platform, rising grandly to his feet.

"Or an angel," cries the woman.

They all talk at once, but I'm not paying attention. It has worked—Will's secret sign between us. He knows who I am. And slowly, even as other certainties are slipping away, I recognize the rest. The robed couple are MacGregor Mathers and his new wife, Moina, priest and priestess of the secret occult society the Golden Dawn. The bear-like man with the broad, hunched shoulders is Will's friend and fellow poet George Russell, whom everyone calls "AE." They're holding a séance in this dingy upstairs room with poorly proportioned fairies painted straight onto the walls. Knowing who they are and why they're here doesn't make them any less silly in their amateur solemnity.

"Where has the essence of Miss Gonne's mind traveled?" AE asks me, and his deep gray eyes, peering from masses of chestnut hair and beard and inch-thick glasses, warm and steady me. If my dreams are teasing me for my sudden interest in the occult, they forgot to make this man ridiculous. Or Will any less attractive.

"I am in Hell!" Ida moans, and the heads all spin back to her.

Or Ida any less frightening.

Her body, geological in its collapse down the frayed upholstery, is so vacated that her voice echoes in the loose flesh. Moina, across from me, shudders.

"She said she had a unique gift," AE admits, studying Ida with grave interest.

"Devil damn you to the maggot-blistering, sexless abyss, Moina Mathers!" Ida screams.

Moina springs to her feet and staggers. Her husband leaps to her, and guides her back to sitting without taking his eyes from Ida. "I should not have admitted her to our circle tonight," he says. "I did so with reluctance."

"I know you did MacGregor," Will says, "and I am still grateful to you for it." He's looking at me now. I try to smile at him, to signal with my eyes, somehow, that all the Ida weirdness aside, I've come back to him, and I'm here more fully than I have ever been. Unlike the first time, when Maud hovered against my left side and could speak though me, and unlike earlier tonight, when I could not walk, nothing mediates between my total self and him. I only wish there weren't so many people around.

"Well, I don't like it," Moina says. "I would believe she was counterfeiting, just for the freedom to speak brazenly, if she weren't also so grotesque."

"No, I'm afraid she's quite authentic." AE traces a faded vine on the dull tablecloth. "And to my surprise, I find I agree with Miss Jameson, Will. It is no devil she has channeled into Miss Gonne. I do not know what sort of spirit has joined us." His eyes search mine again. I'm not sure I know either.

MacGregor reclaims his elevated seat on the platform and repositions his headdress. A strange, reverent silence descends into the drafty room. Even Will does not meet my eyes. Ludicrous as they are in their furs and robes, their fancy hats and pince-nez, the very fact that I'm here to think they're silly, proves these strange people are capable of more than any of us knew. Than I believed. Does real power invest their make-believe props? And is that a scarier proposition than having conjured me out of complete ignorance?

"Had I known her method of contacting the spirit realm required her to go into trance in addition to mesmerizing Miss Gonne, I would not have permitted it," MacGregor grumbles.

"But for Miss Gonne . . ." Will says, and I hear a new shadow in his voice. Some lingering edge of sorrow or longing when he says her name spikes an unhealthy heat in me.

"Yes. Quite," MacGregor says, acknowledging tacitly what neither man can say about the power of a beautiful woman in pain. "She was quite eager for the ritual. And I know she, too, felt Miss Jameson was the only one who could summon a spirit through her. That she herself was not a natural medium."

I'm brewing ugly thoughts about "she herself" and recognize the stabbing heat as jealousy. I resent the dark edge Maud has left on Will and the things they share—their time together and their real bodies—that I cannot. Could I lose him to her?

"Ida doesn't have to be in a trance," I announce. "The first time she brought me through Maud, she was enough herself to knock me out with the fireplace broom."

"How did she summon you?" AE's voice, smooth and deep, touches something calm in me. I close my eyes to feel it soothe me, and gasp with the pain. My whole interior, my throat, ribs, womb, and skin contract in a crushing fist of sorrow. My baby, my child, the little boy whose magical eyes trusted me utterly, whose bones I rocked within my hips and in my arms and finally, a last time, at the side of his little tomb, is dead. I throw my eyes open against the sob. No wonder Maud was eager to have Ida mesmerize her—anything to get away from pain and memory.

Will's tender gaze supports me as Maud's terrible loss becomes something shared between us. I realize he doesn't know the child was hers.

"Speak to us, Spirit, of how you came here." MacGregor's voice is compelling, but Will's mouth stays hard with warning. I must be careful what I say.

"I can come through Maud when Ida calls me," I say. "I hear her voice when I'm sleeping."

"Speak on, O Spirit," MacGregor intones.

"But this time was different. Ida didn't call me." Already, it feels a long time ago, and unimportant how I got here. "This time, I think I just sensed the empty place in Maud. I think Ida was maybe trying to trade places with her," I say. "Or move into her, like I do. Possess her." I'm not sure. I have trouble remembering the transition times, the flowing into this room with these people, this body. I only know Ida didn't pull me this time. It was me, reaching for Will, which carried me here into the space she opened. I wanted to find Will. I want to find him still.

"Extraordinary." AE leans his elbows on the faded tablecloth.

"Whence hale you, Spirit?" Macgregor asks me. "Are you an over-soul? An angel?"

"The restless soul of an Irishwoman who died unjustly?" Yeats suggests.

"The spirit of Ireland herself?" AE asks. "One of the *sidhe?*"

Their sincerity and the utter lack of irony in their trust of the Mysterious Unseen deflates me. I don't know how to answer such earnest interest, but I can no longer laugh at it.

"Send her back to Hell," Ida suggests, her voice slurring. Her body has continued to puddle down the chair, and only her lolling head remains visible above the table.

"Whence come thou, O Spirit?" MacGregor inquires with scientific calm.

"I don't remember," I say. "Very far away."

"Do you know where you are?" AE's beefy hands, folded on the table just inches under his chin, have vanished beneath the wiry chestnut veil of his beard. It hangs over his lips and climbs up his ears. His dark, thick bangs tumble down to meet it over his rounded forehead. Only his eyes, like crows in snow, gleam lively and alert in the thick blanketing of hair.

"Dublin?" I guess. Everyone sounds Irish.

"London." AE's warm, hypnotic voice somehow keeps getting such simple things wrong from being frightening. "Do you know the present year?"

"No."

"Do you count the passage of years, or know the movement of time?" AE asks.

I can feel Will watching me, and both the Matherses. MacGregor has come off the dais to kneel by his wife's chair, and the drafty, shabby room shrinks around us into a nest of protection and curiosity.

"Yes," I say. "But differently than you do, I think." Maud's memory shows me Georges as little boy, maybe two years old. She was pregnant only yesterday.

"Do you feel pleasure and pain?"

"Through Maud's body. But it's not mine. The longer I'm in it, the more comfortable I get, but I'm more aware of my container than feels usual."

"You inhabit other bodies then?" Will asks.

"I think so." I pull my eyes away from AE's deep and dappled pools to look into Will's. The hurt I see there almost deafens me to AE's next question.

"On other planes? Or other times?"

"I guess."

"Is your native plane superior to ours? Or lower?"

"I don't know. It's different. I can't think how."

"Are you one with God?" AE presses me.

"No. No God."

"Do you serve the Devil?" It's MacGregor Mathers who leans in to ask this question. I can feel him tense and flex, as though he might be called upon to duel with me if I answer wrong.

"No. I don't serve. Don't worship anything . . . really . . . I don't think."

"Are the sexes equal on your plane?" Moina asks.

"Not really. I mean we are, but we're not. Same value, different power."

"Like priest and priestess." I love the smile in AE's rich voice.

"Yeah, kinda like that, I think," I say. "Or that's how it should be. Women can run for office, be CEOs, but . . ."

"What is a CEO?" MacGregor interrupts.

"I don't remember," I say. I am adrift in pockets, sliding in and out of what I know and remember, what I experience in this place, with these people, and the things of mine and parts of me that don't fit into even Maud's much larger frame.

AE's kind eyes probe mine. "I have wondered before," he says, "whether things we know as facts and things we believe as Truth imprint our souls in different ways. What our bodies cannot see, and our minds cannot think, our spirit selves sustain. Or rather we use the word *soul* to describe the part of the self containing that which defines us, that makes us who we are, and that does not change. Perhaps a soul is but a symbol."

"I won't let you fuck her," Ida announces from under the table.

The fine prickle of embarrassment pinches my cheeks and I focus with renewed attention on Moina. I straighten up in the tall, full body I inhabit. I want to run my hands across it, remembering the tender fullness of the flesh, and exquisite sensitivity of the skin. My eyes find Will's again, and see the color rise in his face. He will find a way for us to be alone.

"I know those eyes," comes Ida's voice, muffled by carpet and her tumbled hair. "I saw your eyes in a mirror once," she whispers. "They're so very secret, so . . . exotic. Who are you?" she asks.

She gasps suddenly as though throttled.

Will rises from the table, with only the barest glance toward me. "Gentlemen, we should attend to Miss Jameson, I believe she is not breathing."

AE climbs up from his stiff chair to stand with MacGregor over Ida's sprawled and empty body. Moina rises, too, nudging one of Ida's ankles with a booted toe, but Ida has sunk farther into trance, and even her mouth gapes slack and silent. MacGregor, powerfully built and proud of his vigor, hoists her easily into his arms. He holds her like a child made to carry a mangled and now detested doll. His wife follows him from the room. AE glances after them, and cocks his head inquiringly to us. Yeats catches my hands and draws me silently toward the far door, AE smiling after us.

"Laura?" Will whispers urgently, closing the door behind me.

I nod and step into his arms.

Ida would have liked robes.

In the little house where her husband made a meager income arranging and polishing the collected curiosities of the eccentric-but-wealthy Mr. Horniman, the newly married Moina MacGregor swanned around like the high priestess of Isis herself. With no domestic help beyond the occasional charwoman to come in and clean, Moina had opened the door looking underfed and shabby, yet somehow irresistibly grand. She had ushered them upstairs to the long, empty room over the museum's main gallery and insisted on arranging them, Will, Maud, AE, and Ida, side by side, around the parlor table. Then she had left the room.

She had returned, resplendent in her ritual dress, on the arm of her husband, who enthroned himself on the raised stage in his full priest regalia. Ida grudgingly admitted it made a grand effect, but Moina's complicated seating choreography had required Ida to stand in an undignified posture, leaning between the Golden Dawn's grand magus and Maud. Still, Ida had positioned deft fingers on Maud's haughty auburn head and peered into her grief-rimmed eyes. Mayhap Maud's married French lover should have died, and not her son. She could splinter under this loss.

Maud had pulled the pins from her hair herself.

"Close your eyes tightly—tightly—" Ida had whispered, noting how readily Maud complied. Not like the first time when the lids had fluttered and fought with nerves.

Ida's plan had proceeded well enough, at first. The pinch had eased from Maud's face, and the pained plank of her shoulders slid into a gentler slope. Neither of the Matherses had noticed Ida's haste, nor had Yeats taken his eyes from Maud when Ida reseated herself beside him and closed her own.

Quickly, she had recited the incantation, already reaching beyond herself, groping for Maud. It surprised her, how easy it was to see this way, to spot Maud floating, free of her body, fluid and beautiful as smoke. But then she had sensed the other spirit—Laura—pushing toward Yeats.

"Stay away!" she had warned, driving herself through the bruising bone and fiber of Maud, moving into her until, for a single, crystal moment, Ida possessed Maud.

She had opened Maud's eyes, touched her tongue to her lips, and felt Maud's fingers flex beneath the table. And then—

A glint of something, Maud's ring on her finger, not folded in her lap, but vanishing. Ida had closed Maud's eyes again, turned, and saw her slipping away, dissipating.

Impulsively, Ida had reached.

And Laura pushed. Greedy slattern that she was.

"Whore!" Ida screamed, and fell out of Maud.

She had lost Maud's body. She lost Moina and MacGregor and AE and Yeats. She lost her own body sitting in the Matherses' drab upstairs room, in her ordinary, expensive clothes full of envy for Moina's cheap robes.

"Devil damn the Golden Dawn," she wailed.

"Ida!" Maud's accusing voice rang from somewhere above her. "You were trying to take possession of me!"

Ida lifted her face from cold stone and rolled, slug-like, onto her back. Her bleary eyes tracked a turned wood chair leg up to find Maud in a solitary wingback, the proud buttons of her dress undone. Two tender pale pink rounds of flesh shone warm beneath the ghostly lace and white upholstery. Ida pushed herself up to sitting on her rump, her absurd, squat legs poking straight out before her.

"Maud!" Ida moaned. "Where are we? Why am I here?"

Maud cradled a downy baby head against a swollen breast, and the air between her and Ida rippled like the halo of a blue-hot flame. "You're in Hell," her apparition snapped. "Because you deserve it."

Ida daubed fruitlessly at the muddied apron spread over her thighs. Her astral body must have followed Maud's rather than slipping into its vacated shell.

"You would have moved into my body like that other soul does, and no one would ever have known," Maud accused her. "'I see Georges!' you would have cried, and even Will would have believed you for my sake."

The infant Maud held twisted in her arms as if it recognized its name, but Maud placed her fingers on the miniature skull, touching the same places Ida did when she whispered Miss Hunt's mesmeric words in Maud's ears, and Georges went back to feeding, sucking like an eel at Maud's soft, white breast. Ida tucked her bare feet under her and stood up with a grunt. Where were the clothes she and Maud had worn to the Matherses'? They had ridden out to Forrest Hill together, smartly dressed, but Maud was now swathed in white sea-foams of lace, while Ida wore a match girl's rags.

"You intended to keep possession of my body, didn't you, Ida?" Maud raged in an awful whisper through the infant's downy hair. "Did you plan to live through me, when they inducted me tonight? You would have joined the Golden Dawn that way, so that all the magic would adhere to your spirit, and not mine. Why do you not just brave initiation on your own?"

"My family . . ." Ida began, but Maud waved her silent. "Your parents are dead and your brothers are preoccupied with their own families and careers. No one is watching you, Ida."

"Moina Mathers hates me," Ida whimpered. She would not tell even Maud of the humiliating reading she'd watched MacGregor perform, foretelling an order-destroyer with Ida's name and natal date. "The Golden Dawn won't admit me."

Nor had anyone mentioned to her that Maud was to be initiated that very night, on a whim of hers. Just for asking. Ida writhed with the injustice until the sheltering wings of Maud's chair began to swell with her hatred. They opened into pillowed shell halves behind her. Ida blinked, but the illusion persisted. Wherever she was, its reality transformed more than the clothes she wore.

"It's impossible, you know," Maud said, and dropped her head back against the softness. "You can't inhabit another person. You are not your body. You're always yourself, even in other skins. It's just asking for suffering to try."

Ida nodded mutely, but in Maud's arms, the oblong lump of baby thinned and lightened.

"When you want a thing too much, you can't ever have it," Maud said. "Although it may have you." Maud yawned and stretched, and the seat beneath her mirrored her extension, sliding out, lifting her legs, flexing toward Ida. "My boredom used to untether me from my body, and keep me a dull distance from my life. Now suffering drives me away."

Ida could see through the baby blankets to fragile bones and paling blood.

"And of course I've started taking chloroform to help me sleep," Maud noted. Fully bloomed now, her chair opened beneath her recumbent body. "You'll have to want less, Ida, if you want to avoid Hell."

"How do you know where we are?" Ida asked, creeping toward Maud. "And why are we wearing different clothes?"

Maud shrugged. "This is where I always go when I leave."

Ida stood beside the cloud-white bed, looking down at the full length of beauty beneath her. "I thought you could see more of what you left behind," Ida said.

Maud lifted a finger to point straight up. Ida twisted her neck. MacGregor Mathers's fish-eyed profile loomed huge and terrifying from immediately over her head, asking her to speak. His voice shook the soft mattress where Maud lay.

"Go to Hell," Ida advised him, and returned her attention to Maud.

The gentle lines and stitches of Maud's white dress were folding into the whiteness of her bed. Crumpled, deep pink nipples pushed through the thinning fabric. Maud sighed, but did not close her eyes. Her breasts, like sun-warmed cakes, spread away from each other, and Ida slid her eyes lower. Maud's bare belly rose and fell with her breathing. It lifted the secret slit of her navel toward Ida, only to withdraw it again. Maud stretched her arms, dragging her breasts higher, and Ida, keeping her eyes averted, brushed a dangling finger across the reaching, reddened peak.

Maud's smile came slow, but willing.

How well Ida knew that smile.

Her blunt finger described a slow, careful circle around the proffered nipple, then dragged her fingertips down the mound of breast, and up the long throat to the parting lips. Maud's tongue flicked Ida's fingers, the whole exposed length of her naked body on the bed twisting for the taste of Ida's flesh. Ida pushed her fingers between the parting lips, and they smiled again in invitation.

Ida knew she had invented that smile. Hating how she looked, Ida loved what she saw.

This was Maud as Ida dreamed her, naked and hungry. How many others found her here, inside imagination? And possessed her. How could Maud—or anyone—ever belong to Ida, or be hers exclusively, hers alone, if any fool could claim her in imagination? What you share, you do not own.

Ida's eyes raked the exposed flesh, and saw Yeats kneeling, like a praying child, on the bed's other side. He never lifted his eyes to Ida's but ran an uncertain hand over Maud's trembling exposed flesh. Maud sighed and turned her fretting head against the building sensation. MacGregor was there, and AE and O'Kelly, and Emily, Ida's own maid, but not Marie, Maud's little French servant.

Ida watched Maud's body shudder under the hands and mouths.

MacGregor positively bit into her, while Will Yeats hesitated to touch even his lips to her flesh. Maud belonged to so many, in their imagination. There, anyone could claim her. Was it possible that so many eyes and hands, so many minds turned to her did not somehow collect and touch the Maud that sat at the Matherses' table? Did Maud's power over men in the material world come from what they gave to her in this one? Or took from her here, in this place of collective imagination?

Ida dropped to her knees and grasped Maud's head as it twisted against the pillows in a gasping sea of caresses and sucking mouths. O'Kelly, his dignity abandoned, crouched on the open chair between Maud's generous thighs, his ass in the air, his hands full of her regal hips. Emily ran an insolent, cat-like tongue across one panting nipple, while MacGregor nipped at the other, grinding his teeth between bites in a delirium of animal instinct to tear the flesh. Holding Maud's strong jaw in stubborn fingers, Ida thrust her tongue into Maud's mouth.

All the tumult of Maud's incipient orgasm poured through her kiss onto Ida's lips. And Ida clung to Maud's mouth, licking and biting, tasting the pure eroticism of imagination. Emily's wicked licking transferred to Ida's smaller and more tender breasts. O'Kelly's flailing tongue raked between Maud's legs, and on her mouth, in her kiss, Ida tasted desire. It bubbled like the water does from the small and rocky springs once named for fairies but now given to the saints. Ida smelled the cold metal cups often tied to the wells, and the fear of kneeling and reaching with it across the fresh water to dip into the unseen.

This was the power that brought men to their knees. Ida lapped it up. All she wanted, to taste it on Maud's mouth.

But Maud twisted her face away, falling over the edge, tipping into orgasm. And never had Ida dreamed of that. Only the wanting and the getting. Never the having. Wildly, she wheeled around. Maud's long fingers gripped the mattress, stomach rigid. Ida peered into MacGregor's bloated face.

"I won't let you fuck her," she warned him.

Maud's hips pressed up, a whale breaching beneath the tiny ships of the men who hunted her. Ida wanted to thrust a finger between Maud's parting legs, to harpoon that magical heartbeat of sex, but Maud's eyes flew open at the same instant. What Ida saw froze her.

"Those aren't your eyes," she whispered. "I know those eyes."

"I'm coming!" Maud's voice was pleading. Her hips writhed.

MacGregor had forgotten her in his own crisis. Emily's sly hand had snaked under Maud's knee to his trouser front. "Kiss me," Maud begged.

Ida leaned closer. Maud's eyes had gone matte gray. No light reflected in them. These were the eyes Ida had seen in the mirror the afternoon of Kathleen's wedding. A man's eyes.

The violence of Maud's pleasure dragged Ida over her, looking down. Down into the strange, magical eyes. Not Laura's. Not Maud's, but under hers. Beneath the hell of dreams and waiting she shared with Maud. Deeper.

Maud screamed as Ida vanished.

Ida gasped. All she could see was the flat gray of his irises, the forest of dark lashes, and the exotic slant of his fathomless eyes. There was nothing else, not even breath, where he was.

"Hello, Ida," he said. "Welcome to Hell—the place where dreams come true."

His beautiful whisper echoed magic and power in Ida's clouded mind.

"Where we speak with our bodies, and fuck with our words. Would you like to come and talk with me?"

Ida nodded.

The moment my body crashes into his, I know this is improper. My height and the lushness of my body are unfamiliar to us both. But everything is alien and far from me in dreams. Still, I know I will endanger it all if I take his earnest face in my hands and kiss him. I want to, but I only plant my cheek in the strong curve of his neck and cling to his arms. He's tall as I am, and I taste, more than hear, the trembling inhalation he takes at last to steady himself. His careful hands touch my waist. Then harden. Then they are crossed across my back, holding me to him with the same reckless hope mine have. He says my name again, like an incantation, like just the syllables can hold me with him.

"Who are you?" he whispers into my hair. "I must understand. In the half year since I glimpsed you behind Maud's frozen eyes in the hotel, I could think of little else. Laura . . ." He takes my face in his large hands and turns it to his. His eyes touch my lips and cheeks. "There is much to say, to ask and to tell you. Much to protect you against and warn you from."

Protective, he has drawn me away from the uproar in the ritual room over Ida's collapse, and into a narrow, carpeted back hall. His handsome face is a field of conflicting fear, grief, and terrible need, and all I want is to bring my mouth to his. All my longing centers in my lips. What was it Ida said about kissing?

He bows his head. "I had begun to fear you were imaginary, or some submerged part of myself." The pain strafing his confession twists in my belly with the heat of my physical desire. I thought he was the same—a projection of my subconscious. I can't tell if I still believe that.

"I knew that I loved you, but I read the story of an artist in Japan," Will tells me. A whispering draft scurries low to the ground through the corridor. It wraps around my ankles and ruffles the hem of my long skirts. "He painted a herd of running horses on the wall of a temple so perfectly imagined, so meticulously drawn, that at night they became animate, came off the temple wall and ruined a neighboring field of rice." The nearness of his crisp woolen trousers to my thighs, his waistcoat to my breasts charges the air between us with motion equal to the low-lying draft. "In the morning, an aged priest, sweeping the temple floor, felt water fall on his arm and looked up in time to see the last of the horses shaking the morning dew from his mane, and trembling into stillness. The very strength of my belief in you convinced me I had likewise made you corporeal. A modern day Pygmalion."

His eager eyes hold mine, and he turns his head to shake away a fall of brown hair tumbling over them. "I don't think we created each other," I say. I am too alert, too coherent to be dreaming. I am more aware of the air and space, my thoughts and my body, than I ever am at work.

"Nor do I," he whispers.

A door slams under our feet, and staccato little heels rain across the downstairs corridor. The voices of the Matherses trill and rumble beneath us. Everything is ordinary. Our bodies almost touch.

"Laura, you must leave."

"No way! I want to figure this out. Besides, I don't even think Maud wants to come back yet."

"Maud's initiation into the Golden Dawn is to take place tonight," Will explains. "After the séance, we're all expected in Euston Street. She wants to learn the secrets of reincarnation. She must be fully present in her body, or it would be you to whom the powers came."

"Maybe I'm the one who's supposed to have them. Maybe that's how I can keep coming back here," I plead. But he shakes his head.

The pain in his face physically hurts me. I want to touch him and his dark eyes of poetry and magic. "I don't know how to bring Maud back into her body," I tell him. "And I don't know where I am when I'm not with you."

"Close your eyes."

"No!"

"If you leave your body, it will draw Maud's soul back; a body cannot stand empty without a soul."

"Is that why Ida stopped breathing?"

A subtle hardness freezes his gentle features. "I don't know. Her body was empty too long. After Maud is inducted into the Golden Dawn, she will be able to channel you herself perhaps, and we won't need Miss Jameson anymore. None of us trust her."

"But she's the only one who really knows how to find me."

Will nods. "And we had a rare opportunity. Maud was hungry for news of her buried son, but fearful of what she believes to be the evil spirit she channels. MacGregor and AE offered to hold the séance and provide their psychic protection while we determined what you were or weren't and whether any of our rituals might help Miss Gonne."

I want to touch the unconstrained lock of hair, push it back with my fingers, savor the single strands reflecting and burnishing the diffuse hall light. "While you were speaking with AE, I understood that, quite opposite of what Miss Gonne feared, your spirit hales from a higher plane, a guardian soul, perhaps, an over soul, more pure, more enlightened."

I have no memory of what I am, and the tiny air between us presses against my entire body, my breasts—so large—and my lips opening to him, and the secret wakening passage between my legs, all anticipation, all wanting—lusting. "I'm not sure I am advanced," I whisper. No, I am a primitive stew of sex. "It's possible Maud was right. I may be wicked." I lean toward him, swaying in the hallway's whispering drafts and closing doors. I don't think sex is wicked. The magnetic murmur between our bodies closes and drives a quick, arrested panting exhalation from him.

"I don't know what I am," I whisper. It scares me a little, to say the truth out loud.

"And I don't care," he mutters, his hands alive and running over my face, hungry on my cheeks and diving through my hair. "I don't care if you're an evil demon out of Hell or a heroic spirit from our Irish past. I only want to know you."

"Kiss me," I whisper to him.

He hesitates. I know he wants to. Even if his need did not speak through his fingers, even if his eyes were not already penetrating me, skewering me, even if he did not stand hard against my belly, I would know it.

"How can I?" he says. "Maud's lips, when it is you I want?"

He shuts his eyes and drops his head to mine. The stray lock falls against the bridge of my nose. We stand silent, trembling in the empty, dusty hall.

"Even if this were your body, I could still not kiss what I want to taste," he whispers.

I don't know if his hands raise my face or if my mouth moves of its own accord; I only know our lips have found each other's, both closed, both still, just resting. A touch. And then, voracious. Our mouths are beings with their own wills, living, twisting, grunting, biting things, fighting for everything but air. His restraint shatters, he kisses without thought.

What belongs to me, and what is Maud's, my body, my living mouth and starving arms, my whole soul, fits into my kiss. I hear the house around me, smell time whispering down the hall, Moina and MacGregor arguing. The world is not water. A stone falls against our lives and makes no ripple in the people trotting by outside the window, or in the winter weather. Will's kiss pins me to him, pulls me deeper into sensation. It echoes through me like a beaten bell, an insistent ring.

"Can you get that, baby?"

Oh God, no.

"Laura, can you get the phone?"

from *A Servant of the Queen: Reminiscences*
by Maud Gonne MacBride

1938

By chance I was on the boat that bore [Parnell's] dead body back to Ireland, for I had not thought to attend his funeral. There was a terrible storm and all the day of burial it rained as if nature mourned for him. Some said Parnell was not in the coffin and would appear again . . .

I stood in the thick mud of Glasnevin among a dense and silent throng. Dusk was coming on. As the thud of the earth sounded on the coffin, a rift in the leaden sky parted the clouds and a bright falling star was seen. Hundreds of others saw it as I did. The Parliamentary Party was dead before Parnell, and should have been buried with him. It is an ungracious task to kick about a corpse; it is what Griffith and Sinn Fein had to do and I helped because its leaders refused to bury it.

I never ceased to love my old friends, only their movement had to die that the young might live.

Life out of death, life out of death eternally.

———————

5

THEY BUT THRUST THEIR BURIED MEN
BACK IN THE HUMAN MIND AGAIN

While still I may, I write for you
The love I lived, the dream I knew.
From our birthday, until we die,
Is but the winking of an eye;
And we, our singing and our love,
What measurer Time has lit above,
And all benighted things that go
About my table to and fro,
Are passing on to where may be,
In truth's consuming ecstasy,
No place for love and dream at all;
For God goes by with white footfall.
I cast my heart into my rhymes,
That you, in the dim coming times,
May know how my heart went with them
After the red-rose-bordered hem.

—from "To Ireland in Coming Times" by W. B. Yeats

As children, Maud and Ida had walked thus, deliberate and slow, down Donnybrook Road, both of them shaking, although only

Maud with fear. Arm in trembling arm again now, through the dark October graves, toward Georges's tomb, Ida still needed to caution herself against skipping in her first giddy moment since arriving in France almost a month ago. The country irritated her, the rigorous attention the nation paid to beauty, the constant wine in small glasses, and how at home Maud was within it.

Ever the hostess—ever the *French* hostess, for all her Irish color—Maud had brought red wine and flowers to the crypt. Ida, always more practical, carried candles, blankets, and lap rugs. Maud unlocked the metal doors of Georges's little memorial chapel, and Ida stepped into its dark of underground smells and windless cold.

Ida dropped the furs in a corner while Maud cursed benignly, burning matches, unable to make the flame stick to the candle wicks. If they lived together and entertained, they would bustle about thus, in friendly silence, preparing for their guests. But tonight only Lucien was expected, he and whatever spirits came, invited or otherwise. Ida tore the bloom from one of Maud's flowers and scattered the petals over the altar. "Why don't you let me light the candles, darling?" she suggested.

Maud leaned her back against the cold and unadorned stone wall. "Ida . . ."

"I know." Ida kept her smile sympathetic, and took the matches from Maud's ghost-white fingers. "Pour the wine."

"Ida, I don't think I can do what I . . ."

"Go ahead and have yourself a glassful, dear. We have more than enough for our communion."

Maud took glasses from the wooden crate they had provisioned over several trips to the little mausoleum. Ida lit the candles, humming to herself. Maud already had a reputation for pleasant evening gatherings, but Ida would raise the tone of the soirées. She and Maud would talk Art and God with their guests, not only politics. The tomb's rich, under-earth smell of graveworms and mushrooms crept over Ida. Maud had been too frightened of tonight to eat, but when they entertained together, Cook would serve duck in whiskey sauce, or salmon with morels.

The candles blazed like a birthday cake, dancing in the drafts admitted through the glassless windows and the open grate in the door. Possibly too from the colder metal doors in the cold stone floor. Maud sat on the provisions box, wordlessly taking her wine like the poison or medicine it was. "Did you want some, Ida?"

"No."

"He will be here soon."

"Yes, I should think so." Ida stood over Maud, strong and unafraid, behind Maud's sloping, robed shoulders. In Paris, Halloween festivities would be mocking the rites and devils Ida and Maud hoped to make real tonight, in the little village of Samois. Through the provincial streets to its tiny cemetery, Maud had walked, a priestess or a secret witch cloaked and hooded with Ida, her familiar bird, wing-in-elbow beside her. But inside Georges's little burial chapel, Maud shrunk to an Irish crone, her ritual robes a weathered shawl wrapped over curling shoulders and the hollowed-out hole where her heart had been, and Ida, her carrion bird behind her.

She plucked the pins from Maud's hair. "Let's prepare you," she whispered.

Maud did not move while Ida's pecking fingers unwound the braided skeins of rust and shadow. It slithered free over Maud's shoulders, and she absently pushed back the strands snaking into her face. She caught Ida's hand in an icy grip. "Ida, I'm frightened."

Maud choked on the blood-scraped whisper, but Ida had heard, and her smile broke like a towering thundercloud. Maud's deathbed promise to her father broken—to never be afraid of anything, not even death—and Ida here beside her. She sank down beside Maud's shuddering shoulders and wrapped her robe-winged arms around them. "Shhh," she murmured, cheek in flowing hair, lips to sunken throat. "You must master your fear. There is no other way."

Maud nodded her bowed head in Ida's arms. "I know."

Her face, when she raised it in the tomb's guttering light, glowed gold with tears, more beautiful in terror and despair than she had ever been in love or at the viceregal court. But Lucien was on his way. Soon, he would take the robes and wraps from Maud, and place her on the pelts and petals Ida would spread upon the grave. He would open her legs, position himself upon the brown and pink, and dig and grunt his seed between them.

But Maud's penetrated flesh would never open to him as her soul did for Ida now. Maud's brown eyes were deeper and her trembling lips more vulnerable, and never was anything more erotic than her trust. "I will stay here with you," Ida lied. She touched her cautious finger to a tear's path down Maud's cheek. "And you will feel nothing. I swear." A solitary salt drop clung to her fingertip, and Ida hid the tear-daubed finger in her lap to taste when Maud at last took her gaze away. "You will be mesmerized. I will do as I did last time, but you must give yourself to me even more fully. I will make certain all your awareness and sensation have fled before Lucien proceeds." Ida would not let Maud's spirit suffer, although she would not vouchsafe the same for Laura's soul. But Ida no longer needed Laura. All she needed was a ride to Hell.

"Do you swear it?" Maud whispered.

"I will make the trance so deep you will know nothing of what occurs, the way I did the last time, at the Matherses' house, remember?"

Maud's lashes quivered and more honey tears slicked her eyes.

"Yes," she said at last. "I was initiated into the Golden Dawn that night, and I still remember not one thing about it."

Another gift stolen from another humiliation. Ida would have nothing at all without her knack for grubbing through the wastes of hope. She had not been able to possess Maud's body fully, not inhabit her as Laura could, but Ida's long-starved spirit had reached out while Maud's well-satiated one reclined, and it had captured the mark of Maud's initiation. Now, Ida's bold fingers brushed Maud's damp cheek, as if to stroke away the slippery wet marks collecting there. "I can command the magic we need tonight, because of that, to reincarnate your son."

"I know, and oh, Ida, I'm more grateful than I can say." And suddenly it was Maud who was reaching, her grave-cold hands clutching Ida's narrow face.

Ida's body washed ice and then flamed. Pure radiant lust illumi-

nated her. Maud's open mouth—promising, awake, and hungrier than
the so many times Ida had kissed it sleeping—closed over Ida's ragged
lips. And kissed her. Demanding, and wanting, and fully Maud. "I
don't know what I would ever have done without you!" she cried, but
did not offer her mouth again. Embraced her. And before the kiss
might come once more, metal tore over stone, the small gate groaned
open, and Lucien Millevoye ascended to Ida's private paradise.

Maud, a hopeless pupil of Irish despite the earnest efforts of
Douglas Hyde, spewed French like a drunkard pissed. Ida stayed kneeling while Maud poured her wine-sopped words all over Lucien—
the ridiculous, married, minor revolutionary with his silly twisted-up
mustache—with the same unstinting generosity she had given him her
love. He was unworthy of her, and should die wretched and alone.

Maud's fluid French explained she must be mesmerized and passive during the ritual act. The spirits themselves required it. But Millevoye was not unwilling to fuck his darling out cold as Maud had
worried he might be. Ida listened to his barking, and translated clumsily in her head:

"And must this ugly chicken—maybe duckling?—remain while I make love
to my white swan?"

"She is the priestess."

"And will you, poor darling, feel nothing of your huntsman's amorous caress?"

"No."

"You will be rendered quite insensate?"

"Yes."

"As if asleep, or even dead?" He made a moue of pity with his dishon-
est face, but his distended trousers spoke more honestly.

"It is almost time," Ida said.

"C'est l'heur," Maud translated for Lucien and turned to Ida, her
face the stone of angels carved for children's graves. Maud's cold,
unwilling fingers fumbled with the cloak ties, useless in the slick
black satin. All her strength collected in the hollow of her slender
throat where Ida saw the sobs shove and batter for release. Her eyes
pleaded with Ida to say this was all a dream. Or unnecessary. A

test—like Abraham, called to place his beloved son upon the cold rock altar of his god. But Maud's child was sacrificed already, and underneath the stone.

They knelt before it: Ida, Maud, and Lucien. In the glassless window over the altar, the pregnant curve of moon hid for shame behind low clouds. The candles smoked black and flickered, but Maud and Lucien held their eyes to the little portrait of the dead child on the stone shelf.

Maud prayed. Her actress's voice echoed in the closed stone and metal of Georges's patrician tomb. How British, Ida noted, Maud had been in her architecture and grief. No banshee wail, no carved stone icon, only massive square blocks piled up in sorrow, and now the pitiful words of supplication.

All they had rehearsed was over. Kneeling before the shallow altar, their feet and shins rested on the metal doors they now must pull wide and descend. If Ida had not stood and gestured, would they ever have moved? Lucien helped Maud to her feet and Ida led her away from the grunting man and grinding hinges of the doors in the floor.

The sound of the tomb opening almost undid Maud, but Ida pulled the ribbons of her cloak and watched their bow collapse. Hanging in sad streamers down either sides of an unbreachable divide of visible flesh, they tied all Maud's attention. Ida's warm fingers pushed the halves apart, and the cloak fell with an expensive murmur in a pool of deeper black against the darkness of the hollow floor. Millevoye coughed. Maud's bare bottom faced him. He could content himself with that and wait. Ida would not rush this moment. She had earned it with a patience he would not attain until his death.

Still, he was not the only one who kept a lover waiting. Ida brushed a tear from Maud's shivering chest, slid her fingers across the most tender rise where the fine bones, visible beneath the flesh, lost themselves in the swelling ascent of breast. She gazed at the breathless nipple, like a hard matte candy, until Maud gasped, and Ida heard how close to screaming that small sip of air had come. She took Maud's hand in her own then, gold ring to gold ring—Ida had waited four more days while Maud searched her things for it—and turned Maud's body toward the grave.

They climbed down the ladder.

Naked now, and shivering, Maud only must not faint. Ida had tried for two years to find the exotic eyes again, their seductive power, their unearthly beauty. But only by trailing Maud's pilgrim soul from its body to its secret, dark untethered place, could Ida again find the erotic, handsome daemon who had once welcomed her to Hell. It had taken her two years, but never, even for a solitary moment, had Ida thought of anything but finding her way back to him. To claim his love or win his power, Ida could not foretell. But all the omens boded well.

Maud's wild eyes clung to hers alone.

Ida glared up at Mr. Millevoye, and he turned away to fumble with his waistcoat and trouser buttons. He dropped his hat, picked it up, and dropped it once again. He believed he had the most to lose. A wife. A political career. And yes, his enemies would love to find him here. They could ruin him with Maud, like Parnell and Kitty O'Shea. His thoughts must touch his enemies every time he fondled Maud. How exciting that must be.

Ida spread the lap rugs on the ground and eased Maud to the furs and flower petals folded into them. She placed her hand in Maud's unbound hair. "Close your eyes," she whispered.

Maud's terror shot up through Ida's fingertips. Above them, Millevoye tripped over his shoes. Ida would say the phrase three times, and they both recognized the signal. After the third recitation, Lucien was to descend and approach. He should strive to time his climax for midnight.

"Close your eyes," she said again.

Maud's horror, naked and open-thighed, underground beside her son's too-small casket, drained through Ida's arm and slipped away. Maud's legs, her sex, her womb, were open. Her guilt. His grave. Her freedom. Ida looked up to find Lucien watching with eyes that mirrored her desire. She tasted it on the fetid air between them.

"Excité?" she asked and winked at him. He dropped his shoe onto his hat, his fish mouth gaping.

Ida smiled. Yes, she spoke French.

Yes, they were both excited.

"Close your eyes," she said the final time, and knew Maud had slipped away.

"Excitement is the pleasure we feel from danger," she told Millevoye.

No, he spoke no English. He cursed stupidly and stumbled in his naked ass-first descent. Let Laura deal with him; Ida had other fish to catch. The salmon of knowledge was slippery, but tasty with a thick mushroom sauce.

Millevoye gripped his rigid cock in his hand. Yes, Ida would follow Maud, down into the red quiet. Yes, Laura was already slipping in, eager, groping through Maud's mind like Lucien across her belly.

Ida stretched herself on the ground beside Maud, but kept their rings aligned. *Here*, her spirit whispered. *Here, fishy, fishy.*

***

From the seven-figure-bonus banker who steals, to the famous actor in another great role he just can't carry, I keep my most sincere and violent hatred for the only-partial failures, and for myself. Self-loathing is indulgent. I know that, and I hate myself for it. But I've screwed up again. I can smell it—wet autumn leaves and metal. A damp chill running in whispers up my skin. I have to squeeze my eyes shut hard, or I'll open them.

This is my feeble plan. Ridiculously naïve, I know. As if not seeing the bogeyman could make him go away. But what if you fall in love with the bogeyman? No well-adjusted girl would do that. I won't open my eyes, and my dreams won't see me, and they'll go away.

I know I'm not dreaming.

Maud's body thickens around me, and I settle into her heavy breasts and cushioning ass, the weight of her long, unpinned hair and the strong limbs lying still. And naked.

Why am I naked?

I raise a hand reflexively to cover myself, but a hand pushes my modest wrist back to my side. I'm outside, naked and not alone. God, the past was kinky.

With an exploding light like an old-timey flashbulb, I remember Will's kiss in the Matherses' upstairs hall, and a warm flush wakes up in my exposed belly. The same thing happened at the game tonight, the memory and the heat, and soccer is my place for not thinking.

I+D is too small and too arty to field a team, so I still play with my old agency. It doesn't hurt to keep a toe in corporate water anyway. We played a Seattle agency tonight. They're in town pitching NorPac, too. I was more than a little stressed out. Anyway, their striker got a breakaway after a goal kick, and I took off running after him.

My cleats bit into the ground, I locked into my full stride—play the ball, not the player—almost to him, and I then remembered Will. I flashed on Will's eyes reaching through Maud into me, and his mouth tasting mine. The runner heard me coming, looked up for the net, across for the pass, and I went in clean, sliding. Will's lips kissed me, raw as the grass ripped up under my knee. The hard leather of the ball connected with the soft leather of my boot in a damp smack of understanding. The Yeats thing must stop. Hell, I don't even like poetry. Literature is much more Amit's thing. That and music. The ball skittered out of bounds. My teammates caught up. We reset for the throw-in, and I didn't go out for drinks afterwards, although I could have gotten a free beer off our goalie for that one.

I am such an idiot. All it takes is the scratch of a match to make me open my eyes. A short, unattractive naked man with a melodrama mustache is lighting a cigarette in a candlelit, low-ceilinged, marble-walled room. Not outside. Maybe underground?

I did better on the nights I drank. I want out of this.

"You okay?" Amit always feels me get out of bed.

"Yeah, fine. Gotta pee." I stagger into the bathroom and open the cabinet over the toilet. Unisom. NyQuil. Valerian. I have got to get some sleep. Amy's excited about the NorPac concept, and I need to be sharp tomorrow—not dream-addled like I was on Monday. In college, we stayed up all night concepting and still felt great the next day. We rubbed ideas together and played with the sparks. And we dreamed of having jobs like mine.

I pad through our clean, airy loft. Our modern, Zen decor just looks empty in the dark. We bought this place for the massive windows that fill the space with light, but in the middle of a sleepless night, they are only black open holes. Or mirrors. I get a drink from the kitchen and return to my husband.

"Come back to bed," he mumbles, but I stay standing beside it.

I pull my cami over my head.

"Mmm," Amit murmurs appreciatively, "I love you."

I hook my thumbs into my panty-band. "I love you, too," I say.

He holds the blankets back for me, already hard, and I slip in beside him. "Feel better?"

"I'm okay."

I had told him I was too tired for sex when we went to bed—too sore from soccer—thinking sex might be what triggered the Victorian dreams. But I now push my spine against Amit's warm, solid chest, and close my eyes. I smell moss and cigarettes. My husband reaches around to cup my breast, and Maud's nipples tighten atop their generous rounds of flesh. Mine feel small and stingy in Amit's hand, and it embarrasses me when his fingers start to turn them. I know he thinks I'm beautiful, but it isn't what I feel. I make an encouraging noise low in my throat, and hear the tiny hiss of a cigarette dropped into wine. Muttering in French, the mustached man climbs over me and grasps his cock in an impatient fist.

"Are you sure you're okay?" Amit's lips move against my neck, kissing like the fur under Maud's shoulders.

"I've been dreaming weird dreams," I say.

Maud sprawls, legs open, on fur rugs, one arm extended, hand linked with Ida who, equally inert, makes an inverse image on the ground nearby.

Amit's voice still carries the huskiness of sleep. "We've had a lot going on," he observes with his classic gift for understatement. "The wedding, my folks, your work . . ." His cock nudges my rump, but he settles my body against his for sleep.

The Frenchman kneeling astride Maud yanks his cock with such fury it jostles not only her thighs and breasts, but my flung-back face and arms. I let my eyes drift closed and push my back against Amit. He kisses my shoulder blade, and glides his hand between my legs. The Frenchman is gasping now, his short, thick cock jerking. He gropes between my legs.

"C'est presque de minuit," he pants. My high-school French suggests something about midnight. He pushes himself between my legs, Maud's legs, where Amit's heavy fingers stroke me. I peek over his shoulder. I'm in a fucking tomb. Literally.

I roll onto my back beside Amit. The Frenchman falls over me. He roots for Maud's closed sex, even as mine opens under Amit's skillful fingers. I smell woodrot and standing water, and my apartment has no answering smell. Our blackout curtains and white-noise machine cannot compete with the moaning Halloween wind and the circle of guttering candles that ring Ida's body and mine, unconscious on the ground.

Lucien—so this is Lucien—grinds in a mad frenzy over me.

"I think I might go back on the antidepressants I took in college," I mumble.

"Are you depressed?" Amit lifts his head to look at me.

"No." Lucien's squat cock and Amit's tender fingers move in different time. Arrhythmic, but distinct. "But they kept me from dreaming."

"Are the dreams so bad?"

Is married sex like fucking the dead? Is that what my twisted subconscious is trying to say?

"No," I say, "but I want them to stop."

"How come?" Amit's hand has stopped stroking and come to rest on my stomach, low and protective, curled over where I guess my womb is. What a weird word—*womb*—I've never thought of it belonging to my body before. I weave my fingers into his.

"They just don't make any sense."

"Dreams aren't supposed to, you know. They're the one place we're free from the tyranny of reason."

I'm not sure I should have such freedom. Maud's head is banging against the stone. Lucien is gasping. Words and tears pour out of him, and I know Maud will conceive again tonight.

"My dreams are usually ridiculous. Stupid. They're small. These have been . . ."

"Bigger?"

"Too big. I can't figure out what they mean."

"Maybe they don't mean anything."

Maybe they mean I've been married a week and I'm already cheating. Not with my body, because I like to keep my promises, but every night in my mind. "Shouldn't my dreams make some kind of sense?" I ask him.

Amit lifts our hands to his lips and kisses mine. "You're not quite as logical as you think."

"Don't you even try that 'emotional female' bullshit on me."

Amit unlaces my fingers, kisses my thumb, and prods my thigh with his knuckles.

"Ow!"

Lucien grasps Maud's full hips, raises them, and drives his robust thrusts between her fallen-open thighs.

"That's not logical," Amit said.

I rub the achy bruise the tumble with the striker left.

Lucien swears once, and with a hearty grunt orgasms in stout jerks, his eyes squeezed closed.

"That's what I do for exercise."

"Bullshit." Amit curls me into his arms again. "Are they scary dreams?"

Lucien climbs from astride Maud's lifeless form.

"Not scary really. Just crazy."

"Same dream over and over?"

"No. Well, sort of. The same people each time, but different places. There's this crazy woman—Ida. She's been in every dream I've had since we got married. The first time I dreamed about her, we were fooling around."

"I endorse that dream!" Amit says with mock fervor. "You should dream that more."

Lucien gropes on the floor above him for matches and lights another cigarette. He stands over Maud, smoking. Then he looks at Ida on the ground beside me.

"There was a man, too."

And—although Maud's empty eyes show me her lover kneeling beside the grave of their buried child to make certain Ida is fully unconscious before he reaches under her skirts—I see only Will again.

"But that's not the crazy thing," I tell Amit. Sure, the sex is crazy, but it doesn't worry me. It's what I feel without my body, without her body—what I feel bodiless and truer than bodies, that has me running scared.

"Go on," Amit nudges.

Lucien sits astride Ida, one beefy knee on either side of her much narrower hips. Contemplatively, he squeezes a breast. With one hand, he pinches where he guesses the nipple would be, smoking with the other. The sticky trickle of his seed starts to leak onto the fur under me.

"What's the craziest thing?" Amit's voice is sleep-blurred and fur-warm behind me.

"When I dream about Ida and Will, I dream I'm somebody else," I say. "I have a different body, and I live someplace else. Actually some *time* else. It's a Victorian dream." Lucien flips the cigarette into the darkness and grips his cock again.

I close my eyes and find Will's face in MacGregor Mathers's upstairs hall. I see pain twist behind his eyes before he kissed me, and danger. Not in my body, not in Maud's, but in my thoughts, in my head, in something deeper, I feel the heat and hunger for him. And I recognize it. And know Will is right to be afraid.

"I have this Victorian body in the dreams, and I'm really tall, with giant tits." I can hear my voice slipping into sleep after me. Love is dangerous. I only fall into ass-over-elbow, addicted love with men who are bad for me. If I'm crazy attracted to a man, I guarantee you he's crazy. My decision to go out with Amit was the first sane dating choice I ever made. Everyone knows poets are crazy.

Amit's deep laugh rumbles far away. But I can taste Will's consuming kiss again. The hallway draft slips around my naked ankles, and I slide my hand across the warm chuckle in my husband's chest. "Wasso funny?" I mumble into his clean shoulder, loving the smooth muscle under my fingers, the disobedient brown hair brushing my nose just before Will kisses me.

"You have a very literal subconscious."

I kiss Amit's shoulder, Will's mouth.

"Will and Ida, eh?" Amit says. "Do your Will and Id argue with each other, Inky? Do they fight over your old-fashioned, Victorian womanhood, now you're a wife?" He chuckles. "'Longest way round is the shortest way home.'" I think he's quoting Joyce again.

I want sleep to come and claim me, but Amit is sounding more and more awake.

"What's your name, in the dream?" he asks me.

"Maud Gonne," I say.

"Seriously?" He laughs aloud this time. "Maid Gone?"

"Maud," I repeat, but I can't come awake enough to say it clearer.

"Wasn't she Yeats's muse?" He kisses me tenderly "Laura?" he whispers, just like Ida did when she called for me tonight. But I can't hear her now, and I'm trying to.

Amit pulls me closer, wraps around me, chuckling at his own puns. "Laura?" he whispers. "I guess you're Gonne." And after a while, because he can, Amit falls asleep again.

⁂

Ida knew from Maud's face, its softening and smile, that a man was standing behind her who hadn't been there a moment ago. "Perhaps you would settle a debate for us," Maud purred above Ida's prone form. "Miss Jameson and I were just disagreeing about the nature of a promise."

Disagree was an outright lie. Maud had been excoriating Ida, dragging her over the sharp tines of language, combing old words for proof of fresh betrayal.

"I maintain"—the subtle dip of Maud's hard chin told Ida the newcomer must be both handsome and expensively dressed—"if a friend says she is willing to take one's place somewhere, attend an . . . event in one's absence, their obligation is to be personally present at the appointed time."

"And Miss Jameson?" The velvet power in his voice made Ida giddy, despite her rage. Still, she did not sit up. It had spoken only a few words of welcome to her almost two years ago, but she would have broken more than her word to hear it again. More than beauty or even knowledge, it held what she craved.

"I didn't promise Maud a thing," she said, hoping she had managed to keep the elegant robes she had ordered specially to wear to Georges's tomb. They were a very flattering color.

"Miss Jameson promised to take my place tonight," said Maud, "but she's followed me here!"

"I promised to keep you from experiencing the events of tonight," Ida clarified, pushing herself to sitting, eyes drilling into Maud's, "and I have."

"I may still remember it!" Maud never deigned to glance down at her, but held the eyes of the man Ida had not yet turned around to see.

"I made no promises about memory."

"She's quite impossible, don't you think?" Maud unleashed a rare full smile over Ida's head.

"Yes." The succulent depths of his voice slipped into Ida like wine. "What precisely did she promise, Miss Gonne?"

"She promised to be there!"

"And is she not?"

"Well, her body is but . . ."

"We can only promise what we can control," he said. His footfalls made no sound, but Ida knew he drew closer. "A promise is a statement of intent." He stopped right behind her. Close to her. "Perhaps Ida's intentions changed?"

"Pah! She always intended to follow me here!" Maud exclaimed, but Ida didn't care. Maud could say anything she wanted. All Ida's attention was fixated behind her.

"And what did you intend, Miss Gonne?" He stepped over Ida without a glance, giving her no more notice than an amorous client gives a whore's child sitting on the floor. He took Maud's strong shoulders, and turned her body from where it stood, towering over Ida. He tucked it under one of his arms, and murmured into her tumbled hair, "Maud, what was your intention?"

Her body folded itself against his with shocking ease.

He led Maud away, his hypnotic voice low and secret in her ear, with his arm like a wing around her. His beautiful, exotic face had haunted Ida for two years, but she had been unwilling to turn and meet it with her own. She watched his retreat, ushering Maud across the tender, brilliant grass toward the silent river. He moved with the grace of an uncaged animal. His fluid trunk rooted in narrow hips, but spread into shoulders strong and wide enough to support a hundred arms. Ida touched her lips with the tip of a thoughtful tongue and tasted pleasure. She liked watching him; and with his face bent to Maud's, Ida could linger over her uncomfortable joy. The ears can hear, and love, and yet not covet. But what the eye finds beautiful, the body longs to own. Ida stood up and followed them across the garden.

On the riverbank, Maud turned her back to Ida's daemon and listened, nodding and freeing the buttons of her dress. His strong brown fingers moved with an assurance that worked across Ida's body, too, twisting small knots of excitement into her until she had to turn her attention to the yellow flowers underfoot. He spoke to Maud as he undressed her. He spoke of Ireland, and of the noble soul her body housed, until Maud, stripped naked, stepped into the warm, black water while Ida watched, rapt. And his eyes met hers.

Ida focused all of her formidable will into her gaze, willing it not to dart and waver like the nervous chit she felt. She tipped her chin up with a bright smile that broke too early, before his strong legs had carried him across the whispering grass back to her. The too-soon smile locked her features in a rictus of dubious appeal. This she augmented with an inane giggle, cursing herself silently all the while. He should have stayed with Maud; she was not rendered ludicrous by the attention of a handsome man.

He made a slight bow to Ida, offering a tailored elbow. "Shall we?" he murmured.

Ida flapped an arm behind her. "Maud is a weak swimmer; I would not like to leave her alone."

"You would like very much to leave her here; and so would I."

Ida opened her mouth and closed it again. She put her clammy hand in the crook of his elegant arm, and let him lead her from the garden.

Ida walked, shoeless beside him, inventorying the stains on her scullery maid's dress. Why did Maud awake in this place dressed and shod and standing, while Ida found herself belly-to-the-ground in the tatters of a drudge?

"What would you like to see first, Ida?"

"Oh, you needn't show me about. Really. I'll just go exploring on my own. I'm quite capable." She had waited two years to see him again, and all she wanted was to hide.

"Nonsense. This is Hell, my dear. And while it isn't difficult to arrive on your own, the farthest depths are unreachable without the help of someone you love."

They stepped together out of the garden's brilliant, sunless light through a vast gate, into a shadowy hall. Comforted by the box of ceiling, walls, and floor after the limitless sky, Ida stole a glance at the handsome man who strode beside her. He caught her eye and smiled. "Would you like to see the library?" he asked.

Ida considered a moment. "Will it hold books I have not read?" she asked.

His low laugh rumbled off the raw stone of the corridor. "You believe you have created all this yourself?"

"Is it not Imagination?"

"Not yours alone."

"But it is not real."

"It is not material. You must not confuse the two, my love. That which has no being or body may still have power."

"I understand unseen power," Ida snapped.

"You do not." They rounded a rough-carved corner into a wider hall, and Ida stumbled in her surprise to find it flocked with people. "The library must wait," his voice growled in her ear. "There is something I want to show you more than its stories."

He nodded "Sylvia" to a beautiful, red-haired woman with luminous skin who stared at Ida on her daemon's arm. The hallway rustled like a low ocean, lapping in little waves of sound and movement. Small, whispering clusters and strolling pairs watched Ida and her handsome escort. Her fingers clawed reflexively at his arm. But he led her with serene authority into the half-circle of emptiness that opened in the crowd before them and closed again in their wake. Whispers radiated before and behind the inviolate core of silence in which he held her. He inclined his head. "You make quite the sensation, my dear," he whispered, nodding and smiling into the swirl of onlookers. Distant hands flew up like gulls, waving and he made small, precise nods to each of them.

"Just up the stairs on our left, my lady, is what I wanted you to see." He transferred Ida's hand from his elbow to his own and held it up as they mounted a narrowing dais. At its summit he turned her by the fingers to face the room and whispered, "Wave."

Ida put her free hand aloft and turned it stiffly at the wrist. The sea of upturned faces raised their hands and clapped. A woman at the foot of the stair folded her long, white body fully to the floor in a curtsy so graceful Ida gasped. The gesture exposed the tiny sharp vertebrae of her neck for only a moment before she rose fluidly again to standing with a wink of one crystalline, emerald eye. Beside her, Ida felt the devil bow. Then he swept her through a door behind them, out of view, and caught her against his powerful body.

"You did that brilliantly," he whispered, holding her hard against his unmoving chest.

For a moment, Ida did not think how beautiful he was. She did not remember her own ugly face. She saw only her success, and the deep earth-crimson of his lips. They parted slowly to reveal white, sharp teeth, a shocking contrast, like knives in silk. In this place and with this creature, she was beautiful. No—still not beautiful—but here something mattered more than beauty. Here she was like Maud in Europe—a sensation wherever she went, Maud's *inversus*.

Then Ida remembered the wan plainness of her complexion, the fine hair and too-thin shoulders. She stepped away from him, tripped over her skirt, and fell into the wall. He caught her with a speed and strength she knew should frighten rather than excite her. Ida laughed. He reached behind her and opened a door she had not seen in the bare rock.

"My lady." His dark and warm smile murmured invitation, but his powerful body stood quite close, and rather than turn and flee down the stone stairs spiraling away beneath her, Ida met his eyes. He was more beautiful even than Maud. High, hard cheekbones under savage, red-brown skin, his black hair and eyes a mystery. Ida bit her lip, but did not look away.

"Who was the woman who bowed to us?" she asked with a boldness stolen from Maud.

"She is one of Helen's daughters," he said. Ida walked through the door her devil held open. "She is damned by her face." His voice spiraled down the dark behind her. "She cannot see through her own beauty, nor can she own it herself. Kings and armies rent it. Or advertising agencies."

"Are they all damned? Everyone we walked by?"

"Have you ever known anyone who wasn't?"

"I think I have," Ida said. "I have known people who were innocent."

Ida did not allow her feet on the stairs to change their rhythm. She did not slow. But she knew she was not. Her guilt had always held her separate.

"And do you think, my dear, innocence is never cursed?" his voice slid over her in the dark, painting her body with a deeper blackness.

She had never doubted her own difference. She had simply not enjoyed it before.

She stumbled in the total dark when there was not another step to take down, but the devil slipped behind her fluidly. "We're here," he whispered in her ear. "This is what I wanted to show you."

"I can't see."

"Come here." His voice sounded mere inches away, but Ida reached her blind fingers out for him and encountered only rough heavy fabric lining the walls. She took a careful step.

"Do you have a match you could light?"

"Follow my voice."

Ida laughed. Deep underground, in total darkness with a spirit she knew to be dangerous, she was unafraid. In the dark, they were equal. "I don't know your name," she said, groping for what would be polite.

"I cannot tell you."

"Why ever not?" she laughed.

"Ida," his voice was closer.

Ida probed the empty air before her until she realized his voice came from below, and knelt on the hard ground. Warm, strong fingers took her hand.

"Ida?"

"Yes?"

"How art thou damned?"

Her hand felt small and feminine in his. In the dark, she remembered his arresting face.

"I don't know," she whispered, all the laughter gone. His body, strong and lithe, must be just fingerbreadths away. The mere proximity ran across the flesh of her breast beneath her clothes, like a rough caress. Her nipples hardened as if pinched. "I'm bad. I don't know how or why. I only know I am."

"Until you know the nature of your own damnation, I cannot tell you mine."

He released her hand, and Ida bit back a curse. He was a powerful spirit. If only she had his name . . .

A flame bloomed near her feet in the floor. It grew and widened in folding squares as the daemon rolled a cloth away from burnished gold.

"What is that?" Ida whispered.

"What I wanted you to see."

"A metal mirror?"

"Look again."

Ida leaned over the warm, golden plate in the floor. How did it give off such light? She peered hard into its reflective surface. Not to see her own dull face polished bright, but beneath it. Candles set close together ringed a face with fire, another face, buried under hers.

"Georges?" Ida shuddered remembering the October grave where her body lay.

"No."

"Who is it?" she whispered.

"The buried king."

"Which one?"

"Does it matter?" His voice came from far away.

"What is he doing here?"

"This is where his story leaves him."

"Until he comes again," Ida whispered.

He came again, grunting and guilty. Ida opened her eyes behind the layers of dress Lucien had pushed over her face. She focused all her will at once to keep the scream at bay, and turned her head to press her cheek into the filth of the mausoleum floor.

Lucien scrambled off her, tugging down her skirts, doing up his fly. Ida peeked at Maud, still naked by her baby's grave. Ida chewed her check not to cry, but her damnable weakness came welling and she closed her eyes again, swallowing the blood. Lucien touched a match to a cigarette, smoking in the darkness. Maud stirred and yawned like a sun-soaked cat.

"Lucien?" she called, and he rushed to kiss her cheeks and fingers, calling her his love, his wife, and the mother of kings.

from *The Shadow Land, or Light from the Other Side*
(An autobiographical account of mediumship)
by Elizabeth d'Esperance

1897

I feel somebody's arms round me although I sit on my chair alone. I feel somebody's heart beating against my breast. I feel that something is happening . . . It must be my own heart I feel beating so distinctly. Yet those arms around me? Surely never did I feel touch so plainly. I begin to wonder which is I. Am I the white figure or am I the one on the chair? Are they my hands round the old lady's neck, or are these mine that are lying on the knees of me, or on the knees of the figure if it be not I, on the chair? Certainly they are my lips that are being kissed. It is my face that is wet with the tears which these good women are shedding so plentifully. Yet how can it be? It is a horrible feeling, thus losing hold of one's identity. I long to put out one of these hands that are lying so helplessly, and touch someone just to know if I am myself or only a dream—if "Anna" be I, or I almost as it were, in her identity . . . How long will there be two of us? Which will it be in the end? Shall I be "Anna" or "Anna" be I?

6

DREAMER OF DREAMS,
BORN OUT OF MY DUE TIME

The miracle that gave them such a death
Transfigured to pure substance what had once
Been bone and sinew; when such bodies join
There is no touching here, nor touching there,
Nor straining joy, but whole is joined to whole;
For the intercourse of angels is a light
Where for its moment both seem lost, consumed.
. . .

When the conflagration of their passion sinks, damped by the body or
  the mind
That juggling nature mounts, her coil in their embraces twined
. . .

What matter that you understood no word!
Doubtless I spoke or sang what I had heard
In broken sentences. My soul had found
All happiness in its own cause or ground.
Godhead on Godhead in sexual spasm begot
Godhead. Some shadow fell. My soul forgot

—from *Supernatural Songs* by W. B. Yeats

Even before I open my eyes to the cool, Parisian, Right Bank light
pooled behind the gauzy curtains, I know I'm in Maud's body again.
It gives itself to sleep in a way mine never has, and leaves sleep's
pleasure trailing dreams and comfort. Outside my bedroom door,
Cook prattles to Ida, remembering to call her Mrs. Rowley, and no
longer "mademoiselle" since she's married now. They dither amiably
over my health, and whether the afternoon will warm up. Then Cook
takes her basket and tromps off for the market, and Ida comes into
my room to take up her post in the chaise lounge by the big bay
window.

I should speak to her, now I'm certain I can, but I hate to leave
the glow of lingering sleep. I can't quite visualize the body that con-
tains me, but pushing myself into its perimeters, the height and weight
of it feel like home—a natural nest for my spirit. This is my body
for feeling from the inside, not being seen from the outside, and I
love it.

I grin and stretch my long, white arms over my head. "Good
morning, Ida," I yawn.

Ida's eyes pepper across my face and pierce into mine. "Laura?"
I nod.

"You'll be wanting Mr. Yeats to call on Maud today, then?"
"Yes, I believe so."

"I've been having the concierge tell him you're ill. He's been in
Paris four days now—no! Don't sit up yet, I have questions, and this
is when you are best to answer them. Mr. Yeats will be breakfasting
with the Matherses for the next hour anyway."

I don't need much encouragement to linger, floating in the morning warmth, tinged pink now with incipient desire. I will see Will
soon.

"You didn't come when I summoned you," Ida begins.

The red deepens now, prickling into shame. "I remembered," I
whisper, grasping for wisps of memory. "I was running, and I remembered."

"What were you running from?"

"No, I was chasing someone. It was a game. I was . . . Holy shit, Ida! I'm married."

"A grown woman running about, playing games?"

"Soccer. You'd say football . . . Ida, that's not the point. I'm married in my real life. Why do I keep coming here? I told my husband about you, and Will and all this craziness. I didn't come when you tried to summon me because I don't want these dreams anymore. I'm married."

"The future may be so pure that wives no longer make arrangements with other men, but in this time, it is not so unusual."

Ida still lounges in the chaise, but I'm too agitated to be still. I'm sitting up in bed, picking at the fabric of my dress and bedding. "My age more pure? Seriously? We've got twenty-five channels of porn, and condoms at the quickie mart, for fuck's sake."

Ida cocks her head away from me, uncomprehending.

"No," I say. "I'm not even sure my age values purity. We're just not repressed anymore. At least I think we're not. We're supposed to be liberated. There was a sexual revolution."

"A sexual revolution," Ida whispers, and her eyes flare with a heat I've never seen in them before. It makes her color prettily to say *sexual*.

"You told your husband about your lover?"

"Will is not my lover! And yes, we think honesty is important."

"We think it is in very poor taste." Ida blinks her large eyes. "We have our love affairs, but we refrain from their discussion. But you— you reveal them, but do not have them?"

"I think that's right," I say, but the hungry way she looks at me makes me wonder if I was wrong about repression. Maybe we've just shifted its weight from our society to our selves.

"You must not try to deny me again," she says.

"Yeah, no. It didn't work out too well anyway. I didn't drink, didn't have sex, tried thinking about anything but Will while I was falling asleep last night. And I dreamed about sex in a tomb with a French guy." I shrug. "If I'm going to have these dreams, I want Will in them, and he wasn't last night. You were, though," I say to Ida, just remembering. "Did you have sex with the Frenchman, too? Is that who you married?"

The glass shatters behind my head before I see it in her hand. Water explodes across the wall and the flowers land in a tumble on the pillow where my head had been.

We are both standing.

"Goddamn it, Ida," I shout. "I will find a way to reach Will without you, if you keep trying to kill me!"

The anger washes from her face in a wave of ice white. "Find a way into Maud without me," she says, "and I will kill you both."

I sit down. Even through the sleep haze and adrenaline hangover, I know the way she said that means something. The middle of me, tits to bones, runs freezing liquid.

She walks toward me in small, precise high-booted steps. A little woman, bitten off, but fearless. I am so much taller, a soccer player, strong, but hiding, afraid for my life for the first time in it. Ida collects the flowers fallen around me. Her voice is conversational. "That French man was Maud's lover. My husband is Irish. I do not love mine. Eventually, I will destroy hers."

Her quiet reordering freaks me out more than the violence. "Why did you marry a man you're not in love with?" I ask, cautious of the palpable rage pulsing under her.

"We make a good match."

"I get that. You're friends," I say. "I think that matters more." I hate the question mark stealing into my voice. I stay camouflage-still, letting her lean around me, picking up roses by their thornless, hothouse stems. "Love is about being able to live together, right?" I say. "It's practical. It's about having the same values, wanting the same stuff out of life. That's what I have with my husband, and we're very happy together."

"Obviously not."

"We are! I love him very much."

"Love is one of The Mysteries," Ida says. "An inexplicable soul connection that transcends knowledge and proof." She retraces the trail of fallen flowers across the rug until only petals, water, and glittering, splintered glass remain, sprinkled through space between us.

"I don't think I believe in that kind of love," I say.

"You don't think you believe in astral travel, either." She drops the roses onto the breakfast tray, and lies back down on the chaise. "Belief has nothing to do with thought. You may not believe in transcendent love, but here you are."

"I was trying not to be."

"Love cannot be resisted or denied." Ida closes her eyes against the in-rushing light. "It's a thing your soul does."

I don't believe in souls either, but it would be irrational to argue that point from here.

"Okay," I say instead, "you can't control what you feel." I start collecting petals from the bed. "But you can control what you do."

Ida's angular body, against the velvet chaise in the extravagant sun, softens just fractionally, but it's enough. I understand. "You're in love," I remember. "You're in love with Maud. But you haven't tried to kiss me again. Why not?"

"You're not Maud."

"That's not the reason." It's starting to make sense. "No," I say. "You've fallen in love with someone else, too."

"Yes."

"And it's only when you can channel me into Maud that you see him."

"Yes."

"And that's why you'd kill us both!"

My hands brim over with red petals, but I'm afraid to carry them to the tray where their stems lie. I can't tell if Ida is falling asleep or working some terrible spell up in her mind.

"My new love is not afraid of me," she says. "Perfect love drives out all fear."

I stand without making a noise.

"You are afraid," she says, cracking one blue eye at me.

"You threatened to kill me."

"And?"

"And I believe you."

Ida closes her eyes again and settles more deeply into the couch. "Good. But you're a woman. Surely you are accustomed to fear."

"Not really, no."

"No? Any man, at any moment, might kill you, or worse. Surely, in your strange future, all men are still stronger than a mere woman, and they are your only protection from themselves."

I stand there, stupidly, with my hands full of petals, more afraid of a woman half my size than I have ever been of a man twice my strength. "I changed my mind. I'm not afraid of you," I say. I walk over to the tray and dump the fluttering petals. "I'm not buying into that paranoid bullshit."

"No?" Ida doesn't move. "Not even in a body sick with the burden of another life? How will you protect it without men?"

"Maud's pregnant again?"

"And expecting a son, again. Your 'last night' was four months ago. A girl would be a terrible disappointment. What can a daughter do to free a nation? How can she fend off the invader's force? Will she, like Scheherazade, trade stories and sex to the man or nation who owns her?" Ida yawns and sits up. "Why don't you pour us some tea?"

The teapot is buried under stems and flowers. "You need me to keep coming here, coming into Maud so you can travel to the man you love."

Ida doesn't look up, but I know I've surprised her.

"You need me as much as I need you," I say. "I'm not afraid of you."

We face each other across the little table's breakfast tray, newspaper, and mound of dead flowers. Behind Ida, the doors to the balcony stand open, and I can just glimpse the Eiffel Tower through the blowing white curtains. Maud really knows how to live.

"Perfect love drives out all fear," she says again.

"I don't love you."

"I know," she whispers, but she holds my eyes.

"And you're wrong," I say, standing to Maud's full height, strong and certain in her full, lush body. "Love doesn't drive out fear. It's the other way around. "

"Is that why you told your husband your dreams?"

Sometimes Ida just makes no sense. What husband?

I think of Will's fierce eyes and tender mouth, but I know we are not married.

"Ida," I scold her, "silly, it was you who married last month, not I!"

Ida's pink tongue darts out and retreats. "Of course," she says. "You must forgive me. I'm quite clairvoyant, darling, and, on occasion, confuse the present with the future."

I want to ask, but my face burns so hot I keep it turned away from Ida and the window's light. Do her words mean Will and I will one day wed? Or that in some powerful, mystic way, we already have?

"You should dress, my dear," Ida says. "I can show myself out. I shall call again tomorrow."

Had Ida realized the licenses of matrimony, she would have married sooner. Her husband, the right honorable C. T. Rowley, would not accompany his wife on her Bohemian weekends with poets and playwrights, but Ida now made an appropriate chaperone to Miss Gonne, Maud's monkey of the same name notwithstanding.

Ida smiled quietly and motioned for the maid to unfasten her sober matron's dress. This weekend at Douglas Hyde's Ratra House in County Roscommon, many miles west of Dublin, was the closest Ida had approached to an Irish equivalent of the fabled country house parties her English cousins so loved to titter and blush about. Wives and husbands roomed separately to uphold both the national decorum and the national pastime—corridor creeping—an illicit nighttime pleasure Ida intended to both modify and participate in that night, in her uniquely Irish way.

With consummate care and tenderness, she unpacked the gorgeous dress purpose-made for the night's occult occasion. Its heavy white satin flowed thick as peeled flesh beneath her fingers, and the detail work, made from a slender folded tube of the same fabric, was subtle but intricate, sewn in spirals and secret symbolic shapes like a white snake's tracks through bleached sand. Ida's wedding dress. So much finer than what she had worn the day she married Constantine Rowley. But the vows she had taken that day bound only her body. Tonight, she would give her whole self to her daemon underground. Ida closed her eyes, looking for his face. She recalled his predatory gait—a hunting beast from Araby, hungry, sleek and fluid—and the sheer power of him walking beside her through the dark, underground halls ran warm beneath her skin.

Ida sent her daft, hovering maid away and stripped down to nothing in the warm spring country air. All tonight was sacred. Ida washed in the graceful porcelain basin, and anointed her flesh with oil and whispered words. She knew the rituals now.

Ida robed herself in the new linen underthings, a weave so fine they were almost both transparent and weightless. Tiny tucks and seams in the light fabric set it fetchingly over her flesh. She ran her hands across her breasts, smaller than Maud's, but finer and more tender. Could her daemon find her beautiful? She wanted wonder on his face when she disrobed for him.

"Until you know the nature of your own damnation," he had said, "I cannot tell you my name."

She had thought of little since. She was not beautiful. But if her meager beauty was enough to win his love, she would not ask for more, not even his name.

"You did brilliantly," he had said. He held the door open, and she had looked up into eyes that reflected none of the walls' shuddering firelight. His black hair slid forward, a sinuous silk curtaining his face from any eye but hers, and his lips, those velvet cushions cloaking blades, had smiled. Ida bit her own mouth with fierce wanting to feel his teeth take her so.

But she kissed instead the gold ring she had commissioned from Monsieur Dulac and fastened the slender cord around her throat, fingers brushing bone too close beneath the skin. Not soft enough, not womanly like Maud, Ida's body was resonant with feeling and

more awake to touch or scent and vision than Maud could ever
dream.

It was almost time. Dinner in the well-appointed hall below was
winding down at last. Ida unfolded the careful wrappings from two
bottles—the chrism for her, and the chloroform for Maud. She
touched the oil to her crown, her third eye, and to her lips. She had
excused herself early from the Hydes' table, feigning weariness after
traveling. Fortunate she was fasting, she was so nervous. She touched
her throat-base, and between her breasts, her navel and her root.

Through her window, open to the fields of County Roscommon,
she heard the men step onto the back veranda, laughing and striking
matches for cigars, Yeats's strong growl mixed with Hyde's nasal bark.
Maud would come upstairs now. Ida thought she ought to pee, but
found she could not. Never before had her nerves stretched this taut.
Seven years of work had brought her to this moment, to the power
and the skill to send herself after Maud's freed soul, to the daemon
whose exotic eyes and secret power had betrayed Ida's punctured
heart to love. She had married for this, for Rowley's name and because, despite all her skill, Ida could not foresee what lay ahead for
her, and she had witnessed Maud in the claws of Iseult's birth.

Ida had walked with her until she could no longer stand, groaning
with the dropping weight and climbing pain. She had screamed with
it. If Ida were to conceive tonight, her child would have the protection of the Rowley name and fortune. And Maud had suffered her
rending in vain. Iseult would always know, from birth, she had been
a disappointment. A girl, and not the son Maud had lost. But Ida
was not likewise blind. She had spoken with the future and she knew
women's lives would one day change. Her daemon could choose the
body that suited him, male or female, to be born into this world.

Her hand sat on her stone-flat stomach. She squeezed her eyes
hard closed. *Please.*

Why was she praying? Providence was a power Ida had learned to
command. She had no need to wheedle.

*Please let me still be fertile ground, not poisoned by the men who dug unwanted
wells, or by the hate which filled them to brimming over.*

"Devil damn it for Christ's own sin!"

Ida gazed in horror at her dress. Where her praying hands had pressed against it, twisting the fabric in their fervent fists, the fine white satin hung crumbled and oil-stained. Her wedding dress, ruined as she was.

Maud's clothes were never soiled, and Moina would have a scarf of gauze to drape and re-arrange until the blot became a shadow cast by the swirling cloud of silk. But Ida, although she dabbed and swore, only tore the dress a little and spread the ugly gray. She pushed her fingers into her lids and willed the tears away. They would just mottle her plain face. She sniffed and pushed her shoulders down. She would never be beautiful or good. But she could still be clever. She seized the chloroform bottle and left the room. She did not walk, as she had imagined she would do, stately to her bridal hour. She slunk instead, silent as cancer, and as pretty. And less welcome.

❦

I lay their faces out, four rows of five on my left side, another twenty on my right. Charlie will be here any second, but right now, it's just me and these forty faces, half of them dead, in I+D's chilly, airy open space. The coffeemaker, gurgling companionably from the kitchen, adds a rich sepia to the moss-morning smell of incipient Portland summer. I've hidden his face among the dead, second row, third from the left, but just glancing at it drops my pulse between my legs. How can a face do that to me? Why doesn't Amit's?

I know the sounds of Charlie's arrival like a childhood song: the downstairs door flies open and hits the back wall. Silence as he wheels the bike in. *Thunk* when he drops it against the wall. Then the front door bangs shut and the one at the foot of the stairs flies open the same way. A grunt as the bike goes up on his shoulder—he could leave it in the lobby, but he won't. Then his feet in the hard-soled biking shoes come trudging up the stairs. There are twenty-three *scruff-scruff*'s before he'll drop everything—bag, bike, helmet, and coat at the top stair and deliver the entrance line I'm sure he works on the entire ride. But I'll be in the kitchen, pouring coffee.

Except this morning, it's a song. His strong Irish tenor carries U2's "A Sort of Homecoming" into the kitchenette to hurry me until I return with our two cups. "My god, woman!" he stops mid Bono-yodel. "What have you been doing? You're positively radiant!"

"I've been sleeping in." I try to play it casual, hand him his mug, but he's scanning me closely.

"Is that what you naughty newlyweds are calling it these days?"

I spent last night with Will Yeats walking through a Paris spring.

"I slept until six this morning. I guess I needed the rest."

"You surely need something you're getting!"

No, I don't. I don't need these irrational, restless, I-know-they're-not-dream dreams.

Charlie whistles and pours sugar into his coffee in a fat, white rainbow. "You decadent child!"

I am a child. A ridiculous child, who screams and tantrums because she doesn't want to get in the tub, then howls when it's over because she doesn't want to get out. I'm afraid of what my dreams mean, but I want to keep dreaming them. I'm not superstitious. I know imagining other men can't make me cheat on my husband. Dreaming doesn't create reality. But could Charlie and I make an ad we didn't imagine first?

"So these are our choices?" Charlie drapes his brawny arm around my shoulder and pulls me against his side to contemplate the rows of pictures. "We need three?"

"Three sets. Three from the left and three from the right," I say.

"Men, women, couples, families . . ." He's not really talking to me anymore. I lean against him and he shifts to accommodate me under his wing. My body feels runty but safe against his of coiled wire cable. Charlie is muttering, trying out different headlines under his breath. We still haven't found a good tagline, but we trust us. We'll get it. We always do. My eyes keep going back to Will's.

"What amazing outfits. God, wouldn't we all look amazing in clothes like that? Look at the giant bow on this guy. You'd get your ass kicked for that today. Even in Portland. I wish we could see the colors. Where'd you find these?"

"They're scans." But I'm remembering the colors of Paris. My dress, a lilac crepe cut loose to hide the first swellings of Maud's second pregnancy, is trimmed in rows of tiny, hand-sewn beads. More hours went into that dress—the skillful tailoring and intimate understanding of fabric, the detail too small for any but the wearer to notice—than go into many quarter-million-dollar, thirty-second ad buys. Will walks beside me in gray and light blue serge, wonderful to touch, and vaguely crumpled without any rayon to help the ironing. Everywhere we go, eyes follow us. I would hate that, but I never feel self-conscious in my Maud dreams. I don't judge her body the way I do my own, even though it's larger and less fit. It fits me, I guess.

"And the hats!" Charlie unwraps me and picks up the picture of Maud.

I try to see her objectively. Her body is fat by contemporary standards, but from the inside, it's not overly padded, or numb. It's full of feeling. Will's hand on my wrist, and every ounce of me shuddering for more touch, more sensation.

"Is that a whole bird on her head?" Charlie wants to know.

Maybe because it's not my body, I never dream of changing Maud's. I know I don't have that kind of long-term control over it. I can diet and exercise, dye my hair, change my clothes, but in my dream, my body isn't for looking at, although everyone does.

"Oh, no. Look at this one!" Charlie picks up a different woman, in a different hat. "This is perfect! Hang on." He dashes off to Amy's desk.

I put Maud's photo back in the bottom row. Straighten it. She gazes at me with a confidence close to arrogance from under her bird-wing hat. It would never occur to her to work on her body. She wouldn't know what that means. Her body works on her like it works on me when I inhabit it.

This is crazy. Irresponsible. I don't inhabit it. My work bleeds into my dreams. Spend all day collecting Victorian photos, and dreaming about them all night is hardly a surprise. I am so full of shit. Amit guessed his name night before last—W. B. Yeats—a poet, his mom's favorite one. I hadn't been able to remember his name from the dreams, but I've been reading up on him every spare moment since.

"Check it out!" Charlie holds the eight-by-ten of the elaborately hatted woman up before me, his left arm cocked behind his back. She's reclining in a dark wood and striped canvas deck chair on a rocky beach, book facedown in her knee, umbrella over her shoulder, absently watching a boy in a long-sleeved, knee-length knitted jumpsuit. He regards the camera with skeptical, dark eyes.

When he decides I've studied the picture long enough, Charlie whips his hidden hand around with a boxer's speed. "Ta da!" he exclaims, revealing the framed shot of Amy and her daughter he's stolen from her desk. They're at the beach in matching pink bikinis, Amy scowling a little from a steel and plastic folding chair, her daughter grinning beside her prize sandcastle. The book in Amy's lap is turned facedown.

"Very good," I say. "Amy will kill you."

"It gets better." Charlie points at the table, eyes crackling. "Who's that?"

"Queen Victoria."

"Tell me that's her wedding dress?"

"That's her wedding dress."

Charlie practically sprints to my cubby and comes back with one of the formal portraits our wedding photographer dropped off yesterday. I'm thinner than Queen Vicky, and my silk dress is black, but you can't miss the lineage. When times and people have changed so much, women work jobs as equals, vote, make laws, why do we still dress ourselves and pose like this when we marry?

"What about him?" I point Will Yeats out to Charlie.

"Yeah, I saw him. Why's he here?"

"What do you mean?"

"Is he anybody?"

A sudden, Victorian anger rises up in me. I set my coffee mug down carefully.

"He's a poet."

"Christ. We hardly have professional poets anymore, do we? No parallel."

"We have copywriters."

Charlie snorts. "He's cute."

"Do you think so?" I say, loving that he shares my appreciation of this face.

"Yeah. But I like him better." Charlie's finger moves down Will's row. "Look at these whiskers! I mean, damn!"

I want to still be looking at Will. I want to linger over his face with Charlie, and talk about the way his eyes hold you from the page. And what he says.

"If we're going to do one Happy Family shot, one bride and one ordinary guy, we ought to get a really good one."

"What's wrong with him?"

I can feel Charlie's eyes on my face, but I keep mine on the pictures under me. "What's his name?"

"W. B. Yeats."

"And what does this dead poet mean to you?"

"Nothing," I say through the closing knot of my throat. "I just thought he was interesting."

"Is he the Irish writer your husband is so crazy about?"

"No, that's Joyce."

Charlie picks up Will's photo and studies it. The tops of my ears are hot.

"What's the story?" he asks.

Charlie and Chris have been in love for as long as I've known them. Really giddy, crazy in love, and if I had an intelligent question, he would be the expert I'd ask. "No story," I say. "I just like his face."

"Ever the artist," he grins at me, drops Will, and picks up Side-burns Magee. "It's not all about looks, you know."

I have absolutely no right to be angry with Charlie for believing what I tell him.

"Yeah," I say. "I know."

Ida mirrored Maud's pose, leaning her shoulder against the casement, fingertips on the sill, the dull gold of their Eire rings glinting in the wet twilight. Beneath them, the grounds of Ratra House tumbled toward the bottomless Lough Gara, hasty and wild. It took a strength of will Maud could never fathom for Ida to endure the soiled dress and the comparison. And the silence. She wanted to confess, to say, "This is my wedding night and I am afraid," but she gazed toward the distant lake with Maud. They had boated out onto a larger lake that afternoon, with Mr. Yeats and Dr. Hyde, to an island almost entirely covered by an abandoned castle. Ida had wandered the barren rooms like a restless ghost while Will dreamed of an Irish Renaissance, and Maud of revolution. And Douglas Hyde fished.

Each floating his own freedom.

"How I love Ireland," Maud murmured. "Although France's beauty is less tragic."

Only Maud would talk about herself at such length on the night of another's sacrament. "Come away from the window, dear," Ida coaxed. "It's making you sad."

Maud turned her back to the wall, leaning against it still. Ida waited, lonely as the island's ruined tower, and as haunted.

Did Maud stand by windows because she knew the evening light polished her pearlescent skin? She had been touring the famine towns, and already there the country people called her "lady of the *sidhe*." Ida snorted, but twisted the sound to coughing. Fairy indeed! Maud had no magic of her own at all, only enough suffering to keep her soul blowing free as the Host of the Air.

"I could learn to love Will, maybe."

"Love is not a thing one learns to do," Ida snapped. "Artifice is learned. Love is only fanned or smothered. Come lay down."

Maud turned, dreamy, back to the window, to the sloping lawns and dusk-dimmed trees. "I should not have left Iseult in France."

"She was not the child you hoped to have, of whom you dreamed."

"No, but I have learned to love her all the same."

Ida ground her knuckles into one another to keep from saying she would also have a child soon. What a comfort it would be to say the words, *I am on the brink of something I know to be a sin.*

"You have done much good for our country, Maud, but you will become too ill to do more, if you do not rest," she said instead.

"How can I rest? Ida, I saw a woman, starved so thin she could not walk, try to nurse her dying child from a breast that could only bleed."

"Then come and lie down for that poor woman's sake," Ida gentled, tugging Maud's plump arm. "Recover your strength."

"And Will does nothing but dream. His castle of heroes, his vision of an Irish Eleusis. Real bodies cannot be fed on imagination."

To Ida, without imagination, bodies would be just meat and gross sensation, but she said, "I too have seen the soldiers set the battering ram and beat against the door until the whole wall that holds it is knocked in." She eased Maud onto the bed. "I have sat within the houses beside the huddled peasants whilst the law has made its assault, and felt the pounding, thrusting, intruding fist of the queen grind into a family's only safety from the cold and rain."

Maud nodded, and Ida pulled the pins from the thick auburn hair. "And what could those poor people do then but die?" Ida uncoiled the heavy braid and started loosening the strands. "But imagine, what if the family had another house? And all their things and more were there? And the soldiers wasted all their strength against a door nobody hid behind? Would that not make angry fools of them? Would England wear her troops out with hunting us until they died?"

"The queen would send more. There are always more. Land that can grow no food sprouts soldiers in its hungry fields."

"But they do not want to live here. And they are men. All they can do is fight."

"I want to fight!" Maud sat up, her unpinned hair wrapping wild and red around her.

"Yes, you must fight!" Ida seized Maud's arms and gazed into the hasty eyes that could see nothing but the bodies—the hungry bodies, the bloodied bodies, the raped. "But you must be strong to fight."

"I am strong!" Maud's height and defiance shone in the darkening room.

Ida almost hesitated.

"Are you stronger than men?" she asked. "Are you stronger than even one man?"

"No."

Ida took Maud's faltering hands in her smaller ones. "No woman is. You must be beautiful."

Maud sat down on the bed's edge.

"I have this to help you sleep." Ida took the chloroform bottle from her skirt, and saw the fire light in Maud's eyes again.

"Ida, I begged you not to bring that! I have come to need it too much since Iseult's birth."

"You cannot be beautiful if you are ill."

"But is it only my beauty that inspires men, and not my words?"

Ida unstoppered the bottle and inverted it over the handkerchief she had prepared. "Real bodies cannot feed on words," she said.

Maud closed her eyes and allowed Ida to ease her tall body back onto the bed.

When the lids fluttered, Ida took the cloth away. She walked to the bed's other side and lay down, suddenly nervous. It was time. Maud might not know the power of words, but she would recognize the spell of possession if Ida said it now. Instead, she took Maud's hand, twisting their fingers together so their rings touched. Then she shook her hand free and groped at her neck for her husband's wedding band. It was not lost.

"Love can be lost, as well as fanned or smothered," Maud murmured, her voice thick and drugged.

Ida wrapped their hands again. It might well cost her Maud's love to follow her pilgrim soul tonight, but Ida stood ready to pay that price. She held the hanky to Maud's perfect lips, and closed her eyes against the fumes she, too, must breathe this time. In the empty space behind her sight, she sensed Maud's spirit still, weak and hovering nearby. If she and Maud fought side by side, might they not do some good thing? Votes for women, or Home Rule? Something real for the starving country people Victoria would not feed?

She heard the secret whisper of Will's occult name. Had he told Laura this? No matter. It was enough she knew Laura was near, hungry for Will, and Maud was slipping away. Maud's leaving would make a wake Ida could follow from suffrage and nationalism, from Maud's love and her own freedom, to a devil who she knew lied. Laura wavered, her mind touched a man with chestnut skin.

"Doubt is the only enemy," Ida's daemon whispered.

"Yes," Ida said. It was what made Laura weak—the wondering. But Ida knew. Ida knew it all.

⁂

When we say *upright* to mean moral, it must be because lying down makes it easier to sin.

I don't believe in sin.

All the same, lying by Ida, watching her sleeping face, I know what I want to do is wrong. And that I will soon forget that it is. I will forget everything I learned about Will Yeats's future. I will forget the man who gave me his name.

Beside me, Ida is a twisted patchwork of too-thin and baby fat. Her flesh is dimpled and plump, but the bones stick out in a way that makes her look awkward or in pain. Her mouth is close to mine. Maud's fingers, heavy and unfamiliar still, push the damp, sick-smelling cloth away from between our lips.

I have become more aware of women's bodies since I woke up to dreaming about Ida kissing me, and I like the new erotic thrum under my days and in my work. I could lie here with Ida, stay dreamy, and not forget my husband. And not sin. But in the same way I know that's not what I want to do, I know what I will do. Ida's lips move in her sleep. I know she's not sleeping, any more than I am.

I tiptoe across the room, out into the corridor, and close the door behind me. Maud would know where to look for Will, but I have no sense of navigation here. The house stands quiet, but I'm not sure I could hear a whispered conversation over the quick, interior thud of my heart in my ears. The hall is dark and the floor groans with every uncertain step. If I could see which door I came through, I would go back and wake Ida just for the company.

The uprights supporting the vanishing banister loom like ghost-white sentries deeper into the black. Only the first steps of the massive central staircase are visible. The night rises up before me, creeping higher with every step I take down. I keep a hand on the railing until the staircase stops. I follow it across the landing, and move into moonshine with the next flight down. Now I know where he is.

Fear slides its cold fingers down my throat, and holds my pulse against my ears, to grip my belly with a warmer terror. My shadow on the wall distorts strangely, and I touch the great wads of fabric rising from my shoulders and upper arms. It is rich, soft stuff, for all its tortured contours, and I wonder briefly why the arms of all my shirts are always the same profile, just long or short.

I walk soundlessly across the gaping entry hall and through the parlor where the slender, tall doors stand open to the night. I can see his legs through them, one knee crossed over the other, on the stone bench outside. But I can imagine his face, his mouth, his consuming kiss, and I want him. I want him wild and unafraid, not picking my silent way through the abandoned chairs and crowded bookcases, navigating by the ferocious light of lust. I walk through the door into the moon's still purity.

He's holding a sketch pad, drawing with black sticks of charcoal on the luminous white paper.

"Miss Gonne."

I can't see his eyes, but his silhouette rises slowly to standing, a politeness that seems out of place. There is no one with him.

"No," I answer.

He's by my side at once, strong hands on my wrists, eyes reaching into mine.

"*Demon est Deus Inversus*," I whisper.

"My God," he says.

He holds my body against him fiercely, and we are only wrist
bones and ribs, and breath squeezed to almost crying. "Every night,"
he whispers, "I have tried each prayer, every invocation I've learned
to bring you to me here. Last night, I had given up. Tonight, I knew
you would come."

I nod my head against his chest, and he tightens his grip on me.
I know I fell asleep tonight looking for him as well, but it was Ida's
voice that found me. That we cannot reach each other without her
makes a desperate fist of my throat.

His fingers trace the curl of my ear, and a radiant eroticism joins
the bath of sensation. His touch slides down my jaw, and tips my
chin up to him. He will kiss me now. The sensuous sheen seeps from
the surface deeper into me.

"We must find a way to be together more." His voice is heavy with
pain or desire. "I can't live five years between holding you."

His eyes move over my face. My breasts and belly, my thighs and
sex, press snug against him, my lips raised, but it's the way he looks
at me that hollows me.

"You are so beautiful."

"It isn't me you're seeing," I tell him, a quick jealousy in my chest.

"It is," he says. "And it has been five years since I last did."

Relief or anticipation slides my lids closed and lifts my lips in
invitation. He takes it.

His fingers turn my face, feeding it to his mouth. But his kiss is
tender. His lips brush mine without moving, fitting themselves against
my parted ones. His mouth opens only fractionally, but I pulse toward
it, catch the questioning upper lip between mine, and hesitate. His
arms close around me. And his kiss. Drawing on my lower lip, sucking, and my mouth answers—teeth and tongue and sob. In the hard
house of his arms, with the cool Irish night whispering in eddies
around our gripped bodies, I am screamingly awake years before I was
born. And it all makes sense. No part of my mind or philosophy
rebels or questions this. Every beam of flat light, every tree-rustle and
animal smell sing vibrant to me, and even the pain is welcome.

Will takes his mouth away. His forehead touches mine; his eyes plumb me. "Laura?" His fingers slide gentle whispers across my cheeks and hair. "You're troubled."

"Something's wrong with Ida," I confess at last.

"How so?" He makes his voice soft as his hands touch me.

"I don't know. I felt it when I was moving into Maud tonight. Ida was following her, riding Maud away from here. I don't know where she was going—somewhere dangerous. And Maud didn't want her to."

"Is her life in danger?"

"I don't think so."

"Good. No one trusts her, or even likes her well, but she is highly trained in the occult, and very powerful."

I think she may be too powerful. I think the life in danger may be Maud's. Or mine. But I don't say so. My fears are irrational. Maud is upstairs asleep, and I'm a hundred years away. Will never takes his hands from me, or his eyes, but they flicker to my lips and back.

"What about Maud?" I ask instead. "Is she powerful as Ida?"

Will jerks his head impatiently. "No. She was initiated, but has not advanced. She has less aptitude, I suspect. And certainly less interest. All her concern is for the daylight world of action." But his face cannot hold the hard imprint of anger long. In the brilliant moonlight, it is hazy with tenderness. He runs his fingers over my cheek. "But I believe tonight Maud was truly willing, for the first time perhaps, to channel you."

"Why?"

"I spoke to her of you, at last."

He dips his mouth to me again. His hypnotic kiss takes away my worry, and drops my thoughts into a blur of pleasure. "She knew she channeled something, but hated being only a vessel. She did not understand about you, and Madam Rowley had not been truthful with her."

His words and fingers trail over my throat and down my arms. They trace my flesh like magnets, drawing to the surface all the electric, stinging metal of my blood. I am flush with wanting him, over-charged and tingling.

"Maud saw today for the first time, and believed, as I do, that the land itself is holy."

My body is holy.

"That Ireland could one day be our Judea, a land of sacred pil-grimage." His mouth moves across my flesh. "There are places in our land—Tara, Castle Island, the Rock of Cashel—that summon ex-traordinary souls to them."

I cling to his shoulders as he bows his head deeper over me. His mouth travels inexorably down my throat.

"Maud saw today that you must be allowed to come to me in such places, where poets might embrace the soul of Ireland."

"If I could reach you there . . ." I whisper, but his mouth takes mine again, obliterating and inviting, and everything I don't under-stand, or have been afraid of, washes away. I run my hands across the strength of his back, pulling it closer, wanting more. It tugs, retreat-ing, and elongates me. Every open space of my skin, every filament beneath, stretches and quavers taut to his touch, to his insistent kiss. Hands hard on my shoulders, he holds himself away.

"We must go there tonight," he murmurs. "We must become not only the pure essence of our selves, but their symbols as well."

My body, resonate with his touch, drowns out thought. I can only nod.

We slip across the silent black grass under the high, white moon, for the deeper darkness of the secret wood bordering it. We are subtle as hunters, fragile as prey.

from *The Autobiography of William Butler Yeats
Consisting of Reveries Over Childhood and Youth,
The Trembling of the Veil, and Dramatis Personae*
by William Butler Yeats

1916

Speaking suddenly to Madam Rowley, a friend who was present while Maud Gonne was in semi-trance, she had described
herself as a murderess of children. Upon another occasion
this friend, a pious woman, suddenly screamed in the middle
of some vision of Maud Gonne's. She had found herself amid
the fires of Hell and for days afterwards found all about the
smell of sulphur . . . She had a great affection for Maud
Gonne, and certainly suspected neither of us of diabolical
practices.

7

I OFFER TO LOVE'S PLAY, MY DARK DECLIVITIES

When we bent down above the fading coals
And talked of the dark folk who live in souls
Of passionate men, like bats in the dead trees;
And of the wayward twilight companies
Who sigh with mingled sorrow and content,
Because their blossoming dreams have never bent
Under the fruit of evil and of good:
And of the embattled flaming multitude
Who rise, wing above wing, flame above flame,
And like a storm, cry the Ineffable Name,

—from "To Some I Have Talked with by the Fire" by W. B.
Yeats

Ida knew at once she was in Hell.

It wasn't the type of thing a girl was likely to have much confusion about, despite the fundamentally subjective nature of the proposition. Still, she kept her eyes closed. She rolled herself heavily onto her back and sat up. She knew her expensive, exquisite wedding dress was gone, replaced by something loose and shapeless, but her body was anointed for the ritual act of marriage still, and the man to whom she would soon surrender herself for the first time, body and soul, stood somewhere nearby. She climbed to her feet. Still she did not open her eyes. She stood, virginal and pure, a bride, and almost beautiful. When she opened her eyes, she would not be.

But his eyes compelled her, and she gazed into their unshining depths. Not even light escaped them. But the sharp hardness of their sheltering brows, his fierce nose and angry chin lost all sign of brutality in the almost feminine generosity and luxury and scarlet of his lips. Shadows clung to his face—darkness itself longed to caress the hollows of his cheek and jaw—but he wore the tight britches and high, polished boots of the loathed British military men.

"I wondered if you would return," he said. And Ida's mind, even in sleep, scrambled after his words, scratching at them, to shake his "wondered" instead of "hoped" at her in its cruel claws.

"Did you doubt me?" she challenged.

In a sudden blur of movement that did not touch his face, he caught the tips of her fingers, raised and turned her hand, and held it, motionless between their almost-touching bodies. When he dropped his imperial eyes, Ida treasured both the rich sweep of jet lashes on his cheek and the cool touch of his lips on the back of her hand.

"I have another great wonder to show you." He took a step back, extending the arm which held her hand. He drew it over his head, forcing Ida around him in a dancer's promenade while he stood, haughty and strong, the hub of her wheeling. If she were Maud, this would be grand. Ida had been forced, at the false wedding which bestowed upon her her true name, to dance, wincing and burning, before the assembled society of Dublin. But her steps marched somehow surer at her daemon's hand, and she paraded from behind his back to meet his eyes with a proud and truthful smile.

"What do you think of my great hall?" he asked with a pirate's flourish of his mahogany hand.

Ida looked up. She stood in the center of a cavernous stone beehive. Above her, in the inward-leaning walls, she could glimpse small holes, doors into other caverns mayhap, and tunnels leading off in several directions from the uneven, raw stone they stood upon. A dusty haze of light filtered through a jagged opening at the top. Ida's eyes reeled away from the size and scope of the void in the stone.

"Even more lies beneath us," he whispered. "Halls and rooms, the garden you have seen, all populated, but unmapped."

He strode across the rough ground, pointing out a hole in the floor. "I've thrown a stone down this and never heard it land," he called over his shoulder. "And look at this!" He struck a match against the sole of his boot and held it to the naked stone. With a wicked hiss, the small flame caught and spread, like rain down glass, up the bare stone wall.

Ida gaped.

"Imagine how beautiful all this could become, Ida. Hell could grow into a much more inviting place. But it needs a woman's touch."

The flames spread, moving horizontally across the wall, wrapping them, like the thrill of his words blistering Ida.

"Can you envision it?" he asked, striding back to her.

"The walls are burning," she whispered.

His laugh filled the hollow space and echoed, distorted by the flame.

"Yes," he said. "Wonderful, don't you think, that Hell should possess so convenient a source of illumination?"

"Will we also burn?" How Ida would hate it, if the priests were right, after all she had learned.

But her daemon took her shoulders in his strong hands and looked down into her face. Ida's belly contracted and her fingers stretched for him. Yes. Let the flames catch her hair.

"Ida, hold your breath."

Would he kiss her now? She stopped her breathing and only met his eyes, willing her own to radiate the invitation burning on her lips and between her thighs. Every nameless longing of her life coalesced in her stoppered lungs.

The walls went out.

Ida almost missed the flames' consuming danger.

"You are the only breathing creature here." He placed a reverent hand on her chest. "Your breath moves through cracks in the walls. I only set a spark."

"And when I'm not here . . ."

"There is nothing." His eyes dropped to his hand, rising and falling with her quick, small breaths.

He was the symbol of everything Ida had sought without satisfaction from her mother and her minister, throughout her mangled, stolen education, or in prayer. If she had his love, she would not care for his power. "Without you, there is nothing for me," she whispered.

But he laughed and took his palm away.

She had no skill at seduction. And no beauty.

"What if I could bring others here?" she cried. She would lay down on the rock and weep if he walked away. "I could go fetch Maud."

He smiled into her eyes. "Who?"

"Maud Gonne." Ida's cheeks flamed again. He had remembered her and forgotten Maud! "The woman you freed from her clothes on my last visit here. She went swimming," Ida said and at once wished she had not. Idiocy to conjure Maud's full pink breasts in his mind when Ida had only herself to offer. "But I don't know where she is now," she added. "And freedom is ultimately something we must give ourselves." Her shaky fingers touched the buttons of her dress.

"Maud?" He dismissed Maud's image with a wave of a graceful hand. "She is not damned, only cruel."

He turned Ida's back against his adamantine body to point a muscular arm over her shoulder at the scope of empty space. "Ida, I want you to imagine this room filled with all the ruined souls of the world. Can you see a place of comfort here, where the lost and damaged might come to meet? Where they might, for the first time, be not alone?"

Ida tipped her back in a subtle incline toward his strong chest behind her. "A secret order of Heaven's outcasts," she whispered, and felt his hands tighten on her shoulders. "Men and women. Equally damned, equally admitted." Minutely, Ida arched her back to bring the fuller flesh of her rump against him. "This room would become their meeting hall." His arm encircled her. "They will come from far away to be initiated"—she leaned back into the strength and power of him—"by us."

"You can see it, can't you?" His deep voice growled just above her ear sending chill erotic currents washing through her. "Ida, you posses such extraordinary vision."

Ida dared to touch his fine, corded wrists with her fingertips, to stroke the flesh that covered sinew. She tipped her head onto his shoulder, and tried to mimic the resonance of his voice in a sensual moan of abandon.

She made instead a strangled and phlegmatic squawk.

He released her and strode off, toward the far wall.

"What would you put there?" Ida's dashing daemon turned to point over his head at a shallow alcove several feet up.

She mashed her hair flat where it had snagged in the buttons of his coat, and caught a whiff of something spoiled. "A statue," she answered, and coughed to clear her muddy voice and think. "Of Nike. The Winged Victory of Samothrace." Discreetly, she sniffed again.

"You are a wonder and an inspiration, my love," he shouted, and strode along the curving wall toward a gaping hole. *My love.* He had called her his. It was all Ida wanted to be. His long legs, bold and purposeful, beneath the spotless white of his tight breeches, stepped with confident, broad strides over the uneven ground. Ida squeezed her shivery legs together. He claimed her! Strength showed in his every gesture, a latent power, magnitudes more than necessary, and merely hinted at in his restraint. Ida's nervous fingers crept to her collar buttons. He was whistling, his powerful back to her, looking up. She rushed to undo and rearrange her neckline to more seductive effect. The sick smell lingered, but she tugged at the fabric until she heard it tear.

"I'm sorry?" she stammered.

"I said, 'What shall we put down here?' You mustn't make me jealous, Ida. I will not share your attention. One hoards what is scarce." His rich, teasing voice brought a blushing smile to Ida's dry lips.

"How deep does it go?" she asked.

"I don't know."

"We'll have to chart all the halls before we decide how to use them."

"I don't think that's possible." He chuckled again and returned to her, decisive and elemental. She twisted, canting herself to reveal a shoulder to his devouring gaze. That never left her face. "The larger branches, certainly, but where they split and reconnect, where they overlap or narrow into nothing . . . No. We must plan without understanding, my love."

My love—again! Balanced between the animal vigor of youth and the astute wisdom of maturity, in full command of both, her devil prowled, the model of a man in his prime. How but through her own small beauty could she hope to take this power for her own?

"I will learn surveying," she suggested.

"Shall we furnish this room like a club or like a ballroom?"

"Must I make up my mind right away?"

"Not your mind, Ida. It is your imagination I want."

"I will dream of nothing else."

"Then I am satisfied." A muffled roar, that word *satisfied*, in her mind, in her throat, on her skin, with him standing so proud and strong beside her. Without its savagery, his face would be more beautiful than Maud's, but where her high cheeks were rounded and soft, his cut a harsh, hard line beneath his eyes. His nose and jaw made sharp angles against them, all arrowed toward his mouth.

"Close your eyes," his plump and tender lips commanded.

Ida complied, but it made the strange stench stronger.

"Tell me what you see."

Ida rifled her memory, but found only Will's wild dreams from their boating expedition that afternoon. Rowing across Lough Key to Castle Island, the poet had imagined a new Elysium housed in the abandoned castle there. But Ida had already stolen and fed to the devil every image she could remember.

"Tell me, Ida," he said in a tone that should have said, "Kiss me, Ida" instead, low and hungry. How could she think to talk when her body ached to open its real and secret self to him? Against her closed eyes, she could see only her mute yearning and his face framed in a dusty halo of scattered light from the stone hole fathoms over them.

"We will build a spiraling ramp to reach the higher caves," she whispered.

"Yes."

"Wide at the base, but tapering."

"Yes."

"And we will cantilever the platforms—buttressed in brass and ornately wrought."

"Oh . . ." Wonder tinged his voice, and maybe love. Ida's lips opened to give themselves, wanting the assault of teeth, tongue, and annihilation. She peeked through cracked lashes to see if his mouth inclined toward hers at all.

But he stared right up. Chin lifted, broad shoulders thrown back, his eyes had turned from her to the spiraling walls.

"And we'll widen the opening overhead and build a great glass dome in the roof, like the Crystal Palace."

"Wonderful," he murmured.

"And every blighted soul, every lost and broken, ugly, benighted thing will find its way to us." Ida's ice fingers moved down the coarse fabric of her dress, pulling buttons like toadstools from dampening ground. "The filthy and the ruined, the corrupt and wrong will come to us."

"The damned, cursed, and misbegotten," he said.

Ida pulled the halves of her dress apart and wriggled, like a waking moth, free of her confining sack cocoon.

"And what will draw them here?" he whispered.

Ida looked at him, rapt in her words, staring heavenward.

She could tell him the truth. She must swallow her fetid anger or choke on it now. She untied the laces of her chemise and pulled it away. She knew the stink came from her skin.

"They will come here for love," she said.

"Ah." His shoulders fell. His chin lowered.

A space empty as all Hell gaped between Ida's collarbones and chin. She tried to swallow, but only stroked the void's back side. His eyes stayed closed.

"They will come here for what Heaven cannot offer, to trade freedom for belonging," she said.

His arched eyebrows constricted in a *V* of pain. Ida loosened her drawers and used them to wipe away the green trickle sliding down her ribs.

"They will come because Heaven cannot hold them, and their souls' wings are made of stone," she whispered.

He turned his face away, twisted with suffering. Ida lifted the chain from around her neck and undid the clasp. The precious links slipped from the ring and coiled at her feet like a golden snake.

"Heaven cannot give them what they need. But here, they can create it."

The way the agony left his face slipped over Ida's naked flesh in a thousand flames of hunger.

His lips parted, and Ida let herself linger, longer than she should, to watch the softening of his features, how the cruel lines melted into hunger, how desire overthrew his pain. From her sex and shivering nipples her hunger bubbled, wanting to attract and nurture, wanting to enfold and claim. She laid her thirsty body on the dry and dirty stone.

"We will be priest and priestess to them, and welcome all those who have never had a home for their imperfect souls." She centered his ring—made to match the one she already wore—on her navel, and saw the chain that had held it worming away from her into the ground. The fine, invisible hairs of her thighs and arms rose and folded in waves like windblown grass across the fields of her wanting, waiting to be furrowed.

"We will initiate them"—Ida parted her thighs, felt the wild touch of cool air between them, and closed her eyes—"together."

"We will initiate them." His voice was close. Ida dared not peek.

"Together," she repeated, bruised by longing to be half of every *we* he ever spoke, "if you want me."

"I want you more than I want hope." He knelt on the stone beside her. "I want to claim you, fill you up with me, but I can barely touch you."

"Why?"

"I am not human."

"I don't care."

"It is impossible."

"How?" Ida screamed. She had not meant to peek, at his pained face looking down at her; his aching eyes and consuming lips aroused her even more. "How is this impossible, if Laura can reach Yeats through Maud, that I, here before you, cannot touch you?"

"She's only half a soul, asleep in her own time, and content to share."

"He doesn't even know what time she's from! He thinks she is the Irish soul. One of the Host of the Air. Or our goddess. If he is half her soul, surely you're half mine."

"Ida, you know I am half of no one's soul, nor could I be. But you must believe I want you."

"How could you want me? I am poisonous."

"I have already shown you everything you need to understand."

He leaned over her, still on the stone beside her.

"Ida, my love, my own, I want you—want to take and claim you—more than I have ever wanted, and it torments me. I am all but broken by it, on my knees before you, but there could never be enough for us."

Ida dug her nails, like hatpins, against her eyes. "I want nothing else. Not my own power. Or Irish freedom. I only want to belong. Here. With you."

"Ida," he whispered, "I must go, but you can stay."

"I will belong to you then. Take all of me!" she pleaded to the empty air. Alone.

***

"Should you gather the skirts of your dress?" Will asks me.

The ground, slipping out from the woods, sucks at my bare feet, and I gather the folds of fabric in a gesture both familiar and strange.

Not too long ago, I raised the trailing hem of a black dress, a wedding dress, awkward as a high school prom.

But I have done this all my life.

He hands me into the small boat, and it tips and roils under my legs. I have been married. I am married still. The cold certainty closes over me like drowning. I imagine our little boat capsized and the heavy folds of fabric dragging me. He stops it with his hand.

He said I am the Irish soul—no, that's not right—how could that be married?

An Irish soul. That feels true. Yes, something of me comes from here.

Where is the rest of me?

He shoves an oar into the mud beneath the water and the boat slides back. The marshy bank and woods blow away with every sweep of his strong back. There was something I had wanted to tell him about who I am.

"I can't remember . . ."

"Nothing matters but right now," he says.

I know that's not true—this moment has meaning only because of what sits on either side of it—but I'm willing to believe him all the same.

I don't know where we're going. The wooden oars on their metal pins make a shushing, grinding sound, but they dip into the silent water and rise, glistening, only to be dunked again.

"Doesn't it worry you," I ask him, "to be so far from Ratra?"

"I like being alone with you." His smile is quizzical in the moonlight. But I can't shake the unsettling sense of being peculiarly unconnected and adrift, of wanting to be closer, even without more physical nearness, to other people, to help, to doctors.

He pulls the oars up, letting them hang lightly from his strong hands. "When I first saw you, looking out of Maud Gonne's eyes, I believed you were a spirit from Irish legend; that Maud, from her political passion, had channeled Kathleen Ní Houlihan or Maeve, the fairy queen. I began, at once, to write a play for her, thinking only of you. But as I wrote *Kathleen*, I became certain that was not who you are."

"How?" I ask.

"Because I loved you."

The gentle eddies and currents of the lake rock our boat the way a mother sways with a sleeping child. His eyes slip from me to the night beyond. When they return, they hold a whole night sky of sadness. "I love you as a man loves, not as a poet does, wanting to belong wherever you are, to be a part of your realm, and bring you into mine."

The way this confession hurts him pulls me more than drowning.

"MacGregor Mathers thought you were a spirit from another plane; whether benign or malevolent, he was uncertain. Moina, his wife, insisted Ida could only conjure a devil, but I would have risked my soul to love you, demon though you might have been."

I know what Moina means. But I'm pretty sure I'm not evil. Selfish and irresponsible sometimes, maybe. Chickenshit, sure. But not a devil. Not an angel either. Something inconsequential in between. Something boring.

"And now?" I ask him.

"I am a poet. I have dedicated my life to symbols. Symbols of beauty, of love, of truth. But I have come to love you in a way deeper even than symbol, in a way no man can love a generality. I realized my love for you was specific and particular, and I knew your soul must be likewise definite and singular, even if it remained forever a mystery to me."

I can only listen to the thousand small sounds of water under us. "If I'm not your nation's past," I whisper, "maybe I'm her future?"

Something in this feels right to me, too, but he only smiles slowly, and doesn't answer. He drops the oars into the water again and pulls their blunt handles to his chest, gliding us forward soundlessly.

"It's who you are that I love. Let it damn me or inspire me. Demon or symbol. Woman. It matters not. I belong where you are, be it Plato's sunlight realm, Milton's Hell, or some strange corner of our poor and muddled Earth. Only where you are do I cease to be alone. All I need for belonging is you."

I don't know why his sincerity makes me itchy. No one else is watching. But to my imagination, the star-sequined, velvet night, and the gorgeous, earnest man all court ridicule. But his strong strokes send the little boat across the glittering lake in gasps and glides toward the island, and I float with it. He stops again and points into the lake. "Look," he says.

The castle's white rock glows with reflected moonlight, throwing wild, luminescent inverse images of its glass and stone onto the water—three reflections deep from the rational sun.

"We should dive in!" I say. "We'll enter the castle by swimming through the lake door instead. Much more fairy-tale!"

He answers with a laugh, total and warm. "We would emerge together, not on Castle Island at all, but in a strange, inverse land, with others like us, the young discoverers of strange worlds. We would find one another anew as that sacred land's first inhabitants." He starts rowing again, easily, the graceful wave of his body, a larger, slower imitation of the moonlit-risen pulse-and-drop of water radiating from our boat. "We would delight together in everything that has never been seen or felt.

"But it would not be a perfect land. We might glimpse fairies and ghosts prowling the shadows, and one night, upon a haunted hill, we would find a tattered and ancient flag still flying. We would tear it down and fly our own banner." The prow of our little boat impacts the reflected castle, which shudders and vanishes into rippling white. "We would explore and name, claim and revel. We would age. And one day we would discover a fresh band of young adventurers. Although we know the landscape better, and are more entitled to call the island's magic ours, the new inhabitants will only glimpse us in the shadows, and one night, they would pull down the flag we set upon our hill and fly a new one of their own creation."

He leaps from the boat in a sudden, arching bound and lands on a flat rock. He crouches to tie the boat to an iron ring set in the stone, and on one knee still, holds out his hands to me. In the soft rocking boat, I hesitate. The whole lake lies in my belly. Dark and bottomless and blind. I put my hands in his, and he pulls me up beside him. But he stays kneeling, holding my hands.

"Marry me."

I will. I have. I am.

"Oh, get up!" I say. Maud's supper party dress, cut low over her opalescent shoulders, is sewn of innumerable lightweight black cotton panels. It catches the wind in whispers billowing around me in the restless Irish air.

"I feel like a tacky Christmas angel," I laugh, twisting in the blowing fabric.

"You are more beautiful than God."

"Oh, come off it!" I laugh, and try to drag him to standing by the hands he still holds.

But I am Victorian and dangerous, ready to declaim and gesticulate, prone to throw myself off things. "You look ridiculous," I say.

"To appear ridiculous is not a sin," he whispers. "I lay my dignity on the altar of experience."

I want to kneel on the stone beside him. I want to plunge into our underwater land.

"Experience is a cruel god," I say.

"I am a willing sacrifice."

"Oh, would you please get up!"

He stands, tall and strong. My insides are squeezed together too tightly. There is not enough room inside my skin. And on the edge of Castle Island, our little rowboat bumps like a puppy's head against the island's stone thigh. Will Yeats, the wild Irish poet and student of the occult, stands and puts his mouth to mine. His kiss tears a space into me.

All the passion, the wanting, the terror of where I am and what I do not understand brims over and runs slippery over me with his demanding mouth. I step closer, fold my body against his. His angry lips take from my mine the words I could not say. That I love him.

That I am afraid. Under my hands, his arms are taut with the restraint of keeping them from crushing me against him. His kiss is the inverse of food; every taste makes me more hungry.

"How is this cruelty?" he whispers.

I want him to kiss me more.

"Experience is no more cruel than our lake is," he says. "Only as indifferent to whether we poor mortals drink or drown."

His lips brush mine, teasing now, not kissing. I want the obliterating contact of them consuming mine still. But he's whispering against me. "Maud and the dogmatists may stay dry; some don't even suffer thirst. The careless fall in and drown." A soft, anguished squeak twists from my kiss-starved mouth. "We must teach ourselves to swim, and work our way to deeper water."

He turns and strides across the moon-glinting rocks.

"You must have a tour of the castle," he calls back to me.

I consider creeping up behind him and jumping on his back, wrapping my arms around his strong shoulders and whispering "Fuck me" in his ear, but I don't. Instead, I only hold my breath, and test the liquid hunger of my legs against the task of walking.

I follow him through the dense, overgrown yards between the bare rock edge of the island and the castle's looming walls. I don't want a tour of the ridiculous turreted structure. The whole thing is embarrassing and absurd and a little bit dangerous, but he leads me through the empty castle, up spiraling wooden stairs and onto a wide balcony on the second floor.

He stands behind me, pointing out over the water. "Can you imagine a little painted boat coming across the water, bringing the very best and bravest of Ireland's young people, male and female, to us here?" He stands strong and motionless behind me, so close I only need to nod. His gentle fingers weave through my hair, strange and heavy but soft against my flesh, sweeping the long, loose strands away.

His nose brushes my skin, just below my ear, and all my flesh springs alert. He pushes his nose deeper and inhales. "I don't know whether it is your scent, or the way you hold your head, or a change

in your voice or eyes, but I know, almost at once, when it is you and
not Maud with me."

His voice slides over my throat, low and warm. His lips touch me.
He kisses a tiny pilgrimage of flame from my ear, over my shoulder
to the black edge of dress. Under Maud's clothes, inside Maud's
body, some part of me starts to shake.

"In you—in loving you, Laura—I have found an image of myself
in my highest and most sacred essence. And I strive to be, in my daily
life, as pure a presence as you are when you come through Maud
to me."

"But I'm not like this is my real life."

"Love me, and you will be. We both will be."

His deft fingers work buttons and ties and bindings I don't even
know the names for. Things slip and fall from me. He gathers the
final layer in fists, pushing his hands under it and flattens his fingers
against the bare flesh of my belly. I remember Maud's two pregnancies, but he draws my body to his with a deep groan. It is softer than
mine, the skin of her stomach dimpled. I should be ashamed of the
loose flesh, worry how I look undressed, but all I can feel is him.

When his mouth takes my neck again, the tenderness has turned
to need, and my head falls back into his shoulder to expose more
throat for his kissing. My lips puff up with fluid, or sex, or just with
wanting him, swollen to make more surface area for his touch. My
body curls wave-like into his. I want him to kiss me now.

I open my eyes because he is drawing me from the balcony into
the vast, deserted upstairs room of the castle. We walk across the
wide wood planks that form the roof of the Great Room below. The
interior walls of lath and plaster have started to crumble, a telling
contrast to the changeless permanence of the fireplace and exterior
walls made from stone. He kneels again. I wish he wouldn't. The
crazy, dramatic gesture is lost on me, or worse, distracts me. Then his
lips touch the top of my foot. My sex clutches like a fist on empty
air. I gasp. And mock myself for such a ridiculous noise.

"But we have all bent low and low and kissed the quiet feet of
Kathleen, the daughter of Houlihan," he whispers.

Really. It's all too much.

That there's a poet kneeling at my feet. That I'm in a moonlit castle, on an island, in the middle of an Irish lake. That I am not Kathleen or Maud or myself. But his hands glide up Maud's long, soft legs, pushing the linen of her underclothes up with them, his eyes following. He holds the gathered folds of cloth around my waist, and my naked, unclothed sex before his silent face. He pulls me by my hip bones to his lips. And kisses me.

I allow myself a groan as his tongue, reaching out, touches the tiny point of me. I know, more than he does, the names and structures of where he kisses now, but only his imagery touches me. My clitoris has become a silver fruit, and the secret, hungry dark place behind it the dimpled surface of the moon, and my body, even to me, a mystery.

His tongue, a slow, light stroke, glides over the skimming surface of my sex relentlessly, from just before its opening rim, over the fattening lips, to the naked silver apple, high and hardening. I am the lake beneath our boat, his coaxing stroke sliding through me with an inexorable, unhurried force, driving waves before it. His tongue doesn't quicken, but it deepens. Or the flesh of my sex swells around it. His hands slip up the rounds of my ass to tip my hips to him. Unfastened, coming loose, my dress falls over his eyes like a dark veil, and I don't know who he is or why I'm with him. But my soul, or my dreaming mind, or my fundamental self is connected to him, belongs with him, regardless of what I can rationally know or prove. And I am powerless and ridiculous before it. Even if it is all only me and my imagination.

Please, let it be "us."

The tip of his tongue reaches deeper, shunting side-to-side between the heavy folds of my flesh, burrowing for the mouth of sex, the yielding. A liquid weight builds just beyond his reach. He drags his tongue again forward, deeper, and it wells downward. But his mouth presses the tiny hardness trapped under flesh. It slips to one side, a slow-rising bubble, dancing, breaks where the water ends in air, and I do not know the name for the sound I make.

His gentle tug on my wrists brings me to kneeling by him. I could not have stayed standing anyway. My legs are made of water. I open my mouth and close it again. And still he does not kiss me. He pulls my dress away at last, and I am naked.

He runs his hands down Maud's high cheekbones, stopping at my lips. His touch, tender and light, paints shadows across my exposed breasts and thighs. I close my eyes to kiss his fingertips, but they're in my hair, thumbs on my chin, hard and holding me.

"Laura, I don't know what loving you might do." His eyes search me, urgent and afraid. "Kissing binds a soul, but God knows, we are already bound."

I can only nod.

"The Order has rituals of sex, for initiation and for marriage, but tonight is none of these. And I want you, as a man wants a woman. Without magic, without ritual or poetry. I want you blindly, like a stupid animal." He drops his forehead to mine, his shoulders shaking.

I don't know what to do with his confession.

I take his wrists in my hands. "Open your eyes." They are inches from mine and full of anguish. "We will teach ourselves to swim," I whisper, "and work our way to deeper water."

He stands and undresses. I sit back on my heels and watch him, seeing the signs of where and when he comes from fall away. He has never seen himself on videotape. He has never seen porn. A heart-twisting innocence shadows the way he takes his clothes off. He stops, with his pants and tie already on the ground.

"Joining our bodies could trap you here. You may not be able to get back to wherever you come from," he says.

"I know."

"Or you may not be able to hold yourself with me."

"I'll try" is all I can say, but I hadn't thought of that. What if too-strong sensation draws Maud back? Or simply pushes me away? I have a sudden flash of awkward, guilty, teenage memory. Although Maud is not, and I am not, together we have a strange virginity. And it isn't only our own, but time's. And Will's. I shiver, holy and afraid.

Will spreads his coat on the ground and pulls me down to him.

Naked, we are timeless. Our two bare bodies stretch as bodies have forever—fragile and temporary things—facing one another, trembling. And still he does not kiss me.

He pushes my hair behind my shoulder. "There is no ritual for this," he says. His fingers trail my shoulder to my collarbone. "But our bodies create one tonight." His descending hand opens, gathering my breast. An involuntary shudder wracks his body as he closes his hand over the weight of it, but he holds himself still until he masters it.

He releases the full flesh, keeps his fingertips in place and starts to circle. "As we join our bodies tonight, in this sacred place"—the spiraling of his fingers narrows into small, hard circles across the tip of my filling, tightening breast—"let us become the agents of our spiritual and physical connection to our land, even if not to our times." The hard nails and tender tops of his fingers play over my nipple like a harp's string. ". . . to bind our timeless souls, if not to our flesh, to Ireland"—the strumming vibration drops between my legs—"and to each other."

"Can you make up religion, just like that?" My voice sounds strangled.

He smiles. "It's the only way they get made."

"Just some guy talking?"

"Am I just some guy?" All his playfulness is gone.

"No," I whisper. "Not to me."

His stroking fingers slip from my breast up to touch my cheek. "Yes, then. Religions are created by souls made more than they are by love." His eyes leave mine and run across my exposed flesh. "Ritual takes a common object—a cup or cross—and imbues it with meaning." His palm runs across my rigid nipple in a light, teasing, cruciform stroke. "It takes a gesture—a bowed head or a kiss—and gives it power."

"You make sex sound like prayer." I'm reaching for a laugh, but his mouth opens over my breast, and I can't.

"Could it be any other way for us?" his lips whisper over my nipple. "Sex is always a symbol."

He moves over me, tucking my body under his, cushioning my back with his forearms, and I know I have become the water that carried us here. Our bodies entwine fluidly, his broad back keel-hard under my hands, and my legs parting. I want him diving into me, into our inverse island.

Wretched in the bowels of Hell, Ida lay on the golden glass of the buried king and sniveled in the dark and isolation. She had wandered until she found her way back to the king sleeping under the mountain, to wail and whisper and scratch her fingers to bleeding worse than Jamie's for something to salvage from her abject humiliation. She had not found a single ray of hope until at last a small, bright shadow glinted in the glass. She pressed her lips against it and stepped into the large, upstairs front room on Castle Island where she had suggested they eat their sandwiches while Yeats raved to Maud, conjuring the very images of secret, sacred schools and initiations Ida had fed her daemon on. She had been angry they had not heeded her then.

They did not heed her now, and Ida fell back through the glass again, smiling.

Whatever Will sees, looking down at me—my soul or his symbol, my essence or ideal self—is better because he has seen into it. Nothing separates our bodies now, naked on the castle floor. He raises his head a moment, listening, but my lips grope for his, and my fingers in his black hair bring down his face to me. His eyes hold mine. His confidence is gone.

"Do you want this?" he whispers, and in his face I see the doubt and danger that must have always shadowed sex before birth control and C-sections, when childbirth was the most likely cause of a woman's death. "I have never . . ." He does not drop my eyes, but he cannot say the words.

"I have never made a ritual," I say.

"We are both initiates." He smiles, the grin dawning slow and warm. He kisses me with a chuckle in his throat, at the pleasure in my body, with the wonder of it and the anticipation. I slide the soles of my bare feet up the hard length of his calves and legs, opening my body under his. His eyes close. His cock drops against the open liquid of my parted sex, but he makes no volitional movement. He holds my head cradled in his huge hands, and my thighs press against his ribs. His smile does not fade, but his lips part with a low, agonized groan. Beneath my thighs, the tension of his back muscles flexes with ruthless control to hold his body still over me. It's too much—even for him. He drops his forehead to mine and pulls my body to his chest, gliding our sexes to each other soundlessly.

He enters me.

His body slides into mine, a boat into the element it was created for. A deep, joyful pleasure, centered in my sex, radiates in rings from his advancing cock into my liquid core, and with each diving of him into me, the shock waves overlap and magnify. I give myself to our growling, kissing, hungry mouths, making wild, tiny noises. He gathers me like he could drink the water he drowns in, but I am overflowing. I am stronger than water, and his body rides in waves over and through me. Animal pleasure flows beneath us, ferocious and unseen within the depths.

How can everything not be enough? How can this completion open deeper longing? The discordant waves he builds in me are elemental. Will drown me. Without compassion, without concern, miles from telephones and paramedics, years from divorce and therapy.

Will's fingers are in my hair. His mouth finds mine again, but he cannot kiss me, cannot organize his body on the tempest of mine under his; he only holds his lips, open, over mine. I cannot be the water that carried us here. Cannot ride its secret depths above its hidden monsters. It has gotten into my veins, is driven through me with the pounding, pumping heart of Will's body in me. I am the darkness and the face of the deep. I am coming.

Will moves his lips against me, kisses the face of the water, his voice a coarse command in his throat. He comes with me in the same moment of brilliant, hallowed light and blackness. The blinding orgasm is a timeless, glittering fire in the bottomless wet sky. The depths of my body and beyond are obliterated by light, blind as blackness.

"My god," he whispers.

I smile.

"I actually saw stars," I say.

"My love"—his lips move softly in my muffling hair—"same thing."

"Could it be any other way for us?" I answer, and, even though I struggle not to, I fall into the bottomless arms of sleep.

from *The Esoteric Philosophy of Love and Marriage*
by Dion Fortune

1930

When the act of sexual union takes place the subtle forces of the two natures rush together, and, as in the case of two currents of water in collision, a whirlpool or vortex is set up. This vortex extends up the planes as far as the mating of the corresponding bodies takes place, so that should two people who idealize each other, and whose love, has elements of a spiritual nature in its composition, meet in coitus, the vortex so created will extend on to one of the higher planes.

8

HER SOUL IN DIVISION
FROM ITSELF, CLIMBING, FALLING
SHE KNEW NOT WHERE

I have drunk ale from the Country of the Young
And weep because I know all things now:
I have been a hazel-tree, and they hung
The Pilot Star and the Crooked Plough
Among my leaves in times out of mind:
I became a rush that horses tread:
I became a man, a hater of the wind,
Knowing one, out of all things, alone, that his head
May not lie on the breast nor his lips on the hair
Of the woman that he loves, until he dies.
O beast of the wilderness, bird of the air,
Must I endure your amorous cries?

    —"He Thinks of His Past Greatness when a Part of the
    Constellations of Heaven" by W. B. Yeats

Will positioned the small pitcher of flowers on the table between the tea things.

He moved it to the window ledge. Then back to the table again. After many months of hesitant courtship, Mrs. Shakespear, Will's intended mistress, was on her way with her sponsor, Mrs. Fox, to meet him at the rooms he had taken expressly to accommodate their secret affair. After meeting on trains and in museums, awkward and intimate in their public privacy, the love-lost bachelor poet and the lovelessly married novelist had settled on this circumstance. All stood ready. Will threw himself into a chair with a soundless groan.

You have forgotten the cake. Ida took advantage of his agony to make the suggestion, but positioned her astral body between him and the cake all the same. His eyes ran right past it, over her, and he dropped his head against the chair back with an audible sigh.

You must go out for cake.

The poet's distress stained his handsome face, but still Ida was uncertain her suggestion was reaching him. If he left to fetch a cake, she could call the first of her night's two experiments a success.

"I will find you," he whispered, and Ida's spying spirit splattered the papered wall and ceiling in shock.

"I swear it to you, Laura. Even these five months have been too long."

Ida reconstituted her startled consciousness, resenting the energy Will had blown about his rooms by so recklessly talking to himself aloud. She climbed down the window overlooking Essex Street, collecting herself by the fireplace where Yeats's little clay alchemist's pot nestled in the ashes. Yes, the five months since Ida's spirit body had walked straight from Hell through a stone hearth to find the poet in the very rite she had longed to enact with her daemon had been too long for Yeats and Laura to be apart, joined as they now were, physical being to astral, and soul to soul. But it had been scarcely enough time for Ida to learn all that she needed to work the same magic in the opposite direction.

You must go out for the cake, she commanded.

He straightened himself and reached for his Inverness cloak. In every motion of his long arms and strong face, Ida read a suffering she recognized. Like her, he strove to drag a creature he loved from dream into being. There could be no freedom for him, as there was none for her, only gnawing dissatisfaction and rage against the name-less, indifferent powers thwarting them.

Leave the key.

This command made a much better test than the cake. Impatient now to test her new skill on Maud, Ida would not have to wait for Will to make his way to the bakery. All she needed for confirmation her astral suggestions worked was to see him leave without his key. He patted his pockets, imagining his married lover already with him, and Laura moving through her into his arms. No chance of that.

Leave the key.

He passed the table on which it lay and shut the door behind him. Ida smiled in satisfied benediction. *Enjoy your Olivia. She is no threat to me.*

◈

Ida opened her eyes and yawned. From down the hall, her husband's vigorous snores polluted the sacred silence of ritual. She clambered stiffly to standing, stretched, and stepped gingerly over the salt circle mounded on the rich, imported rug. The maid would mutter when she brought the morning eggs and tea, but Ida remembered to be clumsy at dinner and spill other things from time to time. And Mr. Rowley paid the servants well enough to purchase patience with their mistress's peculiar mishaps.

Ida slid another black candle from the packet hidden under shawls in the wardrobe's bottom drawer, and returned to the salt circle. She wrapped the voluminous priestess robes she'd had made—orange, the color of the highest order in the Golden Dawn, and not one she had technically attained—around her thrill-taut shoulders and repo-sitioned herself within the circle. One dispatched. One remaining. The third, she no longer needed. Laura was simply bait.

◈

Maud lounged in the drawing room of her Dublin hotel, and Ida knew at once her second experiment had failed. Maud could see her.

Right there, surrounded by people talking politics and fashion, Maud glanced up and met Ida's eyes. And smiled. The smile made another, more painful failure plain, because it was not a smile Maud had ever given Ida. It was a smile for a man.

I can't speak to you now. Those with me know nothing of the occult and would not understand.

The beautiful head inclined to the woman beside her, proud lips reformed into the demure smile Ida knew too well, but Maud's low voice rang clear in Ida's mind. *Come back to me at midnight, when sleep has set my soul free, and I will go with you, Will, wherever you wish.*

◈

Ida kicked salt into the air. She threw the ash-filled incense burner against the grate and howled. She had studied this. She had struggled with the words. Learned the forms. Maud worked at nothing, yet she had managed to thwart Ida again!

Her husband's fist made raven raps on her locked door.

"Ida? Ida, you're dreaming, my love!" Mr. Rowley cried.

Ida pinched out the candle and bundled it with her invoking wand, chalice, and athame under the bed.

A tenor hail of maid's feet down the hall joined her husband's bass percussion outside Ida's private sanctum. She squared her shoulders at the locked door and inhaled, nostrils splayed. Slowly she collected the air from the frantic whispers and demands to find the passkey. She screamed. Not a shrill lady's terror, but a low roaring, the bellow of outraged denial unnaturally prolonged. Yeats was open. She could have persuaded him, eventually, through accumulated suggestion, to let himself be mesmerized. But Maud! How would Maud now be persuaded to give herself to Will? Ida was certain her daemon could possess Will's body only in the moment of his profound surrender to—no, within!—the body of Maud Gonne. Maud gave herself to no one.

Feet came running with rattling keys. Ida threw the bedclothes into convincing disarray and, at the last moment, tore her nightdress to ravished threads to give those rat-damned maids an eyeful. If she could not channel her daemon into the body of Will Yeats, how could she ever give herself to him?

Her husband's knock-red hands claimed her shoulders. The maids stood appropriately aghast while Mr. Rowley muttered and cajoled her under blankets. He could not raise his eyes from her breasts.

"Another nightmare, my darling, nothing more. Foolish dreams."

He stroked her hair, her naked back, her rump.

"I'm here, my love. Nothing will hurt you."

He wedged his body into the bed beside her. He would fuck her now.

Once he was underway, Ida let herself be wracked by sobs, and her husband mistook even the snot for ecstasy.

⬤

At my deli, there's a guy with two gold teeth and a hairnet on his beard who can slice cheese or meat to within a few one-hundredths of whatever weight you ask for, and right now, I am that guy. I'm down in the pixels, surgically repairing a water spot, and I don't have to look for anything. Every tool, each menu, every layer is what I need and where I want it. I don't know the time, because I haven't remembered to look. I'm not happy or unhappy; I'm gone. Not tuned out or drifting off, but so utterly present I've forgotten I'm here. And I know why Greek artists believed in muses. It feels less like me working, than something sacred working through me. But there's no Muse of Photoshop; and then the phone rings.

"Howdy, darlin'." Amit comes from Canada, but thinks it's funny for a six-foot-tall Indian man to talk Texan.

"Hi, eh?" I say, because I think his real Canadian accent is funnier.

"I'm at the Wok n' Roll. What do you want me to get you?"

At first, I don't understand why he's calling me. "What?"

"Hang on, I'll walk outside," he says.

I don't know why it bothers me that he's bringing me dinner, but by the time he's left the restaurant for the no-quieter street, I'm hungry for General Tso's tofu and broccoli. It'll be at the office in ten.

I walk my feet away from my physioball until my stomach muscles

engage and my back stretches out. I like testing the compact strength
of my core and thighs, and the way the ball rocks me. My arms hang
palm-up, like broken wings, or the arms of a fainted damsel carried
off by the mustachioed melodrama villain.

Instant Messenger pings, and by the time I reply to Amy, who is
working from home with a sick toddler, and check my email and
Facebook, my mind has wandered back to Lough Key. I looked it up
on Wikipedia this morning, and it's really there, complete with the
ridiculous Castle Rock, *an island almost all castle.* My dreams are so
obvious they're insulting. I finally have sex with my wild Victorian
poet (in a castle, of course) in the middle of a lake he pronounces
lock key. Could this be the key to my lock, do you think? God, I'm
ridiculous.

I don't know whether my imagination makes all this stuff up, or
remembers it. And I honestly don't care, so long as it doesn't stop. It
may be corny as hell, but I like feeling like a powerful priestess. It's
fun! I zoom in on Queen Vicky's dimpled arm. For the first time in
my life, I know I'm in the right place doing the right thing. I feel no
doubt. I start lining a thin shadow between the white arm and white
dress. I have it all—a great job, an adorable loft, smart, supportive
friends, a stable husband who loves me. Also, a passionate affair of
wild romance and crazy sex that can't screw up the rest of it. I in-
crease the contrast and consider contouring the arm. I am free and
fearless, but safe. I zoom out and tweak the image contrast. It's a
beautiful balance. I'll keep the dream dreamy and reality real.

God, Victoria was a relentlessly unattractive woman.

The pounce of Amit's feet, coming two-a-time up the stairs, still
sets a fine ripple of disorientation through me. He's a project man-
ager in one of Portland's few proper office towers an easy walk away,
but he seems out of place here, and I feel foreign when I go up there.
I wonder if it's possible to spend enough time in another person's
workspace to stop acting like a freshly sprouted appendage. He drops
two distended plastic bags on the conference table and swoops me
up in his arms to carry me back to the food.

"Hey, Charlie, come eat!" I call over my husband's strong shoulders.

Charlie's head gophers up from behind his cubicle's low partition. "No way. Newlyweds need their alone time." He vanishes.

"Don't be ridiculous, Charlie!" I say as Amit deposits me on the table.

"No seriously, look at the poor man," Charlie re-pops to waggle a reproving finger at my husband.

I look at Amit, and notice again the fierce masculinity even his ironic T-shirts and cuffed jeans can't mask. He raises an overstuffed paper carton in salute to Charlie. "I got you shrimp-and-vegetable fried rice."

"Well, you do know my weaknesses!"

"Lazarus, come forth!" Amit declaims, then sotto voice to me, "and he came fifth and lost the job."

"Joyce, right?" Charlie guesses, emerging from the warren of desks and dividers.

"I'm impressed," Amit grins.

"Don't be," I say.

But Charlie sparkles with energy. "I've been researching Victorians for the last three hours. Do you know they actually sent Oscar Wilde to jail for sodomy? Another page from the *if I ever catch you with a cigarette, I'll make you smoke the whole carton* book of disciplinary genius."

Amit grins and unpacks boxes from bags while I go to the kitchenette for napkins, chopsticks, and beer. At lunch, I learned from Charlie about Mrs. Beeton and her household guide. He's reading to Amit now from something else. "It would be just as injurious for the laborer's wife to give up her daily work and exercise, as for the lady to take to sweeping her own carpets or cooking the dinner." They're laughing at the absurdity

There's only one beer, so I get a Diet Coke and a Mountain Dew and three glasses. Maud never ate out of paper boxes, but we agreed to stop buying disposable plates, and I just can't be bothered to get out the plastic ones we would have to wash after.

"Until 1882"—Charlie has put the book down, but he's still

talking about what he's learned—"what you two did this weekend would have cost Laura her constitutional rights to free speech and due process. A wife became a nonperson under the law."

"You'd never guess you're married to a lawyer," I tease, and share the beer out between the three glasses, hand us each one, and push the Mountain Dew at Charlie.

Amit wheels a chair out for me with a wink. "And don't you know, it's still the woman who sits down last to eat."

I laugh and dig into my dinner. "And it's still the brown man who carries up the food."

"Oh God!" Charlie gasps in mock horror. "The police will be coming for me next!" He twirls a shrimp by its shelly tail. "Mmm, men in uniform!" He toasts Amit and me with his third of beer. "How are my favorite newlyweds managing with so little time to gaze into one another's eyes?"

"God," I snort, "you know we're not the eye-gazing sort. You keep saying *newlyweds* as if getting married turned us into different people!"

"Better than a nonperson," Amit points out.

"Say what you want," Charlie digs into his rice. "Rituals matter."

In the precise way he captures rice grains with his chopsticks, I see the hurt the exclusion he and Chris face causes. "They matter more in their absence than their performance, maybe," I say. "Rituals are just gestures with meaning layered on. Just because you don't have the gesture doesn't mean you don't get the meaning."

"And just because you have, doesn't mean you do," Amit says.

"Deny it all you want, but I swear you're different since you got married. Am I making this up, Amit? Have you noticed how ebullient and beautiful your new bride has suddenly become? How energized and sunny?"

"I've been getting really good sleep," I say, but I know my cheeks are turning pink.

"Nope," Charlie says, "you're in love."

"Well, of course I'm in love," I snap. "We wouldn't have gotten married if we didn't love each other."

Charlie shakes his head over his rice, with its tiny flakes of orange and green "vegetable" mottling the brown grains like scattered stars. "No, you're different since the wedding. Suddenly you look wild, reckless, ass-over-armpit crazy in love."

Amit smiles with a question mark stuck in his teeth. I am writhing in my skin. Right now, Maud's would fit me better.

"Well, I can vouch for the difference in how she's sleeping," Amit says. "She used to have a lot of trouble drifting off, and woke up really easily. Now she sleeps like the dead."

They are all dead. Will, Maud, Ida. And loneliness, with my husband and my best friend beside me, chills me.

Charlie screws a sardonic eyebrow up onto his forehead. "You must be exhausting the poor girl!"

"Clearly. And driving her mad." Amit chuckles. "She's started talking in her sleep."

"No!" Charlie raises both his heavy, unruly eyebrows in mock horror, but I can't take a breath. Have I done that more than once? Amit hasn't said anything about it since our wedding night.

"Yup, the night we got married, fast asleep, she told me her name and birth date." Amit and Charlie laugh, and I pull a shrug, making my best *Oh golly!* face.

"And now, every night, she says something in Latin." Amit winks at me and takes a bite, but Charlie plumbs my eyes with his gemgreen ones before he laughs, and I know he's seen something.

"Sleeping soundly and speaking in tongues. Amit, are you a mere mortal, or has our girl fallen for an angel incarnate?"

I reach out and grab Amit's leg well above the knee. "Trust me, honey. He's all man," I growl.

Amit pulls my roller chair closer and sticks his chopsticks into my carton for a beheaded broccoli stalk.

Charlie is still watching me over his shrimp. "I didn't know you knew Latin."

"I don't. I'm babbling," I say, focused on the food.

"Oh, come on, you had two years in High School." Amit is back in the to-go bags, digging around. "She's deeper than she looks, you know." He tosses a fortune cookie at Charlie.

"So I'm learning," he says.

I'm sending violent *shut-up, shut-up* vibes and almost miss the cellophane-wrapped cookie Amit slides my way.

"Yup, I got a sweet package deal in my wife"—Amit cracks a cookie open—"brains *and* beauty." Charlie has known me longer, and Amit is enjoying knowing more about me.

"And mad Photoshop skills," I add, laughing it off, but Charlie's chopsticks stand up in his rice like covert antennae.

"I never had Latin," he says, "but I was infatuated with my algebra teacher for an entire semester."

"Wow, a whole four months?" Amit pours a few inches of my Diet Coke into his empty beer glass.

"Three. Summer school. But that record stood unchallenged until I met Chris."

"How long have you been together?" I ask, happy to turn the conversation.

"Eleven years in February."

Amit whistles, but Charlie just shrugs. "Monogamy plants a tree in a pipe. When you can't branch out, you have to grow up." Is he trying to say something to me? To Amit? "Or grow all twisted and stunted," he adds with a laugh, and breaks into his fortune cookie.

I'm laughing like a man before a firing squad who has heard the *Fire!* order and seen a row of *Pow!* flags drop from all five guns.

I should really stop.

Charlie starts collecting trash. "Poor darling," he says, patting me dramatically. "The pressure's getting to her." But he stacks his empty box into my full one, hiding from Amit how much I didn't eat.

"How's the work going? Any chance of getting my beautiful and talented wife home before midnight on our one-week anniversary?"

"It's going well," I chirp. "I've got all three ads laid out. I'm having to do some pretty intense color-correction and cleanup on the old images though. I only need a couple more hours. And the body copy . . ." I peer at Charlie.

"You'll get it, you'll get it. You cannot rush inspiration." Charlie makes a stunningly accurate Victorian gentleman. "Genius will not come when called."

"Text her, then," I say.

"Give me another half hour," Charlie's wiry shoulders collapse under the weight of his melodrama. "I'll hurry the bitch up."

"I'll just hang out here, then, and we'll go home together?" Amit drags his laptop bag onto the conference table.

"Yeah, that'd be great," I say. "I need to tweak Queen Victoria a little more."

Charlie's watching me closely enough Amit notices. "It's okay with you, right?"

"That you stay? Of course. I think you should." He turns to me. "You're Photoshopping Mrs. Brown?"

"Not really, but if I don't do a little work on her, it'll look like we're trying to make a point about how much better-looking modern people are; how much healthier and slimmer and younger we are than we were a hundred years ago."

"But it will be less accurate."

"Just a little, but it will look better. Trust me on this, Charlie; I'm the artist."

"So you are," he says, and cracks open his cookie. "The master of appearances."

I raise my Diet Coke in a toast and drink, wondering what either of the men watching me actually sees.

⁂

God would not be wheedled like a father, nor seduced like a man. He could not be bribed like a judge or cowed like a husband. So Ida hated Him. She cursed Him slowly and methodically the entire long, clumsy journey by underground to Maud's hotel in the bloody heart of London. Stepping with grim satisfaction into the blare and chaos of Charing Cross, Ida noted that nothing untoward occurred. God did not punish her. Nor could He. Ida was immune.

But she was not yet more powerful.

She stood before the replica Eleanor Cross, stared up into the face of the dead queen, and waited for a sign. All she saw was pigeon shit.

Ida turned on her pointy heel and breezed through the lobby of Charing Cross Hotel and into the Residents' Lounge unchallenged. Wealth and—if not beauty, the ability to look expensive—solved most problems. Any remaining difficulties had always yielded to cunning or persistence. Until now. She gave Maud's name to the barman and watched for the room number he jotted on his pad. If only Maud could be tricked to yield her body into Will's arms—or her soul into Ida's hands—as easily. But would Will make love to Maud without first finding Laura behind her eyes? Ida took her tea with milk and curses, and left the lounge.

Seated in the hotel's newly installed rising room, waiting to be lifted up, she rehearsed the victories wrested from fate in her constantly thwarted pursuit of occult truth. Had she not, when MacGregor Mathers denied her entry to the Golden Dawn, stolen the power meant for Maud, a stowaway in her august beauty? And when Maud, wary of links to the loyalist Masons, had resigned from the Golden Dawn, Ida had forged a more fortunate alliance such that MacGregor Mathers himself, with apologies and his warm, self-mocking laugh, had welcomed Ida Rowley into the Golden Dawn's most secret circles. He had found her an apt pupil once his foolish misreading of Ida's horary had been cleared up. An understandable mistake, she had murmured, with her birthday the same as the order-destroyer's and his name only an added *C* away.

Ida exited the elevating contraption and marched down the silent corridor. She had met Aleister quite by accident, a naïve and troubled young man, at one of Aubrey Beardsley's decadent parties. She had been examining one of their host's drawings, a monstrously endowed man in a woman's frock and underthings. "Inspired by me, you know," Aleister had whispered lewdly to her.

It had proved sadly untrue.

But they shared a birth date, and Ida had once more plucked gifts from the ashes of disappointment and soiled linen. A single December night had been enough for her to kindle a hungry curiosity in the barren basement of a soul Aleister's scowling, religious mother had scrubbed to clean and powerless.

Ida stopped before Maud's door, and rapped too vigorously, remembering the ease with which she had found a wealthy widower with a closely spelled name in the society pages.

Ida's young protégé, utterly seduced by the occult and tenderly vulnerable to astral suggestion, joined the Golden Dawn, and once within its secret ranks, his gently poisoned nature sewed discord and dissent until, refused advancement on grounds of "sexual intemperance," he had come to fisticuffs with Will Yeats himself in the London street. And Ida, with her private income and explanation, appealed again to the Matherses who had laughed at their mistake and welcomed her into their most secret ranks, fractured though they were. Now she knew more than they did.

But still not enough. She might have to call on Aleister again. Mr. Crowley, now calling himself the evilest man on earth, and breaking ground in black magic, ritual sex, and heroin use, still owed her several favors.

Maud came to the door in her dressing gown.

"Oh, Ida! I wasn't expecting you, but I'm glad you've come to call. I was just writing to Will Yeats. I met his soul at Howth last night."

"I'm sure you were dreaming," Ida said crossly.

Maud laughed, and drew back the curtains to admit the bitter November light. "Did you know the Thames has frozen over?"

Ida jabbed absently at the fire, weighing the little poker in her soot-smudged hand, summoning a thick yellow filth to blanket the wicked city.

"I suspect Mr. Yeats has been engaged in some occult activity touching on me," Maud prattled on. "He walked into the drawing room of the Maples Hotel, where I was staying in Dublin, but it was only his ghost. He will be dining with me here tomorrow night. Do join us, my dear."

"Maud, have you read Mr. Darwin's book?"

"His new one this year? The singing earthworms?"

Ida shook her head. "No. The famous one. I was just thinking, if the fittest survive, we must all be bred for despair."

"Whatever do you mean, Ida dear?"

"Imagine a beast trying to drink from a dry stream. If he never gives up, he'll die of thirst."

"Ida, I'm surprised at you! How can you, of all people, speak of despair?"

"I've just begun to wonder"—Ida walked to the window to hide her face from Maud—"if it's possible to fight too hard for what you believe in."

"You sound like O'Leary"—Maud's bright laugh fell on Ida's ears like snow into open wounds—"who says there are things a man must not do in the name of freedom. And maybe a man may not, but a woman must be willing to do anything."

"You say that"—Ida stopped herself and chewed her lip to sop up the bitterness too obvious in her voice—"but you are beautiful and unmarried."

Maud's voice iced over. "That's not what I meant, Ida. And you know it. I was devastated when Lucien tried to give me, like a common harlot, to advance our cause. It ended things between us."

Ida put her back to the window and studied Maud's taut face. So she had left her married French Boulangist over sex. Maud, who loved violence and longed for war, would willingly give her body to battle, but not pleasure.

"And Mr. Yeats? Has he asked you to marry him again?"

Maud's face froze white.

"He loves you," Ida observed coolly. "You should summon him to Paris."

"He does not like France."

"Call him anyway. He'll come. No one, not even God, denies you."

"That's not true. My little Georges . . ." Maud's voice was very small. "When I forced the hand of God, when you helped me do so at his grave, God mocked me with a daughter."

"Maud." Ida thought a careful moment. No, she was certain now. "Maud, would you like a chance of getting even?"

Maud's eyes gazed into Ida's from her white face like twin fishing holes broken in the ice—dark, bottomless, and deadly. "A chance to get even with God?" She sank onto a horsehide chair, but did not drop her eyes. "How?"

Ida stopped when she realized she had been creeping steadily closer to Maud, and twisted her hands behind her back to steady her patience. "You've always said you are part *sidhe*. Mayhap the spirit you channeled years ago was a fairy mistress seeking William Yeats. Channel her again. He'll refuse her love—you know he pines for you alone now—and so she will have to serve him. Can you imagine what the Host of the Air might create through him? You complain Ireland has lost her wild, fighting spirit. His poems could recall the wandering Irish soul, create it again, and teach it to dream of freedom."

"It must do more than dream of freedom!"

"Maud, dreams are only the beginning. Channel the soul of Ireland for her poet once again," she whispered.

"I would be more than a vessel, Ida!"

"Yes, I know. But we are women. We must recognize our weaknesses, Maud. We must face those places where God tells us *no*, and ask again elsewhere. A woman must be willing to do anything for freedom."

Yeats, she had proved, would take suggestion when simply distracted and sad. How much more when his soul was already half-transported?

Ida knelt beside Maud, and took her hands. "Darling, when we cease to watch after what we cannot change, our eyes light upon those things we can, and we see where our true power lies."

Ida would suggest Will's soul fly away and leave his body open. Open for possession. By the Celtic gods, she might whisper to him. Or Poetry's muse. But in truth by Ida's one—and at last material—love.

"Maud, think what you might do, working within your realm of power."

In Will's body, Ida's daemon would cast Maud aside and come to her. To Ida. Chosen over Maud.

"When you dine with him tomorrow night, invite him to Paris. He will come."

Of course, he might never return. Ida weighed the danger that her plan might kill the poet or trap his soul in Hell, but chose against mentioning the risk.

Yes, she saw with sudden clarity that William Butler Yeats, Ireland's national poet, would die in France.

"Charlie's right, you know." Amit lies beside me, rubbing a contemplative, open palm across my left breast.

"What do you mean?" I ask, imagining myself in Will's trembling embrace on Castle Island.

"You are different since the wedding."

Amit's stroke is too assured and easy, and his voice keeps me from falling into my fantasy. "Different how?" I ask. "I'm not different."

"You're sleeping better."

I remember the way Charlie looked at me, and my guilt when he talked about monogamy.

"And we're having more sex. You were never repressed or anything, but you seem more into it now, since we were married, somehow." Amit's fingers narrow in on my nipples. He does this because he knows they're sensitive, and touching them this way makes them harden, and my legs part.

Will touched me with wonder, like a holy relic or a magic talisman, not a soap dispenser, but Amit's practiced fingers still wake a prickling warmth between my legs.

"Yeah, well," I say, "you know I'm bass-ackwards, right? So if sex is supposed to dry up and get boring after marriage, you should have expected this."

He laughs, but he doesn't stop. "You're less inhibited, too." His fingers curl my spine from side to side, rubbing my bottom across our soft sheets. "Not just sexually, but how you talk, too. You're more emotional—I don't mean fragile, but more opinionated. More your-self, somehow?"

He sounds uncertain, but it makes perfect sense to me. I'm tapping into my subconscious with these Victorian dreams, into my more passionate, sexual, poetic nature. All the restless energy that gets in your way when you're eighteen—that you learn to smother or sail across the surface of—to get through school, to start a job, climb the damn ladder, it's all waking up in me. How could that be infidelity? To find that wildness for your husband?

Okay, maybe not all for him. But having an imaginary lover is just a creative solution to the problem of monogamy, right? And monogamy *is* a problem. Every advertising first-year learns the human brain rapidly habituates to what we do daily until we cease to see what's most familiar. It's why you need things "new and improved." Update your bank's identity. Rebrand.

"Open your eyes," he says.

I slide my hand down his torso to his cock, and shake my head.

"Come on, look at me."

I know the exact amount of pressure it takes, and how to curl my fingers to wring a groan from Amit on the very first stroke. I crack one lid to check. A hard line tightens over his closed eyes. I pull my pulsing, constricting fingers down the shaft of his cock, and back up in an easy, unrepentant rhythm. I like the way my touch constricts his forehead but softens his lips. He opens his eyes.

"I want us to be the eye-gazing sort," he says.

I don't falter in my rhythm. "You want a lot of things."

"I want us in wild, passionate, crazy love. I want to sweep you away on our honeymoon tomorrow to somewhere over-the-top romantic and not even tell you where we're going. Not let you finish the NorPac campaign, just carry you off in my arms."

"I love you," I say. And I do. But crazy in love is still crazy. I'm responsible and sane. And I like it that way. Amit likes me that way. The kind of love he wants is imaginary. Not for real people. Not without affairs and tumult and divorce and kids whose hearts get split up before they ever fall in love.

I roll onto him, straddling the cock I've stroked awake. It pulses between my spread-wide thighs, and I sweep my nipples over his chest, tempting us both. I keep my eyes looking down into his, and kiss him. I taste his mouth, soft and sucking, swaying my body over him. I run my tongue between his lips and coax them apart. His hands curl around my thighs and squeeze hard, just above my knees. Then he slides them up to grip the halves of my ass and pulls me harder down against his straining cock with hungry, strong, unhesitating hands.

I close my eyes.

Maud and Will are looking right at me. Their faces are separated from mine by only a pane of glass. Will's face sends pleasure stabbing through me. I groan.

Amit's mouth moves down my throat. Teeth hard behind his lips, his tongue rakes the flesh as he opens his mouth over it. I raise my chin to give my neck to him. His hands grapple up my body, from ass to hips to ribs. And I want him to bite me, to hurt me, to leave a mark.

Will's lips close around the mouthpiece of a slender black flute. His eyes, fastened to Maud's face, are hazy with longing and denial. She takes the pipe when he hands it to her, and I notice the long, colored cord running from it to a tall, lidded glass vase. They're smoking something in a hookah, but I can't tell what, because I'm trapped on the other side of the mantel mirror, like a vampire at the window.

Amit's fingers dig into my back, holding me over him. His teeth brush my nipple and, from an unnerving distance, I hear my voice in a hungry whimper. My breast swells in his mouth, wet and sucking. My hips twitch. My hands grope for his shoulders to pin me down before I get too carried away.

Ida can scarcely lift the sledgehammer. One hip pinned against the mouth of the fireplace, she grips the rough wooden handle and grunts. The metal impacts the back wall with a dull shudder. Mortar snows over her skirt. She musters more momentum with the second stroke, and a brick cracks.

I slam my body onto Amit's cock too quickly and too hard. It rams against my cervix and binds me up with a deep but momentary pain. He grunts and grips my hip bones. My hands press flat on his chest, and my ass rocks up and back, down and grinding. I'm panting, and my tits are shuddering, jostling, fat with sex and the impact of his body hammering into mine. I accompany the jerking dance of our bodies with a desperate, wordless escalation of cries and breaths. Amit is silent as he will be until he comes, eyes squeezed shut, mouth locked open.

Ida fastens a black cloth over the hole she's made between the rear-adjoining fireplaces and piles the extracted bricks into a wheelbarrow. The massive over-mantel mirror stays propped on the floor opposite. She's cursing in a quiet, fluid, white-rage stream of whispered, monotone violence.

We've rubbed the swollen balloons of our sex to bursting and wait, skinless, breathless, for the thick pulse of rupture. Amit is fractionally first. His cock beats once inside me, and I contract against it in a radiating squeeze of shock waves down my legs, up my chest, and out my arms. In my head, inanely, I count the pulses.

Will raps at the door. Ida opens it and ushers him into the library but does not take his coat.

"Did you and Maud not travel from Paris together? You've been here a week; I'm sure you've seen her before tonight."

"Yes. I've visited her in her rooms to scrye for information, and we're working with MacGregor and his wife, developing rituals for our Castle of Heroes. But I am staying at the Hotel Corneille. It is too painful for me, to be so near to Maud, and so far from Laura."

"Have you tried to summon her without me?" Ida's keen eyes glint danger. Does Will know she's offered to kill me for that?

"No, we have not tried, but I glimpsed her once, in a scrying mirror."

Ida's black ostrich eyes search his face. "And?"

"And we've been taking hashish, but to no avail. Maud and I have both had visions, but nothing of her."

Ida hands him a length of black velvet. "Put this on," she says.

"If you want anything, you'll have to get it yourself. I brought no one with me. Mr. Rowley would not understand a December visit to our summer house."

Amit slides me from his chest, tucks me between his side and arm, and pulls the light, white cotton blanket over us. He rubs his face in my hair with a noise almost like purring. "You are perfect for me," he whispers.

I burrow against him, relishing the perfect safety of fidelity. And the restless, wicked thrill of a new affair. My responsible, rational, modern husband, and my mystical, erotic dream. Perfect: love, re-branded.

Ida and Will wear black robes painted with gold occult symbols. She opens the door again to usher Maud into the cold, quiet house, and hands her a robe.

"Did you set the alarm?" Amit asks me.

I want us to stay perfect like this.

I nod against the soft fur of his chest, and look out at Will from Maud's eyes. *"Demon est Deus Inversus."*

Amit chuckles sleepily. "There you go again."

Will springs to my side with a cry. "You're here!"

"Everything is perfect," I say.

"That's unlikely." Ida's voice grates harsh behind me.

"Yeah," Amit whispers.

Will is struggling not to take me in his arms in the creepy library of Ida's deserted summer house and kiss me in front of its mistress.

"I will show you to your room," Ida says.

I recognize the room Ida takes us to, but I can't place it, until she apologizes for the broken chimney and lights a fire in the little brass brazier standing squat and cold on the hearth rug. The chimney is fine; Ida just spent all yesterday breaking down the fireplace's back wall.

I wonder why she's lying, but as soon as she's gone, Will comes to me and touches my cheeks and eyebrows, forehead and chin with trembling fingers.

"You've learned to find me, haven't you?" he whispers.

I nod.

"You've been here with me, without Ida, and without Maud?"

The battle he's waging with a gigantic grin makes me want to laugh. "Yes," I say.

"I glimpsed your true face in our scrying glass. You are even more beautiful than Maud."

"I'm not, really," I say. "Not actually. Not in real life."

"Is this life not real for you?"

Pain shadows the struggling smile, and I want to cry. How can his face, his eyes, the way every emotion shows on them, affect me with such depth and precision? "No," I say. "It's more than real."

"I have only this one life," he whispers, "but I spread it under your feet."

"I think . . ." I'm groping through memory and imagination. "I think I have only this one, too. Only it starts before I was born."

"I have loved you for that long."

He lowers his mouth to mine, and it isn't until I've closed my eyes to taste him that I feel the tears. They slide down my cheeks, soft as his lips over my mouth.

"Why are you crying?"

"I don't know. Because you love me."

Because it's sappy and pure. A crazy, irresponsible dream.

Because I want it to be real.

He runs his tender fingers down the wet stains on my face.

Because it's dangerous, and I would mortgage everything to keep it.

"You are so beautiful," he says again. Tears threaten in his eyes, too.

"No. That doesn't matter. It's just packaging."

He has to let me believe this. Or it would be Maud he's holding.

I am not my body. It's faithful and asleep beside my husband.

I am here with Will.

Then I am not faithful, am I? If society is only ever three meals away from anarchy, is marriage only one long and perfect kiss away from adultery? Or can I stay hanging on this spider's thread above the ocean, between breathing and drowning, between freedom and possession, between Heaven, and the bottomless, bright blue sea?

"It is your beauty that I love. And when I cannot find it in Maud's eyes, I see no beauty there."

"There is a difference between me and what's beautiful in me," I tell him.

"I love you," he whispers. "All of you. With all my self. And it is all beautiful to me."

I pull the ribbon at Maud's throat and drop the velvet robe to stand naked, holy as a sacrifice before a jealous god.

Will does not move. He stays, his fingers in my hair, his mouth between my eye and ear, but I hear his breathing snag. His lips move in a whispered prayer or tiny kiss at my temple. Then he drops his hands to my shoulders and takes several steps back. I try to meet his eyes, but they slide relentlessly over my body—over Maud's body. The only sign he is not reading something written in my skin, or studying my flesh for a portrait, is the quick, ragged edge of his breathing.

I look down. Maud's breasts are beautiful, truly. High and full, their freckled paleness a stark contrast, even in the dim light, to the deep red-orange of her large, tightening nipples. Mine are small and pale, and it's hard to see sometimes where they begin. My breasts are more like pyramids than burial mounds. They perch on my ribs; hers flower outward from her body, growing toward the light. I cover them with my hands. Because his eyes unnerve me. Because I want to test their weight in my fingers. But touching them wakes a deeper ache at my center, and I drag my fingers over the reddening tips and it uncoils, pushing and reaching.

Will sits on the edge of the fireside chair like a pupil or penitent, and we both watch my encircling hands glide over Maud, setting fine waves of sex into the ritual quiet. The flesh of my belly, when I touch it, is oddly rippled and nerveless. Looking down, I recognize the dimpled gathers I've seen on bikini-moms. Maud's body has carried two children. I drop my hands, and stand still. Does Will know? Is it ugly?

"What are you thinking?" I ask him because he has not moved, and because it's a hundred years ago, and the question isn't ridiculous yet.

He meets my eyes and shakes his head. "My understanding clutches after threads. It cannot hold the mystery. It cannot hold you."

"But you can."

"Yes."

He slides from the chair onto his knees, and the idea of it— of him kneeling before me as I stand naked, arms outstretched in invitation—is ridiculous again. My embarrassed eyes dart from him to the massive mantel mirror on the ground to find myself self-conscious and not holy, reflected in the fireplace's dull glow.

"Laura"—his slender fingers encircle my wrists, draw me toward him—"you are every symbol of Truth to me, of every place where fact and meaning coincide."

I thought the fireplace was broken.

"And I love you. I love you as a man loves a woman, but also as a poet loves the muse whispering through him." He presses a trail of fervent kisses across the puckered flesh of my belly and they drop, like crumbs through honey, to the center of me. I know I watched Ida smash the wall at the fireplace back and hang up the black fabric.

". . . and as you want Maud, not to possess, but to be a part of, to be one with." His uncertain hands move up my thighs, dragging a current of arousal to join the wave his kisses set descending.

The fire I saw must be in the room next to ours. Maybe Ida did this to share heat in the empty house.

"I will not refuse you, no matter what you are, even if it enslaves my soul or carries it away." His hand, clutching the deep flesh of my ass, drives the dropping pleasure up to his mouth again. Why else would Ida be burning all those candles in a circle in the room next door?

"You belong to a deathless time, to the *sidhe* and *Tír na nÓg*, where bodies are not looked at nor judged for their beauty, but lived through . . ." My thinking, my hearing, is dropping under the rolling sensation his mouth and hands ignite. I slip my fingers into his hair, pull him hard against my body. "... and where the claim to another's body in slavery or monogamy is denied."

He guides me down, and we're both kneeling, like prayerful pilgrims, with my weighty breasts trembling between us and his words rolling over us. If he kisses me now, everything will submerge beneath our bodies, into our sex and love.

He glances down to unclasp the belt closing his gown, and something glints beyond the fire. A mirror stands on the other side of Ida's broken hearthwall, too. Will shrugs, and his body emerges from the black of Ida's borrowed robes. The flow of muscle that wraps his shoulders and winds his arms and chest moves with a fluid grace. He pulls the fabric free. Beneath the hard chest and lean waist, his cock stands up dogged and hard. I could bow my head and take it in my mouth, but I look into the fireplace, and see through the black drape. Framed by the ragged edge of old gray and new too-red where the broken brick looks like bloody flesh, Ida's pinched face peers through the knocked-out hole.

Behind her, in the candlelit mirror, I see Will's hands cup my throat and slide across my breasts. His hard palms rub over my nipples, and a hungry pleasure blooms behind them. A groan rises in my throat, my lids slide closed. The sound resonates between my legs, but the afterimage wavers behind my eyes and Ida's face in the other mirror. This body is a story, not of how I look—I don't look like this—but of who I am. Of how I feel. I feel delicious, erotic and alive, fully present to this single moment. This pure moment in the past.

Will's arms, like polished wood under my flying hands, thrill me, and I can't find his mouth with mine quickly enough. My reddening nipples crush against his chest, and every subtlety of our bodies' contact ricochets keenly between their sensitive tips and the blunt lust building between my legs. And Ida is watching.

"I love you." Will's mouth opens over mine, kissing, whispering.

"I love you, too." And I do. I know it. I feel it. The knowing lives in whatever of me isn't body or memory. The way I know women vote and own houses. The way I know how to draw.

His hands move in my hair and across my back. His mouth, without tenderness or fear, wild and mindless across my lips, my throat, teeth against flesh, tongue on shivering skin.

I know Ida watches us, and I don't care. I almost like it. Our sex is more than sex. It is used for something, means something, and she the priestess presiding over it in the sacred In-Between. There, our sex exists not in the facts of bodies touching, but in the meaning of union and creation itself. Her eyes are another kind of stroking me, hers and his, watching. Will's strong fingers touch everywhere, arching me back, neck open to the night, to bring his mouth down to my breasts, but not quite reaching. He holds my face in his hands. Who is standing between us and Ida?

Will's face is flushed with sex, tender and fierce. "The first time we loved one another on a stone floor because the place we lay was holy. Tonight, we have no excuse for refusing a soft bed."

I laugh and follow him to standing.

I walk to the bed feeling disembodied, or extra-embodied. Not moving, but being moved through, the conduit and what it carries, the vessel and the animating soul. If I could bring my body to this, and not Maud's, I would be more powerful than sex, stronger than the elements. Will and I tumble into the soft warmth of bed together, and close ourselves under the mounds of welcoming blankets. Will's cock brushes my knee, and the dedicated strength of it wrings an urgent sound from me. I want him in me. My sex swells almost closed with an exquisite, juicy hunger, but it hollows, too, with needing him.

He finds me and holds me hard against him. His forearm under my shoulders, an open hand flat at the base of my spine. We are both trembling. If all that is me in Maud is my awareness, my soul or consciousness, how can I be losing my mind and still be here? Has he become universal to me now? Is Will all men?

He holds himself over me to watch my eyes as his cock drives, with shuddering caution, into me. He has entered other women since the last time we loved, and does not want to hurt me with his size. His cock is heavy and rich inside me, and I close the walls of my sex around its heft to embrace and savor it; and the man in the fireplace steps into our room. He looks like a pirate, with his broad shoulders, narrow waist, and swagger. He comes toward us with a monster's grace. His beauty alone is erotic, like some summoned, possessing god of sex.

Or the muse of it.

But Will's broad, naked back is open under him, and all at once the blind, muscled flesh seems vulnerable, even in its hard strength. I close my eyes, run my hands down the fine, hard flesh of my poet lover. Driven by something keener than thought, my hips thrust of their own volition to meet his penetrating cock. Ida gets up out of her body and crawls through the hole she made.

From my breasts to deep into my pussy and back again, the pleasure spirals, gathering. With each circuit, more of me comes within the widening edge of mindless sensation. I cling to Will, to the thrum of my orgasm drawing me in, deafening me.

This is your ceremony. Ida's peat-smoke voice reaches across my collapsing tidal center, just as I start to lose consciousness. She isn't talking to me.

"A sacrament." Will's whisper is harsh with the battle to stay present enough for speech. Does he hear Ida, too? She's talking to him: *Float up into it, Will. Be graceful, or your body will know it's dropping behind.*

No, Ida.

A passionate, Victorian rage is rising in me, solid and intense against the drowning rush of pleasure.

I will not let her take him.

Submit your will to mine.

"Will!"

His torso rides above me, his head thrown back, hips driving. Muscular cords dance under his skin, like sand under wind, contoured by restraint. A noise of animal pain stifles in his throat when I shout his name. His cock stabs again, but he lowers his desperate eyes to mine.

"I need you." His whisper is a groan of a man cracked open. "I need you with me."

His soul is fractured. The pieces are pilgrims.

"Stay with me," I tell him, and wrap his slowing thighs with my legs. I twine my arms across his broad back to pull him down over me, under me, and say his name again. There is no space between our bodies now. His cock drives the darkness dropping down and my body draws the tide pouring up. Our voices mingle in a harsh pant of wordless dissolution into something new. We are becoming what we share, what we feel. An experience.

A memory.

The vortexing spirals of pleasure flood from my swollen, open, panting mouth to my folded, arching pointing toes, and center on my rocking clit like lightning on stone. Thunder looses deep behind it in my sex, my cunt, my womb. Where Will is. Coming. Our locked eyes are an anarchy of rough revelation.

And the possessing god, denied, slouches back through the fireplace.

I have turned him away.

Ida is screaming. She beats her fists on the mirror in the next room, again and again and again, but it can't crack. There is nothing solid in her soul, and I have kept Will's body from her.

from *Fairy and Folk Tales of the Irish Peasantry*
by W. B. Yeats

(first published in 1888)

The Irish word for fairy is *sheehogue* [*sidheóg*], a diminutive of "shee" in *banshee*. Fairies are *deenee shee* [*daoine sidhe*] (fairy people). Who are they? "Fallen angels who were not good enough to be saved, nor bad enough to be lost," say the peasantry . . .

In dreams we go amongst them, and combat with them. They are, perhaps, human souls in the crucible . . . Their chief occupations are feasting, fighting and making love, and playing the most beautiful music . . .

An old man told me he saw them fight once; they tore the thatch of a house in the midst of it all. Had anyone else been near they would merely have seen a great wind whirling everything into the air as it passed. When the wind makes the straws and leaves whirl as it passes, that is the fairies, and the peasantry take off their hats and say, "God bless them."

The *Leanshawn Shee* (fairy mistress) seeks the love of mortals. If they refuse, she must be their slave; if they consent, they are hers . . . She is the Gaelic muse, for she gives inspiration to those she persecutes. The Gaelic poets die young, for she is restless, and will not let them remain long on earth . . . To her have belonged the greatest of the Irish poets, from Oisin down to the last century . . .

There is a country called *Tír na nÓg*, which means the Country of the Young, for age and death have not found it . . . One man has gone there and returned. The bard, Oisin . . . [It] is the favourite dwelling of the fairies. Some say it is triple— the island of the living, the island of victories, and an underwater land.

9

OUR SOULS ARE LOVE,
AND A CONTINUAL FAREWELL

Turning and turning in the widening gyre
The falcon cannot hear the falconer;
Things fall apart; the centre cannot hold;
Mere anarchy is loosed upon the world,
The blood-dimmed tide is loosed, and everywhere
The ceremony of innocence is drowned;
The best lack all conviction, while the worst
Are full of passionate intensity.

Surely some revelation is at hand;
Surely the Second Coming is at hand.
The Second Coming! Hardly are those words out
When a vast image out of Spiritus Mundi
Troubles my sight: a waste of desert sand;
A shape with lion body and the head of a man,
A gaze blank and pitiless as the sun,
Is moving its slow thighs, while all about it
Wind shadows of the indignant desert birds.
The darkness drops again but now I know
That twenty centuries of stony sleep
Were vexed to nightmare by a rocking cradle,

And what rough beast, its hour come round at last,
Slouches towards Bethlehem to be born?

    —"The Second Coming" by W. B. Yeats

All things wicked come from the west, and although Ida was not particularly averse to evil, she was now the farthest west she had ever been, and found it did not suit her. The light was too thin, the air too bright, and Will Yeats's legs too long by half. Ida scuttled after them across the rough gray cobblestones of the stableyard at Coole Park House. The poet flourished here, where the magic hung close and Lady Gregory hauled him between peasant cottages in her dog-cart, collecting tales of the *sidhe*. But Ida brimmed and bubbled with wanting to rip the whiskers from their hostess's fat chin and set fire to her big white house.

"Shall we leave the walled garden for another day, Madam Rowley, and stroll the woodland paths?"

Ida looked into the finely sculpted face and nodded. She understood Lady Gregory's yearning to add this elegant luminary to her collection. Both charismatic and irreverent, Will had strung her dinner guests between outrage and adoration in a web of wine and words spinning everyone but Ida into a golden twilight of affection.

"How kind of you, Mr. Yeats, to show me the grounds."

"Not at all." Despite his voice of polished courtesy, something in his brow as he looked from Ida's face into the brilliant green of a leaf-filtered, late-setting sun gave her hope. "I am accustomed to wander in these woods after dinner."

"Beneficial to the digestion," Ida concurred.

Watching him from under soft and lowered lashes, Ida's rapier eyes caught the shadow of an ironic twitch at the edge of his graceful mouth. He had swallowed something evil after all. Ida reached out to stroke the darkness.

"I attended a luncheon with Miss Gonne last week," she said.

Will's head turned sharply in her direction, but Ida kept her eyes on the broad, leaf-dusted path, as a city-bred woman, wary of hidden roots or snakes, might do.

"I saw her a month ago in Dublin," he said, and Ida heard, in his choked voice, proof her rapid and unpleasant trip to the edge of the western world had not been made in vain. His performance over Lady Gregory's silver-laden table aside, William Yeats was in terrible pain. How very reassuring.

"Are you here on her behalf?" he asked.

"No," Ida said, to watch the shadows deepen. "She told me only your concern for her physical safety had forced on her the single cowardly act of her life. I understood, of course, better than she, why you would strive to keep her body safe from harm."

"After two long, terrible days of speeches and excitement over the queen's Jubilee, Miss Gonne and I together led the protest procession down Dame Street to Rutland Square," he said. "We were having tea at the National Club when word came the police had attacked the crowd with batons. An old woman had been killed. Maud was desperate to get into the streets, to join the riot, but I would not permit Lorcan Sherlock to unlock the doors. I have seen too much of riots. But she—I think, sometimes, she longs for violence."

"Of course she does."

"She could have been killed."

"She may long for that as well." The horror-stricken eyes he turned to her justified Ida's trip entirely. "You did right to prevent her," she added, although to Maud, of course, she had said quite the inverse.

"It has not touched her fame," Will groused. "Her absence from the mob was noticeable only to her; but she has written to me since, accusing me of cowardice for wishing to protect her life."

"You need Maud's body to house the pilgrim soul you love."

"I'm no longer certain that I do," Will said, dully. "But I still could not allow her to put herself in danger. Every passionate soul is reckless at times. We depend upon our friendships to shield us from ourselves."

Ida had no such protective armoring, and if Will did not need

Maud's body to hold Laura's soul, he did not need Ida to channel it. But that was impossible. Women are but stables to men, paddocks in which they lodge their aspirations, and children, and cocks. Ida changed her tack.

"It must be terrible for you," she said, and placed a gloved hand on his arm.

"If I had not this place to come to, I don't know what I might have done." Will folded his long and gallant arm, wrapping Ida's fingers into its crook and covering them with a protective hand. "All day, I roam the woods and the shore of this lake for comfort, and at night, I close myself in my rooms and seek her on the astral plane." If he could, he would stride across time to Laura on his strong legs. Thwarted, he paced the woodland path too quickly for Ida to keep up with both his feet and thoughts.

"How tragic," she panted.

His laugh was dark with anguish. "Ours is a tragic generation."

Ida, perplexed, concentrated on not tripping over the gathering dusk and shadow between the tall and ancient trees.

"We are forced into serving as our own midwives. I read my nation's birthing in her hills as clearly as in her newspapers, and the throes of her labor overshadow my love affairs and wrack my metaphysics."

"No," Ida cried, "the clumsy maneuvering of politicians must not be permitted to touch real power or beauty!"

Will shot her a quizzical glance, and took his hand from over hers to point away from them. Ida, mind wheeling, followed his finger across a glass-still lake in which the entire sky, blood-streaked with sunset, lay reflected. On earth—only inversion and illusion masking drowning depths—as it is in Heaven. The bellow of a distant cow moaned across the lake.

"I love Laura the way I love Ireland," he said. "I love her through the darkness."

Ida knew he tortured himself, striving night after night to reach his lover on the astral plane, wanting the peace only their reunion could bring. She understood his longing, being desperate herself for a lover she could likewise not walk beside or own. She peered up at the lonely poet, already shadowed by the coming night, counting gray and white swans on the still water, and realized, with a sudden vertigo, she might fall in love with him herself. He stood at the water's edge, motionless and dark, passionate, wild, and tender. What if poets, in the throes of love, always opened paths into Hell? If Will made love to her, could Ida's daemon step into him directly? Having heard Will was barely eating for grief, Ida had traveled this far west to sell her last secret to find out.

"There will be no moon tonight," Will said.

"You know the woods well enough to thread them in the dark," Ida answered. "And Lady Gregory's little mansion, I'm sure, glitters like the grail flame for you in our wild and pagan Irish night."

He chuckled, and Ida took his arm again, leaning into it and craning her neck skyward. "How beautiful," she said, eyes sweeping the dusk sky.

"Yes," he said. "The beauty of Coole at twilight is like the beauty of Maud when I cannot find Laura in her eyes. It makes me long for darkness."

"I long for darkness, too," Ida whispered, sidling closer to his broad chest. "Darkness without a hope for dawn."

"I'm sorry?"

"Will, the pilgrim soul you love—Laura—she is not a creature disembodied. Nor is she *sidhe* or ghost."

"I know she is not."

Ida pressed her molars into her tongue. How did he know? What did he know Laura to be? Love might have molted secrets even Ida's skill could not pluck, but she dared not gather the windfall now. A moonless night too cloud-stuffed for stars was eiderdown enough. "Laura comes," she whispered, forcing Will to incline ear-to-lip, "not from our Irish past, Will, but from its future years."

A slow smile broke over Will's subtle face. "The coming days bring souls more bold and radiant than even our myths conceive." He laughed with a disconcerting freedom.

"No." Ida stopped him before he could invent another shining race. "She comes from only a hundred years from now."

In the gathering shadows he turned his handsome face to peer down at Ida. She met his questioning eyes boldly, cocking up her chin with pride at the doubt, distrust, and wonder chasing each other across his strong features. In his slow intake of breath, Ida's keen ears caught a note of awe.

"How strange and antique we must be to her."

"No, she cannot remember," Ida said. "Only in the first few minutes, before she awakes fully into being Maud, does she retain memories of things to come. After that, she knows only what one remembers without words, and what she has not done. She has never cut up a chicken, but she knows how to drive a motorcar."

"They still have those in the future, then?"

Ida hated the joy on his face.

"They still have husbands," she said. "Laura is married, Will."

Will's eyes crackled in the twilight with an antic fire. His strong face split in a quick and crooked grin. "But to me, first." And he turned away from her, hands in his pockets, strolling back the path.

Ida picked her peevish way across the tangled underbrush to join him. None of her revelations affected him correctly. "No, not first to you. Maud's spirit, with its *sidhe* knack for theft, carried the soul of your bride away. You met her on her wedding night."

"On her wedding night a hundred years from now."

"It does not upset you? To share your one beloved with another man?"

"She is not mine to share or hoard."

"How can you not want to possess her?" Ida moaned. "How are you not eaten with desire to touch who she really is, to hold her physical being?"

"Who she really is, is not the same thing as her body," he said, and Ida had to hurry back up the gravel path to hear him. "But yes, I do want her—terribly. I want to mingle our days and dreams. I want to create the future she lives in with her. Perhaps it is not her, but me, who belongs in another age. Perhaps she has been sent to bring me home."

"Sent by whom?" Ida snapped.

Will stopped walking and dropped his poet's eyes to hers on the darkening path. Hope and apprehension chased like clouds across his strong face. "Sent, perhaps, by the man I could become. I have often felt I warred with my own age. Maybe love is a summons from our more god-like selves waiting to be born."

"I can help you." Ida touched her fingertips to his arm, warm and inviting under the stiff sleeve of his coat. "I've learned to follow Maud's awareness in the moment it leaves her."

She stepped closer to Will's taut frame.

"I have studied more than you know with MacGregor and with other and more powerful magi. I hold the secrets of The Between, and your soul is ready for the journey, Will."

In the small teeth of time, Ida stood before him with the falling night and expanding possibilities. She could not have said, in those few moments, whether she more wanted to lie down with the poet on the leafy sands of Coole's beautiful tree-shrouded paths, and mingle their bodies like night with shadow, or to see her daemon rising from the depths of his dark eyes.

The confusion excited her.

She took another step to him. Olivia Shakespear, his married paramour, had left him realizing he loved another, and Maud had refused to channel even friendship since the winter bedroom of Ida's summer house. His body must long for a woman's touch. Ida tasted her parting lips with her warm tongue, and put her chilly fingers to his grief-ravaged face. "Your suffering has shown you worthy," she whispered, and slid her thumb into position between his brows and in his soft, rich hair. He closed his eyes.

"Can you send me to Laura?"

"Yes," she lied.

"What must I do?"

Ida let her satin-clad breast slide against his chest and heard him swallow, his agony pleasing to her. "Close your eyes tightly—tightly—and keep them closed."

"Those are the words you said to Maud at the Matherses' séance."

"Yes."

He shook his head. "I promised Laura never to be hypnotized."

Ida's fingers on his scalp, her body against his broad chest stiffened, but did not flinch. She should have waited until she had his cock clasped tight between her legs.

Joint by joint, she loosened her fingers enough to stroke his wild, unruly hair. "I had not thought to do so," she murmured, "only to relax you."

His sad smile and encompassing hand tracked her arm, elbow to wrist, and took her frozen fingers. He held them between his body and hers.

His trembled. "Laura is learning to send her soul to me," he said.

He would not make love to her, or obey.

"The last time we were together," Will said, "Laura saw a figure standing, *like a hungry ghost,* she said, behind me."

A tiny, rebellious sob, like a hiccup, rose in Ida's chest, and she coughed to mask it. How was she always denied? Powerless.

"Laura feared what that hovering soul might do, if ever I tried to leave my body for her."

"I know the man she saw," Ida said dully.

"She said it was not a man's soul, but larger, some vast image of *Spiritus Mundi* ready to work its way into me. I said it was the work of poets to serve such souls, but she said it would break the pipe it played through, either all at once, or over time. I gave my solemn promise not to attempt it. "

Ida nodded her defeat.

"Ida, who is that waiting man? It is not my future self, or Laura would have known me."

Ida combed her mind with furious fingers, raking memory, scrambling for persuasion, and stumbled clumsily headlong over truth. Her soul rang like a black bell, clanging through to her deep bones, with the import and weight of what she had found, and the power of her dark love's will.

Her daemon had shown her this. He had foreseen.

Will was the ideal target for the blow, balanced from a rope of

myth and magic, politics and poetry. The perfect bell for such a ham-
mer to strike, ringing his own death knell.

"He is the king," Ida whispered, "come again." Even as she spoke
it, she heard the stars grind into line. At last, it was in motion.

"Cúchulainn?" The reverberations rang across his face in waves of
shock and promise.

"I don't know," Ida confessed. "Cúchulainn . . . or Arthur."

"Or Christ," Will whispered. "The second coming. This is how
only the hundred years between us creates the new golden age, after
twenty centuries of suffering."

"I don't know," Ida repeated, stubborn. "I only know he sleeps
under a mountain in the place where I follow Maud's pilgrim soul;
and if we combined our power and our will, his hour may come
round at last."

I'm not the sort to fall apart. I keep a pretty tight grip on myself
(time-tripping, body-snatching dreams aside), but this morning,
when the glass body of the French coffee press slips out of my hands,
I have to look a long time to make certain no splinters of me are
mixed in with the shatters on the kitchen's black-and-white checkered
floor.

My breakdown-free life isn't proof of my strength or hard work.
It's lucky, at best, or evidence of something linoleum in me. My
fingers collect the pieces—large and curved like petals off an ice
flower, sharp as thorns.

Amit is in the shower. He doesn't know I'm up and can't have
heard the glass break, but I don't know what to do with the top of
the French press. The metal plunger and plastic lid, the elegant coiled
spring, fine mesh, and disk of punched circles seem too complicated
to throw away, but they're useless.

"I'm running over to Prized Possession," I shout into the tiny,
steam-filled bathroom.

Amit pushes back the plastic curtain. "Hey, good morning!

Why are you up?" He gets out of bed at the same time every day. Weekdays, it's an hour after me; most Sundays, it's four hours before.

"I didn't sleep well."

"I'm sorry, sweet." He's covered in soap, the foam bubbling into the dark hair of his chest and arms like spider nests. "I'll make coffee."

"I broke the pot."

He grins at me and ducks back under the water stream. "Why don't you wait, and we'll go together on our way to pick up the tile?"

"What?"

The water bounces and sprays off his muscular body, healthy and vigorous, his cheerful lather-and-rinsing invigorated by scent and bubbles, by the sheer masculine pleasure of verticality and water. "You remember. The tile for the backsplash came in on Friday. We were going to go pick it up yesterday, but you wanted to go to Powell's."

Yesterday, I woke up having had no dreams at all, and spent the day grubbing through bookstores and the web for anything on dream interpretation or astral travel. I've never hung out in the occult section before, and I felt obtrusive and insincere, but every night I don't dream could be years away from him. What I learned only worked in pieces last night, and I need coffee and time to sort it all out.

"Yeah," I say. "I'm gonna go ahead and walk over now."

"Want me to go while you shower?" He's drying off, scrubbing his sculptured legs without noticing their chiseled beauty. He's beefier than Will, stronger and more forceful. Younger, too, by now. Will was in his thirties Friday night. He could be forty by now, or worse.

"I got it," I say, and am out the door before Amit has time to get dressed and come with me, or to see me cry.

I am going to bits.

In Prized Possession, waiting for our coffees in a crunchy velvet chair, and staring at the pictures, it gets worse. The man with the thundering newspaper next to me looks like Will's dad the night I met him one week—or ten years—ago. A woman in the far corner by the window, tall and elegant as Maud, tears pieces of muffin for a little boy in a highchair. The strings come off the puppet. My body is far beneath me, and the narrative threads I have always used to control it wave gracefully in the hundred miles of separating air.

The pale, too-skinny barista with the white-blue eyes hands me two paper cups with plastic lids in a cardboard carry-thing, and puts our scones in separate bags, and I leave the cast of a week's worth of crazy dreams drinking their coffee and feeding their babies.

Have I made it all up? My crazy imagination.

I push the crosswalk button with my elbow. My hands are too full to shake, but I lean against the coffee shop window to steady my wobbly legs. I should have eaten my scone. Behind my elbow, an infant hand splays its pink starfish-belly against the glass. Maud's son gazes through the tinted pane at me, and my empty womb retracts, remembering.

I want this. I'm strong enough for this, the weight and the debt, the absolute trust in his unglistening gray eyes.

The electric orange hand is replaced by the blinking white *walk* body, and I cross the street bearing only empty calories.

"This is going to be so cool!" Amit is kneeling on our little balcony, examining a bastard child of a potter's wheel and an electric bone saw. He takes the coffee I've brought him and comes inside, leaving the door open to the bright morning air. "I've got the tile cutter all set up. Anyone interesting at Prized Possession?"

"Just the regulars," I say, and take my coffee with me into the shower.

In the bathroom mirror, my naked body glistens slender and fit, unmarred by malnutrition, childbearing, or confining corsetry. I am sculpted by targeted exercises to meet aesthetic goals, not shaped by experience or occupation. I feel untested and too young.

I step under the hot water worrying that, whether to protect herself or to punish me, Ida will never whisper me back in time again. Last night, testing what I had read, I caught glimpses of Will and Maud over and over. I found myself standing at the foot of a little cot while Maud slept as a child. And I saw Will at twelve, playing games with his young cousin. But I couldn't get them to see me, and I wasn't able to find Ida anywhere. I use Amit's shampoo because it seems less lonely, and the lather slides down my smooth legs. We're at the tile store before it opens.

Last fall, I bought half a dozen carved stone tiles from an artist on the Portland Open Studio Tour. Amit's brought one, and we tear open the box of flat-backed river rocks he ordered and arrange a test pattern on the large, craft-paper-covered table in the showroom.

"Well," I say, grinning at our mosaic, "we won't completely recover our costs on these, but they should still boost the resale some. Kitchen upgrades keep their value better than most home improvements."

"And everything we eat will taste better." Amit's tender fingers re-wrap the pieces in nested layers of newspaper. "You're so good at *beautiful*." He winks at me.

"Here's hoping NorPac thinks so," I say.

"You're going to do great tomorrow."

"We're pitching way out of our league," I remind him.

"They're going to love you guys."

"They better! How much would you hate me if I postponed our honeymoon for a pitch I end up losing!" I'm laughing off the anxiety, but Amit knows how much is riding on tomorrow's presentation, and I suspect he's timed our backsplash project to keep me occupied today.

"Would you hate me if I screw up cutting tile?"

"Only if it's ones I bought."

We laugh, and I rest my head on his shoulder. The wipers brush away the fat drops that splash over our glass-and-metal bubble. I yawn and watch the rubber blades clear, and the rain re-freckle, the windshield. Wipe, rewet, wipe, rewet, hypnotically.

About three in the morning last night, I found Maud at last, close in time to the night in Ida's French summer house. I close my eyes, remembering the powerful, alluring man who stood over Will's back, watching us make love. His gaze, touching my naked body, had singed me with a frightening lust. But when Ida had crawled through the cracked-open fireplace, I denied her and refused to let her whisper

Will away. I held his soul locked to me. Ida's scream sends me back to wiper watching, wipe, rewet, wipe, futilely.

Will didn't sense the danger that night, and believed Ida the next morning when she said she was too ill to leave her room. But I knew she was only wickedly and passionately, Victorianly angry. Last night, trying to find any of them again, the closest in time I got was Maud in spring of the same year, traveling the Irish countryside. Standing on the back of a little wagon, in a beautiful green dress before a throng of starving Irish peasants, she harangued them into action. I saw her in a courtroom threatening the magistrates with the mob she'd rallied. Outside, their bare, hungry feet beat the hard ground in a relentless muffled thunder. If he doesn't double the famine workers' wages, and send at once to England for seed potatoes, she will not quiet them or send them home.

A few days ago, I was worried my erotic, Victorian dreams might take over my waking life. I was worried their wild romance and passionate politics might make my real, responsible life look safe and dreary in comparison. I never guessed it would be my crazy imagination that receded like wiper-pushed raindrops slipping with the road runoff into gutters. Were they just dirty dreams?

I want them back.

"Otto called yesterday while you were at Powell's," Amit says, unboxing the tile in the kitchen. He must have spent the whole time I was gone clearing the cabinets and getting everything ready for our work today. "He wants to put the band back together. We should dry-fit them first, don't you think?"

"He didn't say anything at the wedding?"

"No, even he has enough sense not to suggest a ridiculous return to an adolescent dream to a man on his wedding day. Is this section right? The way you want it?'

"What'd you tell him?"

Amit laughs. "I told him no. I'm a married man. I grout tile now, not grind guitar lines."

"You can cut these to fit, right?"

"Yeah."

"I think you should give Otto a chance," I say. "There'd be less drama now everyone's older. And the music was really good."

"Don't be ridiculous." Amit stacks the tile to be trimmed carefully to preserve my ordering of the pieces, even though they're all the same.

"There're worse things," I say, but Amit is already outside.

The thick, white tile-setting mastic gloops out of its tub, and I spread it in toothy swoops between Amit's snapped line and the blue tape. If frosting went on this easily, I would have decorated my own wedding cake. I press the black, flat-backed river rocks into the white paste, and they stick. Amit cuts pieces on the porch and brings me right-sized ones to slot into the gaps. I focus on keeping patterns out of the pebbles.

I should have worn gloves. The mastic dries on my hands, and the stones chap my fingers, but there's something genetically Irish about arranging rocks. I saw their cairns and tombs twice through Maud's eyes just last night.

On my last attempt to dream my way back to Ida, with the Portland sky already paling out of night, I found Maud in a small, stone-lined, underground room, but Ida kept herself distant as the Neolithic tribe who built the tomb, as unreachable as their stories, or the things they dreamed of, and as lost as the reason for the tomb I find Maud visiting. It's September and nearly lunchtime, so Maud and I miss the advancing finger of light climbing the floor to mount the altar stone, whose whirl-carved basin is so ancient and so large it must have been here even before the stone-and-earthen mound which shelters it. Winter ends here each year, when the first shaft of spring sunlight penetrates the earthwork thighs to touch the curved stone cervix of the earth on our shared birthday. I watch Maud scoop dirt from the tomb's center and put it into a little box I know she will mail to Will.

But Ida is lost the way only memories can be—personal or genetic memories, my ten-year-old self, or my grandmother's great-grandmother. I know there must have been one, but that's all I know. A loss that leaves an empty socket instead of a tomb. I count over five and down to where the corner of the first accent tile should go, and press it into place.

The last thing Amit does before he climbs into bed with me tonight, as every night, is to open the curtains, making a night-light out of our plate-glassed city view. My cheek and knees against him, I twist in his encircling arm to see the moon dwarf the high-rises. "The kitchen looks great," I whisper, "thank you."

He rubs his chin in my hair and chuckles. "You're the artist. I just cut things."

"And grout them," I remind him. I had left the stones, gumless mummy teeth, and run out to the Wok n' Roll for our dinner. He had finished the work and cleaned up. "You could have done it all without me," I say.

"Yeah, but without you, it wouldn't have meant anything. It would have been just a stack of rocks."

"Bullshit. You're nothing if not meticulous."

"I would never have thought of it."

I roll over and press my spine against his side. It's dark and warm and my hands are tired and a little itchy. "It was your idea," I murmur.

"I was just trying to figure out something to do with those carved pieces you fell in love with."

"I didn't fall in love." My voice comes heavy and distant. "I walked down."

He chuckles from a hundred miles away. I want to explain myself across the years to him.

"I walked down the stairs at the Studio Tour . . . I don't fall . . ."

"You don't fall in love?" He's teasing, but Maud is asleep, not me.

"I don't fall apart." A part of what? Apart from Will?

"You're going to do great tomorrow. Get some sleep."

Get some sleep, Maud, and dream. Dream about the castle Will still hopes will channel me.

Maud is excited by the idea. She and Will have been traveling Ireland, planning and talking about Castle Island, their holy place for Irish heroes. They imagine it as a retreat for those who work for the Irish cause, or who create the new national literature. It's good.

The shared project unites them. They're bound by what they make together. No.

"What we make together," I correct myself.

"I'll spend my life making things with you." Love warms Amit's sleep-tinged voice.

Make a castle and a backsplash. Makes me smile. Make memories. Make love.

Make Maud find Will while she's dreaming.

"Makes a good story," I whisper.

I feel him nod, but you can't hold a story like you hold cut stone. Or like Maud dreams Will is holding her hands, down on one knee. Marry me?

"Hold on," I murmur.

Amit tightens his arms around me. "I've got you." His voice is husky with sleep.

Not "have and hold," but tell, like a story, together.

"Yes." I am the guardian of Amit's stories.

Yes, I do.

Ida took a silent moment to assess her situation, before beginning to curse.

Her feet were over her head. The trailing nightdress which had tripped her and launched her headlong tumble down the servants' backstairs, was likewise aloft. It had been her intention to spend some of her night in such a posture, but not alone at the bottom of an uncarpeted flight of stairs.

Additionally, both her wrist and tailbone might have cracked in her tumble.

But the midnight boardinghouse stayed quiet, so at least there were no servants coming to bustle her back to bed. Ida rolled cautiously onto her side, legs fanning the wall to rest one upon the other, curled like an infant in the landing's unforgiving bassinet. Suckled on disappointment as she was, Ida did not vomit now, but gulped the winter air and waited for the fresh agonies to fade. She had been foolish to rush so. Maud never snuck down backstairs to hunt a lover. She railed and cajoled, gave lectures and published magazines, nor did she hasten to train stations and carriages when Ida wrote to her.

Ida pressed her unbroken hand to the quiet stairwell's cold floor and pushed against it, still swearing steadily. Maud also did not plunge down stairs. But when she wrote to Ida of her new "spiritual marriage" to Mr. Yeats, Ida had raced from Paris, leaving her house and studies with more haste than planning. None the less, if her trip (despite her fall) bore the ripe red fruit she hoped, and Maud's astral nuptials were enough for Will Yeats's erotic love to open the vortex between planes, Ida's daemon lover might, this very night, take possession of anyone she could find to make physical love to her.

The rear alley door into the kitchen slammed, and Ida muffled her litany of curses. Upstairs, Maud was dreaming, her secret, sex-sweet whispers audible through the listening horn Ida had purchased expressly for use against the thin Hyde Park Hotel walls. For days now, she had hovered at Maud's side, waiting in her adjacent rented rooms; and only tonight, Ida having been summoned home by her husband the next morning, only now, did Maud's spiritual marriage manifest itself in a way Ida might employ. But not from her present position. If Maud's dream lasted, and Ida could pluck a lover from the London streets just one more flight of stairs below, she might bring her true love to her at last, out of Hell, into flesh—alive and bound to her.

Ida grasped the stair rail with her good hand and heaved. Her knees wobbled like a camel's, but she remained upright. She reassessed. Her flesh bloomed in a purple garden of bruises. They trellised her arms, and blossomed across her back and rump. But she could shift her weight between her legs. None of the work she had set Yeats to do—planting the seeds with MacGregor Mathers about the sleeping king—nor any of the researches she had conducted in Paris with the help of the Horoses would be necessary, if she could channel her daemon herself through the portal it seemed Maud's sex opened on the astral plane. Because it couldn't be Maud whom Will had married. It could only be Laura, the future soul, the link through time.

Ida took a careful, aching shuffle toward the final flight of stairs, but stopped when she heard whistling. Damn the fool and her dancehall tune coming in past curfew. And damn Ida, too, for her woman's form. If she were a man, the maid downstairs, caught between dismissal and the chance to win ten shillings on her back, would be easily coaxed upstairs. And if not, a man could still take what Ida sought. But not tonight. Tonight her selection must be willing, open to suggestion, and able, once mesmerized, to send his soul away. No matter. Ida had a lifetime's skill of using what little beauty she possessed. Once on the street, an unbuttoned coat over her nightdress and her loosened hair would be enough to draw a gentleman to the aid of a sleepwalking woman. Ungentlemanly opportunism would accomplish the rest.

The whistle faded into the pantry, doubtless foraging for a bite of cold dinner. Ida leaned against the stair wall and extended a leg in silent descent. Her knee knifed pain through her hip into her belly, locked, and completely gave way. Ida catapulted down the stairs into the kitchen.

"Who is there?"

A glint of blade in the black scullery and the growled question in nearly flawless English revealed the night whistler as male, but Ida's attempt at her own name issued from her lips as a dull moan. A match scratched and set against a wick, spit, and lit a man's rugged face.

"I said, who is there?"

Still unable to speak, Ida tasted the blood-filled space between her teeth and cheek and watched the cruel shadow steal across the kitchen on silent feet behind his raised candle and knife. Mayhap this was how all foreign criminals fed themselves, stealing into the sleeping kitchens of decent English houses.

The thief belted his knife and knelt beside her with a fluidity that returned Ida's voice with a scream. Or with the beginning of one, stifled by his sudden, smothering palm. "Shhhh," he cautioned in a low whiskey whisper.

Ida nodded consent.

He took his fingers from her lips and wiped the blood from them on his breeches. "Can you sit?" he whispered.

Ida nodded again, but before she could struggle upright, her body was banded by oaken arms and hoisted aloft. In two silent strides, the burglar carried her to the kitchen's long table. He kicked a chair out and seated Ida unceremoniously, catching her shoulders to hold her. "Are you steady?" He crouched before her.

Ida tried to smile.

Without warning, his large hands shifted from her shoulder, to run, surprisingly nimble, bold and deft across her body. He handled her feet and knees, twisted her wrists, stopping when she winced, and prodding the pads of her palms. He reached boldly into her hair and felt across her scalp. He poked a finger into her mouth and Ida jerked away with a squeak. He raised a menacing eyebrow and reached again between her lips. They gapped open around the digit's formidable girth, and he ran it without pressure against the fronts of her teeth.

"Would you care to tell me why a lady of your position slips down the servants' stairs at two o'clock in the morning, madam?"

"I'll scream," Ida threatened.

"No you won't." He sat back on his heels with an insolent grin. "You are escaping a reputable address, undressed, at a disreputable hour. You are late to meet a lover who has taken rooms close by."

"No."

From between a rough-stubbled jaw and hanging forelock, a pair of fierce eyes combed Ida's face. The subtle trace of accent was Russian, she decided. "Your husband—an upstanding and prosperous man, no doubt—is in your bed upstairs, and you can no longer bear the smell and the sound of his sleeping. You are out of bed only to be away from him."

Ida stifled a laugh and shook her head.

"Invent a more entertaining lie while I fetch my supper," he instructed, and vanished into the pantry with uncanny speed. He returned with a hunk of the evening's cold mutton and a bottle which he unstoppered, swigged, and passed to Ida. "You've no bones broken, but this will do you good all the same." He bit into the meat with savage teeth. "Talk."

"I must have been sleepwalking," Ida murmured.

"Sleepwalkers don't stop for coats."

"I awoke from sleeping and realized I had left a case downstairs."

Mouth full, he shook his shaggy head. "You would have used the front stairs." He swallowed and studied Ida. "No. You would have rung for someone to bring it to you."

"It was too late to ring."

He laughed. "You're a very dull liar. If you had wanted any decent thing, you would have rung. There are only two reasons to fetch for yourself what others can carry to you, and they're two blades of the same knife. Is it shame or pride, Madam, driving you abroad so stealthy and late?"

Unable to meet his bold eyes, Ida took a drink from the bottle and gasped as the liquor touched the raw, bitten places in her mouth. Her eyes filled with tears and she swallowed with a gulp, blood and whiskey mingling her father's smells and her uncle's tastes.

She hated this Russian lolling in the chair beside her while upstairs Maud dreamed a bridge across damnation that Ida must span tonight, or risk losing forever. Maud would not stay married to Yeats for long, even only spiritually. Her soul paced too restless in her seething brain.

Ida stood up and wobbled. She would have fallen, but the thief caught her once again.

She looked up into the dark at him and cursed her blindness.

He whistled softly. "I've never heard a lady swear so well."

Ida swooned against his heavy, wide chest, and enjoyed the strong arm moving to cradle her again. One of her more artful faints, it dropped her cloak from her shoulder and opened the neck of her nightdress. A slight adjustment, masked by a fevered moan, pushed her breasts into better view.

How could she have doubted her daemon would provide? He had chosen for himself this massive specimen of masculinity. Ida had been a fool, wasting time trying to escape him to the streets. How slow she had been to revise her plan, to realize the gift given when it was not where she sought. Rather than the stableboy she had thought to command, this cretin would obligingly rape her, given half an opportunity. A hard, strong paw skimmed the swells of her breasts. His breath warmed the crown of her head.

"I cannot say I do not appreciate the offer," he said with a new edge in his gruff whisper, "but you won't need to ransom your freedom from me. I didn't mean to keep you past the point I knew you were unhurt enough to leave."

Ida stayed fainted, but let her limp body press against him below where his belt was slung.

"Enough of that." He dumped her onto the chair again. "I did not mean to drive you to such desperate measures. You need not tell me anything. Go. I will not try to stop you."

"Don't you dare believe you held me against my will!" Ida glared at the towering man and took another gulp of whiskey. She held it in her mouth, and let her eyes fill up with tears, the yellow fire licking her tongue's raw places, searing them with rage and doubt.

"Were you going out for gin?"

Ida nodded and let a tear run down her cheek.

"Drink up then, *cherie*. I would not hold that against you."

Ida tipped the bottle to her lips again and drank. She extended it to the tower of man standing over her. He sat and drank, swallowing the flaming amber easily.

"You're still lying," he observed.

"Yes," she said at last.

"Why did you offer yourself to me just now?"

"I thought you intended to take what you wanted, and I would rather give it away myself than have it taken."

"You hold your virtue in such small esteem?"

"No. But it's not really mine, is it? It is my husband's because God says he has a right to me, or yours because you are armed and I am a woman."

"I would never hurt a woman."

"You will," said Ida, angry because she knew he spoke the truth. "Or you will when you have one."

His smile surprised Ida. Not the whiteness of his strong teeth, not the brutal beauty of his lips, but the sadness of it. "I have had women," he said.

"No," Ida snapped, angrier for his tenderness. "You have never had a wife or daughter. You have never truly owned a woman."

"If God ever blesses me with either"—danger now laced his sadness—"I still will not own them."

Ida laughed without sound. "Mayhap I offered myself to you because I wanted to."

One harsh eyebrow rose in surprise, but he did not accuse her of lying again. Slowly, the other brow joined it. He leaned forward in his chair. "Was it a man, then, you were going out to find?"

"It was."

The whistle came again, deep and slow. "In Russia, I read every issue of *The Pearl*, with its stories of wanton English ladies, but I never dared believe they were true."

It was Ida's turn to be surprised. Mr. Lazenby's magazine of "facetiae and voluptuous reading" was well above the reach of common thieves.

"I am married to a much older man."

"You lie to me again."

"Fornicating Christ on the bleeding cross!"

He chuckled low in his throat and sat back in his chair. "I should have known the first time you said that, you were no ordinary woman."

"I have been married to the same man for too many years."

"And you ventured out tonight for one who was not your husband."

"Yes."

"You should be going then."

Ida masked her surprise with a coquette's smile. "You are not my husband," she observed.

"I am not. But I am more than *not* just one man."

"Of course," she sneered. "You must be the hunter, the seducer, and all your conquests come—pure and persuaded, almost unwilling—

to your bed." Ida stood up, and when her legs weakened, she steadied herself with a hand on the rough table. "You may read your stories of women who give their bodies freely, in pursuit of their own pleasure, but you, in truth, would fear such a maenad."

He stood slowly, exaggerating the difference in their heights and strength. "Is pleasure all you were seeking?"

"Yes."

"I wish you would not lie to me."

Ida drew breath to scream and found his hand across her mouth again. "I stopped you from waking this house once in concern for your reputation. Do it again, and I will let them all, concierge and chambermaids, find you out of bed and underdressed, and leave it to your limited imagination to answer their questions."

Ida closed her mouth behind his hand.

He did not smile. "You have lied to and insulted me. I should put you out of doors like a yowling tomcat to find what you need to-night, but you are too bruised to walk and haven't the sense to avoid murdering." In an easy swoop, he gathered Ida into his powerful arms and started up the backstairs with her. At the first landing, he set her on her battered feet.

"What is your name?"

"Ida Jameson Rowley."

"Had you lied, I would have left you here."

Instead, he took Ida's face in his huge hands and kissed her with a deliberate and insistent mouth. Not a hurried kiss, but not the easy lapping of her afternoon ten years ago with Maud, nor the furtive mouthing of her husband. The thief's long and thorough explora-tion made Ida's lips want to answer, and without willing it, her bat-tered mouth responded, her tongue tasting cold flesh and whiskey.

Then she was in the air against his chest again, the steps swim-ming past, two at a time, beneath her. His rough stubble brushed her cheek, his voice spoke hot in her ear. "What room is yours, Madam Rowley?"

"Four," she said against his neck.

The thief strode to Ida's door and put her down again. She leaned against the jamb and waited, afraid he might depart, but after listening to the silent hall, he turned the knob and walked into her rooms. Ida tottered after him.

He prodded the dying fire and seated himself in the best chair beside it.

"Take your coat off, Ida Jameson Rowley," he whispered.

Ida let it fall to the floor.

"Why are you in London?"

"I am visiting a friend."

"Open your nightdress."

Ida's stiff fingers worked slowly, unbuttoning down to her navel the stiff white cotton. Beneath its split halves, her hungry nipples hardened.

"Is your friend the woman in the room next door?"

"Yes."

"Put your hands on either side of your nightdress and show yourself to me."

Ida's hands moved of their own volition, curling around the cloth, pulling it open. Her breasts, small and needle-pointed, stood out from her chest stretching to meet him. "You heard her sex cries through your wall?"

Ida opened her eyes and stared at him. How did he know of the noises Maud made? Between Ida's legs, a thick bubble of anticipation was inflating.

"I have Russian hearing," he said with an easy smile. "Take that terrible thing off."

The buttons and ruffles fell to the ground, eliciting a low rumble of appreciation from the mysterious blaggard Ida was no longer certain she was seducing. Her arms felt extraneous. She clasped her hands before her as she had been taught to stand for singing. His eyes caressed her naked breasts, and Ida swayed, dizzy with the pleasure of it.

"Your friend next door has been enjoying a secret assignation while you, invited to visit, but unattended to, listened from the room next door, until loneliness drove you out of doors for a lover of your own."

"Yes."

He rose to leave.

"My friend next door sleeps alone," Ida quickly corrected.

The elegant, questioning eyebrow arched, but he said nothing.

"And I want to share her dreams."

"Untie the drawstring of your drawers."

Was he trying to humiliate her, forcing her to strip for him? Was he punishing her for lying? But the bubble of anticipation bloomed between her legs, the lips of her sex thickening around it. She wanted this. She wanted him to strip and punish her. Wanted him to meet her shame with shaming, her anger with his rage. Ida unlaced her knickers.

"Is she dreaming of sex with a man you also love?"

"No." Truth came unreadily to her lips, but she dared not lie for fear he would leave her panting on the hearth rug. She knew he was more than the first man she had found.

"Come to me and turn around."

Ida pushed away the footstool, and turned her back to him.

"Put your hands under the fabric of your drawers."

Without meaning to, Ida let a whimper slip from her lips, and felt her face flush pink.

"Sweet Christ, you have a magnificent rump." The Russian rasp sat heavier in his deep whisper. "You like my eyes on you."

It was not a question.

"Yes," Ida said, glad he could not see her reddening face.

"Push the fabric down."

She did.

"Open your legs."

Ida gasped. Her entire face caught fire. Shame and arousal twisted her breasts and filled her swelling sex. She took a tiny step apart, and the night air licked the exposed wet flesh.

"Your friend is dreaming of sex with a man you know, but do not love, and yet you hope to partake in her dreams by giving yourself to me."

"Yes."

"I will leave you, charming though you are right now, if you lie to me again. I swear it."

A trembling took Ida, knowing his eyes roamed her body.

"I believe my friend's dreams open doorways to other times and places, other possibilities," she said.

"Put your hands on your knees."

Ida slid her icy hands down her thighs, rounding her body into an ugly, withered coil.

"Arch your back." A thick trickle slid down the flesh of Ida's thigh. Still, he waited.

With a little sob, Ida cocked her ass into the air.

She quivered, impossibly exposed, her tiny bunghole squeezed and winking, her sex pushed open. She tried to pull it closed, but it pulsed like a gilled fish.

"What do you mean, *other times and places?*" he asked.

And Ida didn't care what vows she broke, what secrets she sold. She didn't care if she never got within twenty miles of Maud's dreams again. Her entire constellation of desire strung between her hanging breasts and gasping sex, her humiliated longing and this man.

"I once channeled a spirit from a hundred years from now into my friend while she was mesmerized," Ida's voice rang high and twisted in her own ears. "I—"

But all her breath had flown away.

The hard tip of his huge finger pressed against the opening of her sex. Her thighs knocked. "Oh," was all her strangled voice could squawk.

"Continue." His breath caressed her asshole.

"I have learned to send her soul away from her body, and trail it with my own," she panted.

"Push back onto my finger."

"I, I . . ."

Ida's body convulsed. Her breasts hung heavy from her chest, huge and weighted by her need. Her sex twitched against the invading finger. Her ass stretched open. How could she do what he asked of her? Must she fuck herself on his unmoving finger, push onto its girth and summons? She would go mad.

"I have seen the place spirits go—"

"Push back onto my finger."

Ida pushed.

His finger mashed liquid from her sodden tissues, forcing itself—no it was she who forced it—deeper, wringing squeezing spasms from her stretching sex, until her impalement was complete. She drew a shuddering breath.

"Shall I bring you off like this?" He fractionally curled his finger.

Ida moaned. She had emptied many men. She had forced the helpless spasms from them, their abandoned grunting a welcome sign her work was done.

"No," she pleaded.

He pulled his finger out so quickly Ida's sex made a humiliating slurp. He slapped her hard across the ass.

She screamed, but bit the sound back at once.

"I said I would not stop you," he said, and smacked her burning flesh with his broad hand again.

Ida knew, in that instant, she was going to come. She would orgasm, open before this man she did not know, with nothing in her pussy, no touch upon her bursting breasts. His palm cracked a third time against her shuddering flesh and Ida, lost to caring, grasped her sex with her open palm, twisted herself upright and came without a sound.

The thief stood and turned her by shoulders, still shaking in silent sobs that might be laughter. She dropped her reeling head against his wide, immobile chest.

"You are an extraordinary woman, Ida Jameson Rowley," he whispered into her hair. "And I believe you."

She looked up into his face, harsh and solemn. When he kissed her now, he closed his eyes.

Ida fell into his kissing, her pale nipples against his black coat, her stair-bruised arms closing over his strong chest. When he stretched her body by the fireplace, she saw a tender admiration in his eyes. Never had anyone looked at her so.

His body, as he shucked his clothes from it, was lean as a horse's and as large. He gathered Ida against his strength and sucked the sorest places where stair edges and banister had bashed her.

Graceful in his arms, Ida twined over his muscled thighs and strong chest like an eel through water. He was under her, and then above, his mouth an obliterating exploration, diving and lapping until the tide pulled inside her, too.

"You can set a soul free of its body?" he asked.

"Yes."

"You know the secrets of where the wandering spirits go?"

"I do."

"And all the secret words and phrases?"

"Yes."

"Tell me."

He rolled his body under hers and set Ida astride his broad hips.

"What?"

"Anything true." His hands held her by the hip bones, his cock a rigid oar on the hard plane of his corded belly. "Tell me everything."

Ida looked down at his cock. For the first time, she understood the beauty, the magic, of the phallus—the ritual object made of leather or carved totem on the altar—in its true living perfection laid bare beneath her. She took it in her hand. It pulled against her fingers. She squeezed it, and he groaned. She stroked it, mesmerized.

"Close your eyes," she whispered.

She watched her fingers close around him, her narrow, gold-encircled thumb at the center of the high, hard head, and pulled down the shaft until he shuddered.

"Close your eyes tightly—tightly—and keep them closed," she recited mindlessly, repeating her hand's sliding stroke again to draw him, bowstring taut, between her trembling thighs. His cock, harder, huger than his finger, pushed into Ida's sex, slow and shuddering. She aped her hand's stroke with her sex.

For a single perfect moment, Ida held his body in hers alive, flooded in pleasure and beauty.

He opened his eyes.

Ida stared into their flat gray surfaces, without light or depth, without reflection or sight.

Did she shake her head? Did she whisper, "No"?

His hands collapsed to his chest, curling all his muscle-wrapped strength around it, but they could not restart his seized heart, nor stop his agonizing death. He died with his cock still hard inside her.

Ida screamed.

She screamed again knowing, and not stopping, that people would come, that she would be ruined, the body of a dead Russian thief beneath her.

She took his handsome face, pain-twisted, in her hands, still screaming. Maybe it was then she cried, "No." Maybe her daemon could believe it was he whom she mourned. Too powerful a spirit for a common man, or too wicked for a good one. Either way, they had both abandoned Ida.

She howled.

She hated running feet in the nighttime, but could still only wrap her arms around the man she had killed, and cry. She curled her body like a fetus over his. But it was gone.

Ash fell from her womb, and all she could smell was sulfur and her own blood in her mouth, naked and pinned to nothing before the cold fire.

She held the door open, her nightgown pulled back on, to the swarm of sleepy housemaids who chattered and cooed and brought hot water bottles for the missus alone in her iced-over rooms with the faulty, sulfur-smoking fireplace and bad dreams. Management apologizes, there had been no problems with the flue before, and the night will be gratis, of course, but has anyone seen the Russian prince staying in the double suite upstairs? His rooms are likewise full of smoke, but he is gone.

from *Ulysses*
(set in Dublin on June 16, 1904)
by James Joyce

1922

Well: slainte! Around the slabbed tables the tangle of wined breaths and grumbling gorges. His breath hangs over our saucestained plates, the green fairy's fang thrusting between his lips. Of Ireland, the Dalcassians, of hopes, conspiracies, of Arthur Griffith now. To yoke me as his yokefellow, our crimes our common cause. You're your father's son. I know the voice. His fustian shirt, sanguineflowered, trembles its Spanish tassels at his secrets. M. Drumont, famous journalist, Drumont, know what he called queen Victoria? Old hag with the yellow teeth. *Vieille ogresse with the dents jaunes.* Maud Gonne, beautiful woman, *La Patrie*, M. Millevoye, Félix Faure, know how he died? Licentious men. The froeken, *bonne à tout faire*, who rubs male nakedness in the bath at Upsala. *Moi faire*, she said. *Tous les messieurs.* Not this *Monsieur*, I said. Most licentious custom. Bath a most private thing. I wouldn't let my brother, not even my own brother, most lascivious thing. Green eyes, I see you. Fang, I feel. Lascivious people.

The blue fuse burns deadly between hands and burns clear. Loose tobacco shreds catch fire: a flame and acrid smoke light our corner. Raw facebones under his peep of day boy's hat. How the head centre got away, authentic version. Got up as a young bride, man, veil orangeblossoms, drove out the road to Malahide. Did, faith. Of lost leaders, the betrayed, wild escapes. Disguises, clutched at, gone, not here.

10

LOOKING FOR THE FACE I HAD
BEFORE THE WORLD WAS MADE

Gaze no more in the bitter glass
The demons, with their subtle guile,
Lift up before us when they pass,
Or only gaze a little while;
For there a fatal image grows
That the stormy night receives,
Roots half hidden under snows,
Broken boughs and blackened leaves.
For all things turn to barrenness
In the dim glass the demons hold,
The glass of outer weariness,
Made when God slept in times of old.
There, through the broken branches, go
The ravens of unresting thought;
Flying, crying, to and fro,
Cruel claw and hungry throat,
Or else they stand and sniff the wind,
And shake their ragged wings; alas!
Thy tender eyes grow all unkind:
Gaze no more in the bitter glass.

—from "The Two Trees" by W. B. Yeats

Charlie and I sit like a pair of trained seals down the desk from Amy and her PowerPoint bucket of fish. The bank boys thumb their paper packets, and everyone drinks sparkling water in discreet sips and smaller smiles. The final slide stays on the wall, our logo:

$$I + D^2$$

(Identity + Definition) (Information + Design)

But all of us—the four of them and three of us—are all watching Mr. Shell. He sits on his back, hands folded over his belly, and frowns. Amy asks again if he has any questions, but he just shakes his jowly head.

"We want to look modern," he grumbles at last. "Bunch of old-timey folks in my grandma's dresses aren't gonna do that for us."

"We do have the contemporary pictures alongside them, Mr. Shell," Amy points out, sliding the eleven-by-seventeen print of Victoria and me in our black-and-white, inverse-but-identical wedding dresses across the table. "And bear in mind, they are real people, not models, staff members and family friends. NorPac bank customers."

Mr. Shell chews the air, unimpressed. "But where's the high-tech wizardry? Shouldn't there be stuff moving around on a website?"

"We could certainly animate portions, if you'd like. Cross fade between the old and new, maybe morph between the faces . . ."

"I don't want cartoons. I want sophisticated. We're trying to look relevant here."

"Don't look relevant, be relevant," I mutter.

Under the table, Charlie places a cautioning hand on my leg. Amy shoots me a cub-clubbing glance, but I keep not shutting up, even though I know I should.

"The cutting-edge design work, the stuff winning industry awards, delivers exactly this sort of undersell. If you want to play catch-up, slather Flash over every click and see how quickly people get frustrated with your UI."

"My what?" Shell's raw hands clutch his distended middle.

"Online user experience is the new customer service. It's the gorgeous teller who knows everyone's name and sends them home with the right number of lollipops for the kids. The future is all about ease-of-use and customization. That's what people want. That's what will make you relevant."

NorPac's president smoothes the shirt over his belly and examines me with rheumy eyes that chill the film of sweat I've sprouted with embarrassment for my overly emotional outburst.

"Well, thank you for your input," Shell says. "We'll discuss all our options and be in touch."

And that is how accounts are lost. The prospective client feigns polite interest, we file out, and his lackey emails later, saying our proposal, although interesting and well thought-out, wasn't quite what they were looking for. It's all very nice. No one shouts or argues. Nobody acts like they care too much. Everyone wants to be likeable. We're grown up. Modern. Nice.

I stand with Charlie, wickedly, passionately angry, waiting for Amy to gather her things.

She doesn't say anything in the elevator, and we stop in the lobby of the tall building to study our good shoes against the slick black stone.

"Lunch?" Amy suggests, and Charlie and I fall into lockstep beside her across the courtyard. The sidewalk narrows under new trees, and we end up single-file, like a miniature army, in a line behind Amy to Dim Sum.

"I'm sorry," I say after the waiter leaves.

She shrugs, embarrassed. "It was already gone."

"I'm sorry anyway."

"It's okay, really." She meets my eyes this time. "I understand. You're exhausted. You put a lot of yourself into this one, Laura. You delayed your honeymoon, worked nights and weekends. Hell, it was your face on one of them."

On two, actually, but I don't say anything. I'm remembering Maud and Will's father. I have never been to a dinner in Portland where anyone got angry. Not over politics or religion. Not that anyone could see, anyway. When did passion become passé?

"You ought to call Amit," Charlie says. "He'll have your honeymoon re-booked before you get home."

"No lie," I say. "The man is efficient."

"And eager for a little one-on-one."

Of course, no one around the Yeats table ever said anything that overt, either.

I call Amit. "I blew it," I say to his voicemail. But Charlie takes the phone away and leaves a more detailed message. He also tells my husband where we're eating, in case we stay late. It's a good idea.

"It was a cool campaign," Amy said. "Don't take it personally."

"Why not?"

Amy and Charlie stare at me.

"I mean, seriously. Why not take it personally? It's my work—our work." I nod to include Charlie. I want to, but can't quite bring myself to call it *our art.*

Charlie pokes a dumpling. "I know, sweetie, of course it is. You got invested. That's why Amy gives you the big gigs. Because she knows you're going to give it everything you've got, right?"

Amy gives me her quick, professional smile. "That's right."

She's managing me.

I am ashamed in a flood of hot, sticky prickles. I've always taken pride in not doing the temperamental artist thing, in bringing work in on-time and under-drama.

"But, darling"—Charlie refills my wine glass—"even if you love fucking, when you take cash for sex, you're a whore. This is your job. Don't take it home with you."

"I spend more time at work than at home."

"Not for the next two weeks, you don't." Amy is crisp. "You're officially off the clock. Honeymoon vacation starts now!"

On cue, Amit strides through the door and sweeps the empty dining room with his dark eyes. His beautiful face is marked with concern, and he leans over the booth to kiss me. "You okay?"

"See?" I say. "Amit takes it personally, too."

"He takes you personally," Charlie leers from under his unruly brows.

Amit backhands him on the shoulder, and Charlie scoots over to make room across the table from me. Amit works for a big, creaky corporation where the workers are treated like schoolchildren, and thus do what is asked for rather than what's needed. He hates it, but the money's great, there's health insurance, and he's never tempted to bring anything home.

"I need to get back to Abby." Amy hands the company Amex to Charlie. "Stay as long as you want, it's on us." She smiles at me. "Laura, you've done great work for I+D, and we want you to take an extra week for your honeymoon. Paid time off."

I stand up and hug her good-bye, thinking maybe *nice* isn't so bad. My boss is a single mother, my coworker is married to his man. Oscar Wilde and baby farming seem more than only one hundred years away.

Amit is grinning when I sit back down. Winning the pitch would have meant another month before we could leave.

"Italy, here you come!" Charlie winks. "You just need to change the dates on your tickets, right?"

"Actually," Amit says, "I've been thinking about Ireland."

The second time Ida rang for the parlormaid, the little brass bell flew out of her hand and chipped a divot in the morning room's new plaster mantel.

"Ma'am?"

Ida stared from the girl to the fireplace, unable to make a sound. The sudden shock of terror enveloping her kept seeping deeper in.

"You must run right away and fetch a policeman," Ida finally whispered.

"Ma'am." The girl bobbed a quick curtsy, and ice swam into Ida's lungs at the absence of surprise in the simpleton's voice.

"No." Ida stopped her. "First, turn out the gas. And lock and bolt up the house."

"Ma'am." A chit from some western fishing town, she was a new hire with eyes like the creatures her father drew from the ocean to put on her plate. "Go!" Ida shrieked. "No, I'm sorry. I didn't mean to raise my voice, Mary."

"Maggie."

"Maggie, of course. Maggie, I'm not angry with you dear."

"No, ma'am."

"Please go now."

"Yes, ma'am."

The door closed behind her perfidious back, and Ida could not breathe. She clutched the arms of the chair from which she had presided over a generous tea just a mere half hour hence, unaware, innocent.

Well, no. Ignorant.

Rage at her own blindness galvanizing her at last, Ida beat the padded chair arms with her closed fists only once, and sprang for the sideboard. Poisoned pearls in the silver shell of her card tray, the four white slips which announced her morning's callers rested pale and ominous. Dr. Sanbourne had rung after nine. Dr. Linley not an hour later. Their interest had flattered her, curious as they were about Ida's expertise with mesmerism, intrigued by its possible medical application, they had said.

How had she, so skilled in reading the subtle signs of secret nature, missed the gross marking of a man's intent? Two medical men in independent interviews. It was all that was necessary to commit her as mad. That and the signature of any male relative.

Ida stifled a scream and ran up the stairs to her room. How could she be anything but terrified? Yet any outward sign of distress would only prove the case against her. She had never guessed her brother's embarrassment over her mystic studies would extend to this. She tore into her hidden library for the name of *The Spiritualist*'s editor, certain it was in that magazine she had read the cautionary tale of a woman confined to a lunatic asylum for her occult beliefs. "Nothing is easier," she remembered the poor creature having written, than to dispose of "women in general, and wives in particular."

Ida scrawled two notes to be sent by telegram, one to the magazine's editor, one to her husband, and reached out to ring for Stephen, but withdrew her reality-stung hand. What sane woman would throw about shreds of newsprint for the maids to clean? She dropped to the ground, gathering the loose magazine pages to her bosom like a pauper grubbing carriage-tossed coins. She despaired of the job and clattered down the steps to find the stableboy.

The kitchen staff jumped like caged hens when Ida tore into their belowstairs sanctum.

"What are you gaping at?" she shrieked. "No, never mind. Stephen, take these telegrams to the office and wait for a reply. Speak to no one on your way. Return with all haste or I shall make certain . . . Return quickly and I shall give you a shilling."

The wretch beamed and fled.

Ida's wild glare swung from the cook to Kate to little Brigit. They stood in the gloom of an inside afternoon when all the lights have been ordered put out. The bell rang and Ida screamed again. The servants jumped, and she clamped her teeth together to silence herself.

"Shall I go to the door, ma'am?" the parlormaid ventured.

"No!" Ida looked from her to the cook, a crone who had worked for Ida since before her marriage. If anyone in her household owed her fealty, it would be this shapeless drudge. "No, Kate. Stephen will return soon with a telegram from Mr. Rowley to clarify things. In the meantime, we mustn't allow those men inside."

From the cook's cataract-fogged eyes, lightning struck Ida below the sternum. Their bright flash of triumphant hate illuminated a lifescape more blighted than nightmare.

"Cook," Ida's voice echoed behind her own blind eyes. "If the policeman I've sent Meggie to fetch demands to see the lunacy certificate, will he find my husband's signature upon it?"

The old cow tipped her waddled, defiant chin. "I'm sure I couldn't say, ma'am."

The bell rang again, insolently loud and long. The cook made an arthritic curtsey. "I'll just be having Kate answer the door now, ma'am."

Ida stood gasping.

Cook abhorred her.

Her husband believed her a dangerous lunatic, or was willing to

attest to such, to be rid of her. The Horoses, the closest approxima-
tion Ida had to respectable friends, had just been arrested in France
for rape. Of the many who owed her favors, most would find her dire
state a convenient excuse for forfeiture, rather than an opportunity
for repayment. Yeats, whose dependence she had nurtured now for
years, no longer needed her; and Maud, ever foolish and shortsighted,
had renounced all work on the spiritual plane in preference to her
futile publications and speaking tours.

Maud's last letter to Ida, some months ago, spoke of the *strange
places, from which I, less darkening in thought, if more daring in action, than Willie, drew back, least it might lead me away and not into the heart of Ireland's hidden
strength.* The fool! But had Maud written from France or Ireland? How
quickly could she come to Ida's aid?

Hearing the doctor, his two burly assistants, and the parlormaid
parading the hall above her head on their pallbearers' feet, Ida spun
with enough speed to startle the wicked cook and little Brigit into
inaction.

"May the souls of your children rot in their stillborn graves!" Ida
shrieked and scrambled up the backstairs. Up three flights on the
narrow, twisting wood she scampered to the quiet of her bedchamber.
She hesitated only a moment, panting, before she dug with resolute
fingers into the stacks of books—expensive, rare, and powerful—that
comprised the library hidden in her massive wardrobe.

She raked the volumes onto the ground and leapt until she
grasped the ornate copula at the wardrobe's front corner. With one
hand clawing that, and the other on the silver door pull, Ida tugged
with all her frail, woman's strength until the overwrought piece tipped
up onto its two spindly side legs, teetered, and fell with a splintering
crash before the door. It lay, disemboweled of her precious books,
spilling knowledge and power and a last, insane bid for rescue over
Mr. Rowley's expensive parquet.

There was no time to search for an address. Ida's little writing
desk trembled with the force of her desperate pen.

The door crashed against the wardrobe's back.

"Mrs. Rowley? Ida? This is Dr. Sanbourne. I'd just like a quick word, madam."

Ida must not stop writing to curse him.

"Ida, your husband was certain you would wish to avoid making a spectacle of yourself."

The wardrobe sustained a battering series of blows, but Ida sealed the letter and crammed it into her bosom. Maud, she knew, kept a small glass vial of poison on a cord around her neck against the possibility of capture on one of her vainglorious spy trips. She had offered to procure another for her confederate once, but Ida had laughed and told the truth. "No, thank you, my love," she had said. "I should forget, and drink it on a whim one day." Now, she wished she had accepted.

"Mrs. Rowley, I'm Dr. Linley. My wife and I run a quiet, respectable establishment in Sussex. I do believe you'd find it quite restorative there."

Ida plucked the wicked little letter opener from her stationary box and thrust it into the bodice of her dress, between her bosom and the stiff fabric. It would do some damage to one of the worthies chasing her, at least. The wardrobe shuddered, hemorrhaging wood splinters and book pages as the door bashed it with the dull repetition of whip tongues biting into servile flesh. It would not sustain much more. Ida peered through each of her bedroom windows and threw up the sash of the farthest street-side one. She wadded up the trailing lace and, terrified, clutched the curtain, against the sealed envelope and the letter opener, to her chest. She poked a scrawny leg out the window.

The wardrobe rang hollowly, a tuneless wooden bell.

Ida shifted her weight from the trembling leg she stood upon to the thigh resting on the window ledge and the fistfuls of fabric in her arms.

The curtain rod groaned beneath her weight, but held, even as the wardrobe's back gave way.

"Mrs. Rowley, if I am unconvinced you are a reasonable woman,

I will have to refuse your husband's request for your accommodation in our private sanatorium. And I am afraid, my dear, he might then feel compelled to house you at St. Patrick's."

Ida's mouth filled with bile. She had prowled Dublin's ancient hospital for the insane once, looking for a fabled seer, and been disgusted by the grotesque mad and syphilitic. That must never be her fate. She pushed her forehead against the window glass and eased one shaking hand from the bunched-up curtains. The billowing fabric flapped indecorously out the gaping window, but Ida didn't dare lift her clawed hand from the window ledge to push it back inside. Her stomach churned and twisted, coiling with fear at the drop beneath, and with nausea at the treacle-kind voice of the man whose minions had broken the back of her secret library.

"Mrs. Rowley, I have a policeman here. He's examined my warrant and will take you in charge himself, if you will not come along with me discreetly."

Ida eased her head under the sash and into the icy January wind. Only her bony knuckles remained indoors. She pressed her slippered feet to the cold brick wall and drew a long, knifing breath through her reddening nose.

Ida Jameson took flight.

Time, always malevolent toward her, ground to a frozen crawl. Every splintering second twisted into a still life of Ida moving—ice under glass. She pushed her body straight from the window, arms splayed, knees rigid. The upward rush of winter billowed the silk skirts of her dress and the sleeves of her jacket like so much laundry from an East End slum. She sailed, belly down, flapping fruitlessly as a sky-thrown, wing-snipped chicken, to hit the leafless branches of the spreading tree below in a single clump. Ida hung, not gracefully swinging from a bough, but pinioned on a thousand spiking, scratching tines of twig, like a cat too deep for blackberries. Her polished boulevard stood empty. All decent Londoners sat to their suppers, at home or with their mistresses, closed within the frowning edifices, beside smug fires, while Ida drowned in sticks. The scratches on her face stung, hot blood in the cold air. She scrambled and plucked, working her feet onto a stronger branch, pulling her hair and clothes free, climbing down.

She stood, cheap rag and bone, before her own expensive, bolted front door until the pavement bled snow up through her slippers, and the doctor's beefy jowls emerged from the window overhead. Ida ran. Flailing down the icy Kensington sidewalk, trailing specks of blood and strands of hair, splinters of tree and streams of branch-ribboned silk, Ida wheeled down the graceful terrace like a seizure at a funeral.

In the winter silence, the ragged, angry choking of her cold-shocked lungs rattled through her with the sound of polished black shoes down her front hall stairs. She spied the postal pillar box as she reeled around the corner, red and virginal in the thickening snow. Ida groped in her collapsing bosom for the envelope, kissed it and pushed it—flecked with spittle and blood—into the upright crimson column. It was sacred now.

Nothing was sacred.

The doctor would thrust his fist inside and drag her secret out.

Her husband would have the postbox opened and her letter found.

The letter opener slipped out of Ida's numb fingers pointing at the letter box to give her away. She kicked it with a sodden toe, and it scuttered up the sidewalk. She ran after it, fell, and crawled to bat it, like a blind kitten, away from her.

And so they took her. A dangerous lunatic. Lifted from her game, played with a knife, not a ball—a phallus, not a womb—for a child's toy, and sobbing. They took her, pliant and serious, back to her house to undress and redress her for winter travel, the doctor watchful and upright behind his thick glasses and beneath his pressed trousers.

After the train ride, there would be a thorough physical examination, and tuppence for Kate, Cook, and the copper. Tea all around once the mistress left—the rabble in the upstairs parlor with the good plates, laughing, telling tales, and free.

And Maud, returning triumphant from speaking before a French audience alongside a new and dangerous Irishman, would find a crumpled, bloodstained letter, and put the ugly thing aside.

"Seriously? Ireland?"

The idea has stuck in my throat since Amit mentioned it two hours ago. I throw a quick look behind me, but Charlie has already melted into the warm rain Amit and I are walking through, home from Dim Sum.

"Why Ireland?" I ask my husband.

"Because it's where you're from."

"I'm from New Jersey."

"You know what I mean." Amit takes my hand and beams at me through the street's damp light. He walks in the rain the way he makes love. "Ireland is where you're from genetically."

Ireland is where I go when I fall asleep. When, irresponsibly, I lose consciousness or let it wander off, it wanders there.

"I don't know that," I say.

"Bullshit."

"I don't. My adoption records are sealed tighter than a spaceship."

"You've always said you're Irish. You look Irish."

"I know, but it's sort of a fake. *Irish* is sexier than *European mutt*, and it saves explaining being adopted. People get all weird when you tell them that. They always say, *Oh, I'm sorry*, like it's cancer."

"Did I say *sorry* when you told me?"

"Probably." But it pleases me he thinks I look Irish. My natural hair color is between dark auburn and ash blond. I dye it black, and I like it. I wear it short and smart. Very urban-looking, I think, but maybe I'll try red next time. Maud's shade would be too rich on my skin, but something a little cooler might work. I'll ask Grant.

"Ireland would make a great honeymoon. We could do one of those Joyce pub crawls, rent a car, drive the country, stay in little bed-and-breakfasts. Very romantic." He elbows me gently in the ribs.

I've seen Ireland through the window of the Dublin–Sligo train. I've seen the famine cottages and the Neolithic tomb at Newgrange. And last night, I gave my word to marry Will Yeats there. What would happen if my two honeymoons coincided—or collided—in that country's savage romance?

"It's not like we could retrace my roots, you know. I don't have any."

"But that'd be part of the fun, yeah? Because you don't know which village or hilltop is in your blood, anything you see could be yours, right? I mean the whole country would be a possibility for you."

I grin at my husband through the shadowy dusk. I love his optimism, his blind courage. How can I be tempted to use our honeymoon to chase another man? What the hell is wrong with me?

"I'm not a changeling, you know, some weird, magical Irish baby left on my parent's doorstep. I really do come from Jersey. Or the tristate area, anyway," I say. "Just because I'm not excessively close to my family, like some people, doesn't mean I'm pining subconsciously for the motherland."

"Hey, my folks have been gone a whole week." He pulls me against his side, and my arm wraps around him. Under my palm and fingers, his muscular waist undulates with the relaxed and easy stride of his long legs. "It could be a really good experience for you," he says into my hair.

It could. It could also be a terrible idea to layer my dark sleep-life over my real awake one, to be in the same places with Amit and Will, with only time between them. It might open, crack—even just an instant—and my two lives collapse into each other. Time could, or I could. That either seems equally possible should worry me more than it does.

"Do you ever wonder," I ask my husband as we turn onto our stoplight-illuminated street, "about what's up that road?"

"Which one?"

"The one we're about to cross." I point ahead to the only road intersecting our busy, blinking thoroughfare without a crosswalk, signal, or street-name sign.

"I don't come home this way much."

We stop at the corner and look both ways down the quiet, darker street. Without the traffic and the storefronts, it's fully night in each direction.

"Want to check it out?" he asks, looking left, away from me. When he looks back, I push myself onto the balls of my feet to kiss him.

"Not tonight," I say.

We cross the untraveled street, and by the time we're in the elevator up, its mystery of shadows and disjointed midnights hang distant as my college romances and postgraduate heartbreaks. Amit leaves our long cityscape windows unveiled and gets us each a beer. We sit on the sofa looking out at the night.

"Italy would be safer," I say.

"You mean emotionally?"

I nod. Maybe my dreams are a premonition of a man I'll meet if I go to Ireland. I fell in love with a dream man on my wedding night. What if I meet a real one on my honeymoon?

I toy with the label of my beer, unable to look at Amit. His fingers are gentle through my black hair. Crazy in love is still crazy. And I'm responsible for a marriage now, a weighty thing to carry, like a car or a condo, something with a maintenance schedule and insurance policies paid against loss. Or theft.

Not that the insurance company's "replacement value" for things ever replaces their actual value. A replacement ring in not the one you married with, not the one your grandmother wore. It's never the stuff, it's what it means. It's the children you didn't have with the last man you didn't marry. It's the dreams you kill that bloody your hands, and the roads you turn down you can't wake up from. Is adultery—that magic, archaic word—one of those one-way sins? Even if my body isn't committing anything?

"I want to see Ireland, but Italy would be smarter right now."

Amit whispers kisses against my temple. "It's our honeymoon. Let's go with *want* over *smart*, okay?"

"Does it have to be a choice?"

"Everything is a choice." His fingers move through the tiny buttons of my expensive silk pitch blouse. "NorPac made the wrong choice. I made the right one."

Right and wrong.

Want and think.

Unforgivable.

Amit's strong, dark palm disappears under the fabric of my shirt, sliding across the delicate mesh of my bra, and my attention drops into my body, away from coherent lines of questioning and images of Mr. Shell and Amy.

I can feel Will wanting me.

My husband closes thumb and forefinger on my nipple, already standing up for him. If I shut my eyes, it will become Will's hand. Can I stay safe in the light and still invite the shadow in? Can I only *play* with darkness?

Amit's hand cups my breast, kneading and stroking. He lifts it free of the confining lace, raises it like a chalice to his lips, head bowed to taste it. The lightless glow of increased blood-flow raises heat beneath his crisscrossing tongue, and my legs push open under my too-stylish skirt.

I am married to two men, in love with two men. Can I choose both and not between?

I close my eyes and take him, dreaming our shared past—or future—deeply, strongly between my thighs, all the way to Ireland.

From the transcripts of court trials and letters of Louisa Lowe

1871

Mr. Wilkes condemned me "because all spiritualists are mad"—ipso facto, irrespective of their conduct in life; and now I am indefinitely re-consigned to this hideous doom—this lingering death in life, this moral torture of incarceration among maniacs—on pretexts that would not deceive a child.

It is now about eighteen months since I became convinced of the truth of Modern Spiritualism that is, of the reality of an unseen, impalpable agent acting on persons and material objects. I attended a séance at Mrs. Mary Marshall's, and saw a table tilt and rap in a wonderful way . . . Therefore I tried to develop in myself the passive-writing power, and after some weeks of daily, short solitary séances, unintelligible strokes gave way to letters, and passive writing recorded the names of all I loved best in Spirit-land, with many sweet words of affection and comfort. Soon, very soon, after this I became a fully-developed writing medium, of unusual power I believe . . .

. . . [T]hey caught me up and incarcerated me . . . because two sapient doctors chose to say spirits were non-existent, or, at any rate, incapable of communicating with man. What shall be said of the stolid, heartless indifference to human suffering that inflicted moral torture of eighteen months on a mind they must have known to be perfectly fit for self-government?

Two Childhood Friends Meet Again Under Sad Circumstances—a parent's funeral mayhap. Maud checked her hair in the mirror, and Ida swept into the room holding out her arms.

"Maud!" she cried through a sad, brave smile. "So good of you to come." Her small, buttoned boots rang sane and sharp across the new, hard, hygienic lino.

"Ida!" Maud's perfunctory embrace softened in relief. "How long has it been?"

Over Maud's fashionable arm, Ida caught a reflected glimpse of her faded, unraveled self, and turned away. "How long, indeed?"

She waved at the tea-things in invitation and sat. "How long since I wrote pleading for your help? Three months. Or how long since we last saw each other? Two years. Won't you have some tea?"

Ida poured for them both because Maud held her hands twisting in her lap.

"Prince Machabeli was never seen again," Maud whispered, without lifting her eyes.

A fine skin of ice spread across Ida's flesh under her clothes. No, her daemon had misunderstood the limits of the material plane he strove to enter—the world not of minds, but of brains; of books, but not ideas. He took possession of both the specific instance of Ida's thief-prince in the moment she embraced him, and of his past and future. He wanted to possess the Russian's very self, rather than just the body alone. And that was not possible. The prince became symbolic, and so ceased to be as an instance.

"I'm so very sorry, but I'm afraid I don't know of whom you speak," Ida said, remembering all her good manners, although she only wished her soul could make the prince's pilgrimage, and her body, disappear.

"The Russian Shakespeare enthusiast. He was leasing the best suite in the boardinghouse where you visited me last."

"You were traveling with Will Yeats then, on the astral plane," Ida said. "I had forgotten."

"Yes, well . . ." Maud fidgeted with the handle of her large bag. "I'm working with him again, actually. On a more practical project."

11

LOVE HAS PITCHED HIS MANSION IN THE PLACE OF EXCREMENT

Empty your heart of its mortal dream.
The winds awaken, the leaves whirl round,
Our cheeks are pale, our hair is unbound,
Our breasts are heaving our eyes are agleam,
Our arms are waving our lips are apart;
And if any gaze on our rushing band,
We come between him and the deed of his hand,
We come between him and the hope of his heart.

—from "The Hosting of the Sidhe" by W. B. Yeats

Because she was a woman, and because they were convinced she was no longer dangerous, her warders at St. Patrick's Lunatic Hospital had moved Ida to one of the wards updated by the new superintendent. Soundlessly, she crept along the wide, carpeted corridor and dropped to her knees. Low to the ground, she poked her head around the corner to discover who waited for her in the patient's drawing room.

Maud Gonne stood, tall, elegant, and more beautiful than was fitting for a woman of thirty-six, dancing her long fingers on the polished wood of a small table which had been laid for tea. So they were to play

"Oh?" Excitement blocked Ida's throat. She had given the poet her best and most secret gift, and would add her forgiveness like a bow for both him and Maud if their work together to locate and wake the king under the mountain was what kept them from finding and freeing her. She cleared her throat with an ugly sound. "Can you tell me anything of your new venture's nature?"

"Of its nature?" Maud hid her quick, puzzled smile behind her teacup. "It is of a dramatic nature."

Ida struggled to keep her grin a sane smile. "And are you working with the Golden Dawn?"

Maud would not know Ida's spiritualist beliefs had earned her her present, formidable and ancient Dublin address, but Ida found herself whispering all the same.

"No," Maud replied. "Will received a spiritual warning last year that adversaries on both planes were seeking my destruction. I put a barrier between myself and whoever was there beyond the shadows. No, Will has written me a play!"

Ida pushed air up through her mouth, but no words emerged. Yeats was not working to wake the sleeping king. He was not using the collected power of the Golden Dawn to open a portal through which Ida's daemon might reach her on the physical plane. Worse, the very spirit she had struggled blood-tinged years to bring into her world, and on whose behalf she had sacrificed even her physical freedom, had been chasing after Maud, until she, the blind cow, had put a stop to it.

"In October"—Maud hurried to fill the empty space left by Ida's gaping, soundless lips—"Will invited me to the Gaiety for the opening of their first play in Irish."

"You don't speak Irish," Ida croaked.

"No, but the people, Ida! The performance so moved the crowd they strove to unhitch the horse from our cab and pull us themselves— the people's poet and Ireland's Joan of Arc—through the streets to our supper party. I stopped them, of course, but, Ida, the galvanizing energy of the stage! I had no idea. I should have understood before, from our very first Nationalist efforts together, when I read Mr.

Todhunter's poem and you sang "Let Erin Remember" instead of "God Save the Queen." Do you remember? The storm of letters in the papers? I don't know why we haven't made better use of the power of theater!"

"October, yes," Ida said. While she had been driven mad in the madhouse, Maud drove adoring men in teams from plays to parties. Ida took a careful sip of tea, watching the flush creep up Maud's cheeks the way it did when Laura lived in her, and wet her lips for kissing.

"Will and I now understand we have been running down the wrong avenues to find our public. He's writing a part for me. Kathleen Ní Houlihan."

"The mythical queen of Ireland," Ida said. "Again."

"Yes." Maud's depthless brown eyes met Ida's with the thrill and innocence of their Donnybrook days. "Maud, the Gray Lady, the one I've seen all my life, the one you channeled through me; I believe she may be the spirit of Kathleen herself!"

"When did you receive my letter?"

Maud hesitated. Ida could see the scales behind Maud's eyes weighing whatever it was she wanted enough to bring her to Swift's famous lunatic hospital against how little she wanted to acknowledge either of their presences there. "I was in Paris when it arrived."

"How long since you returned to Dublin?"

"I have taken new lodgings, a place in Rathgar. There was some confusion with my mail."

"How long have you been settled here?"

"A few weeks. A month, perhaps. But we've been terribly busy with the rehearsing."

"But now you've come to me." Ida rose, utterly bereft.

Her husband, her lover, her poet, her friend, and now—she saw in the wood-framed glass again—her youth, and the last of her always grudging beauty, had abandoned her. No, they had more than left—like Cook, they had come to abhor her. They conspired together against her. Her reflection reddened with a thorny, rising wave of scorn, a crown of whispers biting into her head. Her lip oozed blood from under a protruding tooth. Her eyes lost their sheen. They lost their color. And Ida gazed into the matte gray irises of the only man—no, not a man—the only *being* she had ever wanted and not won.

"Two years since I have seen you," she accused him in the mirror.

You stopped trying to find me a way into your world. His voice was a warm rumble behind her eyes, and Ida closed them to let its beauty roll through her. She was angriest over his betrayal.

"I killed that man," she whispered.

"I know." Maud spoke from behind her teacup.

Ida sat back down. She had both Beauty's and the devil's ear. She must speak with terrible care.

"Ida, I won't hold the murder of a Georgian nationalist against you, but even O'Leary says there are things we must not do in service to a cause. He says a man must not cry in public, and, Ida, you jumped from a window! It's just unseemly for a Nationalist to look mad. You disgraced yourself, and us!"

Ida turned her eyes back to the mirror. Back to her truest love.

"Ida, what can you do for Ireland, looking like you do?"

Ida choked on a sob, and closed her eyes to listen to him speaking: *I wanted you without bounds, my love, Ida, my own. It was wrong of me to force my way, but I am so in love with you, carried away by my desire, I had to possess you.*

"Why have you stayed away since?" Ida asked them both.

"You have been ill."

To keep you safe.

"And why have you come back to me now? I have been so alone so long."

Because now there is another chance.

"Tonight is our premiere. Tonight, I must play Kathleen in Will's play for the first time."

Ida dragged her eyes across Maud's still flawless skin, the looped twists of blood-gold hair, and said nothing.

"Ida, can you try to channel my Gray Lady through me again? Tonight, I want to be, truly, the soul of Ireland!"

And Ida saw Maud was the only madwoman in the room.

"Even if I can find Laura—I mean, Kathleen—again, how could she possibly play your role on stage? She would not know your lines."

Tell her something magical.

"Ida, I don't want to play her, I don't think I can. I want to become her!"

"But I might channel her spirit myself, and you could ask her for a blessing."

Your genius is boundless. I want only to love you, to touch you, to make you my queen.

"Oh, Ida, could you?"

Ida beamed an imperial smile. "You must both keep silent now."

"Both?" Worry clouded Maud's bright eyes; but she was a woman, and had scented what she hunted, so she quieted herself.

Make me a king.

Daemons, Ida already knew, speak in the face of desire. "Close your eyes," she whispered.

What penance will you require, Ida? Justice is sometimes free, but never inexpensive.

Ida closed her eyes and saw Moina MacGregor, in her robes and paper crown, elegant in her performance. Ida was absurd just taking tea.

"Close your eyes tightly," Ida whispered, "tightly—and keep them closed."

Ida studied the milk-smooth eyelids she had not seen for years. "Kathleen Ní Houlihan," she intoned, "I conjure you by name." Her voice creaked, straining after majesty. She cleared her throat and felt her daemon's cool thumb touch her forehead.

Should she pretend to be Kathleen herself, or to hear the spirit speak and pass her words along? She didn't have a plan. Her lover's fingers moved into her hair.

"I am the queen of Ireland." Ida sounded like a schoolboy reading Dante before a cruel headmaster. "I come to bring a message to you, Maud Gonne."

The daemon's smooth, slow strokes down Ida's forehead, sliding again and again from her hairline to between her tightly closed eyes, eased away the world of pride and shame, of Maud's tempting, close-by closed eyes.

"Some call me the Poor Old Woman." The words came from Ida's softening lips without effort. "And there are some that call me Kathleen, the daughter of Houlihan. I will give you my blessing, but it carries a price."

"Anything. I swear it," Maud whispered.

Well played, my love! Will you have her give herself to you? Or require some humiliation to debase her pride?

"I am Ireland's mythical queen. My husband lies sleeping under the ground, awaiting the day Ireland can restore her king."

"Parnell!" Maud cried.

Suffering Christ! Has this woman no imagination?

"Many believed he would return to lead his nation," Maud whispered. "I thought so myself the day we buried him in Glasnevin Cemetery and that blazing star fell from the sky."

"Yes. Parnell." The calm words came through Ida's mouth over the hiss of her greedy daemon and the exaltation of her lost friend. "You must enlist MacGregor and Yeats to wake him."

"Ida?" Maud whispered.

But Ida was coming unmoored—mind from worry, muscle from memory—drifting up. "Swear to it, and in twenty months, you will conceive a fully Irish child, a son destined for our freed country's senate and a golden prize."

"I swear."

"Go now, with my blessing."

Ida?

But Ida was falling apart, the pilgrim pieces wandering like a whore's smile, or a rebel's attention. "The hunt begins," she whispered, and slid from her chair, twisting and defecating on the silent lino.

In the airport bookstore, I pick up a copy of *Scientific American* and flip through its smart, crisp pages.

"Considering a career change?" Amit is reading over my shoulder.

"Yeah, and a move to a new city," I grin. "See if I can't hit a stress triple play."

My husband adds a *Wired* to our arsenal of defense against a mind-numbingly long day in body-cramping spaces. At the register, I snag a celebrity rag, too, with an embarrassed shrug. "Rock stars in rehab." I point to the headline. "Who can resist?"

Amit grins. "Well, it's travel research anyway. One of them has checked in some place in Ireland."

We fold our bodies into the C-shaped seats and belt ourselves in for the Portland-to-Newark leg of our itinerary. "God, there's got to be a better way to move your carcass from one place to another," I grumble.

"Seriously. Can't they just shoot us up with sodium pentothal and stack us like cordwood?"

"That would have to be cheaper," I agree. "No cheap plastic cups of soda to dispense. No sick bags. No boredom."

"No jetlag," Amit adds. "You'd arrive well-rested, caught up on your sleep instead of your reading."

"You know what would be even better?"

"Teleportation," Amit says with authority.

"Or if you could just leave your body at home," I muse. "Send your consciousness into a body that's already there. Remap their neurons to match yours or something."

"That'd be cool." Amit shifts against the worn-thin foam to accommodate the seatback reclining onto his knees. "And remap yours when you come back to account for the new memories. Hell, you could set up switching stations. We'd borrow the bodies of an Irish couple, they can use the ones we left here, and see Portland."

"Oh God, she'd spend two weeks eating like an American, and I'd come back and be fat."

"I'd love you just the same," Amit says virtuously.

I smack his armrest-wedged arm.

"Hey!" he grins, "I'd get to do an Irish chick."

I smack harder. "It'd still be me," I remind him.

"I know," he replies. "That's the best part."

"Of course, anyone who borrows my body could fuck other guys with it while we're gone."

Amit grunts and reaches up to receive his ration of soda, an airborne penitent taking his in-flight communion of Coke and pretzels.

"I'm not sure I like this idea anymore," he says, but on the window side of me during the Newark-to-Dublin leg of our journey sits a woman beautiful enough to make him reconsider. She's the living embodiment of his type of woman, which I know I'm not. She's Maud—tall, with hair blacker than mine, even though I've just re-dyed it.

"I'm going to Ireland," I say inanely, but after a few attempts to engage her, I decide she won't be drawn into conversation. Too bad for Amit. I pull out my magazine and read up on medicine's twenty-five most lifesaving advances over the last one hundred years. By the time we're across the ocean, I feel like I could make a convincing doctor.

We land in Dublin on the morning of a day that hasn't dawned yet in Portland; the perfect inverse of the night, nine nights ago, when I fell asleep beside Amit and woke up with Will, backwards in time. I stand outside the Dublin airport, beside a statue of a winged pig, and confess to myself, for the first time, I have come here for him.

The haughty lift of Maud's strong chin, the careless grace of her long legs, did not distract Ida from the shadow in Beauty's cheek hollows, or the fractured crazing around her eyes. Maud looked in a poor state indeed.

"I had a son. Another son. Sean," Maud whispered. "He's just turned three."

"Who is his father?" Ida asked.

"I've divorced him."

Of course, Ida knew that; she had started getting the newspapers when they moved her from St. Patrick's in Dublin to St. Ita's in the little seaside town of Portrane, north of the city. Maud's divorce from the Boer War veteran, Major John MacBride, not to mention the allegations of sexual abuse between him and Maud's "adopted" daughter Iseult, had quite obsessed the newsmen. Ida remembered being angered by it. Back when she got angry.

"He'll die violently." Ida offered, in way of apology. "Soon."

"You look well, Ida." Maud's tight smile acknowledged her own life-stained beauty.

"I like it here. My daemon is closer to me." Ida watched Maud's slacking lips rewind. "Madness has an interesting freedom," she explained.

"I have often thought"—Maud's smile and voice gave up the strain of smiling and lying—"that were it not for the work I know I still must do for Ireland, I should run quite lunatic myself."

"My doctor says we all must have a cause." Ida gave a sage nod, and held up three straight, white fingers in imitation of his gnarled ones. "A requirement to live: worthwhile work, or at very least a hobby, or children. That's first." She folded the rigid worm of her digit back into the dirt of her fist.

"Regular physical exercise." She folded a second finger and jabbed the remaining one at Maud. "And regular and thoroughly purified bowels," Ida intoned over her closed fist. "These form the three vital pillars of mental hygiene and moral health."

Maud looked away.

"Projects, push-ups, and poop," Ida translated helpfully. "Know what to discard, and what to keep. He's two-thirds of a cure."

"It was wrong of me to come here." Maud turned away from their companionable strolling and leaned against a brick wall of the main building, toward which Ida had been leading her.

Portrane Hospital did not provide the formal visiting rooms of St. Patrick's, but a honeycomb of hallways to wander and out-of-doors yards for purposeful walks and gardening. A massive campus, St. Ita's offered a choice of two churches on either side of the main building—one Church of Ireland, one Irish Catholic—because no matter how mad the inmates, they were Irish still.

Ida had enjoyed strolling the grounds with Maud, but proudest of the main building's clean halls, the stained glass in the massive, shiny wood doors and huge windows, she had steered them toward it. It was beautiful—elegant and airy, like a cloister, except for the double locks on the doors and the big clock tower; like a statue to time, instead of a steeple.

"You came with a question," she whispered, up on tiptoe to reach Maud's nautilusing ear. "Why don't you ask it?" Ida slid her arms around her old friend's thicker waist and noted the shudder of revulsion passing through the still tall, still proud frame. "It has been a long time since anyone has been kind to you," Ida whispered. "I understand."

Her thumb itched with the proximity of the true third pillar of mental health, and opened the door for her friend. "Tell me all," she offered.

Maud could not meet her eyes, but her voice did not quaver. She nodded her stylish, broad-brimmed, veiled hat to the guard at the front desk and lowered her voice to speak to Ida. "When I saw you last, the night I played Kathleen in Will's play, you said I would have a child—a son."

"Yes," Ida agreed.

"And I have. Exactly when you predicted."

"Yes."

"And I have to know . . . Ida, in Sean, have I reincarnated the soul of Parnell, or Georges?"

"Which do you wish?"

Maud closed her fingers across her collapsing face. "I don't know."

"Are you faint?" Ida whispered, but Maud shook her head, and Ida quickened their pace toward a private bench in an alcove down the long hall. "You are impatient," she chided Maud gently. "The child is only three."

Maud nodded. "Older than Georges lived to be."

"He will outlive you by years." Ida eased Maud's long arms from the stylish and expensive overcoat she wore, and draped it with care over the bench's coiled black metal arm. "And he will have more in common with Will than with you. Senator and Laureate." She guided her pale friend onto the wooden seat, and took Maud's too-small hand. "All your life," she whispered, "since Lucien whispered revolution in your rain-drenched ear, you have believed, and never doubted, what you were meant to do.

"He kissed you, and you recalled your heartbreak over the peasants you watched your country weekend's host throw out-of-doors to die. Your passion has always been in rebellion."

Maud swallowed audibly, and Ida's dirty fingers touched the white hand where it lay, clutching her bag in her lap. Ida stroked it to keep Maud from choking on the thick broth of a life regurgitated by a lifelong friend—never a sweet mouthful, but healing.

"But now your certainty grows slippery," Ida continued. "Doubt pulls back your fingers, and you wonder if you can ever know anything absolutely. You want to make a fist around the truth, to clutch it to you, to have it and hold it, to possess it."

"Yes."

"You want to have the truth the way you have a lover, or a memory. For how can you ever give all of yourself to anything—believe in anyone or anything with absolute faith—if you are not so possessed of the truth?"

"Or by the devil," Maud accused herself.

Ida's own laugh, unheard for years, alarmed her, until she recognized the sound and bit it back. Pain blinded Maud to the beauty of her words. Ida's daemon was the only thing of hers Maud had never claimed. And now she was coming undone.

"No, love," Ida soothed. "You were never evil."

"I sold my soul to the devil to buy my freedom."

"That is its price," Ida said. "But mayhap you can ransom it today."

"By being possessed again?"

Ida nodded, and Maud's body lost its stitching. Every seam and sinew gapped and sagged. She would not hold on to consciousness for much longer, but lose it, too—reckless girl. Maud's face crumbled into tears beneath her bright and rigid hat. It did not know how much had changed. It could not droop or dull to match the loss of sense and certainty its owner suffered, and its simple unchanging made it ridiculous. It would suit Ida better now. She was no longer mad.

"But no sooner than you wish to, sweetheart. There is nothing to hurry you," Ida whispered. Poor Maud was suffering too greatly, and Ida, for the first time in years, had a plan once more. She unwrapped Maud's coiled fingers from her fabric bag, smoothed them flat with soft strokes, and administered the final dose.

"All your life," she whispered, "you have wanted and believed in your father or your god, your lovers or your destiny. Now you fear you have waited too long. You have wheedled and groveled, prayed, charmed, and tantrumed to nothing for everything, and all you have left is a life of small things."

Ida reached across Maud's unstuffed body, and over their clasped hands, to lift the bag from her limp thighs. "No one is coming to save you," she whispered.

Tenderly, Ida helped Maud find her way to the ground, and arranged her inert form into not-too-undignified a posture. "The good news," she whispered, "is you can no longer fall down from where you now are."

Ida buttoned Maud's distinctive coat over her white hospital dress. It was too large, but French and overtly expensive. Dubliners would doubt their tailors before her taste.

"First"—Ida bent over Maud—"you must assess. Day still dawns on the battlefield. Now you see all that is impossible, everyone who is lost, the buildings razed, and you can discover at last where your power lies." The fancy, huge hat, mashed between the floor and falling hair, mangling itself, shrouded Maud's beautiful, lost face.

"Maud, you must wear our Eire ring again." Ida rescued the giant hat and tethered it with Maud's sharp hatpins to her own, small head.

"Parnell?" The honey-brown eyes, now swimming red and frightened, pleaded, but Ida shook her head.

"He can never be your savior, Maud. Or anyone's."

"But Ireland's?"

Ida bit her lip, and touched Maud's weeping cheek with love. "Ireland is only an idea."

Maud's lost eyes moved as if to track the separating pieces of her soul. Ida pressed her lips to the pain-ploughed brow. "And ideas without believers die. Ideas need minds to house and channel them."

"Possessed," Maud whispered.

"And words."

"Will!" Maud jerked her head up from the floor. "His words!"

Ida ran a hand across Maud's scattering hair, and smiled at her through the net now veiling her eyes. Maud's hat was not a perfect fit, but a superb disguise. "Rest," she whispered. "Dream. Find Will again on the astral plane; renew your spiritual marriage now, recall your vows."

Three years ago, Maud had promised Ida to set Yeats and Mathers to work locating the sleeping king. If Maud had borne the child the daemon had promised as a prize, Ida knew there must be new work to do.

St. Ita's smooth, black floors reflected Maud's radiant, wet cheek as it came to rest like moonset on a midnight lake.

"Close your eyes tightly," Ida whispered, "tightly—and keep them closed." Maud's bag held her visitor's pass and a little money, enough for train fare. "This is an excellent place for the work you need to do," Ida added. "You can hear all your devils here."

I know Maud can hear me.

Amit's in the shower. Will Yeats is down on one knee. Again. How many times has he asked her?

"Say yes," I whisper.

It might as well be him as another, Maud answers me, her voice in my mind, cracking with irony or pain.

"Yes when I put the rose in my hair like the Andalusian girls used or shall I wear a red yes," Amit recites, emerging from bathroom wrapped in a lurid, blood-colored towel. He's been quoting Joyce all day.

"Did you have a good shower?"

"There's no shower, just a tub; but I had a nice bath." He's rubbing his hair with the red towel, like a percolating head wound.

I make a face. "God, we've gone back in time."

"History is a nightmare from which I am trying to awaken." He holds the towel to his chest with one hand, stretching the other to me dramatically. *"I go to encounter for the millionth time the reality of experience and to forge in the smithy of my soul the uncreated conscience of my race."*

I may have missed some secret-handshake-level of education going to art school, but Amit's found a use for his English degree at last, mining it for an agenda today, arriving jetlagged in Dublin, with nothing planned. Normally, I like to have a list of sights to check off, but Dublin isn't like Paris or London, with an automatic ordering from Eiffel or Buckingham on down, and if you ask a local, he's more likely to point you to his favorite pub than to the Book of Kells or the Martello towers at Sandycove or Bray.

Amit drapes the towel over his head in scarlet pigtails. "Yes, and how he kissed me under the Moorish wall and I thought . . ." He bats his eyelashes until I throw back the covers for him.

He leaps in bed beside me, grinning, and draws my body up against his bath-warmed one with a strong arm. "Say yes, my mountain flower." He nuzzles into my neck.

"Did he write that about his wife?"

"Joyce wasn't a huge fan of marriage." Amit's lips move against my throat, and his hand slides over my belly. "He had two kids with the wonderfully named Nora Barnacle of Galway before he married her. But he wrote her the dirtiest letters . . ." His fingers dip between my legs.

"Those Victorians were a whole lot less Victorian than you'd expect," I murmur, my thighs unhinging.

My breathing deepens.

Maud is back in Paris, alone, but thinking about Will more than she expected.

"Joyce was post-Victorian, but yeah. They were cheating and whoring and fooling around, just like today—more than today, probably. They just didn't go on TV and talk about it."

Amit presses his finger deeper and opens his mouth against my throat. My pulse under his lips knocks a fast and frightened, unheeded warning. I know what I'm risking.

"No wonder divorce rates stayed low," I say. "If monogamy was something you could work around . . ." I say it lightly, but Amit is up on one elbow, looking at me through the dark.

"Are you worried I'll cheat on you?"

"No."

I run my hand over the dark, hard sweep of his shoulder. I'm worried I'll cheat on him.

"But I know you'd like to *get to do an Irish chick.*"

"I was joking!"

"I know. Don't be defensive."

Maud's silk nightdress skims her body like a reverent touch. She's written Will that she will try to dream of him tonight. I know she would not suffer my doubt.

"I'm not being defensive," my husband says. "You know I belong to you, right?"

I glide my hand from his back around to his chest and stroke the flat-carved plane of pecs. His eyelids come down with gratifying speed, and he has to pull them open by lifting his eyebrows.

"What does belonging mean?" I ask him. "Does it mean you'll never want anyone else? Never be attracted to another woman? Never think about anyone else?"

He stops my hand.

Crap. I should have known I don't have Maud's skill with this stuff.

"Laura, what's going on?" The trouble in his soft voice touches me like a caress.

"Sometimes," I say very quietly, "sometimes, when we're making love, my mind wanders."

Amit relaxes, glad it's about me and not him, but I'm almost shaking with nerves. "It's not like I start thinking about work or anything, I just . . ." But now I've pushed the first shoulder strap down in this terrifying new striptease.

"You have fantasies?"

"Yeah."

What if what he sees disgusts him? Maybe I look better dressed.

Amit grins, teeth carnivore-white in our dark room. "Sweetheart, I think everyone has fantasies."

"I have them while we're having sex."

Maud's eyes are closed.

There's my other strap off.

"Sometimes, I imagine I'm someone else."

My voice sounds shaky and far away.

"A movie star, or someone from a book."

First button open.

Amit shrugs. "Sometimes, when we're walking Mount Hood, I pretend I'm a Masai warrior," he says. "No reason old married folk can't play pretend."

"I pretend I am a different person when we're making love sometimes. I have a different body . . ."

There go buttons two and three.

". . . much bigger tits."

My hands shake. I grip the halves of my tear-away top, look up and wink.

He laughs, and relief warms me. "It's just play," he tells me, gathering the flesh of my small breast into his hand and squeezing. "Besides, I love your tits."

"I know, but wouldn't you like some variety?"

I'm bare-breasted in pasties, swinging my tassels hard.

"Yeah, of course. But I promised not to."

Maud imagines a moth-like body with gold-edged wings and reaches out for Will.

"No, you didn't," I say, holding my voice steady, fingers in my waistband. "We wrote our own vows. We promised to love each other forever, but nothing about sex."

Will is searching, too.

He and Maud are almost touching.

"Sometimes, I pretend you're someone else," I whisper, and there go my pants. I'm terrified again.

Tears fill Will's eyes. Maud, for all her height, staggers with the impact of his body against hers. He takes her face in his beautiful hands, hungry, almost mad, and looks into her eyes, staring, searching, finding me. Amit stays very still.

"I close my eyes, and another man makes love to me," I say.

Will's kiss is shattering.

Our mouths open, grappling, devouring. We cannot taste or consume each another. When he stops, I am panting.

Amit holds up his left hand. "See this?" The small, soft gold of his wedding ring mirrors the diffuse light squeezing through the cloaked windows. It's a thinner band than I would have chosen for a man's hand, but it's a family heirloom. Amit's mother would have been crushed if we had used anything else. "It means we belong to each other," he says. "I share my life with you, and get to be a part of yours. But we both have plenty. I'm not starving here. I don't need all the space inside your head."

"What about my body?" I ask, his cock hard against my thigh.

"I'll take care of your body." He growls it like a pirate and pitches himself over me, the weight of his hips parting my legs. I wind my legs over his back, grip my wrists behind his neck, and look up at him.

Will is waiting for me.

"So really? You don't care what I do in my head?"

"What I don't know can't hurt me, right?" He's playful, rolling his hips in a dogged rhythm, dragging the fat head of his cock in invitation across my clit. It feels wonderful. Am I so spoiled I can't be happy with this? I close my eyes.

Demon est Deus Inversus.

If this isn't adultery, is it consummation?

Amit's deliberate, skillful mouth moves down my body, licks my breast. Will's soul melts into mine.

"I love you."

Amit's tongue slides between the folds of my sex, and my hips arch up to meet it, hunger for hunger.

Ida's husband won't tell me where she is. Maud swears she doesn't know. Laura, it's been ten years. I cannot live this way.

I make a noise like a sob, and Amit's cock touches the mouth of my sex.

Will takes me in his arms, and I am torn in half—mind from matter, muscle from memory. Not cleanly bisected at the waist—but chewed off. Ragged. Rusted through.

Amit's slow, delicious mouth on mine swells my lips full and soft. My throat chokes on the empty aching there. His chest brushes my tiny, plucked nipples; his cock pushes into my peeled sex. Behind my breasts, beneath his body plunging into mine, a flesh sobbing grips me.

I have, and I want. *Deus* and *Demon.*

Amit tucks me against his chest afterwards and pushes my hair away from his face. "I was thinking, you know . . . about tomorrow," he whispers.

"Newgrange, right?" I mutter, trying to remember what we planned through the tumble of sleep.

"Let's go west instead."

"West?"

I can't remember what in Ireland comes from the West.

"Yeah," Amit says, his voice sleep-sloppy, too. "I want to see Galway . . . Yeats country. Think you'd like that?"

I can hear sheet after sheet of writing paper being wadded up and thrown away.

"Yes," I say. "Yes, I will."

Ida rested her cheek against the warm wood and closed her eyes. "Not much longer now, my love."

Even though he would not speak to her through it, Ida was certain her daemon hid in the polished wood and gleaming brass of the magic box—the Metallic Medium—whose lid she now carefully wiped clean of the bootblack her cheek had smudged on it. It was the only explanation that made sense of her escape from Portrane, and her possession of this infernal machine which had brought Will Yeats once again within her reach.

She took a fortifying swallow of whiskey from the tumbler on the desk, and raised the box's lid. The metal drum and little glass lens gleamed erotically in the brave electric light she must remember to extinguish before her guest arrived. She unrolled the sleeves of her shirt, pushed up the knot of her necktie, and addressed the box directly.

"An article appeared this afternoon, my love, which puts us in grave jeopardy. *The Sphere*, in proclaiming your many wonders, listed German among the languages you speak. You are wise in every way, but time is a bath more than a stream to you. German armies are now only miles away, and our countries are at war. If you do not seize the chance tonight to put your plans in place, I fear the authorities will come and take your voice from me. Our years of effort will be lost. My love, bring me into your service tonight."

Ida watched the brass and glass eye rotate within the metal drum, hating the note of pleading in her voice. But it was, already, so much longer than she imagined it would take when she sold Maud's French coat, and her own body, to a tailor named Bates for two days of his work—and his secrecy. Since then, her life as David Wilson, neighborhood pharmacist and shy bachelor, had served the mysterious machine the real Mr. Wilson had carelessly advertised in his shop window as his "Ear-Hole to the Unknown." He had not realized the power of either his own creation or a seduced man's shame. Ida had hidden the one and advertised the other, and soon the curious and bereaved were traveling from London to Mr. Wilson's dusty little shop in St. Leonards-on-Sea to hear Ida's daemon speak in Turkish or gibberish, or simply amplify the whispering dead.

The bell rang, and Ida, who had not employed domestic service since the day her maids turned Judas, put out the electric light, pulled on Mr. Bates's coat, and opened the downstairs door herself.

"Mr. Yeats!" she exclaimed heartily, open hand held out to shake. "How very good of you to travel all this way."

"Mr. Wilson," beamed the poet, clasping Ida's hand. "How kind of you to allow me a private audience with your metallic homunculus."

Ida stood back to allow the tower of a man inside her little chemist's shop. With a stiff bow, she directed the now-famous, now-monied, now-impressive poet away from the modest interior of her dusty hall.

"We're upstairs again, are we?" Will sprang up the stairs ahead of Ida on his long legs. She locked the door and followed him, cautious always not to walk before a man. Her trousers and braces, jacket and collar, all did nicely to conceal her breasts and hips, but nothing hid the woman in her walking when seen from behind. It created a confusion in men which tonight, at least, would not serve her well.

Will settled himself at Ida's modest table, and produced a notebook and pen. "Brilliant things, these," he grinned, brandishing his new lever-filled fountain pen at Ida. "How we ever managed with inkpots and blotters, I'll never fathom."

"Will you take whiskey, Mr. Yeats?"

"I think not tonight, thank you. I must return to London by the last train."

"I fear Messieurs Ross and Dulac were not so taken by my device."

"We had more promising results on my first visit, my friend. Perhaps I should not have brought additional witnesses the second time. But, I should confess, I have hopes beyond the ordinary run. Your device may be a vessel for voices of the dead, and although that is what so many have made the pilgrimage to see, I harbor even bolder hopes. What else might we learn from it beyond the words or cares of the specific dead, but of the *Spiritus Mundi*, the World Soul, they now inhabit? What universal truths might your machine reveal?" Will drew a soft, brown leather case from his breast pocket and removed a deck of hand-fashioned cards. He grinned at Ida. "I have brought my symbol cards and a list of questions."

The brass drum began to spin, and a deep, low rumble, like the growling of an animal terrible in size, crept from the metal and glass. The strange heaviness of the sound tugged it from the machine, to spill over the table and pool on the floor, piling up on Ida's shabby carpet, whispering around Will's expensive ankles.

It had never made this sound before. Mayhap Ida's daemon would heed her pleas tonight at last! Will had his eyes closed, listening with rapt wonder on his innocent face. But Ida was terrified. Will's optimistic imagination reached only to hoping the device and the mildly deranged, but likeable, David Wilson were not frauds.

The sound vibrated up their legs, rattled their shin bones and banged their knees.

"Too much! Too strong!" Ida cried.

Mr. Yeats occupied himself with jotting in his white notebook to spare his companion's dignity after such a hysterical, high cry. But the machine's sound twisted, softening into a wordless, closed-lip hum which, just as stealthy, ran over Ida's thighs and arms.

Yeats tipped his proud head to listen, eyes unfocused, and a shock of hair, no longer only brown, but edged in pewter, swept like a caress over his high brow, more handsome, mayhap, than he had ever been. And handsomely dressed. His suit would have cost more than Ida had between her legs. Will matched the machine's note with his voice, but no human sound could hold such power; and when the box began to sing, the poet fell silent.

"The hottest places in hell are reserved for those who in times of great moral crises maintain their neutrality," the box intoned, somewhere between chant and song.

"Dante," whispered Yeats, eyes closed.

"Active Evil is better than Passive Good," it sang.

"Blake." Will's face, when he turned it to Ida, had lost all hard thoughts of proof. "My two great masters." He held her eyes a long time listening, and smiled. "For years, I tried to find a way of freeing the power of a voice this way, to create a sound powerful as a visual symbol, as resonate on the mythic plane. Florence Emery with her psaltery came very close, I had thought, but never attained such power as this."

"She had only a human voice," Ida said.

Will's eyes sharpened. "You believe this voice is divine?"

"No," Ida answered truthfully.

"Surely some new generation will learn the trick of this, of packing such depth of emotion into sound without words, or some ancient race could chant so."

"Irish poet, learn your trade, sing whatever is well made," said the box.

"Those are my words." Will chuckled, leaning closer.

A hard flush of jealousy struck Ida beneath her eyes. Will's long, graceful fingers rested on a wooden corner, ear turned toward it, eyes abstract. He look liked a physician listening for a stopped heartbeat, or a lover for a secret knock. But Ida and the poet were kindred souls in this. Will had been likewise spurned by his love, played for Maud's politics and denied her bed, as Ida had been by Mr. Rowley.

And they both loved daemons far away.

And they both had learned, finally, love was not enough.

"An ancient bridge, and a more ancient tower, A farmhouse that is sheltered by its wall, An acre of stony ground, Where the symbolic rose can break in flower."

"I know of such a place!" Yeats whispered, notebook forgotten. "In County Galway, not many miles from Coole Park; a derelict, old square castle called Ballylee, lived in by a farmer and his wife. They have built a little cottage by it, where their daughter and her husband live. I visited several times some years ago, to try and discover what an old wise woman from Clare meant when she said, *a cure for all the evils of the world might be found between the mill-wheels of Ballylee.* I've often imagined buying it myself one day to realize a dream I once cherished for Lough Key. In fact"—his keen eyes lit on Ida's—"Lady Gregory wrote just recently, suggesting it might be for sale."

"Set all your mind upon the steep ascent, upon the broken, crumbling battlement," the box sang.

The poet turned keen eyes to Ida's. "In your experience, Mr. Wilson, does this device speak directly to men about affairs of the world? Or is it a material mouthpiece for the *Spiritus Mundi*, choosing universal symbols to resonate with each instance of individual lives?"

Ida's fingers twitched beneath the table. She longed to take the box with both her hands and smash it to the ground. In the four years she had possessed it, it had never sung for her. Never drenched her in the rich comfort it wrapped her grubby room in now. And shortly the authorities, alerted by a silly magazine, would come and David Wilson must, by criminal necessity, dissolve into the *Industrious Mundi*.

"I think it speaks to you," she said. "It did so to me about you before you arrived," she lied.

"Oh?" Yeats straightened in his chair and regarded Ida with new interest. "What did it say to you?"

The humming mouth opened, the long *"mmm"* becoming *"ah,"* almost imperceptibly.

"It asked if you remembered Ida Jameson."

Will Yeats sat back against the meager cushions of the room's best chair and touched the lean pads of his fingers together, but the song was climbing Ida's legs again.

"What can be shown? What true love be? All could be known or shown if Time were but gone!" The words formed in the torrent of sound like constellations, appearing and disappearing through attention, rather than arrangement.

All the poise and swagger drained from Will's face.

"Love is all unsatisfied that cannot take the whole, body and soul."

"Mr. Wilson," said the poet in a voice flayed of all its detached confidence, "you're a metaphysical man, and so I trust you'll understand when I say to you that, although I cannot tell you why, this contraption's legitimacy in now proven beyond all doubt to me."

"That's very gratifying, Mr. Yeats."

Maybe he no longer loved her. Maybe her daemon, in his damnable box, had found another way to command the lives of men. Now he talked to Yeats of bodies and souls and towers, and silenced her when she spoke her own name. She would have his love, yes. But she would also have his power.

"Devil damn it, Will!" the box shrieked.

Yeats sprang to standing, towering and formidable in the cramped room. Despite her horrified shame at the box's new voice, Ida was forcefully reminded Will was still a magus, Imperator of Mathers's Golden Dawn, with dangerous powers of his own at his command, while she cowered in her chair.

"Was Maud's divorce not enough for you?" howled the box in uncanny mimicry of Ida's own voice again.

"The ghost of Ida Jameson," Will breathed.

"I had your rival executed by firing squad," Ida heard her own voice complain, *"and still you cannot manage to marry the widow!"*

"It was never Maud I loved."

"It must be her!"

"No." Will reached across Ida and slammed the box shut.

He stood over it a moment, rigid, daring it to make another sound. Finally, he spoke without dropping his vigilance. "Ida Jameson . . . Mrs. Rowley was a woman very gifted in the occult."

Will groped for his chair back and sat down. No color, no power, remained in his face, although Ida's still burned brimstone-hot. "But she went quite mad. Her husband, poor man, had her put away, but she escaped one day and drowned herself in the sea."

Will took the whiskey bottle in a shaking hand, and poured for himself, without asking or offering. Ida realized he could not see her own distress. His eclipsed it utterly.

"She was a medium. The only person who could . . ." Will drained the glass without blinking. "When I learned of her death, I could find no symbol of hope. I despaired."

He touched the box's brass-embossed lid with a cautious finger. Ida did not move.

Will filled another glass, and his eyes finally moved again. He lifted the unstoppered neck to Ida, who nodded. "It has been almost ten years since I saw her last."

"Mrs. Rowley?"

Will poured like a rich man, careless of the cost, and Ida wondered if he no longer knew, as she once had not, what whiskey or tea or sugar cost. "No. The lady I speak of, I cannot name."

Ida nodded.

"I loved her," he said, and Ida looked away like a man, embarrassed by indiscreet glimpses of another man's genitals, or soul.

Will ran a finger across the box the way he might strop a razor to test its edge, and Ida no longer envied the touch. If souls bled, it would have been a lethal stroke.

"When Maud Gonne allowed it, she—my unnamed lady—could come to me astrally, or bodily, but that . . . But years are long when empty. And a man is not only a soul."

"No," Ida agreed. "Nor is a woman only a body."

Will emptied half the tumbler without taking his eyes from the box.

"We are all of us more than our bodies, more than the mere sum of our parts." He drained the glass and put a hand on each of the box's beveled corners.

"But all our parts are material," Ida said. "A soul is but a symbol for the sum."

"In vain, in vain; the cataract still cries," boomed the resonant, caressing voice from the metal drum. *"The everlasting taper lights the gloom; All wisdom shut into his onyx eyes, Our Father Rosicross sleeps in his tomb."*

"The last stanza of my poem 'The Mountain Tomb.'" Will hung his head. "It mocks what I know. With what I have written."

"You must arise and go now," the box sang.

Will nodded and stood with a wry laugh. "Mr. Wilson," he said, his long fingers buttoning his coat. "There is work I must do. I should have undertaken it while some were alive and others unmarried, but still, it seems, I must begin. There is a great deal to do. I shall write to Mathers in France, and use what influence I have on your behalf; but I must beg you not to speak of anything you heard tonight."

Ida nodded.

He turned to leave, and the box began to sing again.

"Mr. Yeats," she shouted over the drone, "The future still waits for you, and Ida Jameson did not drown."

⬥

Will spreads his hand over the page like God's across the water, and just as easily, an entire continent of thought is destroyed. Outside, an impatient wind rattles the wooden windows.

Ashdown Forest Hotel, Sussex. Will's hand carves new black rivers into the pure white page. *My dear Lady Gregory.*

My field of vision widens and retreats, and I move away from the space between Will's pen and eyes. Ten years must have passed for him since I last saw him. Gray winks through the dark of his hair like early gloaming stars, but his broad shoulders hold more power in stillness than they had in their more restless youth. His hands have not lost their grace or agile competence, but I know he is in pain. Through the rain-hammered glass, I can see flood-flattened fields

and a distant copse of trees, whose red and yellow leaves thrash in
the rough wind. There's a woman humming in the next room.

I've never seen her before. She's arranging a velvet shawl over her
dress, and turns her profile to the mirror to study the theatrical effect. It's underwhelming. She is short, vague and dumpy compared to
Maud, and eccentricity is not beauty, or even a good mask for its
absence. But, pleased with herself, she swirls the other direction, flip-
ping the hem out in a sensual arc. She could be Guinevere awaiting
Lancelot, with the secret way she wraps herself in its green folds.
"Will," she calls, "the rain has lessened. Shall we take our walk?"

Often, Maud can see me when I dream about her, but Will never
has. Sometimes I can manage enough of a form to throw pebbles
against a mirror, or whisper loudly enough to make myself almost
heard, but usually, when he's quiet, Will simply senses me there. He
must feel me now, because he appears in the door between the two
rooms like an insomniac called from his sleepless bed, somewhere
between relief and exasperation.

"Do you have anything to post?" she asks, because he has not
glanced at her in her new cape, but reached past her into the wardrobe
for his overcoat.

"No," he says. "I cannot write."

He puts his arms into his sleeves, and in the space between his
shoulders and his coat, the time we've been apart slides over me. I can
feel his age on him like a cramp, a hardening down of sinew and sap.
An ache. I want to slide my hands up the sleeves and climb inside his
coat with him. He leaves the room with the woman he called "Georgie," holding the door open for her with a bow neither of them notice,
deferent, courteous, remote. Whoever she is, he does not love her.

I cannot unfold the mangled pages, the pencil sketches of storm-
whipped trees wadded into a gradually unfolding ball, the unfinished
letters and fragments of a poem awash in angry strike-throughs and
crammed second or third tries at lines: *A strange thing surely that my heart
when love had come unsought . . .* I read.

Of the letter he started, all I can read is, *marriage not a success.*

I stretch myself out in their bed. Georgie is his wife. Of all the parallels I had imagined might appear in Ireland, that I should find Will, both on our honeymoon, had not occurred to me. I am hollow as the howling wind.

But my marriage is a success. Amit and I are both adults. We talk about things. When I tell him I sometimes dream about other men, he reminds me it's our actions, and not our imaginations, we police.

I can live without Will. I know it now. This dream is showing me how soon wild, Victorian love gets old and withers. I can keep my body roped off for Amit, like so much surveyed real estate. *Posted: No Trespassing.*

Georgie is years younger than Will, and they come back from their walk with her cold-flushed face turned up to his, the radiant young bride of a famous man, the helpmeet, the enabler. I wonder why I hate her. Is it the property of his body I still want?

They sit on either side of the fire he stirs to glowing with a little wood-handled poker. She reads. He broods. She does not see him watching the flames like a beached fish looks toward the sea. He runs his hand over his eyes, and for a second, looks right at me. "Will!" I shout, but he grinds his lids into his eyes and does not open them. I never meant to cause him pain. I just wanted to supply the erotic spaces of my marriage, to replenish my stocks from the romantic, poetic past.

"I am having a premonition," she says.

He drags his eyes to her face.

"I feel I have lived all this before, in a past time."

"Yes," he says, "the past comes close to me as well." The pain in his voice curls up like a snake inside me.

"I want you to hypnotize me, Will."

He is too much a gentleman to deny her, but there's something Kabuki in the way he draws the footstool up beside her and takes the pins from her hair. He puts his fingers on her scalp, and I can feel the threads of arousal his touch pulls tight in her. She longs to bind him to her. He touches his thumb to her forehead and strokes it down to between her brows. "Close your eyes tightly," he intones, "tightly—and keep them closed."

Her lids fall and her lips part with an eager little sigh. He has not touched her this way before, and she wants him to.

There is none of Maud's beauty in Georgie. If I could move into her body like I have into Maud's, would Will still love me as intensely without Maud's dangerous beauty? Would I want to love him with Georgie's body? She lets herself go slack in the chair, and her head falls against the upholstery. She makes sleepy little moaning sounds, but there's no space for me. I try to drop into her, to melt into her, and finally, to slam into her. Nothing. I'm afraid if I do more, I'll wake myself up back in Dublin with Amit. I wonder whether I should kiss her. I try shoving in from the left side instead, and although I impact hard enough to knock her arm off the chair's armrest, I get no traction in her soul.

I wet my lips with my tongue.

"Georgie, did you move your arm?"

"No," she says, too soon and too awake. "I shall try automatic writing," she announces and closes her eyes again.

Will strides into other room for paper he has not balled up. He drags the little writing desk to her side and puts his pen into her hand. Georgie grips it with rigid fingers, and I wrap mine, cold and nervous, over them.

Nothing.

Will leans in toward Georgie, eager and intent. It's the closest their bodies have been, and she's as aware of it as I am. I want to touch him, to put my fingers to the new furrows in his face, to kiss his softer mouth. I can't stop watching his lips as he whispers encouragement to her—to relax, to let her mind come unfettered. His tender lower lip is larger than his upper, and I remember it skimming my mouth in the infinite, playful, patient exploration of his kisses. None of us are watching the pen when it starts moving.

Deus . . .

Georgie looks from the page to her new husband, whose eyes hold wonder and excitement and something like love.

"Did you write that?"

Georgie shakes her head.

"Laura?" he whispers, but I didn't write it either.

Or I must have, but I don't know how.

"Who?" Georgie asks, all at once very alert, but I'm concentrating on my fingers wrapped over hers trying to push the pen along again.

"Close your eyes," he whispers, and the anguish in his voice draws mine shut, too. "I had given up hope."

Never. My fingers shape the letters, but I dare not open my eyes. I know, absolutely, if I look right at what I'm doing, I won't be able to do it.

"Oh, Laura, my world has changed. It's a new century. A terrible war . . . Hope went out of fashion, along with dreams. I've been writing plays. Pieces of action and drama. I never forgot you, but I stopped believing." He drops his head into his hand. "Forgive my unbelief."

I open my eyes. His are only inches away, warm behind the frameless glasses, and deep.

He was dead before I was born. He is not real, but my corpseless body flows like the ocean under his moon. It pulls me into swells and tides, crashing and drowning for him. My subconscious mind must be isolating physical attraction, pure sexual desire to remind me to . . .

. . . or not to.

"And then a year ago, I heard your voice again," Will says. "After all that time, I heard you, not in my sleep, not with my astral body, but with my living and awake and human hearing. Your voice spoke from the most remarkable machine. The next day the man and his apparatus had vanished, but I . . ." His voice breaks, and I fall through it into him. Into the spiritual communion we shared, when I don't believe in spirits; the nights I knew we were married, and dreamed him through Maud's dreams.

"Georgie, can you hear me?"

She doesn't answer, her breathing soft and rhythmic as a heartbeat. Only her hand moves.

It's been less than a week for me. Will, I have come to Ireland.

His bolt to standing nearly costs me my hold on Georgie's hand. "I'll go home directly. Where are you?"

Galway tomorrow.

But if he cannot feel me here, right beside him, will my being there matter? Is there a connection between people and land that's enough to ground us? "The tower!" Will cries. "The box gave me instructions—mad ones—but I have tried . . ."

His head drops into his hands, and all the weight of the years he's carried without me bleeds over me.

Will, I'm so sorry. You're in pain.

"I am, but I would not have lived without it. Art does not come from pleasant things, but from these battles with the soul."

I love you.

He smiles, and all the suffering in his face vanishes. He looks like he did the night on Lough Key in the abandoned and haunted castle, when we made love for the first time, and our bodies opened a space for us to be together—and I saw a ghost step through the fireplace and back again. And I wonder: These times inside time, do they always hang there for us, and we just don't notice, don't worship, don't concentrate? Just a touch, just a look, makes them significant, like courtyard gardens not glimpsed down alleyways we flash past. But spiraled into; every petal tasted, sticky on my tongue, dripping dew and shooting roots into my belly—longing and wanting. If I just paid attention, could it feel like this with Amit? Would I want it to? Or would I be someone else if I did?

Rather strange things have been happening here, of which I can't altogether understand the meaning.

I don't know if you know a life size portrait there is of mine—painted by an Alsatian artist, standing in a white dress. It is much the best portrait there is of me—

The other day Iseult came to me with much excitement saying she had been sitting in the drawing room opposite this picture when suddenly she saw it move, the eyes opened & shut. Then the lips moved and the face contorted. Then it became black then appeared again but quite changed. It seemed like a figure in stone with a green veil over the head, the eyes half closed and a strange smile on the lips, the hands instead of hanging down were together yet different. Iseult got so frightened that she fled—

Next day some people were at tea with me suddenly I caught sight of the picture in the mirror opposite to it & sure enough the eyes opened & shut. I said nothing for the people there would have thought me mad if I had but that evening I told Ella Young & my cousin May, & we three went into the drawing room & invoked. *We all saw* the picture move & change in the most extraordinary way—Something has taken posses-sion of the picture—I think it may be the grey woman who I had to get rid of—there have been several other rather curi-ous manifestations which as it is very late I have not time to describe—

12

SO I LIVED, AND LIVED NOT, SO WROUGHT I, AND WROUGHT NOT, WITH CREATURES OF DREAMS

Vague memories, nothing but memories,
But in the grave all, all, shall be renewed.
The certainty that I shall see that lady
Leaning or standing or walking
In the first loveliness of womanhood,
And with the fervor of my youthful eyes,
Has set me muttering like a fool.

—from "Broken Dreams" by W. B. Yeats

The rain just sounds like static until the thunder. Its collective grumble, growing in layers over itself, doesn't scare me. It locates me. And then I am frightened. A week has passed, feels like a decade, and for the first night since my wedding, I fell asleep not looking for what I've found. I open my eyes, and I know where I am, although I've never been here. I'm in Thoor Ballylee, the Galway tower Yeats bought, the place Amit and I will visit tomorrow, an easy walk from the B&B where we're sleeping now. We drove the rental car out from Dublin this afternoon.

"Will?" I whisper, and he turns to me, away from the massive stone fireplace he's been sketching. A cautious smile cracks the stern lines of his face. The drawing pad falls to the floor unheeded as he stands, unsure no longer. He's lost none of his grace.

"Laura."

I'm not yet integrated into Maud's body enough to stand, but I nod her proud head.

"Ida swore she would summon you tonight, but I feared you might be unable to come through." He drops his eyes from mine, kneels by my chair and takes my hand. "Or unwilling," he whispers. I squeeze his hand with mine, and he raises the knuckles to his lips.

If my eyes could see only the deep velvet brown of his, and not look any wider—to his face and my body, to the yawning fireplace, to the four weird three-legged wooden chairs drawn before it, or to Ida's and MacGregor Mathers's slack, inert bodies slumped in them— I could nurture the spark his kiss on the back of my fingers ignites.

He stands, drawing me to my feet, and Maud's tall body unfolds on tighter springs than it once had. But his hands touch my face, Maud's hair, and his liquid, Irish voice, murmuring quiet, secret things, envelopes me. The pain and wonder in his eyes tell of our years apart, what he has done, and been unable to do, without me. He opens his arms and draws me against him. My body, solid for a moment, melts into his tender, fierce embrace. I mold against him, wind my arms around him, and hold on.

Memory pulls like a receding tide, inviting and just beyond reach; and Will tightens his grip on me, as though it tugs his body, too. "I married," he whispers. "I never ceased to love you, but our spiritual unions were both relief and torment to me. I wanted you. Loved you to distraction, but, my love"—he is almost rocking me, held against him, in his anguish—"*our* love was not enough. I am not so pure a being. I needed you—body *and* soul. Needed to weave our days together, to share the small things I have with Georgie, tea and what color to paint the bedroom . . ."

"I know," I tell him.

He holds my face between his hands. "Tell me it doesn't matter."

My eyes swim between his urgent face and the two limp bodies, lumpy bundles in their heavy winter coats propped into the weird wooden chairs. "I don't know," I whisper, muted by the beauty and pain in his face.

I don't know anything, if this is sin or necessity, imaginary or dangerous. But I'll sacrifice my need to know on the altar of love. The thunder growls like a vast, empty belly over us. I want to smash into him, to collapse ourselves into one self.

"Laura," he whispers.

Maud's body sits heavier from the bones than it did and, mixed into my wanting for Will, I wish for a different self to give him—a less honest, more beautiful being, or my actual self—and that desire poisons the other. I walk to the window and look into the wild night from what must be forty feet above a swollen river, drawing Maud's warm sealskin coat closer around her aging joints. The rain comes with more force than falling; it is thrown down or flees earthward of its own accord from hands that would hurl it.

Across the backs of the four chairs ringing the hearth, from behind Will's long legs, the fire winks at me conspiratorially.

Will shrugs. "We carried the chairs over from the cottage. It's just across the road, and much more habitable than my vain tower," he explains, as though the furnishings were the strangest feature of the night. "Do you know what Ezra calls this place? Boggyphallus! Will's phallic symbol in the bog!" He chuckles. "He thinks I'm quite mad."

His impish grin catches on my lips, and even with the rain drilling the thin glass behind me, I feel warm and cosseted. But the thunder roars again, almost overhead, and the echo of it rings the tower like encroaching dogs. The fire behind Will shudders. "Why the company?" I ask him.

His short laugh carries an angry edge. "There are four of us here— five, if we count both you and Maud—plus my wife in the cottage next door. She would have no part of this. Her automatic writing warned against tonight's endeavor."

"What endeavor?"

Why would tonight be about anyone but us?

"Ida Jameson has returned at last. And she has convinced Mac-

Gregor Mathers"—Will gestured at the body collapsed in the chair beside my empty one—"the high priest of the Golden Dawn, that Cúchulainn is sleeping in the tomb the locals call *Maeve's Hill*, and that now—with the world at war, and the Golden Age that Mac-Gregor foretold not dawning—now is the time to wake the sleeping king under the mountain. She told him what an extraordinary carrier Maud makes, and appealed to his pride and to her patriotism."

"And to your . . . ?"

Will's smile carries an apology. "My love for you, of course." But he comes across the room to me, hands out, and brave. "I had argued against this mad plan, too, until Ida told me privately she could bring you to me tonight. I had to see you. Even knowing this must be our final time. I have never—can never—stop loving you." He collects my limp hands in his warm ones. "I swear it."

"Don't swear to things you can't control," I tell him, sounding very modern. "You can't control how you feel, only the actions you chose in the face of your feelings. But feelings change. And so do people. How can we make any promises about the future at all, not knowing how we will feel, or who we will become?"

It's cold by the window. I let a shiver creep over me, and Will pulls me back to the fire. "You're right," he whispers, but I'm not sure if he's admitting to our powerlessness over what's coming, or just soothing me. The drawing he dropped lies on the ground between our empty chairs. Ida and MacGregor droop with an obscene gravity against their hard and modest chairs.

"Why would Ida risk incurring Maud's anger to have your cooperation? She's not the type to believe in a savior king."

Will's laugh is tonight's thunder stripped of its menace, resonant, benign, but powerful. "No, she has been disappointed too many times, and she's hardly a selfless soul. I believe she would sell us all to the devil for the fun of making the deal."

I find myself leaning over Ida's inert body, an inverse image of the way I first woke up with her face peering down at me. I wonder what she wants. Her face has coarsened with age, larger pores and thicker folds, and she's abandoned her expensive hats for what she must intend as an artistic silk headscarf. "What does it mean that Maud is a carrier?" I ask.

"Her soul, when it wishes, can transport with it the souls of others. It is a kind of charisma, I think, tied to her beauty—this gift for carrying others away with her. A glamour like the fairies have."

"And Ida and MacGregor followed her soul to find this king?"

Will nods. "The work I've done with Georgie validated quite a lot of what Ida has promised. We've been working on a taxonomy of souls since."

I imagine the two of them fitting souls together into charts like colored tiles.

"Maud has a *sidhe* soul," he says, voice shy as if afraid of startling me. "Because she is indeed part fae, she dreams only of revolution. She lacks the imagination for anything more. But still, Ireland is indebted to her fairy soul. Made of air, it wanders from her body easily, on any gust of air or pang of human suffering. It carried away your new bride's spirit, and set your imagination on its pilgrimage to me. Without it, I could only have dreamed of freedom. You taught me to love it."

"And what category of soul am I?" I ask him.

When he doesn't answer, I turn away from Ida's slack, ugly face.

"We have a titanic soul," Will says.

"You and I have the same type of soul?" The idea is childish, but I like it.

"No." He takes my hands again. "We share one between us. We are descendants of the primal beings Plato gives to Aristophanes to describe. We were a single thing once, you and I."

"I think I knew that," I say slowly. "I've always sensed some part of me was missing. Like it had wandered off one day when I wasn't paying attention." He looks relieved. He had dreaded telling me, afraid I did not know I was broken, and finding out would make the pain start. "Have you felt that way, too?" I ask him, "Like you're only half there? Half asleep in your own life?"

"Not asleep," he says, "but dreaming."

As if it might break, as if it were itself a dream, he turns my face up and touches my mouth with his. His kisses land like soft rain-drops, tiny on blades of grass, but they bend me. "My soul doesn't wander," he whispers. "It conjures."

In some cloud-cloaked distance, I remember sketching an unfa-miliar hillside on the edge of a map. Immediately above me, thunder snarls in overlapping growls of hunger and rage.

Pilgrim or mage, seeker or creator, my mouth opens under his, and our lips come together as droplets, joining and separating with the same distending pull. All the doubt and questions in my mind scatter under the torrent of my body's absolute sensation.

I want this. I want to stand naked beneath the downpour, to soak it in and drown in it, but Will keeps his kisses small, each one single, a slow treasuring of my mouth. I stroke his lingering lips with my tongue, and his teeth capture it. With a groan, his mouth opens over mine, all the fine smallness abandoned. My body twists against his with the pleasure of our mingled hunger and the deepening need to fulfill it at last. I put my hands flat on his chest, not so supple as it once was, and slide them down his unfamiliar body.

But he stops and looks at me, stares into my eyes. His lips are dappled red with kissing, and his eyes flame behind his crooked glasses. A suspender droops off his shoulder, and all the button studs have worked themselves free from his shirt cuffs. Without the pins to close them, the cuffs fly like wild wings around his beautiful hand. And at last I understand what loving me does to this cultured Ed-wardian gentleman, this elegant man of letters. I am the stray corner of his soul unpinned. And he is mine.

"I love you," I tell him.

"I know," he says.

I know I am selfish to keep a raw edge flapping in the free fairy wind; I should tidy up, pin myself together, be presentable. But my fingertips trace his jaw, clenched hard against wanting me, and I am alive and irrefutable as the rainstorm. I may live my life among the better-tailored, but Will wears his poet's raw tatters like a tailcoat, and he wraps his fingers over mine. "I love you," he says. "And it has noth-ing to do with what I can and cannot see of the future."

He kisses me again, tenderly, fresh and sweet. "My love, your future, Maud's Ireland, I am magus enough to know I have no power there. But what I feel for you—the terrible and primal energy of love—possesses a fierce magic all its own. We may have no dark or occult power over what is to come, but in love, we find the bright inverse of the power over. We find the power to."

I nod, and he takes my hand. The dark stone stairs spiral down, and I follow his broad shoulders into the darkness. We descend, two torn halves of one split soul, a raggedy edge shredded by, or proud flag streaming down, the howling wind of life; of sensation and emotion, of risk, of magic and of love.

It should have been the sort of perfect moment Maud wore in a long, shining strand around her careless swan's neck. Ida, who had possessed one such single, pinpricked moment once but lost it, would have set it in a ring as a solitaire. There she could have seen it always, a constant happy reminder of this reunion, when her years of sacrifice were rewarded. It would have been enough.

But every gem-like moment Ida sought to fashion for herself turned to a dirty paste of disappointment while unexpected opportunities inevitably found her unprepared, in her worst dress or bad skin. Ida met her lover, not swept into his joyful orbit, but acutely grounded in her own muck. The night's scheme required she seduce MacGregor Mathers, and lacking confidence in her own waning charms, Ida had brewed a new love potion—and all her hair had fallen out.

"Ida," her daemon murmured in a voice sleek and supple as black sealskin.

He had not aged, nor had the slow deliberation of his smile lost any of its glittering danger and invitation. His beauty made Ida pluck at her skirts and almost wish herself back with men she could control. He sat on the ledge in the naked rock she had designated for the stone-winged Victory of Samothrace in the cavernous, empty room whose very bareness of brass-veined glass dome, statues, and spiraling ramps accused Ida of her failure.

"I have brought with me the mind of MacGregor Mathers," Ida said stupidly, because of course he would know who waited for him here.

"Yes."

Ida shambled across the uneven floor to stand before the crude throne of her lord. "He is Imperator and Hierophant. I have brought him without his wife, lest she recognized the change in him should we succeed in our night's work. Although powerful and skilled, his body is not . . ." Bold though she was becoming, Ida hesitated. "He will be a strong enough vessel for you."

"My love." Ida's daemon leapt from his pulpit to land beside her with nimble stealth. "I know everything you've done, and all you have planned." He stood close enough she could have counted the black lashes bordering his hypnotic eyes. "And I know you love it here, and have longed to return to me."

Ida met his direct gaze. His black hair fell around his beautiful face, a contrast of soft sensuality and harsh strength. Only his lips combined them.

Ida pushed herself onto her tiptoes. Her daemon's brows contracted, and she put her mouth to his. From her open lips, down her throat, through her thighs, into her feet, the shock of his single kiss skipped through her. She closed her eyes to feel its scorching trail.

"Ida," he whispered against her lips, "tonight I will be born from my hell of thought into yours of body. Soon, I will be a thing that can possess you, and claim the thing that you are."

Ida started to say *God willing*, but reconsidered.

"Tonight," she said instead, "I will give myself to you. I have always loved and served you, believed in you, and longed to belong to you." Her breasts pressed against his hard chest, her breath coming too fast. Her whole being trembled with the approaching storm of orgasm.

If he chose to, leaning over her without kissing, without touching, just whispering to her, he could bring her body off. Her mind was thundering. "I have brought you MacGregor Mathers and Maud," she moaned.

"Join them," he whispered into her upturned face.

Ida opened her eyes. "To one another?"

"No, Ida. Go to them."

Ida collected her scattered self from nipples and sex, from lips and thighs and racing heart, and shoved the whole mess back behind her eyes. "Yes," she said, and felt her daemon take her arm. "I brought them with promises about the buried king. I will send Maud to her sleeping river and Mathers to the secret chamber, and you . . ."

"I will be waiting."

He smiled at her, and they walked, arm in arm, to collect Maud and MacGregor from a small room, square like the Galway tower in which their bodies slumbered. There, her daemon left her; and Ida, silent and regal, a hostess of her own domain at last, led their new guests down the long, raw halls to the spiral stone stairs twisting down and down into the dark belly of the earth.

In the cloth-hung chamber, Maud sank with grace to her knees and began to pray as though she knelt before the body of the slumbering Christ. Her recent conversion to Catholicism had only enhanced her natural genius for dramatic gesture. But MacGregor prowled the room, holding the contraband candle he had hidden in his suit jacket to the tapestries and muttering to himself.

It made Ida fidgety.

"Maud," she said at last, "if you are to continue your work, you must care for yourself. You come here to escape, not to pray."

Maud looked up at Ida from a face still lustrous and fine, despite its patina of disappointments and ill health. "I look for the resurrection of the dead," she whispered, "and the life of the world to come."

Well, it would make sense for her to, after everything. About the best she could hope for, really. But why was she still beautiful? "Go back to the pool you know," Ida instructed. "Bathe. Rest, and recover your soul."

Ida watched her only friend climb the stairs from the tomb, and then she turned to MacGregor.

"Ida, I owe you an apology," he whispered. "I would never have guessed . . . I still do not fully understand. When you came to us in

France with your tales of a buried king, we believed, at best, you were sensitive to the world soul, the vast *Spiritus Mundi*, and had conjured a dream based in the stories Mr. Frazer has shown all people share; but I never imagined it a place I could visit, a thing I could see with my own eyes. These tapestries . . . Ida, do you know how ancient they must be?"

Ida shook her head. She knew only two things at the moment, and both worried her. Most urgently, she knew she must lure Mac-Gregor away from the damn curtains before he discovered what they concealed. "Did you take notice of the markings framing the mirror?" she asked.

MacGregor climbed to his clumsy knees, and crawled the floor, muttering and translating to himself from the arcane symbols Ida had dismissed as decorative. His tedious, disciplined study allowed her a moment of contemplation. She had almost decided on a direct assault, when the grand master sat back on his rump, his muscular legs thrust straight out before him like an infant's. "Gods," he whispered.

Only genuine revelation could account for such a betrayal of his manicured dignity.

"What?" Ida dropped to her knees beside him.

He traced the raised letters with a broad finger. "This word, it's feminine. And again, here," he pointed across the under-lit rectangle of burnished gold. "This is not Arthur, or Cúchulainn."

The shock chilled Ida. Had her devil lied?

MacGregor leaned over the glowing ground, peering intently through his own reflection into the tomb beneath. "Ida!" he beckoned.

She pressed her numb face to the warm metal.

"Can you see how beautiful?" MacGregor almost moaned. "It is a woman, surely. And we were not far from Knockma. I would die happy tonight, to have seen this."

To her bitter draught of truth, Ida extemporized a drop of sweet. "You must pretend I am she," she told the Hierophant of the Ahat-hoor Temple.

"I do not understand."

"There is a ritual we must perform."

"The Augoeides Invocation?"

"No. A ritual of sexual alchemy."

"Mrs. Rowley, I am married and sworn to celibacy."

"Celibacy is an affront to the divine," Ida answered, "more foolish than eating your plate and leaving your host's best food to rot. Besides," she wheedled, "your vow belongs to your body, and it sleeps now in the topmost storey of Mr. Yeats's Galway tower." Ida's sharp eyes caught the flicker in Mathers's iron will, and she gave him her most Maud-like smile.

"Sex is a mystery, MacGregor." Ida began to work the buttons of her dress. "Its power is occult and its discussion forbidden, and yet even men of science credit it with everything from neurosis to inspiration." Mathers's eyes turned from the face beneath the floor to Ida's deepening décolleté. She tugged up the fabric to open more of her body to his gaze. "Sex is a conduit of the life force," she said, unbuttoning the tented mound in his trousers. "What other force could we channel for resurrection of the body and life in the world to come?" She gripped Mathers's own fleshy resurrection and wrung a groan from him with her practiced fingers crowning its anointed head.

"I am familiar with all alchemies and with the teaching of the Indian mystics"—his voice was choked, and his eyes squeezed closed against surrender—"but nowhere have I read it could be channeled to this end."

"Does it matter?" Ida whispered, and pressed her unbound breasts against his chest. She knew it did not. There was no ritual to enact, only fucking. But they must fuck. That was mandatory.

His body jerked with an agony of thought-destroying pleasure. "I fear I am led astray," he whispered.

Ida peered into the lust-distorted face of the man who had denied her entrance to the Golden Dawn, and she worked her hand harder between the buttons of his fly. She held him, who had lorded his knowledge over her and closed the doors of the temple before her surely as the Dublin priests, rigid and powerless in her hand.

The small, white, shoeless feet spiraling into view did not register in Ida's victory-clouded mind until they had been joined by the entire length of chinchilla-trimmed, ridiculous green dress and the pinched, flushed face of William Yeats's ugly new wife.

Georgie gawked. "Mr. Mathers?" she whispered.

But his eyes were closed and her voice was small, and Ida worked his swollen, stubby cock defiantly, aware her tits, thrown into motion by the action of her arm, flapped more than bounced the way Georgie's high, young, pregnant ones would if equally exposed.

Georgie thrust hers forward with a defiant squaring of shoulders. "Mr. Mathers!" she said again, not looking at Ida's flapping breasts, the still-motionless wall hangings, or the glowing plate of backlit gold. And still, the magus Georgie shouted for only grunted and twitched in Ida's relentless hand.

"Go away, Georgie. You have no business here," Ida warned.

"I'm not afraid of you, Ida Jameson," the pale little thing said with a quaver that betrayed her. "I know what you're up to, and I intend to stop you, too."

"Ida?" MacGregor muttered through slack lips. His sluggish eyes moved between the standing, dressed, and righteous woman, and the one with a grip on his drooping cock. Ida gave it a firm squeeze and he groaned. "This is all a dream, isn't it?" he muttered. "Georgie, why don't you come over here a moment, darling?"

"You are not dreaming!" Georgie shrilled. "Ida has lied to you! She is using you to force an evil spirit from this plane into my unborn child!"

Georgie paused for dramatic effect, but MacGregor's eyes were drifting closed, and his cock thickening. "No"—he made a helpless gesture toward the glowing golden floor—"it's female."

Georgie beamed. "I knew it! I told Will it would be. We're reincarnating the Countess of Ossory's child. She's an ancestor of Will's from hundreds of years ago. She came to us during one of our automatic writing sessions. We even went to Kilkenny looking for her grave."

"Maeve," MacGregor groaned. "Queen of the *sidhe*."

If Georgie kept prattling about Yeats's dead aunties, Ida might still manage.

"No, not Maeve!" Georgie marched to the head of the buried king and hesitated. "Look, Ida, won't you please stop . . ."

Ida flailed MacGregor ferociously.

Georgie could not find a decent place to direct her eyes. "You should do up your dress," she fretted.

Ida had noted MacGregor's pleasure matched her mounting desperation, and she cranked at him without mercy. He started to twitch.

"No, not Maeve," Georgie tried again.

MacGregor grunted.

"Mr. Mathers!" Georgie shrieked. "Mr. Mathers, it isn't the fairy queen at all!"

Ida noted with glee the pleading tone creeping into Georgie's rehearsed revelation. How satisfying to see someone else's anticipated climax carried away.

"It's not Maeve or Arthur or Cúchulainn Ida plans to incorporalize." Georgie spun away from the gasping magus and Ida's smug smile, and wound her ugly hands into the back wall's curtaining tapestry.

She yanked.

The cloth came down in a silent thunderclap of dust and horror. "It's this!"

Ida's devil stood, naked and erect, gagged and chained against his lust like Odysseus.

"Devil damn you!" Ida howled. She lunged, struggling to stand through the disarray of her unbuttoned dress, but MacGregor gripped her arm and held her to her knees beside him while Georgie danced out of Ida's clawing reach.

"Here stands the soul Ida enlisted you and Maud to incarnate!" she squawked, pointing as though MacGregor's eyes needed any directing. "He's chained to the rock lest he leap from hiding and kill you himself. That is their plan. His and Ida's! To arouse such hate and jealousy watching you possess Ida to force him into existence. Into the body of my unborn child!" Georgie clutched her barely swollen belly dramatically. Ida lunged for her again.

"You stupid, irrelevant cow, I want nothing from your spawn.

Do you believe he would consent to be born of woman and suffer childhood?"

Georgie's hands slid off her paunch. MacGregor's grip relaxed a fraction.

Ida twisted on her knees and faced the grand magus with her best seductive smile. "I'm sure this explains why Georgie would make a poor Praemonstrator for the Order. She's given to these bouts of hysteria. And monomania. She thinks all ritual centers around her." Ida's thigh found MacGregor's still-exposed, but fainting, cock, and pressed against it.

"But what is he, then?" MacGregor jerked a belligerent chin at Ida's daemon. "And how did Georgie know he was there concealed?"

"I knew because he told me he so," Georgie fumed.

Ida sat back hard on her heels.

"No, now I understand!" Georgie took a step forward. One more and she would be within reach of Ida's hands. "His jealousy would have pushed him into your body. And your soul would have been trapped here. It wasn't my child they intended for their vessel, Mr. Mathers, it was you!"

MacGregor's cock bumped Ida's cheek as she bowed her head, but neither of them cared. "Where is *here*?" he whispered.

"I don't know," Georgie confessed. "It's where the thinking part of me comes when Will and I have our automatic writing sessions. I had been jealous of Maud Gonne, but when Will at last confessed it wasn't Maud he loved, but a spirit from another time, I started looking around while I waited here, exploring a bit, instead of just resting in the river's warm water."

MacGregor released his grip on Ida's arm slowly, forgetful he held it. But Ida could no longer hear even her own murderous thoughts. She sat, hands in her lap, head down, sightless eyes pointed at the gleaming gold floor.

"Will believes Laura is half his split soul," Georgie shrugged. "But I thought . . . I hoped . . . she might be a future incarnation of me. I looked for her here, but I haven't found her."

"You won't," Ida mumbled.

"Why not?"

"Because your future self is not your husband's true love." On the dead tundra of Ida's soul, a spark of cruelty caught and lit. "But Will is wrong about her, too."

"I don't believe you," Georgie said.

"You can believe what you like," Ida said, watching MacGregor fold his forlorn cock back into his pants. "But Laura is not a piece of Will's fragmented self. She's part of mine."

Georgie blanched a gratifying white.

MacGregor and the chained devil stayed absolutely still.

Ida looked back at the radiant ground beneath her knees and smiled. "You have no idea, do you, Georgie, why I needed Will and Maud tonight? Did none of your truthful men—above or below—explain it takes more than sex or jealousy for possession? No? No, I needed one more crucial thing."

Beneath her knees, beneath the reflection of her inverse self towering down, Ida caught a second glimpse of exotic eyes. "You may be able to just drop into Hell, my little Persephone, but MacGregor and I needed Maud's pilgrim soul to guide us. We all left our bodies empty, but Maud's didn't stay deserted." Ida giggled. "And it's about to get a little less empty still."

Poor Georgie didn't get the joke. The stupid cow.

"Your husband is alone with Laura," Ida explained. "You left him with his soul's true love, channeled by Maud's beautiful body." Georgie's eyes, flickering between Ida and the stairs, told her that, although Georgie might just fall into Hell, she would have to climb her way back out. There was time for savoring.

"When they make love," Ida whispered, enjoying the taste of the words in her mouth, "when your husband takes his goddess, his muse, his pilgrim soul in his arms . . ." Ida checked the reflection a final time. The eyes were neither Maud's nor Will's, and the vision rolled in honey down her throat.

"When he takes her in his arms, and *takes* her"—Ida thrust her hips lewdly—"when he possesses she who is herself possessed, it opens a mirror, an inverse image through time between us. Between

Laura and me. I walked through it the first time he fucked her on Lough Key, but they couldn't see me. Come closer to me, Georgie, I'll show them to you. They're climbing down the tower stairs."

Georgie threw a wild look between the manacled devil and the crippled priest. Then she turned and started running up and up Hell's maddening, dizzy spiral steps.

"You would have killed me," MacGregor gasped, rounding on Ida at last.

"Don't be silly," she said. "Your body lies safe in the tower. I would have married you. Of course, you would have been *him*." She jerked her bitter thumb at her captive love.

"Ida," her devil whispered, but Ida refused to give even her eyes to him. How could he have told their secret to Georgie?

Ida slithered down and pressed her still-naked breasts to the warm gold and heard a distant voice whisper, "Laura?"

Ida peered deeper and deeper into the exotic eyes. No man in her age would know to call Laura by name.

"Laura?"

His whispering, sleep-soaked voice reached Ida, from an easy walk and a hundred years away, just as she started to lose consciousness.

No, she would not lose consciousness when she fell. That would be fatal.

⬬

I follow Will down the winding stairs into a room ridiculous as it is romantic.

"It isn't finished," he says, pulling me in, holding both my hands.

"It's perfect," I tell him, and it is. It is the ideal Irish bedroom, accessible only by a spiral stone stair, on the third floor of a time-ravaged, ivy-robed tower beside a thin, wild river in the drenching rain. It is a distillation across time of everything irresponsible and unforgiveable done in the name of poetry and dreams. I will come back here again and again; weave it into me as Will is woven.

His fingers are in my hair, his mouth over mine, and we are an instant tangle of clutching and kisses, of caught breath and crushed ribs. His hands and lips touch everywhere, on my chin and earlobes, wrists and back. His hair, fish-scaled in silver now, falls into my face, and I claw at the hard, wide shoulders under the heavy, soft folds of his coat. His delicate, strong poet's hands slide between Maud's coat and dress.

"I cannot lose you again," he groans against my throat. "You fill my soul to overflowing, where all my life it has been but a stingy trickle." He lifts his face from my skin, looks into my eyes with an urgent, desperate courage. "I have sought for God and conjured spirits; I have dredged the banks of the *Spiritus Mundi* for a solitary drop. In you I find a torrent, and a wellspring of love."

It's that sort of tumult and danger I'm trying to keep confined to this safety of dreams. I don't have his reckless daring. His courage. His tender fingers smooth the tears across my cheeks and brush my withdrawn lips until they soften. Open. Kiss the smooth, caressing tips.

I taste the salt memory of his mother shut into the upstairs room the first night I met him, and the bitter times Maud turned his love away when I could not reach him through her. I kiss the shadows of his solitary childhood and strange youth. His lonely tower, and his regret. He opens the buttons of my dress.

"I spent my young man's life combing my country's past, searching through the Celtic Twilight, when my perfect love was a creature of the dawning world."

And mine is already dead.

He shakes his head, and the storm-blown air runs cold behind his fingers over my skin. "All my visions, the supernatural sights and dreams have all been you—the wandering awareness of a woman not yet born. I have, all this time, been reaching forward, not back. Not into memory, but imagination. There are no gods or fairies." He pushes his hands under the open halves of my dress, and gathers my breasts against his loving palms. "There is only the future."

"I'm so sorry," I whisper. I have brought my tired, modern loneliness, my god-abandoned fatigue, to him. "Have I cost you your faith in God and the muses?"

"You are holy to me. You are poetry and time to me. You are the supernatural."

His gentle stroking against my nipples, the pain in his voice, and the love in his eyes, combine to drive an aching deep maternal swell within me. I run my hands up his coat sleeves, absorbing only the soft luxury of the fabric, and the increasing pleasure of my body. I reach out and unfasten the hard collar at his throat. All his gods are gone.

All he has is me. How could I ever be enough?

I press the length of my body against him, and his hands tighten on my breasts. I touch my lips to the revealed flesh beneath his stiff collar and kiss my way up, pushing onto tiptoe, until my mouth reaches his ear. "Aren't you afraid?" I whisper.

"I am afraid I will hurt you with what I feel." His voice is choked with emotion and restraint.

I put my mouth against his throat. "Yes," I whisper. I want him to.

"I am afraid our passion is too much, too strong, too unstable to last. That it will flame out or set fire to everything I cherish."

I lick the hollow of his neck where it dips into his collarbones. I open all the buttons of his shirt. "Yes," I whisper. "We can unloose more power than we can control. And there are no gods to stop us." His love has invested me with the terrifying power of God, to create and distribute, to channel and contain. And he stands so brave in the face of his power, and so willing to face mine. How can I be anything less than god-like; how can I not claim this power we share?

"I fear I will cease to work. That all my thoughts and drives will flow through you and there be nothing left for poetry."

I unfasten his belt. "Yes." Fear is part of the price. And dignity.

"I fear losing you again."

"No. As long as Ida is alive, I can find you here." I don't know what my time-spanning means, or if it means anything at all. All it has proven to me is I know less about the past than I thought, and nothing about the future. And that it doesn't matter. Beliefs are things we choose, and we leap before we look. I never knew I needed gods, until I saw that without them, we must become everything they provide for one another, through love or art.

My eyes and Will's stay open as our mouths and bodies touch. Our hands work to free each other of coats and clothes and shoes and jewelry. His mouth will not leave my flesh, not stop biting and kissing my lips, my tongue, my shoulders, my breasts. We stagger across the floor like a blinded animal, four-legged and drunk. I am more comfortable, more at home in Maud's no-longer-young body, at home in this distant time of unselfconscious confessions of love and art. I had to come back here for this, for me; and I had to bring it here, to him.

His hands keep finding new places to touch me, new ways to streak my flesh with fire. We hit the wall at the foot of the bed, and he twists us, my body held tight against him, to take the impact on his shoulder. His hands and chest and cock are all hard shadows over my skin. Turning again to hold my back against the wall, he runs his hands across my naked, shivering breasts. My hips ride up in a hungry undulation toward him, but he holds himself away.

"You're cold," he pants.

I can only shake my head.

In two long strides, he's reached our discarded tumble of clothes, and I climb onto the wooden bed on my shaking knees. Without him, I am cold. He stands over me, naked, our coats in his hands.

"My god," he whispers.

Maud's body is no longer my ideal. Three pregnancies and too many years, her recent illness and unfamiliarity with any exercise outside of walking, hang and droop in her flesh. Will's body, too, is a topography of time and imperfect circumstance.

But he kneels beside the bed, and I roll onto my side to stroke his graying hair. His face rests on the pillow by mine. We watch each other's eyes, and he runs a tender, questioning hand down the slope of my body, into my waist and over my hip. He slides it between my legs, reaches with his poet's fingers into the closed folds of me, and my body is perfect. I have earned and I claim the lines and dimples. I love the ache and fat and the history.

He meets my eyes and slides a finger into me. My mouth opens with a little pop. He holds me on his finger, and for a moment, I will come this instant, with only his eyes and finger in me, touching deeply and deeper, something completely mine. But I don't. I don't come, don't contract—I open.

The threshold of awareness expands. It swells, and I can contain more, feel more, channel more through me. He climbs over me, opens my legs for his body, and enters me. His cock pushes against my desire-stuffed flesh, presses against me, rising to receive him. His arms wrap me, body covers me, hands hold me. Our hips groan into each other. Our souls swell with the meaning we have made. Made and given to each other.

He kisses me once, and drops his head, temple to my temple. I can hear his wrenched breathing in my ear. Our orgasms gather like twin thunderheads, piling sensation on sensation, pleasure rolling over pleasure, a cumulative roiling mounting against itself within us. We are overfilled, uncontainable. And still gathering.

Gathering the incipient cloudburst, gathering his body to mine, mine into him, a singularity. Pleasure arcs between my breasts and sex until too many tracers scorch the surface in concentrated flares. Orgasm cracks between us and collapses into a single strike, a depth charge at the seat of my soul, my sex—not clutching, but radiating. The pulsing waves discharge outward and in. We implode. We twist open time.

⬮

Ida opened her eyes in the candlelit gold pane, and fell into the future.

A wood-dark face rested beside hers on a pillow, its eyes closed. Beneath their exotic, black-lashed slant, sweet, somnolent lips formed an unintelligible question and Ida mimicked the man's sleep-heavy mumble despite the interior keen, sharp squeal at the genius of her night's work.

Everything was perfect.

As nothing Ida had done had ever been perfect. Her daemon lover had vanished, tower and cavern dissolved, and the future waited just beyond the bedspreads for her exploration and conquest. She had reversed the game and woken up the future.

Warily, Ida folded her body away from the sleep-muttering man, and knew his name was Amit. Her husband. And her body, younger and taut, fit into his bare chest when he curled around her in his sleep. But the window was not curtained, and the smoky gray of almost-dawn hovered at the edges of pushed-back, oddly patterned drapes that did not reach the floor.

Agonized by the delay in learning all that had evolved, Ida disciplined her joy, knowing this powerful body, this thrilling freedom, had waited for her for a hundred years. It would wait another night. But if she was going to channel her daemon into the future with her, she must gamble that some things never changed.

Mr. Rowley would never have noticed anything different in her eyes, as she had seen in Maud's, but it occurred to Ida not all husbands were the same. Hers had never slept undressed beside her. Never held her with easy familiarity while he slept. She would need to keep Amit's attention from her eyes until she had him mesmerized.

Ida fingered the quilt's fine stitching—the precise, identically sized stitches, the almost invisibly small needle punctures—and pulled the blanket over her head, reaching for the heavy vulnerability men so foolishly keep outside themselves. She gathered the sleeping weight of him with her new, stronger but not larger hands, and gentled the warm mass forward and up.

Ida nuzzled into the timeless, dark salt and warm yeast smell of kneaded testicles and encircled the root of Amit's sleeping cock with one hand. She dragged it from its drowsy nest, and licked its sleepy head once like a wide-tongued cat. His hard stomach tightened in a spasmodic clutch against her cheek. Ida grinned in the quilt-dark, and tugged up the length of his fattening cock again.

Amit sighed and coiled his fingers into the strange, closely cropped hair of his wife's head, and Ida wondered idly as she lapped whether Laura had recently had lice or fever. Still, she worked both her hands in a baroque unison of rolling squeezes until they wrung a groan from over her head, and an unambiguous thrust toward it. Smiling, she put the full flower of her efforts into her mouth and sucked him. Amit's hips lifted off the soundless bed. Leaving one hand to tend him, Ida leveraged herself with the other and suctioned a vine of kisses across his taut belly, up his ribs and around and across and against his hard chest. This should keep his eyes from hers. Ida pulled the blankets back.

More than her daemon in his fitted white military pants, more than her Russian prince in his careless thief's coat, this man, in his undress, made the image of perfect masculinity. Ida marveled at the ideal made manifest in flesh sculpted like dark Grecian marble. She ran eager hands over his delineated form, relishing the carved mass and line, the silent shape and structure. She pushed her blunt fingers into his shoulders. Never had a thing so hard also been so warm, like a horse's flank without its coarse hair, or an eel without wet scales. Ida nuzzled into the rich interior scent of Amit's body and hoped, when it housed her daemon, it would keep this smell.

His skilled hands, sliding up her legs, rounded over her ass and drew her pliant body over his. Ida stretched a thigh against his hip, kissing up his throat. She almost reached his lips, almost had his kiss to bind him, but he turned his head from her with a groan, and his cock twitched up between her open legs.

And Ida could not chase it. Could not trail his strong jaw to his open mouth, because his hard hands ran over her ass, up her back and forward to cup her breasts. It dropped Ida's jaw with the jolt of pleasure coursing over a body which had never known an unwelcome touch, a stabbing hatpin or uncle, and Ida held it—once Laura's body, now hers, her strange, new, nubile body—over his—larger than the bodies of men she knew—and the weight of wetness building in her sex spread open over him. His fingers on her puffed nipples rubbed her hips into movement, and his fierce cock rose to meet it. Ida had to keep her eyes buried. She held her face against his, panting in his ear, but that was all she could manage.

His hands reached from her breasts to her hips and held them, his thumbs on her hip bones, fingers insistent in the flesh of her ass, but

Ida needed no prompting. Nor could she savor the hard glide of his cock driving up into her, but threw her body over it, gasping. She knew herself alive at last, a hundred years away and free. She rode Amit's strong cock with all the demanding vigor of the health and youth she had stolen, somewhere between laughing in victory and sobbing with relief. She understood now how Laura was so safe and free. A strong, beautiful man lay on his back and gave his sex and power again and again to her soaking, swallowing need. Ida threw her head back, and dug her fingers into his chest. His fingers caught her nipples, and all Ida's schemes and thinking left her. She rode into her destiny—sex blazing, tits bouncing—a radiant being, finally beautiful. Good, and where she belonged.

Powerful at last.

Ida collapsed on his broad chest without shame, and Amit stroked her weird hair and back like a cat curled over him. She could almost just stay this way. But she kissed the tender indent behind his ear. He smelled like out-of-doors, almost scentless below the line of his soft hair. Ida's lips dappled her husband's jaw to his lips to kiss him, to touch her mouth—her mind—to his, but he pinned her against his strong chest, moving already back into the rhythm of sleep. If Ida could confidently stay here, simply take Laura's body, time, and husband for her own, would she still want her devil with her here, where women held power of their own? Ida sighed within the warmth and strength she only borrowed. Had Amit's eyes in the reflecting gold of the king's tomb been a gift from her shackled daemon, or just Ida's lonely talent for plucking advantage from catastrophe? It didn't matter. If Laura's reunion with Will had opened this vortex forward into time, Ida's union with Amit had surely opened one back to her daemon. All she needed now was to send Amit's spirit after his wife's.

"Did you know I was gone?" Ida made her voice into a small bone, dry and stripped, and held out in a careful, dimpled hand to a blind witch.

Amit's "eh?" was a grunt muffled in her short hair.

"Was I not different to you?"

He nodded against her scalp, and Ida reached back, not into her cloud-damped memory of the days before her own wedding, but for the self-altering nerves of normal brides.

"I have not been the woman you fell in love with, have I?" She hesitated, but he didn't answer, and she didn't wait for him to consider, whispering swift and secret against his taut chest. "A spirit from another time took possession of me, Amit. But tonight I have returned to you. Now I need your help. I must mesmerize you and send your soul with me to avenge the theft so I can stay with you always."

"Yeah, bullshit."

Ida could not speak. Amit did not move, and his arm draped over her like a boat chain.

"Amit . . ."

"I don't know who you are, but go to sleep, I want Laura back."

"Amit, I am Laura!" Ida did not need to conjure panic into her voice now. "You do not know me because my soul was carried away on our wedding night!"

"No." He shook his head against her hair. His sleepy, calm drawl infuriated Ida. Devil damn him to an eternity of premarital non-consummation. He knew.

Could she escape him and run? If she took Laura's body to Thoor Ballylee, might she bridge the gate by positioning body from soul across time, in the same place? A hundred years later did Yeats's tower still stand?

"You're shaking." Amit took her chin in tender but undeniable fingers and turned her face to his. "Look at me."

Ida seethed and would not.

"Laura, wake up."

Ida laughed and looked up.

Amit's strong fingers tightened a moment where they had lingered on Ida's jaw and she briefly reconsidered how powerful her modern self-portrait should be. But, deliberately slow, he uncurled them, dropped them to her shoulders and set her body away from his.

"Your eyes . . . Where the hell is my wife?"

"Exactly there!" Ida crowed.

"I'm going to ask you again, just in case any part of what I thought was going on is actually happening, and you're a . . . personality . . . Laura was just dreaming. Or pretending to be."

A cold and raging wonder ignited in Ida. "You thought we were but playacting?"

Amit shrugged once. His bare, broad shoulders, whose strength and comfort Ida viscerally remembered under her fingers and cheek, flexed danger now.

Was it possible he and Laura—just on a lark—could simply make up the ritual sex Ida had labored years to master and never found a man to enact?

Her mind slipping, Ida considered the truth, and found an unexpected angel. It nearly knocked her speechless with astonishment. "You knew Laura did not animate her body when you satisfied yourself upon it?"

"She was enjoying it. Her body was . . ."

Amit faltered. Ida leapt.

"No, *I* was! Adultery!" Ida hooted and sprang from bed. Or tried to. Disconcertingly, she moved very little actual distance from Amit's strong arms. In his eyes, she could see only distance. He was already there, in Hell's waiting room, banished by a pain too sudden and too sharp to bear.

"No." He shook his head.

"I'm glad you think not," Ida chirped. She must not let denial protect him. "Because your wife has done the same with another man. I channeled your wife into a body from another land, and another time, and there she fell in love. When you believed she lay with you, she betrayed you in his arms. Even if you held her this tightly." Ida thrust hard at his enclosing arm and found it opened easily. She sprang to standing, Laura's compact, strong body making the jump fluid and easy, despite having to adjust for his lack of resistance.

All his strength was marshaled to the task of understanding. "How long?" he whispered.

Ida edged in front of the window to put the heavy dawn light behind her. He was not a man she wanted to see angry, but if she could keep him weak with shock and pain, she might yet draw her true devil through him. "Years," she whispered. "Since 1889. Since your wedding night."

"That was when she started talking in her sleep." Amit's voice rumbled slow and thoughtful.

Ida said nothing, but glanced around the room. Beneath her, a carpet that touched every wall of the room absorbed her bare feet like a deep-knap velvet. Ida worked her anxious toes into its soft, summer-grass warmth. But there would be time enough soon to explore the future's luxury. Right now, all her attention must go to keeping Amit unbalanced and in pain. "I know what she said that night," Ida taunted. "She said her name, her true full name, and gave her natal date."

Amit's eyes, even through the muddy light, gazed keen and frightening.

"She was giving them to me," Ida whispered. "So I could call her back into our time. She wanted to come back."

Amit's eyes flashed danger and the kindlings of rage.

"Who is he?"

"A poet." Ida shrugged to show herself unimpressed.

"What's his name?"

"Will Yeats."

Amit let his body fall back on the bed. His eyes searched the ceiling over him, and Ida allowed herself a small smile and a fractional scoot backwards to the bed.

"William Butler Yeats," Amit growled.

"You know him?"

Ida moved a little closer.

"He's a family favorite. I prefer James Joyce."

Ida had met the young writer Joyce at the Nassau Hotel once, and she knew Will had lent him money, but little else about the man, so she didn't say anything now to distract her new quarry. She must keep the pain keen. "Did you love her very much?" She sidled farther up the bed.

"I love her completely."

"Love is sacrifice." Ida leaned closer. "Laura belongs more in our time than yours. She could live happily in the past."

Amit nodded, eyes still distant with heartbreak.

"Her only suffering comes from being unrooted. This body can call her back too easily, and then she loses the home she has, and the man she loves in my time. If you really love her, you must set her free."

"She's already free."

"No." Ida encircled his wrist with a tender hand. "This body traps her. Holds her to this time. But you can release her. If you love her enough. I can show you how."

Amit's eyes closed. Ida leaned over him.

"Where is Laura now?" he asked.

"Her spirit animates the body of another in my time, even as my spirit inhabits her body in yours."

"I have to see her. I have to know what she wants."

The delicate skin of Amit's eyelids, paler than the deep red-brown of his strong forehead, twisted with the same constricting pain. Ida had lived in Paris and London, had seen the exotic Indian mystics and the American Negroes, but they did not socialize, and even the swamis Madame Blavatsky imported had seemed always vaguely sinister to her. Still, a strange, urgent treble of desire trilled between her thighs at the anguish in his beautiful features. Ida was intimate with soul-sundering pain and could recognize it on even the strangest face. "Kiss me," she whispered. "Kiss me and I'll show you how to talk to Laura across time."

Amit's eyes met hers. And even through a host body, and out of time, Ida knew he saw her. Saw her like her lovers and father, her servants and husband never had. She caught a glimpse of her image, not powerless, not scorned, but full of a wild imagination, and free. It made a sudden sense of everything she had done and thought. Ida recoiled in surprise, but his hand caught the back of her head, keeping her face only inches from his. He had fought his way back from the numbness, and was fully on fire with his pain. And anger. But he kissed her. Nonetheless.

They were linked.

The blanket slipped from Ida's unclenched fingers and fell away. She didn't understand how he had found the courage to face the truth she'd fed him and return, fully present to feel it, so freshly drawn and so keen, but there was no doubt. He was fully incarnated. Her daemon would find no easy home in Amit now. Why had he kissed her knowing what she truly was when he opened his eyes?

What had he seen while they were closed?

"You must go to Thoor Ballylee," she whispered.

She had his kiss. Let it be enough.

"It's not far. Come to the fireplace on the fourth floor. You can talk to Laura there."

He swung his powerful legs out of bed, naked feet on the inviting, soft floor, and waited, muscle-carved back to her. A superb housing for her beautiful daemon in the future's exciting freedom. If only she could detach herself from everything this future promised long enough to find Amit's injured soul in Hell, all the rituals she had planned to enact on MacGregor Mathers, she would work on this younger, stronger, more magical man instead.

"Go to your wife," she told him and stretched herself on the re-silient mattress.

Ida folded her hands over her flat belly. She would come back and claim Laura's modern body and give it to that alluring man with her devil housed inside him. And together they would be beautiful and modern and alive. And very powerful. Ida forced herself to close her eyes.

Will swings his long legs out of bed, sock-feet to the bitter floor, and twists his lean back to gaze at me curled under our coats. The uneven mattress sits low to the ground, and his knees stick up like fieldstones. We bask in the contended quiet together, but morning lightens the fabric pinned over the window, and its rain-chilled clarity excites me. I spring out of bed with a creaky bound and stumble. He catches me around the waist without standing up, and pulls my body closer, pressing his stubble-grazed cheek to the skin of Maud's loose belly. I cradle his head against me.

"Once I thought"—his lips move against my flesh in tiny, vivid word-kisses—"that you were sent to me so we might fashion the future of my country together. That we would conceive a child, that you—the spirit of my nation's future goodness—and I—her poet— might make something to outlast us. To improve and inspire us."

His words whisper into my belly, and it contracts in an ache of longing. I can almost touch the fat, baby palm against Prized Possession's window.

"But Maud's body is old to risk that now, and there was once before talk of an illegal operation." He stands up and wraps me in his arms. I am almost as tall, and our bodies, matching year for year, absence for loneliness, lean into each other. "My wife is pregnant."

"That's good," I say, but I shiver. He kisses me, and stoops to hand me my clothes.

I wish I had a pair of jeans and a sweatshirt. There is nothing comforting about stepping back into Maud's buttoned, belted, high-necked dress, but for his sake, and hers, we should be presentably clothed and back with the inert bodies by the dying fire upstairs before it is fully light.

We are spiraling up the stairs to the top-floor ritual room when a door slams hard below us, and I have a vague sense that it was a similar sound, in this time or some other, that woke me. We step over the raised threshold between the anteroom and the larger, windowed space where Ida's and MacGregor's abandoned bodies still droop in chairs before the gaping fireplace. Will throws peat from a basket onto the fire and prods it with a rustic poker. He looks from my face to the arched wooden door we left open as his wife flies through it. I recognize her at once from the honeymoon hotel I dreamed last night, but she's grown into herself in an unexpected way. Georgie Yeats runs across the room and plows her hands and forehead into her husband's chest with the confidence of frequent corporeal collisions. It almost knocks me down.

"Will!" she pants. She meets Maud's eyes. "No, Laura!" she says.

I stagger, but she grasps my elbow and shakes me. "Listen! Your adventure has gone awry. Ida has no intention of rousing the king under the mountain, although he truly is sleeping there. I have seen him. But Ida plans to use MacGregor's body to channel an evil thing she has fallen in love with from its mythic plane onto our material one!".

The cold pours through me, furious and blinding as last night's rain. This is Will's wife and unborn child. He loves her. And I am also someone's wife.

I should sit down.

Will takes Georgie by the elbows, looks over the top of her head to me, but she twists out of his hands. Her bony fingers bite into my arms just as I'm about to have a seat on the floor face-first. She guides me onto a stone bench set into the wall. "Will, come, sit beside her," she commands.

He walks to me, but Georgie steps over to the massive fireplace and touches the mantel with questioning fingers.

"Georgie, what happened?" he asks.

"I don't really know." She lifts the poker and replaces it.

"The first time I suggested we try automatic writing," she says, "I was intending to pretend for you." Georgie unpins her straggling hair and shakes it out impatiently. "I knew you didn't love me, and I hoped to invent a trick for speaking more candidly to each other." Will can't hold her eyes, but he does not look to me. "But I swear to you, Will, that first time, I did feel something. A ghostly hand gripped mine and moved my pen."

"Yeah," I whisper from the wall ledge, "that was me."

Ashamed, Will only nods, but Georgie's strange face splits in delight. "I thought as much!" she crows. "But then you didn't come again." She's looking brightly right at me.

I shake my head. "That was just last night for me."

"You know I have also been trained in occult practices." She glances at Will, but her hungry eyes snap right back to my face. To Maud's. "MacGregor taught me, before we met, how to free my imagination in a trance and let it wander. I tried that, hoping to find the hand that guided mine the first time. Hoping to find you, I guess." She holds her steady eyes to mine. "But I didn't. I found what

I thought was fairy land, but Maud was there, and she said it was Hell."

Will shakes his head, and Georgie drops the urgency and strain from her voice. She tries to make it gentle. "I met the thing Ida loves. He is truly wicked—her daemon. He nearly seduced me, but I moved beyond him into love. And I saw the king under the mountain. That much of what she's said is true. King Arthur really waits to come again. Or Christ, although I don't know why either of them would be buried in Ireland. But when Maud, Ida, and MacGregor came to you last month with stories of astral travel, I knew the only place one can go in such journeys is the very place I travel in our automatic writing sessions; so when you all left the cottage to come up here for your great séance, I sat in my room and went into my trance to follow my husband and his friends on their reckless quest. But you stayed here." Her eyes move from Will's to mine.

I cannot hold them. I am ashamed.

"I didn't understand at first," Georgie continued, "until I saw Ida trying to seduce MacGregor. We have to wake him!" She points frantically at MacGregor's limp frame. "If we don't bring his consciousness back into his body . . ." Color flooded Georgie's face behind the dammed-up words she could not bring herself to say. "If Mr. Mathers and Ida . . ." she stammered, trying for a delicate way to convey the sexual act. "If MacGregor *takes* Ida, her daemon will possess him."

She stares from Will to me. "His soul will be lost, ransomed by Ida for her daemon," she whispers. "We must bring his mind back to his body!"

"I don't know how." Will's serious eyes turn to me at last. "Laura, how do you wake up to your own time, when you have wanted to?"

I shake my head. I never wanted to.

Georgie's wild eyes fly between us.

The way her small body is framed by the fireplace prods my memory.

"How do you return to me, Georgie, when we do our writing?" Will asks.

"I climb out. Sometimes it takes me days to feel completely myself again."

I remember, with a blade of sudden recognition, the ghost standing bodiless before the dusty hearth where Will and I made love on the floor of the castle surrounded by lake.

"Was it different this time?" I croak.

She doesn't answer. Will looks between us without understanding.

"Georgie, was it different this time, the way you came back?" I ask.

"A gateway opened right before me," Georgie whispers. "From that plane into this. And I walked through."

"Laura, do you know how these portals are made?" Will's urgency is painful. "Can we create one for MacGregor to return through?"

But I can't take my eyes off Georgie. "Into your body, right away?" I ask her.

Finally she shakes her head. "No."

"You came back disembodied?" I ask. "Like a ghost?"

She nods. "I knew where my body was. I only needed to walk the little distance back to it."

"From where?" I ask.

Georgie bows her head and jerks it behind her. "I came through here. Through the fireplace."

Will's hand clutches convulsively on the stone of the mantel.

"You were sleeping," she says without looking at us.

Will goes to his wife and puts his arms around her.

We all understand. Will and I create a bridge across planes and over time, in our love made physical. Ida walked over that bridge from Hell into the Castle Island fireplace the first time we made love. And the second time, in her closed-up French summer house, she called her devil across it. I saw him. Georgie is right to be afraid. And tonight, leaving Will with me, Ida must have planned to do the same, but Georgie interrupted her. But how could Georgie have crossed back here?

Unless two spans were made tonight.

Understanding claws at me, and I cannot scramble back from it fast enough. *Two* bridges opened over time. The knowledge catches my ankle and clambers up my legs. Links through time made by bodies linked in love, and souls. Ida moved forward, and not back, in time tonight over the bridge made by my sex with Will. And Georgie came back to us over a bridge Ida made. In the future. The same way.

"You were sleeping," Georgie whispers. "And I walked down the stair and out the door. I closed the door, maybe a little more loudly than I needed to, just to know that, even bodiless, I still could."

I heard that door slam.

I hear it again now.

"I walked across to the cottage." Georgie is still whispering. "And I felt perfect, at peace and alive. I saw my body on the bed, hands folded over my belly, like they were already holding my child."

My hands close over my flat modern belly.

"And I kissed my own mouth, and I opened my eyes."

I open my eyes.

The little B&B bedroom holds only sunlight and the quiet. And from the window, when I can lug my body to it, I see my husband walking, tall and purposeful, down the road to Yeats's tower.

from "Magic"
an essay by W. B. Yeats

(first published in *The Monthly Review*, September 1901)

I have now described that belief in magic which has set me all but unwilling among those lean and fierce minds who are at war with their time, and who cannot accept the days as they pass, simply and gladly; and I look at what I have written with some alarm, for I have told more of the ancient secret than many among my fellow-students think it right to tell. I have come to believe so many strange things because of experience, that I see little reason to doubt the truth of many things that are beyond my experience; and it may be that there are beings who watch over that ancient secret, as all tradition affirms, and resent, and perhaps avenge, too fluent speech.

We who write, we who bear witness, must often hear our hearts cry out against us, complaining because of hidden things, and I know not but he who speaks of wisdom may sometimes, in the change that is coming upon the world, have to fear the anger of the people of Faery, whose country is the heart of the world—"The Land of the Living Heart." Who can keep always to the little pathway between speech and silence, where one meets none but discreet revelations? And surely, at whatever risk, we must cry out that imagination is always seeking to remake the world according to the impulses and the patterns in that Great Mind, and that Great Memory? Can there be anything so important as to cry out that what we call romance, power, intellectual beauty, is the only signal that the supreme Enchanter, or some one of His counsels, is speaking of what has been, and shall be again, in the consummation of time?

13

BETWEEN MY HATRED AND DESIRE, I SAW MY FREEDOM WON

"Speaking of love through other lips and looking
Under the eyelids of another, for it was my craft
That put a passion in the sleeper there,
And when I had got my will and drawn you here,
Where I may speak to you alone, my craft
Sucked up the passion out of him again
And left mere sleep.

. . .

Woman,
I was your husband when you rode the air,
Danced in the whirling foam and in the dust,
In days you have not kept in memory,
Being betrayed into a cradle, and I come
That I may claim you as my wife again."

—from "The Two Kings" by W. B. Yeats

It surprised Ida how quickly the air opened her compressed layers, like the wind must touch a flying bird, not only under the outspread wings, but between each feather. Every articulation of her mind lifted. Each thought separated. Navel to the cold stone, Ida hovered, buoyed by success. She knew the nature of her particular damnation brought her into this place easily, but from it she had reached forward into time and come—with less effort than ever—back. Mayhap, in the future, the veil between these worlds wears thinner, and the coming generations live closer to Hell.

Still, Ida's victory made it no easier than ever to roll over. Better to lie on her belly, bathed in her dreams, than to put plans into action, stand, and drag them into being.

She opened her eyes into the vast, empty space of the entrance hall. Flocks of the restless damned, beautiful and brooding, and the ghosts of her glass-and-brass architecture mocked her in shimmers. Ida wiped her future-blinded eyes and almost fell off the high, narrow ledge she lay upon. She pushed her legs into the empty space to dangle. Her daemon had sat just here. Her daemon who, even now, chained to the naked rock in the bowels of Hell, awaited her.

She should probably go see about that. Set him free.

Ida's sharp shoes rang like hooves along the bare corridors, but still she ran, her urchin rags replaced now by a harlot's tawdry regalia. In the future, carpets reached the walls, but she would never return to tread them if she failed now. She stumbled on the spiral stairs, tripped, and landed in a clump at the feet of her manacled love.

"Whore!" he howled.

Ida righted herself, and pushed the flame-red dress away from her face. "No, my love, it's your Ida. I have returned!" She stood up, stepped on her hem, staggered and wrenched the dress front from its wad between her armpit and hip. Her breast plopped out.

"Whore!" Her daemon lunged against the heavy manacles which had already chafed angry purple welts to bleeding on his throat and wrists.

Ida stood silent a moment, suffused with joy.

He cared!

She stuffed her breast back into the strumpet's dress and smiled. She preferred its tawdry charms to the scullery rags, anyway. And mayhap she preferred her daemon chained. It made a nice change from the impotent years of chasing-after she'd done in his name.

He growled with suppressed loathing. "Did you sell yourself to a man on the other side of time?"

"No," Ida demurred. "I gave myself freely."

Face locked in a rictus of pain, Ida's daemon stopped, froze, and sagged in his chains. "Do you not comprehend?" he whispered. "Your generosity is the one thing that can destroy me."

Ida fell from glory at her power to pity at his loss in less time than it took her to throw herself into his chain-wrapped arms. "I don't understand!" she cried.

"Fucking in her body, you opened a bridge not only from here into Laura's time, but also back to yours. And Georgie—damn her faithful soul—walked through it back to her poet."

"It doesn't matter," Ida purred against the blood-flecked chest. "I can reach my old life all too easily. It pulls upon me still. But if we are brave"—Ida raised her face from her daemon's chest and met his ravenous eyes—"if we have true courage, you and I can create a new life in the future. It is a time better suited to both our natures, an era in tune with both possession and possibility." Ida formed her best seductive smile. "And Laura's husband is younger than MacGregor, brave, strong, beautiful. And willing. I can deliver him to you."

Ida's daemon slid his hands, in their shivering metallic bonds, down her back to gather the loose flesh of her ass and squeeze it through the tasteless red silk. "Ah. Well, it isn't really generosity when you stand to gain so much by your giving," he said, mischief and pleasure glinting in his dark eyes.

"I am not your apotheosis." Ida grinned. "I am your wife. It is only mostly the same thing."

He kissed her, fierce and happy.

"We should go," Ida murmured through the teeth biting her lip. "Amit is walking to the tower. He's had a bit of an emotional blow, so he's halfway here already. We will show him his wife in the arms of a poet, and his soul will slip away to the pool where Maud waits."

Ida pulled her kiss-swollen mouth away and ran her hands along the chain manacling the arms that held her. "Do you have the key?"

He shook his head. "You must unravel it yourself."

Ida plucked at the cruel but gorgeous gold encircling his proud neck, and a single thread came loose. She trailed it backwards, unwinding and unpinning it from the interlocking loops and knots. "I wish," she whispered as she worked, "for a magic to pierce and hold open the paths we walk between our worlds."

"I've heard stories," he answered, "of such a thing."

Ida brushed the untangled cords from her lover's throat, and set to work on those binding his hands.

"I'm afraid Amit is not the sort of misbegotten soul who wanders off hunting the things that lead men here," her daemon fretted.

"I have given him directions, and he comes to the threshold already in pain."

"And even blameless souls can find their way through the labyrinth to Hell"—Ida's daemon closed his eyes with the erotic pleasure in the unraveling threads against his skin—"when they are led by love."

"Once I have gathered all his thoughts to me," Ida whispered, "I will take his body."

"Yes, my love," her daemon purred. "And I will live through him."

"Yes." Ida's blunt hands were full to overflowing with a chaos of gold thread. "And draw me into the world Laura leaves when she dreams of romance and the past."

Ida gazed into the face of the being she loved beyond caution and reason, the dream she would soon wake to find realized. "But the sun was already sucking magic from the night when I arrived, and if Maud reclaims herself before we finish, Laura will awaken in her own body, and I will have nowhere but my own life to go."

The tangled strands ran from between Ida's slackening fingers. A cold bubble of fear rose in her throat. She would have nowhere but her past to go. But her daemon grasped her wrist and leapt up the spiral stairs. Ida lurched like a vivified corpse behind him.

And Maud and MacGregor, Yeats and Georgie would know at last who she was, having met her here. They would see what Amit had in the moment he kissed her. And they would hate her. She would be worse than friendless. Worse than mad. She would be revealed and rejected. Seen, finally. Heeded, finally. And turned away. Again.

"Love," she whispered as they emerged together into the aching, empty hole that welcomed all Hell's new arrivals. "Love, you must promise me . . ."

He turned to her. "Anything."

"Laura has not yet come to herself, has she?"

Her devil's tongue touched his lips. "She holds even now, at this very moment, her poet to her heart."

❦

I cannot blink or swallow. My forehead presses against the glass like it would push through the frozen pane. Unfastened, fragmented, I slide my back against the wall to sit on the ugly shag carpet.

I don't know how long my eyes are pointed at it before the first hints of morning sun strike gold, glint, and capture my attention. I know what I'm seeing, but I won't believe it.

I won't.

I could be sleepwalking, for all the awareness I have of standing up and walking from the window to the bedside table. I grope for the lamp. I fumble with the ridiculous thing so long and so clumsily I almost drag it off the table. Which might be better. Better never to reach my numb fingers down for the dull gleam, not pick it up.

So I don't. I can't. I sit on the bed beside it. Look at the spot where he took it off and left it.

Amit's wedding ring.

We wrote our vows around our rings. The band I picked out for myself and the one handed down in his family several generations to him. It was Amit's idea. We each kept our own until the ceremony. I handed him mine, and he put it on me. He gave me his and I did the same. I put that ring on him and promised to be his wife.

I've never touched it without him. But I pick it up at last.

Inside, faint and almost worn away over time, flowing letters wink inside the small gold band.

I am not crying, but have closed my eyes, when I feel the old pull back in time. The Irish voice. Will calling my name, quiet but urgent. I hold Amit's ring against my heart, and again and again, repeat the words inscribed inside it: *Demon est Deus Inversus.*

❦

Hand in hand, Ida and her daemon blew into the cavernous hall of Hell, victorious. Ida was Maud on the night she had heard rehearsed a hundred times, Maud's debut at the viceregal court, in a gown of her own design—white satin and gauze flower petals, iridescent beads and appliquéd train. The Prince of Wales had knocked aside his son to escort her to the Royal Dais. And Ida was no less honored. She was Cinderella announced at the ball. Falling asshole over elbows down the grand stair.

When she possessed Laura's stingy, modern frame, mayhap she would be allowed an elegant descent at last, but now she flung her free hand against her devil's chest to stop him tumbling after. Georgie stood in one of the floor's deep pits, only the top of her shoulders and head visible above the rock floor. Ida pressed her daemon's body against the jagged stone ledge into the shadows there, and gaped.

He grinned and pulled her body against his, cock hard in her fall-bruised flesh, but Ida stayed rigid, fixated by the sight of Will Yeats's wife trying to lever herself out of the stone like a self-weeding root. What was Georgie doing back in Hell? Ida chewed her lip, confident she and her daemon were hidden where they crouched. Even her lover, who belonged here, could not see as well into Hell's dark shadows as Ida could.

But Amit was walking to Thoor Ballylee, and Georgie showed no sign of working her ass out of the hole. If Ida waited, hidden and hesitating, Amit might arrive before Georgie freed herself and left the entry hall in search of Maud and MacGregor. But if Ida plucked her out, Georgie might never leave. Finally, Ida could stand the worming and grunting no more, stormed over, seized Georgie by her rock-scraped wrists, and dragged her free. Georgie's feet scrabbled on the sheer stone of her pit, but her body twisted as it emerged, protecting the second body stuffed between her hip bones.

"What?" Ida demanded, her voice irritatingly shrill in its fury. "Did your husband not want you? Did Will and Laura send you back?" Ida glared at the torn velvet and beading hanging from Georgie's curled form. Why did she get to keep her nice dresses here? "Or maybe you were just unable to find your way out?" Ida's tromping toes itched with the proximity of Georgie's rolled-up fingers.

Georgie lifted her head from the stone. Ida looked from the crumbled velvet shoulders to the beautiful swagger of her devil sauntering toward them from the shadows.

"I already told you." He held Georgie's eyes even though he spoke to Ida. "Georgie walked directly through to her world and husband when you opened your legs for Laura."

Georgie smiled, and Ida could not have said which of them she hated most. What ran between them? Why had her lover ever spoken to Will's wife? Ida seized Georgie around the throat and dug her chewed-sharp nails into the pasty skin. Ida dragged Georgie's face to within biting distance.

"What's so goddamn funny?"

"Laura is with him now."

"With who?" All Ida's assault had accomplished was helping Georgie to stand up. "Is Laura is back in her own body?" Ida's eyes swung to her devil. He had lied to her.

For the first time, Ida was fully in Hell.

Georgie drew her hands down her shredded velvet dress and over the round of her stomach. Short, tattered, and pregnant, a nobility clung to her that Ida could never capture. "And I've told Will to kill you," she said with the same, regal calm. "He will destroy your body, and you will be trapped here, where you can sleep with your devil but never wake. Serves you right."

Ida held a weary hand out to Georgie. "Maud and I wear matching rings. I will ride her soul back."

"Maud's not going back that way." The triumph on Georgie's dull face was unbearable. "Will and MacGregor have secrets you never learned."

"I fixed that! I belong to the inner temple!"

Georgie's lack of concern was almost a flirtation. "They learned them from me."

"You?" Ida shrieked. "What could *you* teach them?"

Georgie dusted herself off. "More than you can imagine. I taught myself. I'm going to find MacGregor now."

"Your husband won't kill me," Ida called after her. "I am Will's only way of reaching Laura. He won't give that up. Laura is his soul mate."

Georgie stiffened, and Ida's devil slipped behind her back. "Laura is his metaphor," Georgie said.

"Laura feeds him—emotionally, spiritually, and sexually. You can't begin to do that." Ida shouted, feeling every one of her own inadequacies.

"Laura feeds only his poetry," Georgie said, but Ida's keen eyes saw the shadow stroke Georgie's pale face with caressing fingertips.

"Can you do that?" Ida whispered.

"No." Georgie turned away, and Ida's devil slipped around her to hold both his open palms to Ida. "I can't. It's why I gave her to him."

"You did what?"

"Will made a portal, a circle on the roof of Ballylee, and I fell through. The magic will draw Laura's spirit into my body. I'm not a natural channel, not like Maud, but I think I heard her whispering, calling for Will by his occult name, as I floated free."

Ida blinked. "You drew Laura into your body deliberately and came back here? You left Will with Laura in your body? On purpose?"

Georgie met Ida's incredulous eyes with frank courage and pride, if not with understanding. "It was a sacrifice," she said.

Ida did her level best to keep from dancing, but laughter raised her jaws in a wolf howl, and she had to thrust her teeth into the meat of her palm to keep from capering.

Laura was again with Will. Amit might still come to Ballylee. He might still be drawn to Hell.

"I'm sorry, Ida," Georgie said.

Ida struggled to bring her focus back to Georgie's strange, but somehow beautiful face.

"I'm sorry, Ida, but you are just too dangerous for freedom. It is better if you live here, where you can't hurt anyone."

"Only here can anyone be hurt," Ida crowed. She wanted to revel and bask, but she knew she must set Georgie on her way. "And Mac-Gregor is to make the portal on this side, is he? You returned to instruct him?" Ida's groping mind impaled itself on a spur to set against Georgie's tender side. "MacGregor and Maud will leave here through it."

Georgie nodded.

"And, Georgie," Ida whispered, "what did Maud and MacGregor come here to possess? Not you. Not your husband or his mythic love."

Georgie blanched. Ida covered her face with her hands to hide the radiance streaming, surely, from her transcendent eyes. Now was her kingdom coming. "They will come to the portal you and Will created with the soul of the buried king, that he may be reborn."

"Into what body?" Georgie quavered, her hands protecting—or were they offering?—the child she could hold no other way. Ida hesitated.

Her devil stepped from behind her to take Georgie's ringless hands. "It would be your decision, Georgie. MacGregor is willing to make the sacrifice. To stay here and leave his body empty as a vessel for"—he met Ida's eyes for a secret moment—"the buried king."

"No," Georgie whispered. "I have to find them. Ida . . ."

"I'll take care of Ida, my love," the devil whispered to Georgie. "You should go."

Georgie popped onto her tiptoes and kissed him. Then she turned and ran.

"Laura?"

Will is holding me upright. A matte gray sky frames his strong shoulders and terrified face.

"Laura?"

I close my eyes against the vertigo and hear the rain-filled stream boiling over stones—it sounds miles beneath us. We're standing on the square roof of his tower, the first gray light of morning beginning to drag itself from the black of trees. I straighten my knees, test them, and meet his eyes. His gentle hands reach into my hair. He kisses me, holding me like new cheese—like I might run out between his fingers. He must bend to kiss me. Maud is his height. My lips feel thin returning his kiss. I push my awareness over my wind-touched surfaces, and they form an unfamiliar container against the Irish air. I am in the body of Will's wife.

"I had to say good-bye," he whispers. He gestures at the pattern of words and symbols on the roof's black surface. "I opened a portal and Georgie, er . . . She fell through it. We're attempting to retrieve Maud and MacGregor in a way Ida's soul cannot follow. To leave her spirit there."

My mind is stretched so thin I can see through it. And I'm shaking. Inside Georgie's body, I am jerky and strained. Each dark hair on her arms rises in the predawn breezes blowing across an ocean of treetops, across the dangerously low wall of stone around the tower's flat roof. I am only glued-on. I look down and press small hands to her breasts. They ache. I touch her stomach, hard and round under a deep green velvet and fur dress. I look back to Will.

"I'm pregnant."

He puts his dwarfing hand over the soft fabric in an accustomed, proprietary gesture.

"Yes, we're expecting a son."

His kiss, delicate and tender, sends a slow stretch of delicious shivers and the promise of first light after torrential rain through me.

"We should go inside," I whisper into his caressing lips.

He murmurs against my mouth and slides his hands over my strange body.

"Do we need to haul Maud and MacGregor—their bodies—up here to the roof?"

He shakes his head, hair brushing my forehead. "Disembodied spirits cannot last long on the material plane. They will be frantic to return to their beings. They will reach their bodies down the stairs or chimney faster than we could chase them. The only danger would be if there were no body waiting."

"And Ida?"

He holds my face in his strong hands and looks into my eyes. Into the eyes of his wife. I am his wife at last.

But in her body, I wish for Maud—for her passion and easy certainty, more than just years distant from my modern ambiguities. On my wedding night, ambivalent about giving up my freedom to marriage, my wandering mind found Will. In Maud. Unmarried, she had two children, buried one, then married a man with whom she had another.

"What are we going to do about Ida?" I ask him.

His fingers trace my forehead and lips. "Georgie said we must kill her," he whispers. "It would not be the first time," he says, scrubbing at a painted symbol with his toe, "that my words and Maud's beauty have fatally combined."

Georgie's stout, strong legs take the spiral stair, cautious of their unsteady quaver. It wouldn't be murder. I'm not born yet, not here, and by the time I am sleeping in a Galway B&B, Ida will be long dead, no matter what I do this morning. Still, violence seems so primitive, millennia older than the regressions I've already made. And I know I am a pacifist.

But this can't be on Will's hands. It is my fault. It must be on mine.

"I'll smother her," I say. "She wouldn't struggle, right? She won't even know until she tries to reclaim her body."

Will leaves, going down another flight of stairs to the bedroom to fetch a pillow, and I am alone in the top floor ritual room with its massive fireplace, secret doors, and doorless rooms. I sit down in the empty little three-legged chair beside Ida's collapsed body. The vivid scarf wrapping her head makes an unflattering contrast to her pallid, sinking skin. Age has intensified both the angularity and pudge of her uncomfortable frame. She has done nothing but make trouble for me. She dragged me backwards in time to a freedom and a passion that have become hard to leave or manage. Still, I can't work up a hatred of her. Or even rage. I can't imagine what I would have done growing up in a world as small and cruel as hers. She brought me here, but I'm not sure if anything she did, or anything I did, was wrong.

Still, I know I would be safer with her gone. I take Ida's limp hand and hold it in apology for what I'm about to do. If I can summon the will to do it. I turn the gold ring on her thumb and remember the one I wore like it when I had Maud's small hands, and not Georgie's capable ones.

"Laura, I cannot." Will stands in the doorway, a twisted pillow in his hands. He drops it and comes to kneel at my feet. "I cannot let you destroy even this portion of yourself."

"I know," I tell him. "Maybe we've gotten too weak and timid in the future, but I can't do it either. Maud could have."

Will wraps his large hand over Ida's and mine clasped in my lap. "Maud understands just one kind of freedom—the kind she has seen the English starve, execute, and imprison." He grazes my knuckles with his lips. "Maud hasn't the imagination to see Irish freedom as any but a blood-soaked thing, an *inversus* of British subjugation, never as a thing in itself. A created thing. An ideal."

The cruelty of it chokes me. This man, this poet, who works solely in the meanings of things and not their physical manifestations, because of me, has been compelled, all his life, to love a woman who can see nothing of him. Or me.

"Maud could never imagine, could she," I ask, "what you were trying to create? She never saw the birth of something in language, in symbol; that the deliberate, collaborative creation of the Irish soul is what will make you free. It isn't the body." I slide Ida's cold, limp left hand from beneath his warm one. "It's the symbol. Oh god, Will, check Maud's hands!"

Will is on his feet and working the ring from Maud's thumb in a sudden blur of passion and grace. He gazes over at me with radiant eyes, and slips Maud's band onto his hand. "It fits me. Laura, how did you know?"

I didn't.

"Just a feeling," I say. "There's something about rings I can't remember from my real life."

I slide the gold band off Ida's thumb and try it on all my fingers. It doesn't fit. I drop it over my ring finger and it loops the two gold rings—my wedding rings—already there, a curving diagonal line across their parallel two, like a cancelled equal sign.

Will kneels before me stricken. "Could not this life be real to you?" Passion and pain twist his beautiful face. "I would not ask you to stay here as my wife; but you could always find me, whether Ida returns or not, if we have their rings. They possess all the power of symbol."

His eyes, emotional and masculine, mirror the earnest unselfconsciousness of my hopeless, romantic dream. From which I must awake. I shake my head.

"Maud didn't understand, Will, but I do." I tell him. "No matter how bodies change—live or die, are imprisoned or set free—until minds change, nothing real can. This is real." I close my right hand around the rings on my left finger. "Maud could have suffocated Ida's body," I whisper, "but it would not have freed us of Ida. She would still be true. I can't kill anyone and I can't destroy myself, but I can sacrifice who I am right now for who I want to be when I wake up. Smother the dream of myself for my real self." I open my hand. "It's not Ida—it's the rings we have to destroy."

Will slides Maud's ring from his finger onto mine. It's a sublimely erotic gesture. And I know it is our last. Will's ring falls over Ida's, over mine, encircling the circle. I close my hand again. Without a word, he stabs the fire to an orange roar and holds the ash-smeared, sharp-ended poker up to me. I kneel at the wide, shallow hearth, almost blind with the tears I'm not crying. I slide the symbols from my finger and drop them over the poker's cruel point, gold over ash black. Erotic again. And although they are not our souls, any more than bodies feel the flames of Hell, still, I feel something inside me twist and close as Will tips the rings off the poker and into the fire.

"Will you ever come back?" he whispers.

I wish I knew. I wish I knew if, one or two more times, I would be carried away by the crazy delirium of consuming passion. That I would fall asleep and into love. Or lust, or infatuation, or whatever this romantic, Victorian, tumult of emotion is. "No," I tell him, "but you can know, absolutely, that the future looks across the years at you with love. And I will know the same about my Irish past."

He touches my face to kiss me, and it feels—as it always feels—like the first kiss. His lips hesitate before they take mine, a tiny hiccup in time stretching into the interminable, a suspended anticipation of *will he or won't he?* I open my eyes, and am staring again at the B&B's ugly rug.

Ida allowed herself a wordless scream at Georgie's retreating back. But Amit and the future beckoned. He might have reached the tower by now. She scrambled around the cavern floor, collecting gleaming red rocks to build a hearth. Laura had taught her modernity did not wait around for magic.

"You just made your first mistake, my love," her devil whispered.

Ida stopped, arms piled with stones. "No, we don't need Georgie anymore. We're going forward. To Laura and Amit. We needed to get rid of her, and we don't need Maud and MacGregor's damn devil—king or queen under the hill—at all. It's into time they're taking him. He will have lived and died again by the days we shall inhabit." Ida stacked the rocks against the wall.

"Ida, do you truly have no idea what is buried here?"

"Very well, *she'll* be bound by time, like everyone is, once born. Another half-child of myth and motherland, she'll belong to neither world, but she can find her own way back here. Through suffering or study. Whatever she does in time, will be done before our time. And I, my love, have never cared for history. Now help me build this damn gate!"

"Once upon a time, there was a gate," the devil said.

Ida whirled around to curse him, but motion in the stone behind her caught her eye, and she turned back. "Amit!" she screamed into the empty fireplace. "Amit, quickly!"

I go through the ritual of the frantic search, although I know it's meaningless as praying to dead gods. Amit's ring is not where he left it. It is not in my closed hand. I dropped it on the tower roof when I fell into Georgie's body, or it went into the fire with the ones we burned. Still, I shake out my clothes and crawl on the carpet. Then I do it again, as though I could convince the ring to be found by the sheer force of my upset. But things are pitiless as lakes.

I run down the stairs, and almost into our hostess. She has yogurt and cereal waiting, and would be happy to make us some eggs, or a full Irish breakfast with "bacon from our own pig." I promise to be hungrier after a brisk walk, and dash out the door.

I know better than to start sprinting for the tower, but the sun is gilding the edges of puddles and leaves, and I run not quite hard enough to drown the questions.

What will I say to Amit? That I didn't do anything wrong? That we talked about this? Maybe the Victorians had it right—you should do more, but talk about it less. I know you can never be completely yourself around the people you want to love you. You always have to tidy yourself up a little, pin yourself together, to be worthy of love. In telling him about my ridiculous Victorian dreams, I let Amit see too much of what was messy and crazy in me. I never wanted to hurt him. But I took risks with both our pain, and I don't know if I had a right to.

The sound of my accelerated breathing, in rhythm with my running, stifles my thoughts, and by the time I turn onto the narrow, treelined street to Ballylee from the main road, my pace has panned the slurry of thought down to gleaming, particulate gold fragments.

I am not Maud. I know no matter what we lock away or suffocate, our minds will change. And we can take them in our hands ourselves and change them. Carve them with words made into symbols, and engrave them with actions that we create as ritual. I know the dangerous, fierce, and primal energy of love possesses a terrifying creative magic of its own, but I also know I am strong enough to channel it. Amit and I can create the story of our lives with its energy. And maybe it won't be poetry, maybe not even a romance, but I will invest it with meaning.

Carved into stone on the outside wall of Will's symbolic tower are his words: *"May these characters remain / When all is ruin once again."* He knew what time can and cannot destroy. I pull open the cottage's barn-wide green door and hear it slam behind me.

I take the winding stone stairs at a full sprint. The ritual room on the tower's top floor is tidier than it was last night. The four chairs are gone and the fire is out, but the grate still stands on the too-clean hearth, and my husband is down on one knee before it.

"Amit!"

He looks back at me, but doesn't say anything. He turns again, staring into the fireplace, but in the moment his broad shoulders are turned, I see what they were blocking—Ida's pinched face peering through a ragged edge of gray and too-red stones. It wears a hungry look I recognize.

She's whispering to Amit, quiet and urgent, and I cannot take a step toward my husband. The story of us doesn't stop our personal tales from going forward I guess, and sometimes his narrative thread weaves over mine, and mine supports it silently.

Amit's strong back blocks Ida from me, but I'm listening hungrily once again for her husky, Irish whisper.

"Close your eyes tightly," she tells my husband. "Tightly—and keep them closed."

I want to scream, to pull him away from the fireplace, from the grate whose metal bars have begun to glow with a weird, internal light. I want to silence her, smother her, whack her with a poker for once. But her hypnotic voice pulls at my eyes, too, singed as they are by lack of sleep.

Amit's wide shoulders sag. Fear grips my lips, and an icy terror shoots into my stomach and feet. She will summon Amit to her, away from me. I can't force my voice to work. Amit steadies himself briefly, bending down beside the glowing bars, with a hand on the orange-hot grate. His fingers contrast solid, unreflective flesh against the luminous gold heat. I hear his flesh sear, and he swings his legs over, blackened fist clenched, and vaults into nothing.

Amit is gone. Gone for real.

He has not leapt through the hole in the back of the fireplace.

There is no hole.

The bars are icy black. The stone is solid and a fine black grit of dust, not ash, stays on my fingers when I touch the cold hearth. This must be what Will felt every time I fell out of his world. I do not want him to have been this alone.

I close my eyes. I close them tightly.

I stood with Will right here, and he put his hands on my face to kiss me.

I keep my eyes closed. We are linked. I claim my Irish history. My Irish soul.

My imagination reaches back between worlds for Will's story as it must have gone on without me. With his fingers woven into the hair of his pregnant wife.

I open my eyes.

Oh.

He was less alone. He took Georgie back downstairs that night, after I left him the last time, and made love to her there. Then.

Now.

I run so fast, it feels like flying. Out through the anteroom. Up the spiral. Up the spiral again, and onto the roof. *Please.* Why am I praying?

Please let Amit not have been poisoned by the restless wandering and the craziness that damn me.

I don't believe in damnation.

Amit vaulted through the same hole from which Ida had dragged Georgie's floundering body, and landed in a deep crouch on the ragged rock behind her.

Ida spun around. "How the hell did you do that?"

"I've come for Laura."

Ida turned savage eyes to her daemon, lounging against the rock wall by his new fireplace, and saw him rake slow eyes down Amit's lean body. "What did you say about him, Ida, my love? *Brave, strong, and beautiful*, I believe?"

Ida flushed. Everything was wrong. How could her daemon take possession of this body she had intended as her offering, if Amit was so woven to it he could leap, body and soul, across time and into Hell?

Whose sex was he riding? What magic?

"Amit's not the sort of Misbegotten who tumbles easily into Hell because he's at home here," Ida's daemon drawled. "Nor is his a pilgrim soul prone to wandering."

"Not misbegotten?" Ida found herself turning her whole body, fish-like, between the two men, Amit and her daemon, the shrug and the sneer. The faithful husband and the jealous love.

"Yes, my damned darling. You threatened what he loved, and freed his mythic soul. You made him heroic. Without temptation, there is no virtue. Without danger, he could never have been brave. A hero is created by the ordeal he faces. It is because of you that he could come here—heroic body and poetic soul—to ransom his pilgrim love. You woke the Orpheus in him. You made him a hero."

Ida faltered. She wanted to sit down. She was soaked in weakness.

"You almost had it," her devil whispered.

Ida turned to face him. "Had what?"

"Power, belonging, even love lay within your grasp. Everything I offered you, laid out within your reach. You wanted it. You sacrificed. And learned patience. You did everything even to perfection, and yet still, you lose. You lose because you know you always lose, Ida my own, and everything you know is true."

She had lost her daemon. Even his eyes left her.

Ida followed his mutinous gaze to the opposite wall, and felt her jaw slacken. All the flesh and sinew binding the bones of her face and holding her teeth in their places unmoored. She gaped. From the dark recesses in the wall of the cavern, from one of the limitless corridors and tubes, Maud and MacGregor emerged, with what could only be a real ghost glimmering between them.

Despite her séances and tap-rappings, channeling and visions, Ida had never seen a real spirit, serene without a body, and all she knew for certain was it was not the soul of Charles Parnell. No one merely mortal. It might be the spirit of Arthur or Cúchulainn. Maybe even Maeve. Nothing to help her say. Ida's knees twitched to kneel, but her eyes fixed on her daemon, and he did not.

Nor did he move. "Welcome to the New Age, O My Origin."

The ghost stood in the center of the open space. Its eyes moved through waxing and waning, swelling and shrinking like the moon. "No. Not just yet, O My Possession."

Ida screamed. Rather, she stopped struggling not to scream, and the wild sound rose from her mouth and chest unbidden, a sonic tangle of confusion, outrage, and fear—unfettered, reckless, and inarticulate.

"Hello, Ida." The voice spoke straight to her hearing, without touching her ears, and as if her howl of soul defiance were its familiar salutation. Ida closed her lips. Maud and MacGregor came forward to make a ragged crescent before the fireplace, standing in the corona of spectral white light Ida's daemon had never ceased from watching, that cast no shadow, and glowed gold at the tips of its hands.

"I made it." Ida's daemon ran his velvet hand over the fireplace's rough mantel. "I don't suppose you'll let me take it back? MacGregor never got his portal made."

"It isn't possible." The words formed as thoughts in Ida's mind, and she could not have said with confidence who shaped them. "Once told, it's here."

Amit cocked his head and studied the cold hearth.

Ida and Maud, MacGregor and even Ida's daemon, his long, languid arm draped across the framing stone, followed Amit's beautiful eyes. Against the stone wall, but confined within the rocks Ida had heaped there, a slick of fire spread.

Ida held her breath, but Amit, present body and soul with nothing left on earth to chain him, kept the fire from going out. Under its shimmering surface, with the uncertain visibility of trees drowned beneath a moonlit lake, the half-circle of chairs in Will's tower's top floor swam into view. They were not burning, but in the flames, Maud, Ida, and MacGregor saw their three slumped bodies sprawled. Maud's long torso dropped against a bare wood arm. Ida's knees fell wide on either side of her flat body like a dissectionist's frog. MacGregor looked ready to tip onto his head.

"The distance between our worlds must lengthen now," Ida thought, or heard the ghost say. "I will return your spirits to your flesh, but spirit and body will no longer bide so close, nor will your astral bodies cross between the planes again this way. Magic is at an end."

Maud nodded solemnly as though she had heard something grave and wise, and had understood. But MacGregor, bless his blunt soul, protested. "And my years of study and practice? The knowledge and experience I now possess? How can I live in a world without that power?"

Through the mantel-framed stone hole, Ida saw Maud's body stir and shift. Stretching herself gracefully against the chair's stiff back, Maud woke up from Hell, tipped her head at some distant sound, blushed, and smiled a distinctly uninnocent smile. Where were Will and Georgie?

Ida looked for guidance to her daemon leaning against the rock, but he barely glanced from the fire-filled opening he watched.

"No," she whispered. In the moment she understood, Ida's daemon turned and slid, like smoke beneath a door, away from her, through the veil of flame and into the tower room. Will and Georgie had gone downstairs. And made this final bridge.

In Thoor Ballylee's hard, wooden chair, Ida's hands clawed her chest.

"Ida!" Maud started to stand, but, her legs still too weak from trance, failed.

All Ida could think, watching her body writhe was how ugly and small she was. And Maud would see her as such, watching her die. Ida's wretched body could never hold the soul of all she longed for, nor could her daemon possess her. Her distant, earthly face bloated with the force of her devil-filled flesh. Her body contorted and snarled. It ran in a powder of ash and yellow smoke, out onto the chair and over the fireplace rug.

Ida was dead.

Her spirit staggered. Strong hands gripped her waist. Amit caught Ida and held her upright while her eyes wheeled across the raw rock where they stood, and back through the fireplace where her daemon blew in a fetid raging wind through the tower room. Maud rose slowly to her feet, real tears for Ida on her cheeks. Her hair flew a million ways, picked apart by tiny hands, but her eyes were terrible.

"I have fought all my life for freedom!" she screamed into the frantic air. "I will not be possessed!"

"Maud!" Will's shout reached them across the distance. He came, at a full run, into the upstairs room, the halves of his unpinned shirt flapping in the gusty morning breeze.

Will slipped in the ash that had been Ida, and gagged on her stench. "MacGregor!" He grasped the inert magus by the shoulders of his coat and shook the slowly reanimating body. MacGregor staggered to his feet, and looked from Maud to Will.

"Stand aside!" MacGregor roared. He clapped Will on the shoulders once, turned and stepped into the fireplace at Thoor Ballylee, through the flames, and into Hell.

He turned and called Maud by her married name. "Madam McBride, tell my wife I was taken by the Host of the Air. She always thought you were part fairy. She will believe you. Tell her my pilgrim's soul is peaceful because with the *sidhe* it wanders at last without searching, no longer able to imagine what might be."

Swaying in Amit's solid hands, Ida spun her gaze to the ghost's changing eyes.

"The spirit gate is closed" was all she knew. Magic was now impossible.

Through the fire in the glowing grate, Ida saw Georgie run full tilt into the tower room. Holding her husband's great coat closed around her gently swollen body, Georgie stared from Maud, strong and defiant, to her husband, slender and bereft in the putrid smear of ash between the fireplace and the four empty chairs.

"This is all that's left of Ida," he told his wife.

"Good riddance," Georgie said.

"No," Ida whispered, but only Amit heard her.

Maud crossed herself conspicuously, and Georgie padded on white, cold feet to stand beside her. In the comforting hand Georgie laid on Maud's still shaking arm, Ida saw the stupid, pregnant cow believed Maud had crossed out of Hell on the bridge made of Will and Georgie's martial reunion. But Ida knew her daemon had taken it. Maud had been sent across. Either way, for both living women, Georgie had reclaimed Will forever from Maud, on every plane.

"I believe"—Will Yeats waved a disgusted hand at the smear of cinder and ash on the ground—"Ida may have always been a devil, and not a woman at all."

"I've seen that stain before," Maud whispered. "We will never see her again."

Standing beside Maud, Georgie's ordinary features and shapeless dress looked dull to Ida's future-awakened eyes, but Will's love-filled ones never left his wife's face in the dawnlit tower room.

In the sunless cavern, MacGregor turned to Ida, who still stood only because Amit had not yet let her go. "Your beloved killed you," MacGregor said. "What you most wanted has claimed your life."

"It always does," Ida answered. "My daemon could possess only, not share."

"Did you know he would attempt to claim your body for his use?"

"No," Ida said. "But he had tried with others. I don't know why I presumed to be different."

"I'm sorry, Ida," MacGregor said. And something in his eyes or voice convinced her, but it didn't matter.

MacGregor turned and addressed the ghost. "I offer myself to you—be you Holy Spirit or *Spiritus Mundi*—so although you have closed the pilgrim's path between the mythic and material, you may bridge it still, to carry the things from our world you will need to outfit yours, do your work in new ways in the coming times."

The changing, mobile shadow-light of the magic that could speak into Ida's mind without words, fell over the face of MacGregor Mathers, and washed it with an erotic joy. He moved his lips in a single, orgasmic gasp and kiss.

"Kiss me," Amit said in Ida's ear.

She was dizzy with not breathing.

MacGregor's hair, glowing with his possession, was turning a red-tinged white, and growing long. And he was aging. "Wanting a thing is better than having it, but not as good as getting it," Ida told the old man. "My daemon will not die."

MacGregor's lips moved in words like kisses. "No," he said. "He will pace the mountains overhead a while, but come down quietly enough after the war."

Ida's despairing eyes registered his matte gray ones. Mathers's pinstripe tailcoat and stylish spats did not disguise the magic he was now. And his hands, once the blunt tools of a self-taught polyglot and amateur boxer, were lengthening, tapering into perfect teardrop-shaped matte gold nails.

"Who are you?" Ida whispered.

"Kiss me," Amit said again.

MacGregor answered with a word part Gaelic and part god.

❧

When I get to the flat roof of Thoor Ballylee, Amit is already there, standing in the center of Will's portal ring, his strong arms holding up a reeling Ida. She looks like hell.

"Kiss me," he says into her thin hair.

I've run up the stairs too fast. I can't catch my breath. Can't say his name or even point to the shadow of the glowing gold circle Will made, that I woke up inside, its ash-drawn inverse on the flat black of the modern roof. But he is here.

Ida turns her ugly face to him.

And he kisses her. I watch his mouth that I have only felt, kissing her, and I feel . . . not angry, not jealous, but very far away. And cold. I think how much like fighting kissing is, the way we bite and scramble open-mouthed, wolves at each other's lips and throats. But his mouth on hers is tender, despite his strength. If she already knows his name, she now has enough for power over him. He bends, catches her beneath the knees and shoulders, arcs her legs up into his arms, and carries her across the black symbols encircling them.

His arms are empty.

The circle is gone.

My breath flies back into me with a shout. And Amit is holding me again.

"I'm so sorry," I tell him.

"Don't be," he says. "I love you."

It's the only story I need.

The stairwell is dark after the brilliant morning sunshine and, spiraling down, I miss a step. It's not just the quick reset I should have earned in the hours I spend staying fit, but a full crash-and-roll down four stairs onto the bedroom landing. Amit helps me up, but neither of us glances into the intimate, private space behind the green wood door.

We walk home holding hands. We could be any young couple on their honeymoon, wandering the romantic Irish country roads. A sudden gust of wind blows around us, whirling, in the open roadside field, the mown grass and fallen leaves into the air. Amit puts an arm around me and pulls me closer to him. I notice he keeps his other, grate-burned hand protectively curled closed, but he's humming low under his breath, and I can feel the music rumble in his chest against me. "I think I'll call Otto when we get home," he says. "Maybe restart the band."

I grin. I can see it already. Otto has been crazy to get back into music for years. Since he and Amit and the rest were in school. They've all played with other folks since then, except Amit, but not together without him. Amit has a beautiful voice, and a kind of powerful charisma onstage that makes me think of Maud. "You'll be his hero," I say.

"Now, let's not get carried away," he laughs.

"Why the hell not?" I say.

Amit looks down into my eyes and I meet them recklessly, daring him to make me ridiculous. "You're a poet," I say. "You have a responsibility to sing."

He doesn't say anything, but he leans down and kisses me as we're walking up the driveway.

The bustling B&B landlady offers us breakfast again, but Amit tells her not to hold up her day on our account. We may go back to bed.

"Sure, it's jetlagged you are." She gives us a wise nod, but there's a wink that comes with it, and I grin back at her as I follow my husband up the stairs.

No, it's honeymooners we are, but devil damn if I can tell the difference.

Amit is still chuckling when he shuts the door and pulls me against him.

"You should let me take a look at your burned hand," I say. It's a rational suggestion, but I feel ridiculous. His hard chest spans strong and solid, and his arms surround me, one open palm and one closed fist against my back. "I'm sorry," I say again. "I wasn't trying to cheat on you. There was never anything real. Just dreams and my ridiculous imagination. But our love is powerful enough to anchor me, I promise, and keep my imagination from wandering."

"No," Amit says, and I cannot breathe. "I've seen what happens to a wild imagination when it's pinned down or ridiculed. Pilgrims need freedom to follow their gods. I'll wander with you."

His stubbled jaw nudges my temple. His lips move in my hair. "I'm not interested in your body as real estate, and I don't want to wall off trespassers." His voice grates with emotion, stripped raw of its usual beauty, bristling with power. "But it's the only place I can find you. Your body is the land of where you are, and I love you."

I raise my eyes to his. "I love you, too."

"I don't know how we make promises about the future anymore," he tells me. "But I figure a promise is just a shared plan. And maybe that's enough. Maybe sharing a plan makes it more likely to come true."

"But not like a wish comes true," I say. "Not by magic."

He shifts my body against his to position his closed hand between us. He opens it.

In the soot-blackened palm, he holds a single, simple, thin gold band.

I take the ring from between the smoky imprints of the grate bars, and hold it.

He rests his forehead against mine, and we both watch the ring as I turn it in my careful fingers. "Plans are different from dreams," he whispers. "You have to work them. You have to drag them out of there," he jerks his head out the window toward the tower, "and into here. Out of imagination into reality. We make our dreams real."

I meet his eyes at last. "I've always liked making things with you. Memories, tiled kitchen walls . . ."

"Our future . . ." he says.

"A family?" I whisper.

He grins. "Okay then. We have a plan."

Tears press up my eyes like filled blisters. If I blink they'll spill down my cheeks. "I want us to make it," I whisper.

"We will," he tells me. "We're strong"—he tips my chin up with soot-smudged fingers—"and we're good with our hands."

He holds his ringless one out to me.

I slide the band onto his finger. "I promise," I whisper.

He *is* good with his hands. They slide up my back, under my sweatshirt, leaving tracks in my flesh like the shimmering tails of shooting stars. I can feel each one of his finger pads. Their firm strokes arc up my spine and separate in bursts over my shoulder blades. My body resonates with the delicious humming songs of spinning brass drums, glass lenses, and polished wood. On tiptoe, every point of me shimmers alert, almost anxious, almost afraid of what will happen next.

What happens next is just ridiculous.

Amit lifts the bottom of my sweatshirt to pull it over my head. I raise my arms, but tangle my elbow in the sleeve, and I'm stuck with my face in the fabric, off-balance, one arm sticking through the neck, the other folded in at my ear. I reel sideways, blind and clumsy. A weird noise of alarm gets muffled in my mouth against the shirt's fleecy skin-warmed insides, but the cool air brushes my unclothed breasts. Amit catches me around the waist, laughing, tugs the ridiculous thing free, and lands on the mattress over me.

"What's gotten into you?" he laughs. "You're never this clumsy." But topless under him, breasts against his chest, arms above my head, I recklessly hold his eyes again.

Love is a sacrifice. Of dignity, mayhap, but not of self. It expands the self. Slowly, purposefully, my body rolls beneath him in an inviting wave of hip and belly. His smile softens from humor into appreciation.

Love requires your attention, but not your freedom. Amit carried my freedom back to me when it wandered off. He ransomed it. I send the same undulation through my body again, and Amit has to close his eyes.

Love asks for your imagination. And I want to give it mine. To keep reimagining with my husband what marriage means.

His hips answer in a steady push, solid and directional, but I am a chaos of small ripples and breezes blowing out from a motionless center that will not hold. Only bodies live and die. Diffuse, and coming apart, I wrap around him like a funneling wind. He weaves his fingers into mine, flat on the mattress over my head. His kiss is serious. His mouth opens mine and opens it again, and his lips inscribe me with permanence and determination. His hands, lips, and hips pin me, and I buffet between them the way a breeze whips and mounts in a narrow alley with an abandon it never shows on an open field. When he stands up to undress himself, I am blowing away, but not falling apart. We are more than our bodies, but without our bodies, we are not. The self is more than the sum of our parts, but all its parts are here.

His shirt comes off easily. He has already unbelted his jeans, and freed one leg, when I fly at him. I don't know where it has come from, this maelstrom of need in me. I am irrational and irresponsible, reckless and Victorian, and free. I vault out of our bed, into his chest, and he catches me. Now there is nothing to hold back. His hands are hard on my hips, his mouth bites my neck. The orgasms rise and rupture in rings over me. His cock is the only solid thing I can find. It thrusts into me, an ancient standing stone in the storming Irish air, and my body ripples from my skin downward in rivulets of welcome. His hands and mouth struggle not to crush me. His face twists with the effort. We've fallen on the floor, between the bed and the wall, against the ugly carpet.

He almost throws me onto him. I ride with my legs open, his cock under me, within me, a witch on a sex-tossed sky, a kite pinned to a single point, torn apart in the crosswinds and lightning. I plant my hands on his strong chest. I am made out of the storm and cannot breathe. He takes my face and drags it down, and kisses me completely. We are bound to one another.

"*Demon Inversus est . . .*" he whispers against my kiss-bruised lips.

Us.

My hips lift under his hands. My legs open.

He is responsible for being the hero I see him as.

As he created and ransomed the artist, and loves the pilgrim soul in me.

His cock slides between my legs.

He closes his eyes tightly—tightly—and we are both entranced. I try to keep my eyes on his, but tiny lights are winking at the periphery of vision. The tender tips of my nipples scrape the rough twists of hair on his dark chest. I am falling—not apart, but together. My sex spirals inward, drawing his cock deeper. The orgasm blowing back and forth between us finally coalesces. It arcs. Every part of me, my pussy and my future, my imagination and my sheet-gripping toes beam and radiate. The blackness of eyes squeezed tightly closed explodes into constellations. I cannot see his face. It is hidden in a crowd of stars.

We are responsible for and to the dream we will reimagine together.

I close my eyes tightly—tightly—and drift up into dream, unpinned by a man both hero and poet enough to walk into Hell and carry my wandering freedom back to me in his strong arms. "I love you," I say, and there's peat-smoke in my voice when I whisper, "Amit Armstrong."

Epilogue

BEING DEAD, WE RISE, DREAM, AND SO CREATE

Nine months (or ninety years) later, Laura gives birth to a daughter conceived, despite modern birth control, on her Irish honeymoon. The child is unusually tall and red-headed, with a soul for music and imagination. They name her Kathleen.

Six months later, Georgie Yeats gave birth to a daughter she and Will named "Anne" after his distant ancestor, the Countess of Ossory, whom they believed reincarnated in the child.

That spring, an American gentleman traveling in the south of Ireland, possessed by a sudden spirit familiar to many in general, but to Ida most specifically, was inspired to buy land near Cork and establish the country's first automobile factory there. His name was Henry Ford.

Both W. B. Yeats and Maud's son Sean MacBride became senators of the Irish Republic, and recipients of the Nobel Prize. Yeats for Poetry, MacBride for Peace.

Neither the body nor the grave of MacGregor Mathers was ever found, and no cause of death is given on his death certificate.

When your pilgrim soul finds its truth or god or you, its roadside shrines are the eyes of those who love you. Its gods are the inverses of all your demons. And its freedom, no longer mistaking possession for belonging, will never again say "I."

Now "I" means Laura. But even within an artist's mind, Ida Jameson is more free than when a father or husband housed her. A wild, unpinned spirit in modernity's clean black lines, she is, even now, falling wildly, Victorianly in love. Amit is powerful. And—although to tell her real and secret story, she must learn to speak of the past in its own tense, and to write herself as "she"—still, Ida will not be silent.

WORKS CITED

Bennett, Bridget. *Women, Madness and Spiritualism, Vol. 1.* New York: Routledge, 2004.

Besant, Annie. *Theosophical Manual No. VII: Man and His Bodies.* London: Theosophical Publishing Society, 1909.

d'Esperance, Elizabeth. *The Shadow Land, or Light from the Other Side.* London: George Redway, 1897.

Fortune, Dion. *The Esoteric Philosophy of Love and Marriage.* York Beach, ME: Samuel Weiser, 2000.

Jeffares, A. Norman, ed. *Yeats the European.* Savage, MD: Barnes & Noble Books, 1989.

Joyce, James. *Ulysses.* New York: Vintage International, 1990.

Lightman, Alan. *Einstein's Dreams.* New York: Vintage, 2004.

MacBride, Maud Gonne. *A Servant of the Queen: Reminiscences.* Edited by A. Norman Jeffares and Anna MacBride White. Buckinghamshire, UK: Colin Smythe, 1994.

Michaelsen, Scott, ed. *Portable Darkness: An Aleister Crowley Reader.* Washington, DC: Solar Books, 2007.

Owen, Alex. *The Darkened Room: Women, Power and Spiritualism in Late Victorian England.* (From the transcripts of court trials and letters of Louisa Lowe.) Chicago: University of Chicago Press, 1989.

White, Anna MacBride, and A. Norman Jeffares, eds. *The Gonne–Yeats Letters 1893–1938.* Syracuse: Syracuse University Press, 1994.

Yeats, William Butler. *The Autobiography of William Butler Yeats Consisting of Reveries Over Childhood and Youth, The Trembling of the Veil, and Dramatis Personae.* New York: The Macmillan Company, 1953.

———. *The Collected Letters of W. B. Yeats, Vol. 1, 1865–1895.* Edited by John Kelly. New York: Oxford University Press, 1986.

———. *The Collected Poems, Revised 2nd Edition.* Edited by Richard J. Finneran. New York: Scribner, 1996.

———. *Essays and Introductions.* New York: Collier Books, 1961.

————. *Fairy and Folk Tales of the Irish Peasantry.* London: W. Scott, 1903.

————. *Under the Moon: The Unpublished Early Poetry by William Butler Yeats.* Edited by George Bornstein. New York: Scribner, 1995.

————. *Writings on Irish Folklore, Legend and Myth.* Edited by Robert Welch. New York: Penguin Books, 1993.

Young, Ella. *Flowering Dusk.* New York: Longmans, Green and Co., 1945.

THANK YOU

"There have been men who loved the future like a mistress," Yeats wrote of William Blake, "and the future mixed her breath into their breath and shook her hair about them." The writing of *In Dreams Begin* put me in a similar relationship with the past. She proved a difficult mistress, and I have many people to thank for their help in my wooing: John Gallagher of the Gresham Hotel, who dug books up from cellars for me and gave me the best tea of my trip; Kevin Flynn of Ratra House, who very generously spent a morning letting me poke around Douglas Hyde's place, which he has so beautifully restored, and Liam Byrne for introducing us; Peter Walsh of Lough Key Boats, who taught me how to row and gave me an afternoon's worth of stories—spooky, historic, and erotic; Peter Murray of the Bedford Park Historical Society, who emailed me JPEGs of floor plans and put me in touch with his society's library; Cornelia Maynard Smith for the hospitality in London; and Frances McDonagh, the impossibly genial proprietor of Lough Key House B&B, in whose delicious breakfasts and peat-fire-warmed bedrooms many of my keenest Irish sense-memories are grounded—my god, the plum preserves!

The past may have shaken her hair about me, but she has also opened her arms. I have been unrealistically lucky with history, and I owe more than gratitude to Will Yeats and to Maud, Georgie, MacGregor Mathers, Aleister Crowley, and the others who came out to play.

My present luck continues in my editor, Leis Pederson, at Berkley, who did more than any living person to facilitate this intermarriage of history and fiction. I'm very grateful to her for her work with rights and permissions, as well as for everything she did to improve and shape the progeny. The book is stronger for her insight and opinion.

My agent, Holly Root, has been a wonderful friend through the cold feet and fretful uncertainties that attend all love. She is relentlessly upbeat, clear-eyed, and the literary equivalent of the years-long, crazy-in-love marriage every young couple needs as proof of what is possible.

I am also grateful to the folks of Berkley who have been both generous and brave in their support of the new and unusual. Thank you to my publicist, Rosanne Romanello, and to Craig White, who has again provided beautiful art for the cover.

My final professional thanks goes to the impressive body of reviewers and bloggers for their fierce love of books, and for their time, careful thought, and curiosity. Thank you especially to Jackie Morgan, Andy Boylan, Paul Goat Allen, Veronica Huerta, Derek Tatum, Doug Knipe, Misty Braden, Kelly Lasiter, Michelle Hauf, and Rebecca Baumann among many others for their excitement, kind words, and excellent questions.

Personal thank-yous begin with my parents—again and always—for providing me with a rich childhood of poetry and art, and for encouraging me to play with what I loved, even when it was messy. Or far away.

Thank you to my sister, and to my extended family, the aunts, cousins, and in-laws who have encouraged, cheered, and apologized for me.

Thank you to my writer friends. To Julie Kenner and Anya Bast for the generous gifts of their time, words, and names. It meant a lot not to take the first leap alone. To David Bradford for the careful reading, Michael DiLeo for the coffee (still), to the Pitts for reading and re-reading, and to ARWA for the solidarity. I also want to thank Alan Lightman for his generosity in allowing me to quote him, and for his kind words.

Thank you, my reader friends, for the emails and letters, for the questions and the ongoing conversation. A special thanks and a juicy wink to everyone who sent photos of their "Damned" tattoos to the web gallery!

Thank you to Steve Dutton for sharing his experience and his city. Thank you to Molly Hayden for the inspiration and the excellent example. Your friendship has let me live two lives.

Thank you to my children. On this one Yeats was wrong. I love you for yourselves alone.

Thank you to Scott. For the support and belief, for the friendship and for the love, for the writing and rewriting, and for the continued reinvention.

Think where man's glory most begins and ends,
And say my glory was I had such friends.

—W. B. Yeats

ABOUT THE AUTHOR

Maud Gonne McBride, born on the winter solstice 1866, Dublin, Ireland.
Skyler (née Laura) White, born on the winter solstice 1966,
place of birth uncertain (adopted).

SKYLER WHITE crafts challenging fiction for a changing world. Populated with angels and devils, rock stars, poets, and revolutionaries, her dark stories explore the secret places where myth and modernity collide.

She [Maud Gonne] had a borrowed interest, reminding me of Laura Armstrong without Laura's wild dash of half insane genius. She interests me far more than Miss Gonne does and yet is only as a myth and a symbol.
    —Letter from W. B. Yeats to Katharine Tynan, March 21, 1889

There is some one myth for every man, which if we but knew it, would make us understand all that he did and thought. —W. B. Yeats

How Art Thou Damned?
www.skylerwhite.com